Lydia could **between the** **tease before they met.**

Then they met.

And all that had been missing was suddenly there.

At first taste she was Raul's and he knew it, for her hands moved to the back of his head and he kissed her as hard as her fingers demanded.

He slid one arm around her waist to move her body from the wall, closer to his, so that her head could fall backwards.

If there had been a bed, she would have been on it.

If there had been a room they would have closed the door.

But there wasn't, so he halted them—but only their lips.

'What do you want to do?' he whispered against her skin, and then he blew on her neck, still damp from his kisses, and raised his head and met her eyes. 'Tonight I can give you anything you want.'

Dear Reader,

This is my 100th title for Mills & Boon!

Rather than use this space to tell you about Raul and Lydia, I would like to thank you.

Whether this is the first or the hundredth time you have read me, I am so grateful to my readers. Even if we haven't met face to face, or online, hopefully we've shared some time through words on a page, and had a smile or three when one of my heroes misbehaves, or one of my heroines messes up. They tend to do that a lot.

I often cry when I'm writing, but I also laugh often too.

I hope, in some way, my stories let you do the same.

Happy reading, and love always,

Carol xxxx

THE INNOCENT'S SECRET BABY

BY
CAROL MARINELLI

First Published in Great Britain 2017
By Mills & Boon, an imprint of HarperCollins*Publishers*
1 London Bridge Street, London, SE1 9GF

© 2017 Carol Marinelli

ISBN: 978-0-263-92513-5

Printed and bound in Spain
by CPI, Barcelona

Carol Marinelli recently filled in a form asking for her job title. Thrilled to be able to put down her answer, she put 'writer'. Then it asked what Carol did for relaxation and she put down the truth—'writing'. The third question asked for her hobbies. Well, not wanting to look obsessed, she crossed her fingers and answered 'swimming'—but, given that the chlorine in the pool does terrible things to her highlights, I'm sure you can guess the real answer!

Books by Carol Marinelli

Mills & Boon Modern Romance

One Night With Consequences

The Sheikh's Baby Scandal

The Billionaire's Legacy

Di Sione's Innocent Conquest

Irresistible Russian Tycoons

The Price of His Redemption
The Cost of the Forbidden
Billionaire Without a Past
Return of the Untamed Billionaire

Playboys of Sicily

Sicilian's Shock Proposal
His Sicilian Cinderella

Mills & Boon Medical Romance

Their Secret Royal Baby

The London Primary Hospital

Playboy on Her Christmas List

Visit the Author Profile page
at millsandboon.co.uk for more titles.

For Lena, my mum.
You were wonderful as both and I will love you for ever.
Until we meet again…

PROLOGUE

SURELY NOT?

As Raul Di Savo thanked the mourners who had attended his mother's funeral a figure standing in the distance caught his attention.

He wouldn't *dare* to come here!

Not today of all days.

The tolling of the bell in the small Sicilian church had long since ceased, but it still seemed to ring in Raul's ears.

'Condoglianze.'

Raul forced himself to focus on the elderly gentleman in front of him rather than the young man who stood on the periphery of the cemetery.

'Grazie,' Raul said, and thanked the old man for his attendance.

Given the circumstances of Maria's death, and fearing Raul's father's wrath, most had stayed away.

Gino had not attended his wife's funeral.

'She was a whore when I married her and she goes into the ground the same.'

That was how he had broken the news of her death to his son.

Raul, having been told of a car accident involving his mother, had travelled from Rome back to Casta—a town on the Sicilian wild west coast—but he had arrived only to be told that she had already gone.

He had been too late.

Slowly, painfully, he had pieced together the timeline of shocking events that had led to Maria's death. Now Raul performed his familial duties and stood graveside as the line of mourners slowly moved past him.

Condolences were offered, but small talk was strained. The events of the last few days and the savage condemnations that were now coursing through the valley made even the simplest sentence a mockery.

'She was a good…' A lifetime family friend faltered in his choice of words. 'She was…' Again there was hesitation over what should be said. 'Maria will be missed.'

'She will be,' Raul duly replied.

The scent of freshly dug soil filled his nostrils and lined the back of his throat, and Raul knew there was no comfort to be had.

None.

He had left it too late to save her.

And now she was gone.

Raul had studied hard at school and had done so well in his exams that he had received a scholarship and, as he had always intended, been able to get out of the Valley of Casta.

Or, as Raul and his friend Bastiano had called it, *the Valley of Hell.*

Raul had been determined to get his mother away from his father.

Maria Di Savo.

Unhinged, some had called her.

'Fragile' was perhaps a more appropriate word.

Deeply religious until she had met his father, Maria had hoped to join the local convent—an imposing stone residence that looked out on the Sicilian Strait. His mother had wept when it had closed down due to declining numbers, as if somehow her absence had contributed to its demise.

The building had long stood abandoned, but there was not a day Raul could remember when his mother hadn't rued the day she had not followed her heart and become a novice nun.

If only she had.

Raul stood now, questioning his very existence, for her

pregnancy had forced Maria into the unhappiest of marriages.

Raul had always loathed the valley, but never more so than now.

He would never return.

Raul knew his drunken father's demise was already secured, for without Maria's care his descent would be rapid.

But there was another person to be taken care of.

The man who had forced this tragic end.

Raul had made a vow as he'd thrown a final handful of soil into his mother's open grave that he would do whatever it might take to bring him down.

'I shall miss her.'

Raul looked up and saw Loretta, a long-time friend of his mother's who worked in the family bar.

'No trouble today, Raul.'

Raul found himself frowning at Loretta's choice of words and then realised why she suddenly sounded concerned—he was looking beyond the mourners now, to the man who stood in the distance.

Bastiano Conti.

At seventeen, Bastiano was a full year younger than Raul.

Their families were rivals.

Bastiano's uncle owned most of the properties and all of the vineyards on the west of the valley.

Raul's father was king of the east.

The rivalry went back generations, and yet their black history had been ignored by the young boys and, growing up, the two of them had been friends. They had gone through school together and often spent time with each other during the long summer breaks. Before Raul had left the valley he and Bastiano had sat drinking wine from the opposing families' vines.

Both wines were terrible, they had agreed.

Similar in looks, both were tall and dark and were opposed only in nature.

Bastiano, an orphan, had been raised by his extended family and got through life on charm.

Raul was serious and mistrusting and had been taught to be fickle.

He trusted no one but said what he had to to get by.

Though different in style, they were equally adored by women.

Bastiano seduced.

Raul simply returned the favour.

There had been no rivalry between the young men—both could have their pick of the valley and the fruits were plenty.

Yet Bastiano had used his dark charm on the weakest and had taken Maria as his lover.

Pillow talk had been gathered and secrets had been prised from loose lips.

Not only had Maria had an affair—she had taken it beyond precarious and slept with a member of the family that Gino considered his enemy.

When the affair had been discovered—when the rumours had reached Gino—Loretta had called her to warn her Gino was on his angry way home. Maria had taken out a car she didn't know how to drive.

An unwise choice in the valley.

And Raul knew the accident would not have happened but for Bastiano.

'Raul...' Loretta spoke softly, for she felt the tension rip through him and could hear his ragged breathing. She held on to his hand, while knowing nothing could really stop him now. 'You are Sicilian, and that means you have a lifetime to get your revenge—just don't let it be today.'

'No,' Raul agreed.

Or did he refute?

Raul's words were coming out all wrong, his voice was a

touch hoarse, and as he looked down he could see the veins in his hand and feel the pulse in his temples. He was primed for action, and the only thing Raul knew for sure was that he hated Bastiano with all that he had.

He dropped Loretta's hand and brushed past her, then shrugged off someone else who moved to try to stop him.

'Raul!' The priest shot him a warning. 'Not here—not now.'

'Then he should have stayed away!' Raul responded as he strode through the cemetery towards the man who had sent his mother to an early grave.

Raul picked up speed—and God help Bastiano because hate and fury catapulted Raul those last few steps.

'*Pezzo di merda...*' Raul shouted out words that did not belong in such a setting.

Any sane man who saw murder approach would surely turn and run, but instead Bastiano walked towards Raul, hurling insults of his own. 'Your mother wanted—'

Raul did not let him finish, for Bastiano had already sullied her enough, and to silence him Raul slammed his fist into Bastiano's face. He felt the enamel of Bastiano's tooth pierce his knuckle, but that was the last thing he felt.

It was bloody.

Two parts grief, several belts of rage and a hefty dose of shame proved a volatile concoction indeed.

Raul would kill him.

That was all he knew.

Yet Bastiano refused to go quietly and fought back.

There were shouts and the sounds of sirens in the distance as the two men battled it out. Raul felt nothing as he was slammed against a gravestone. The granite tore through the dark suit and white shirt on his back with the same ease that it gouged through muscle and flesh.

It didn't matter.

His back was already a map of scars from his father's beatings, and adrenaline was a great anaesthetic.

Only vaguely aware of the wound that ran from shoulder to flank, Raul hauled himself up to stand, took aim again and felled his rival.

Yet Bastiano refused to submit.

Raul pinned Bastiano and slammed his fist into his face, marring those perfect features with relish, and then he held him to the ground and told him he should have stayed the hell away from his mother.

'Like *you* did!'

Those words were more painful than any physical blow, for Raul knew that he had done just that—stayed away.

CHAPTER ONE

ROME AGAIN... ROME AGAIN...

The City of Love.

Wrapped in a towel, and damp from the shower, Lydia Hayward lay on the bed in her hotel suite and considered the irony.

Yes, she might be in Rome, and meeting tonight with a very eligible man, but it had nothing to do with love.

There were more practical matters that needed to be addressed.

Oh, it hadn't been said outright, of course.

Her mother hadn't sat her down one evening and explained that, without the vast and practically bottomless pit of money that this man could provide, they would lose everything. *Everything* being the castle they lived in, which was the family business too.

And Valerie had never *said* that Lydia had to sleep with the man she and her stepfather were meeting tonight.

Of course she hadn't.

Valerie *had*, however, enquired whether Lydia was on the Pill.

'You don't want to ruin your holiday.'

Since when had her mother taken an interest in such things? Lydia had been to Italy once before, on a school trip at the age of seventeen, and her mother hadn't been concerned enough to ask then.

Anyway, why would she be on the Pill?

Lydia had been told to 'save' herself.

And she had.

Though not because of her mother's instruction—more because she did not know how to let her guard down.

People thought her aloof and cold.

Better they think that than she reveal her heart.

And so, by default, she had saved herself.

Lydia had secretly hoped for love.

It would seem not in this lifetime.

Tonight she would be left alone with him.

The towel fell away and, though she was alone, Lydia pulled it back and covered herself.

She was on the edge of a panic attack, and she hadn't had one since…

Rome.

Or was it Venice?

Venice.

Both.

That awful school trip.

She had said yes to this trip to Rome, hoping to lay a ghost to rest. Lydia wanted to see Rome through adult eyes, yet she was as scared of the world now as she had been as a teenager.

Pull yourself together, Lydia.

And so she did.

Lydia got up from the bed and got dressed.

She was meeting Maurice, her stepfather, at eight for breakfast. Rather than be late she just quickly combed her long blonde hair, which had dried a little wild. She had bought a taupe linen dress to wear, which had buttons from neck to hem—though perhaps not the best choice for her shaking hands.

They are not *expecting you to sleep with him!*

Lydia told herself she was being utterly ridiculous even to entertain such a thought. She would stop by for a drink with this man tonight, with her stepfather, thank him for his hospitality and then explain that she was going out with friends. Arabella lived here now and had said they should catch up when Lydia got here.

In fact…

Lydia took out her phone and fired off a quick text.

Hi, Arabella,

Not sure if you got my message.

Made it to Rome.

I'm free for dinner tonight if you would like to catch up.

Lydia

And so to breakfast.

Lydia stepped out of her suite and took the elevator down to the dining room. As she walked through the lavish foyer she caught sight of herself in a mirror. Those deportment classes had been good for something at least—she was the picture of calm and had her head held high.

Yet she wanted to run away.

'No, grazie.'

Raul Di Savo declined the waiter's offer of a second espresso and continued to read through reports on the Hotel Grande Lucia, where he now sat, having just taken breakfast.

At Raul's request his lawyer had attained some comprehensive information, but it had come through only this morning. In a couple of hours Raul was to meet with Sultan Alim, so there was a lot to go through.

The Grande Lucia was indeed a sumptuous hotel, and Raul took a moment to look up from his computer screen and take in the sumptuous dining room that was currently set up for breakfast.

There was the pleasant clink of fine china and a quiet murmur of conversation and, though formal, the room had a relaxed air that had made Raul's stay so far pleasurable. There was a certain old-world feel to the place that spoke of Rome's rich history and beauty.

And Raul wanted the hotel to be his.

Raul had been toying with the idea of adding it to his portfolio and had just spent the night in the Presidential Suite as a guest of Sultan Alim.

Raul hadn't expected to be so impressed.

He had been, though.

Every detail was perfection personified—the décor was stunning, the staff were attentive yet discreet, and it appeared to be a rich haven for both the business traveller and the well-heeled tourist.

Raul was now seriously considering taking over this landmark hotel.

Which meant that so too was Bastiano.

Fifteen years on and their rivalry continued unabated.

Mutual hatred was a silent, yet daily motivator—a black cord that connected them.

And Bastiano would be arriving later today.

Raul knew that Bastiano was also a personal friend of Sultan Alim. Raul had considered if that might have any bearing on their negotiations but had soon discounted it. Sultan Alim was a brilliant businessman, and his friendship with Bastiano would have no sway over his dealings, Raul was certain of that.

Raul rather hoped his presence at the hotel might cause Bastiano some discomfort, for though they moved in similar circles in truth their paths rarely crossed. Raul, even on his father's death, had never returned to Casta.

There had been no respects to pay.

Yet Casta had remained Bastiano's base.

He had converted the old convent into a luxury retreat for the seriously wealthy.

It was actually, Raul knew, an extremely upmarket rehab facility.

His mother would be turning in her grave.

Raul's black thoughts were interrupted when the portly

middle-aged gentleman sitting to his right made his dis-
gruntled feelings known.

'Who do you have to sleep with around here to get some
service?' he muttered in well-schooled English.

It would seem that the tourists were getting impatient!

Raul smiled inwardly as the waiter continued to ignore
the pompous Englishman. The waiter had had enough. This
man had been complaining since the moment he had been
shown to his table, and there was absolutely nothing to
complain about.

Raul was not being generous in that observation. Many
of his nights were spent in hotels—mainly those that he
owned—and so more than most he had a very critical eye.

There were certain ways to behave, and despite his accent this man did not adhere to them. He seemed to assume
that just because he was in Rome no one would speak English and his insults would go unnoticed.

They did not.

And so—just because he could—Raul gestured with his
index and middle fingers towards the small china cup on his
table. The motion was subtle, barely noticeable to many, and
yet it was enough to indicate to the attentive waiter that Raul
had changed his mind and would now like another coffee.

Raul knew that his preferential treatment would incense
the diner to his right.

From the huff of indignation as his drink was delivered, it did.

Good!

Yes, Raul decided, he wanted this hotel.

Raul read through the figures again and decided to make
some further calls to try to get behind the real reason the
Sultan was selling such an iconic hotel. Even with Raul's
extensive probing he could see no reason for the sale. While
the outgoings were vast, it was profitable indeed. The crème

de la crème stayed at the Grande Lucia, and it was here that their children were christened and wed.

There had to be a reason Alim was selling, and Raul had every intention of finding out just what it was.

Just as Raul had decided to leave he glanced up and saw a woman enter the dining room.

Raul was more than used to beautiful women, and the room was busy enough that he should not even have noticed, but there was something about her that drew the eye.

She was tall and slender and she wore a taupe dress. Her long blonde hair appeared freshly washed and tumbled over her shoulders. Raul watched as she had a brief conversation with the maître d' and then started to walk in his direction.

Still Raul did not look away.

She made her way between the tables with elegant ease, and Raul noted that she carried herself beautifully. Her complexion was pale and creamy, and suddenly Raul wanted her to be close enough so that he could know the colour of her eyes. She lifted a hand and gave a small wave, and Raul, who was rarely the recipient of a sinking feeling where women were concerned, felt one now.

She was with *him*, Raul realised—she was here to have breakfast with the obnoxious man who sat to his right.

Pity.

The blonde beauty walked past his table, and he could not help but notice the delicate row of buttons that ran from neck to hem on her dress. But he pointedly returned his attention to his computer screen rather than mentally undress her.

That she was with someone rendered her of no interest to him in that way.

Raul loathed cheats.

Still, the morning scent of her was fresh and heady—a delicate cloud that reached Raul a few seconds after she had passed and lingered for a few moments more.

'Good morning,' she said as she took a seat, and unlike her companion's the woman's voice was pleasant.

'Hmph.'

Her greeting was barely acknowledged by the seated Englishman. Some people, Raul decided, simply did not know how to appreciate the finer things in life.

And this lady was certainly amongst the finest.

The waiter knew that too.

He was there in an instant to lavish attention upon her and was appreciative of her efforts when she attempted to ask for Breakfast Tea in schoolgirl Italian, remembering her manners and adding a clumsy *'per favour'*.

Such poor Italian would usually be responded to in English, in arrogant reprimand, and yet the waiter gave a nod. *'Prego.'*

'I'll have another coffee,' the man said and then, before the waiter had even left, added rather loudly to his companion, 'The service is terribly slow here—I've had nothing but trouble with the staff since the moment I arrived.'

'Well, I think it's excellent.' Her voice was crisp and curt, instantly dismissing his findings. 'I've found that a please and a thank-you work wonders—you really ought to try it, Maurice.'

'What are your plans for today?' he asked.

'I'm hoping to do some sightseeing.'

'Well, you need to shop—perhaps you should consider something a little less beige,' Maurice added. 'I asked the concierge and he recommended a hair and beauty salon a short distance from the hotel. I've booked you in for four.'

'Excuse me?'

Raul was about to close his laptop. His interest had waned the second he had realised she was with someone.

Almost.

But then the man spoke on.

'We're meeting Bastiano at six, and you want to be looking your best.'

The sound of his nemesis's name halted Raul and again the couple had his full attention—though not by a flicker did he betray his interest.

'*You're* meeting Bastiano at six,' the blonde beauty responded. 'I don't see why I have to be there while you two discuss business.'

'I'm not arguing about this. I expect you to be there at six.'

Raul drained his espresso but made no move to stand. He wanted to know what they had to do with Bastiano—any inside knowledge on the man he most loathed was valuable.

'I can't make it,' she said. 'I'm meeting a friend tonight.'

'Come off it!' The awful man snorted. 'We both know that you don't have any friends.'

It was a horrible statement to make, and Raul forgot to pretend to listen and actually turned his head to see her reaction. Most women Raul knew would crumble a little, but instead she gave a thin smile and a shrug.

'Acquaintance, then. I really am busy tonight.'

'Lydia, you will do what is right by the family.'

Her name was Lydia.

As Raul continued to look at her, perhaps sensing her conversation was being overheard, she glanced over and their eyes briefly met. He saw that they were china blue.

His question as to the colour of her eyes was answered, but now Raul had so many more.

She flicked her gaze away and the conversation was halted as the waiter brought their drinks.

Raul made no move to leave.

He wanted to know more.

A family had come into the restaurant and were being seated close to them. The activity drowned out the words from the table beside him, revealing only hints of the conversation.

'Some old convent…' she said, and the small cup in his hand clattered just a little as it hit the saucer.

Raul realised they were discussing the valley.

'Well, that shows he's used to old buildings,' Maurice said. 'Apparently it's an inordinate success.'

A baby that was being squeezed into an antique high chair started to wail, and Raul frowned in impatience as an older child loudly declared that he was hungry and he wanted chocolate milk.

'Scusi…' he called to the waiter, and with a mere couple of words more and a slight gesture of his hand in the family's direction his displeasure was noted.

Noted not just by the waiter—Lydia noted it too.

In fact she had noticed him the moment the maître d' had gestured to where her stepfather, Maurice, was seated.

Even from a distance, even seated, the man's beauty had been evident.

There was something about him that had forced her attention as she had crossed the dining room.

No one should look that good at eight in the morning.

His black hair gleamed, and as she had approached Lydia had realised it was damp and he must have been in the shower around the same time as her.

Such an odd thought.

That rapidly turned into a filthy one.

Her first with the recipient in the same room!

She had looked away quickly as soon as she had seen that he was watching her approach.

Her stomach had done a little somersault and her legs had requested of their owner that they might bypass Maurice and be seated with *him*.

Such a ridiculous thought, for she knew him not at all.

And he *wasn't* nice.

That much she knew.

Lydia turned her head slightly and saw that on his command the family was being moved.

They were *children*, for goodness' sake!

This man irritated her.

This stranger irritated her far more than a stranger should, and she frowned her disapproval at him and her neck felt hot and itchy as he gave a small shrug in return and then closed his computer.

You were already leaving, Lydia wanted to point out. *Why have the family moved when you were about to leave?*

Yes, he irritated her—like an itch she needed to scratch.

Her ears felt hot and her jaw clenched as the waiter came and apologised to him for the disruption.

Disruption?

The child had asked for chocolate milk, for goodness' sake, and the baby had merely cried.

Of course she said nothing. Instead Lydia reached for her pot of tea as Maurice droned on about their plans for tonight—or rather, what he thought Lydia should wear.

'Why don't you speak to a stylist?'

'I think I can manage. I've been dressing myself since I was three,' Lydia calmly informed him, and as she watched the amber fluid pour into her cup she knew—she just knew—that the stranger beside her was listening.

It was her audience that gave her strength.

Oh, she couldn't see him, but she knew his attention was on her.

There was an awareness between them that she could not define—a conversation taking place such as she had never experienced, for it was one without words.

'Don't be facetious, Lydia,' Maurice snapped.

But with this man beside her Lydia felt just that.

The sun was shining, she was in Rome, and the day

stretched before her—she simply did not want to waste a single moment of it with Maurice.

'Have a lovely day…' She took her napkin and placed it on the table, clearly about to leave. 'Give Bastiano my regards.'

'This isn't up for debate, Lydia. You're to keep tonight free. Bastiano has flown us to Rome for this meeting and housed us in two stunning suites. The very least you can do is come for a drink and thank him.'

'Fine,' Lydia retorted. 'But know this, I'll have a drink, but it's not the "very least" I'll do—it's the most.'

'You'll do what's right for the family.'

'I've tried that for years,' Lydia said, and stood up. 'I think it's about time I did what's right by *me*!'

Lydia walked out of the restaurant with her head still high, but though she looked absolutely in control she was in turmoil, for her silent fears were starting to come true.

This wasn't a holiday.

And it wasn't just drinks.

She was being offered up, Lydia knew.

'Scusi…'

A hand on her elbow halted her, and as she spun around Lydia almost shot into orbit when she saw it was the man from the next table.

'Can I help you?' she snapped.

'I saw you leaving suddenly.'

'I wasn't aware that I needed your permission.'

'Of course you don't,' he responded.

His voice was deep, and his English, though excellent, was laced heavily with a rich accent. Her toes attempted to curl in her flat sandals at its sound.

Lydia was tall, but then so was he—she didn't come close to his eye level.

It felt like a disadvantage.

'I just wanted to check that you were okay.'

'Why wouldn't I be?'

'I heard some of what was said in there.'

'And do you *always* listen in on private conversations?'

'Of course.' He shrugged. 'I rarely intervene, but you seemed upset.'

'No,' Lydia said. 'I didn't.'

She knew that as fact—she was very good at keeping her emotions in check.

She should have walked off then. Only she didn't. She continued the conversation. 'That baby, however, *was* upset—and I didn't see you following him across the dining room.'

'I don't like tantrums with my breakfast, and the toddler is now throwing one,' he said. 'I thought I might go somewhere else to eat. Would you like to join me?'

He was forward *and* he lied, for she had seen the waiter removing his plates and knew he had already had breakfast.

'No, thank you.' Lydia shook her head.

'But you haven't eaten.'

'Again,' Lydia replied coolly, 'that's not your concern.'

Bastiano *was* his concern, though.

For years revenge had been his motivator, and yet still Bastiano flourished.

Something had to give, and Raul had waited a long time for that day to arrive.

Now it would seem that it had—in the delicate shape of an English rose.

Raul was no fool, and even from the snippets of conversation he'd heard, he had worked out a little of what was going on.

Bastiano wanted Lydia to be there tonight.

And Lydia didn't want to go.

It was enough to go on—more than enough. For despite her calm demeanour he could see the pulse leaping in her throat. More than that, Raul knew women—and knew them well.

There was another issue that existed between them.

She was turned on.

So was he.

They had been on sight.

From her slow walk across the dining room and for every moment since they had been aware of each other at the basest of levels.

'Come for breakfast,' he said, and then he remembered how she liked manners. *'Per favore.'*

Lydia realised then that every word she had uttered in the restaurant had been noted.

It should feel intrusive.

And it did.

But in the most delightful of ways.

Her breath felt hot in her lungs and the warm feeling from the brief touch of his hand on her arm was still present.

She wanted to say yes—to accept this dark stranger's invitation and follow this dangerous lead.

But that would be reckless at best, and Lydia was far from that.

There was something about him that she could not quite define, and every cell in her body recognised it and screamed danger. He was polished and poised—immaculate, in fact. And yet despite the calm demeanour there was a restless edge. Beneath the smooth jaw was a blue hue that hinted at the unshaven, decadent beauty of him. Even his scent clamoured for attention, subtle and at the same time overwhelming.

Raul had her on the edge of panic—an unfamiliar one.

He was potent—*so* potent that she wanted to say yes. To simply throw caution to the wind and have breakfast with this beautiful man.

She didn't even know his name.

'Do you always ask complete strangers for breakfast?' Lydia asked.

'No,' he admitted, and then he lowered his head just a fraction and lowered his voice an octave more. 'But then you defy the hour.'

CHAPTER TWO

THEY DEFIED THE HOUR, Lydia thought. Because as they stepped outside the hotel surely the moon should be hanging in a dark sky.

It was just breakfast, she told herself as his hand took her elbow and guided her across the busy street.

Yet it felt like a date.

Her first.

But it wasn't a romantic Italian evening, for the sun shone brightly and Rome was at its busy rush hour best.

Yet he made it so.

The restaurant he steered her to had a roped-off section and the tables were clearly reserved, yet the greeter unclipped the rope and they breezed through as if they were expected guests.

'Did you have a reservation?' Lydia asked, more than a little confused as they took their seats.

'No.'

'Then…' Lydia stopped, for she had answered her own question—the best seats were permanently reserved for the likes of him. He had a confident air that demanded, without words, only the best.

Coffee was brought and sparkling water was poured. They were handed the heavy menus, but as the waiter started to explain the choices he waved him away.

Lydia was grateful that he had, for there was a real need for the two of them to be left alone.

He was an absolute stranger.

A black-eyed stranger who had led and she had followed.

'I don't know your name,' Lydia said, and found she was worried a little that it might disappoint.

'Raul.'

It didn't.

He rolled the *R* just a little, and then she found herself repeating it, *'Rau—el...'* Though it did not roll easily from her tongue.

She waited for his surname.

It didn't come.

'I'm Lydia.'

'I had worked that out.' He glanced down at the menu. He never wasted time with small talk, unless it suited him. 'What would you like?'

She should be hungry. Lydia hadn't eaten since the plane, and even then she had just toyed with her meal.

She had been sick with nerves last night, but now, though still nervous, the feeling was pleasant.

'I'd like…' Lydia peered at the menu.

Really she ought to eat something, given that breakfast was the reason she was here.

But then she blushed while reading the menu, because food was the furthest thing from her mind.

'It's in Italian,' Lydia said, and could immediately have kicked herself, for it was such a stupid thing to say—and so rude to assume it should be otherwise.

But he did not chide her, and he did not score a point by stating that Italy was, in fact, where they were.

He just waited patiently as she stumbled her way through the selections till she came upon something she knew. But she frowned. 'Tiramisu for breakfast?'

'Sounds good.'

Perhaps he hadn't heard the question in her voice, because Lydia had assumed it was served only as a dessert, but Raul was right—it sounded good.

The waiter complimented their choice as he took their orders, and very soon she tasted bliss.

'Oh…' It was light and not too sweet, and the liquor made it decadent. It really had been an accidental perfect choice.

'Nice,' Raul said, and watched her hurriedly swallow and clear her mouth before speaking.

'Yes.' Lydia nodded. 'Very.'

'I wasn't asking a question.'

Just observing.

He looked at her mouth, and Lydia wondered if she had a crumb on her lip, but she resisted putting out her tongue to check.

And then he looked at her mouth, and the pressure within built as still she resisted that simple oral manoeuvre. Instead she pulled her bottom lip into her mouth and ran her tongue over it there.

No crumb.

Her eyes met his and she frowned at his impertinence as they asked a question—*Are you imagining what I think you are?*

Of course she said no such thing, and his features were impassive, but those black eyes offered his response.

Yes, Lydia, I am.

Had she had her purse with her, Lydia might well have called for the bill and fled, because she felt as if she were going insane. She looked around. Almost certain that the spectacle she was creating would have the world on pause and watching.

Yet the waiters were waiting, the patrons were chatting, the commuters were commuting and the word was just carrying on, oblivious to the fire smouldering unchecked in this roped-off section.

And so too must Raul be—oblivious, that was. For his voice was even and his question polite. 'How are you finding Rome?'

Lydia was about to nod and say how wonderful it was, or

give some other pat response, but she put down her spoon, let go of the end of her tether and simply stated the truth.

The real reason she was in Rome.

'I'm *determined* to love it this time.'

'Okay...' Raul said. His stance was relaxed and he leant back in the seat, seemingly nonchalant, but in his mind he was searching for an angle—how to get her to speak of Bastiano without too direct a question.

Lydia was terribly formal—very English and uptight. One wrong move, Raul knew, and he would be the recipient of a downed napkin and he'd have to watch her stalk off back to the hotel.

She was so incredibly sexy, though.

A woman who would make you *earn* that reward.

Lydia did not flirt, he noted.

Not a fraction.

No playing with her hair, no leaning forward, no secret smiles and no innuendo.

Really, the way she was sitting so upright in the chair, he could be at a breakfast meeting with Allegra, his PA.

Except Raul was aroused.

He was here to garner information, Raul reminded himself, and took his mind back to their conversation.

Or tried to.

'How long are you here for?'

'Till Sunday,' Lydia answered. 'Two nights. How about you?'

'I'm here for business.'

Raul should not be taking this time now. He had a very packed day. First he would meet with Alim and his team. Then, if time allowed, he would drop in unexpectedly on the other hotel he owned in Rome.

But he always made Bastiano his business.

'When do you leave?' she asked.

'When business is done.' Raul's jet was in fact booked for six this evening, but he did not share his itinerary with anyone outside his close circle. 'So, you've been to Rome before?'

'Yes, I came to Italy on a school trip and had a rather miserable time. I don't think my mood then did the place justice.'

'Where did you go?'

'Rome, Florence and Venice.'

'Which was your favourite?'

Lydia thought for a moment. 'Venice.'

'And your least favourite?'

Oh, that was easy—Lydia didn't have to think to answer that, even if he didn't understand her response. 'Venice.'

He *did* understand.

So much so that Raul again forgot that he was trying to steer the conversation. Even though Bastiano was the reason Raul was there, for now he left Raul's mind.

He thought of Venice—the city he loved and now called home.

Not that he told *her* that.

Raul gave away nothing.

Then suddenly he did.

For as she looked over she was rewarded with the slow reveal of his smile.

And his smile was a true and very rare gift.

She saw those full dark lips stretch and the white of his teeth, but the real beauty was in eyes that stared so deeply into hers she felt there was nowhere to hide.

And nor did she want to.

'Venice,' Raul said, in that deep, measured voice, 'can be the loneliest place in the world.'

'Yes,' Lydia admitted. 'It was.'

It was as if she was seventeen again, walking alongside the Grand Canal alone and wanting to be in love with the city.

To be in love.

Of course nearly every schoolgirl on a trip to Italy secretly hoped for a little romance.

But on that day—on that terribly lonely day—Lydia would have been happy with a friend.

One true friend.

Raul was right. Lydia had felt utterly alone then, and for the most part she had felt the same since.

She was looking at him, but not really, and then his voice brought her back.

'And you forgive her because how could you not?'

'Her?' Lydia checked, her mind still on friendships that had failed.

'Venice.'

'I wasn't there long enough to forgive her,' Lydia admitted.

'What happened?'

'Just being a teenager…'

She could easily dismiss it as that, but it had been more. Oh, she didn't want to tell him that her father had just died and left behind him utter chaos, for while it might explain her unhappiness then, it wasn't the entire truth—it had been more than that.

'Schoolgirls can be such bitches.'

'I don't think it is exclusive to that age bracket.'

'No!' Lydia actually laughed at his observation because, yes, those girls were now women and probably still much the same.

She glanced at her phone, which had remained silent.

Arabella hadn't responded to her text.

Neither had she responded to Lydia's last message.

And suddenly Lydia was back in Italy, hurting again.

'What happened in Venice?'

Raul chose his moment to ask. He knew how to steer conversations, and yet he actually found himself wanting to know.

'We went to Murano…to a glass factory.' She shook her head and, as she had then, felt pained to reveal the truth.

It felt like a betrayal.

Money should never be discussed outside the home.

'And…?' Raul gently pushed.

Why lie? Lydia thought.

She would never see him again.

It wasn't such a big deal.

Surely?

'My father had died the year before.'

He didn't say he was sorry—did not offer the automatic response to that statement.

It was oddly freeing.

Everyone had been *so* sorry.

If there's anything I can do… The words had been tossed around like black confetti at his funeral.

Yet they had done nothing!

When it was clear the money had gone, so had they.

'I'd told Arabella, my best friend, that my mother was struggling financially.' Lydia was sweating, and that wasn't flattering. She wanted to call the waiter to move the shade umbrella but knew she could be sitting in ice and the result would be the same.

It wasn't sexy sweat.

Lydia wasn't turned on now.

She felt sick.

'I told Arabella that we might lose the castle.'

She offered more explanation.

'The castle was in my mother's family, but my father ran it. I thought he had run it well, but on his death I found out that my parents had been going under.'

Raul offered no comment, just let her speak.

'He took his own life.'

She'd never said it out loud before.

Had never been allowed to say it.

'I'm sorry you had to go through that.'

And because he hadn't said sorry before, now—when he did—she felt he meant it.

'I still can't believe he left me.'

'To deal with the fallout?'

He completed her sentence, even though Lydia thought she already had. She thought about it for a moment and nodded.

'Things really were dire. My mother kept selling things off, to pay for my school fees. The trip to Italy was a compulsory one. I got a part-time job—saved up some spending money. Of course it didn't come close to what my friends had. They were hitting all the boutiques and Arabella kept asking why I wasn't buying anything. In the end I told her how bad things were. I swore her to secrecy.'

He gave a soft, mirthless laugh—one that told her he understood.

And then they were silent.

In *that* moment they met.

Not at a breakfast table in Rome but in a bleak, desolate space a world away from there.

They met and he reached across and took her hand, and together they walked it through.

'At the factory, after a demonstration, everyone was buying things. I held back, of course. There was a table with damaged glassware and Belinda, another friend, held up a three-legged horse and suggested it was something that I might be able to afford. I realised then that Arabella had told everyone.'

She could still feel the betrayal.

Could still remember looking over to her best friend as everyone had laughed.

Arabella hadn't so much as blushed at being caught.

'She suggested that they all have a whip-round for me.'

'So you walked off?' Raul asked, impatient to know and understand her some more.

'Oh, no!' Lydia shook her head and then sighed. 'I used up all my spending money, and the money I'd been given for my birthday, and bought a vase that I certainly couldn't afford.'

It was that response in herself she had hated the most.

'How shallow is that?'

'People have been known to drown in shallow waters.'

'Well, it's certainly not easy to swim in them! Anyway, I didn't see them much after that...'

'You left school?'

'I went to the local comprehensive for my final year. Far more sensible...but hell.'

Everything—not just the fact that she was a new girl for the last year, but every little thing, from her accent to her handwriting—had ensured she didn't fit in from the very first day.

Raul knew it would have been hell.

He could imagine *his* schoolmates if an Italian version of Lydia had shown up in his old schoolyard. Raul could guess all she would have gone through.

'I was a joke to them, of course.'

He squeezed her hand and it was the kindest touch, so contrary to that time.

'Too posh to handle?' Raul said, and she nodded, almost smiled.

But then the smile changed.

Lydia never cried.

Ever.

Not even when her father had died.

So why start now?

Lydia pulled her hand back.

She was done with introspection—done with musings.

They hurt too much.

Lydia was somewhat appalled at how much she had told him.

'Raul, why am I here?'

'Because…' Raul shrugged, but when that did not appease her he elaborated. 'Maurice was getting in the way.'

Lydia found herself laughing, and it surprised her that she could.

A second ago she had felt like crying.

It was nice being with him.

Not soothing.

Just liberating.

She had told another person some of the truth and he had remained.

'Maurice is my stepfather,' she explained.

'Good,' Raul said, but she missed the innuendo.

'Not really.'

Lydia didn't respond to his flirting as others usually did, so he adopted a more businesslike tone. The rest they could do later—he wanted information now.

'Maurice wants you to be at some dinner tonight?'

Lydia nodded. 'He's got an important meeting with a potential investor and he wants me there.'

'Why?'

Lydia gave a dismissive shake of her head.

She certainly wasn't going to discuss *that*!

'I probably shan't go,' Lydia said, instead of explaining things. 'I'm supposed to be catching up with a friend—or rather,' she added, remembering all he had heard, 'an acquaintance.'

'Who?'

'Arabella.' She was embarrassed to admit it after all she had told him. 'She works in Rome now.'

'I thought you fell out?'

'That was all a very long time ago,' Lydia said, but she didn't actually like the point he had raised.

They hadn't fallen out.

The incident had been buried—like everything else.

She conversed with Arabella only through social media and the odd text. It had been years since they had been face-to-face, and Lydia wasn't sure she was relishing the prospect of seeing her, so, rather than admit that, she went back to his original question—why Maurice wanted her to be there tonight.

'The family castle is now a wedding venue.'

'Do you work there?'

Lydia nodded.

'Doing what?'

'I deal with the bookings and organise the catering...' She gave a tight smile, because what she did for a living was so far away from her dreams. When her father had been alive she had loved the visitors that came to the castle. He would take them through it and pass on its rich history and Lydia would learn something new every time.

'And you still live at home?'

'Yes.'

She didn't add that there was no choice. The business was failing so badly that they couldn't afford much outside help, and she didn't get a wage as such.

'Bastiano—this man we're supposed to meet tonight—has had a lot of success converting old buildings... He has several luxury retreats and my mother and Maurice are hoping to go that route with the castle. Still, it would take a massive cash injection...'

'Castles need more than an injection—they require a permanent infusion,' Raul corrected.

All old buildings did.

It galled him that Bastiano had been able to turn the convent into a successful business venture. On paper it should never have worked, and yet somehow he had ensured that it had.

'Quite,' Lydia agreed. 'But more than money we need his wisdom...' She misinterpreted the slight narrowing of Raul's eyes as confusion. 'A lot of these types of venture fail—somehow Bastiano's succeed.'

'So why would this successful businessman be interested in *your* castle?'

Lydia found she was holding her breath. His question was just a little bit insulting. After all, the castle was splendid indeed, and Raul could have no idea what a disaster in business Maurice had turned out to be.

'I'm sure Bastiano recognises its potential.'

'And he wants you there tonight so he can hear your vision for the castle?'

Lydia gave a small shake of her head. The truth was that she was actually *opposed* to the idea of turning it into a retreat—not that her objections held much weight.

'Then why do you need to go?'

'I've been invited.'

'Lydia, I have had more business meetings than I've had dinners.' Raul spoke when she did not. 'But I can't ever remember asking anyone—*ever*—to bring along their daughter, or rather their stepdaughter.'

She blushed.

Those creamy cheeks turned an unflattering red.

Lydia knew it—she could feel the fire, not just on her skin but building inside her at the inappropriateness he was alluding to.

'Excuse me?' she snapped.

'Why?' Raul said. 'What did you do?'

'I mean you're rude to insinuate that there might be something else going on!'

'I know that's what you meant.'

He remained annoyingly calm, and more annoyingly he didn't back down.

'And I'm not *insinuating* anything—I'm telling you that unless you hold the deeds to the castle, or are to be a major player in the renovations, or some such, there is no reason for this Bastiano to insist on your company tonight. '

'He isn't insisting.'

'Good.' Raul shrugged. 'Then don't go.'

'I don't have any excuse not to.'

'You don't need one.'

It was Lydia who gave a shrug now.

A tense one.

She was still cross at his insinuation.

Or rather she was cross that Raul might be right—that he could see what she had spent weeks frantically trying *not* to.

'Lydia, can I tell you something?'

She didn't answer.

'Some free advice.'

'Why would I take advice from a stranger?'

'I'm no longer a stranger.'

He wasn't. She had told him more than she had told many people who were in her day-to-day life.

'Can I?' Raul checked.

She liked it that he did not give advice unrequested, and when she met his eyes they were patient and awaiting her answer.

'Yes.'

'You can walk away from anyone you choose to, and you don't have to come up with a reason.'

'I know that.'

She had walked off from breakfast with Maurice, after all.

It wasn't enough, though—Lydia knew that. And though Raul's words made perfect sense, they just did not apply to her world.

'So why don't you tell your stepfather that you can't make it tonight because you're catching up with a friend?'

'I already have.'

'But you don't like Arabella,' Raul pointed out. 'So why don't you meet me instead?'

She laughed a black laugh. '*You're* not a friend.'

He wasn't.

'No,' he answered honestly. 'I'm not.'

She was about to take a sip of her coffee when he added something else.

'I could be for tonight, though.'

'I don't think so.' Lydia gave a small laugh, not really getting what he had just said—or rather not really thinking he meant it.

'Do you have many friends?' she asked, replacing her cup. Perhaps her question was a little invasive, but she'd told him rather a lot and was curious to know about him.

'Some.'

'Close friends?' Lydia pushed.

'No one whose birthday I need to remember.'

'No one?'

He shook his head.

'I guess it saves shopping for presents.'

'Not really.'

Raul decided to take things to another level and tell her how things could be. In sex, at least, he was up front.

'I like to give a present the morning after.'

Lydia got what he meant this time.

She didn't blush. If anything Lydia felt a shiver, as if the sun had slipped behind a cloud.

It hadn't.

He was dark, he was dangerous, and he was as sexy as hell. Absolutely she was out of her depth.

'I'm here to sightsee, Raul.'

'Then you need an expert.'

Lydia stared coolly back at this man who was certainly that. She wondered at his reaction if she told him just how inexperienced she was—that in fact he would be her first.

Not that it was going to happen!

But *what* a first, Lydia thought.

She went to reach for water but decided against it, unsure she could manage the simple feat when the air thrummed with an energy that was foreign to her.

He was potent, and Lydia was tempted in a way she had never been.

She glanced down to his hand, and that was beautiful too—olive-skinned and long-fingered with very neat nails. And it was happening again, because now she imagined them inside her.

Oh!

She was sitting at breakfast, imagining those very fingers in the filthiest of thoughts, and she dared not look up at him for she felt he could read her mind.

'So what are your plans for today?' Raul asked.

His voice seemed to be coming from a distance, and yet he was so prominent in her mind.

She could take his hand, Lydia was certain, and be led to his bed.

Oh, what was *happening* to her?

'I told you—sightseeing, and then I'm shopping for a dress.'

'I wish I could be there to see that.'

'I thought men didn't like shopping.'

'I don't, usually.'

His eyes flicked to the row of buttons at the front of her dress and then to the thick nipples that ached, just *ached* for his touch, for his mouth. And then they moved back to her face.

'I have to go,' Raul told her, and she sat still as he stood. With good reason: her legs simply refused to move. Standing would be difficult…walking back over to the hotel would prove a completely impossible feat.

Please go, Lydia thought, because she felt drunk on lust and was trying not to let him see.

He summoned the waiter, and though he spoke in Italian he spoke slowly enough that she could just make out what was being said.

Hold this table for tonight at six.

And then he turned to where she sat, now with her back to him, and lowered his head. For a moment she thought he was going to kiss her.

He did not.

His breath was warm on her cheek and his scent was like a delicious invasion. His glossy black hair was so close that she fought not to reach out and feel it, fought not to turn and lick his face.

And then he spoke.

'Hold that thought till six.'

Lydia blinked and tried to pretend that she still felt normal, that this was simply breakfast and she was somehow in control.

'I already told you—I can't make it tonight.'

Then he offered but one word.

'Choose.'

CHAPTER THREE

WHAT THE HELL was happening to her?

Lydia watched him walk across the street and then disappear inside the hotel.

He did not turn around. He didn't walk with haste.

She wanted him to hurry, to disappear, just so that she could clear her mind—because in fact she *wanted* him to turn around.

One crook of his finger and she knew she would rise and run to him—and that was so *not* her. She kept her distance from people—not just physically but emotionally too.

Her father's death had rocked every aspect of her world, and the aftermath had been hell. Watching her mother selling off heirlooms and precious memories one by one, in a permanent attempt to keep up appearances, and then marrying that frightful man. Finding her friends had all been fair-weather ones had also hurt Lydia to the core. And so she held back—from family, from friends and, yes, from men.

She was guarded, and possibly the assumption made by others that she was cold was a correct one.

But not now—not this morning.

She felt as if she had been scalded, as if every nerve was heated and raw, and all he had done was buy her breakfast.

She sat alone at the table. There was nothing to indicate romance—no candles or champagne—and no favourable dusk to soften the view. Just the brightness of morning.

There had been no romance.

Raul had offered her one night and a present the following morning. She should have damn well slapped him for the insult!

Yet he'd left her on a slightly giddy high that she couldn't quite come down from.

Sightseeing as such didn't happen.

When she should have been sorting out what to do about tonight she wandered around, thinking about this morning.

But finally she shopped, and accepted the assistant's advice, and stood in the changing room with various options.

The black did not match her mood.

The caramel felt rather safe.

But as for the red!

The rich fabric caressed her skin and gave curves where she had few. It was ruched across her stomach and her hand went to smooth it before she realised that was the desired effect—it drew the eye lower.

Lydia slipped on the heels that stood in the corner and looked at her reflection from behind. And then she looked from the front.

She felt sexy, and for the first time beautiful and just a touch wild as she lifted her hair and imagined it piled up in curls. And *his* reaction.

It wasn't Bastiano's reaction she was envisaging—it was the reaction of the man who had invited her out this evening.

Only that wasn't quite right.

He hadn't asked her out on a date.

Raul had invited her to a night in his bed.

'Bellisima...'

Lydia spun around as the assistant came in, and her cheeks matched the fabric as if she had been caught stealing.

'That dress is perfect on you...' the assistant said.

'Well, I prefer this one.'

She could see the assistant's confusion as she plucked the closest dress to hand and passed it to her.

Caramel—or rather a dark shade of beige.

Safe.

Bastiano was *not* a safe option.

Raul knew that as fact.

'I trust you were comfortable last night?' Sultan Alim asked when they met.

Raul had met the Sultan once before, but that had been in the Middle East and then Alim had been dressed in traditional robes. Today he wore a deep navy suit.

'Extremely comfortable,' Raul agreed. 'Your staff are excellent.'

'We have a rigorous recruiting process for all levels.' Alim nodded. 'Few make it through the interviews, and not many past the three-month trial. We retain only the best.'

Raul had seen that for himself.

Alim was unhurried as he took Raul behind the scenes of his iconic hotel. 'I have had four serious expressions of interest,' Alim went on to explain. 'Two I know have the means—one I doubt. The other...' He held his hand flat and waved it to indicate he was uncertain.

'So I have one definite rival?' Raul said, and watched as Alim gave a conceding smile.

Both knew Raul was a serious contender.

He didn't have to try hard to guess who the other was—not that Alim let on.

Raul had done his homework, and he knew that Alim was not just an astute businessman but very discreet in all his dealings.

He would have to be.

Allegra, Raul's long-suffering PA, had found out all she could on him.

Sultan Alim was a playboy, and his palace's PR must be on overtime to keep his decadent ways out of the press.

Alim kissed but never told, and in return the silence of his aggrieved lovers was paid for in diamonds.

And in business he played his cards close to his chest.

The latter Raul could attest to, for Alim did not bend to any of Raul's mercurial ways.

By the end of a very long day Raul was still no closer to finding out the real reason for the sale.

Alim had dismissed his team and was taking Raul for one final look around.

'I haven't seen Bastiano,' Raul commented as the elevator arrived to take them down to the function rooms. When Alim did not respond, Raul pushed. 'I see that his guests are already here.'

Still Alim gave nothing away. 'I shall take you now to the ballroom.'

Raul had no choice but to accept his silence.

He knew that Alim and Bastiano were friends, and in turn Alim would know that Raul and Bastiano were business rivals and enemies.

So, instead of trying to find out more about Bastiano, Raul returned his mind to work.

'Why?' Raul asked Sultan Alim as they walked along the lush corridors. 'Why are you selling?'

'I've already answered that,' Sultan Alim said. 'I am to marry soon and I am moving my portfolio back to the Middle East.'

'I want the real reason.'

Alim halted mid-stride and turned to face Raul as he spoke.

'You have several hotels throughout Europe that you aren't letting go, yet this jewel you are.'

'You're correct,' Alim said. 'Hotel Grande Lucia *is* a jewel.'

As Raul frowned, Alim gave a nod that told Raul he would explain some more.

'Come and see this.'

They stepped into the grand ballroom, where a dark-haired woman, dressed in a dark suit that was rather too tight, was standing in the middle of the dance floor.

Just standing.

Her shoes must be a little tight too, for she was holding stilettos in one hand.

'Is everything okay, Gabi?' Alim asked her.

'Oh!' Clearly she hadn't heard them come in, because she startled but then pushed out a smile. 'Yes, everything is fine. I was just trying to work out the table plan for Saturday.'

'We have a large wedding coming up,' Alim explained to Raul.

'And both sets of parents are twice divorced.' Gabi gave a slight eye-roll and then chatted away as she bent to put on her shoes. 'Trying to work out where everyone should be seated is proving—'

'Gabi!' Alim scolded, and then turned to Raul. 'Gabi is not on my staff. *They* tend to be rather more discreet.' He waved his hand, but this time it was to dismiss her. 'Excuse us, please.'

Alim, who had until now been exceptionally pleasant with all his staff, was less than polite now. Raul watched as a very put-out Gabi flounced from the ballroom.

'She is a wedding planner from an outside firm,' Alim said, to explain the indiscretion. '*My* staff would *never* discuss clients that way in front of a visitor.'

'Of course.' Raul nodded as the huge entrance doors closed loudly, and he resisted raising his eyebrows as the crystals in the chandeliers responded to the pointed slam.

It was actually rather spectacular to watch.

The reflection of the low, late-afternoon sun was captured by several thousand crystals, and for a moment it was as if it was raining sunbeams as light danced across the walls and the ceiling and the floor—even over their suits.

'It's a beautiful ballroom,' Raul commented as he looked around, though he was unsure exactly why Alim had brought him here instead of to a meeting room, when it was figures that Raul wanted to discuss.

'When I bought the hotel those had not been cleaned in years,' Alim said, gesturing to the magnificent lights. 'Now they are taken down and cared for properly. It is a huge undertaking. The room has to be closed, so no functions can be held, and it is all too easy to put it off.'

Raul could see that it would be, but he did not get involved in such details and told Alim so.

'I leave all that to my managers to organise,' Raul said.

Alim nodded. 'Usually I do too, but when I took over the Grande Lucia there had been many cost-cutting measures. It was slowly turning into just another hotel. It is not just the lighting in the ballroom, of course. What I am trying to explain is that this hotel has become more than an investment to me. Once I return to my homeland I shall not be able to give it the attention it deserves.'

'The next owner might not either,' Raul pointed out.

'That is his business. But while the hotel is mine I want no part in her demise.'

Raul knew he was now hearing the true reason for the sale. To keep this hotel to its current standard would be a huge undertaking, and one that Raul would play no major part in—he would delegate that. Perhaps he'd do so more carefully, given what he had been told. But at the end of the day managers managed, and Raul had neither the time nor the inclination to be that heavily involved.

'Now you have given me pause for thought,' Raul admitted.

'Good.' Alim smiled. 'The Grande Lucia deserves the best caretaker. Please,' Alim said, indicating that their long day of meetings had come to an end, 'take all the time you need to look around and to enjoy the rest of your stay.'

Sultan Alim excused himself and Raul stood in the empty ballroom, watching the light dancing around the walls like a shower of stars.

He thought of home.

And he understood Alim's concerns.

Last year Raul had purchased a stunning Venetian Gothic *palazzo* on the Grand Canal.

It required more than casual upkeep.

The house was run by Loretta—the woman who had warned his mother of Gino's imminent return home all those years ago.

She ran the staff—and there were many.

Raul looked around the ballroom at the intricate cornices and arched windows.

Yes, he knew what Alim was talking about. But this was a hotel, not a home.

Raul would play no part in her demise.

He was going to pass.

So there was no need to linger.

His mind went back to that morning and he hoped very much that Lydia would be there to meet him tonight—not just to score a point over Bastiano and to rot up his plans.

Raul had enjoyed her company.

His company was not for keeps.

Lydia knew that.

She sat in her button-up dress in the hairdresser's at four and asked for a French roll, but the hairdresser tutted, picked up a long coil of blonde and suggested—or rather, *strongly* suggested—curls. After some hesitation finally Lydia agreed.

Whatever had happened to her this morning, it was still occurring.

She felt as if she were shedding her skin, and at every turn she fought to retrieve it.

Her lashes were darkened, and then Lydia opened her eyes when the beautician spoke.

'*Porpora…*'

Lydia did not know that word, but as the beautician pushed up a lipstick Lydia managed, without translation, to work out what it meant.

Crimson.

'No.' Lydia shook her head and insisted on a more neutral shade.

Oh, Lydia wanted to be back in her cocoon—she was a very unwilling butterfly indeed—but she did buy the lipstick, and on her way back to the hotel she stopped at the boutique and bought the red dress.

And then she entered the complex world of sexy shoes.

Lydia had bought a neutral pair to go with the caramel dress and thought she was done. But…

'Red and red,' the assistant insisted.

'I think neutral would look better.'

'You *need* these shoes.'

Oh, Lydia *was* starting to take advice from strangers for she tried them on. They were low-heeled and slender and a little bit strappy.

'It's too much,' Lydia said, but both women knew she was not protesting at the price.

'No, no,' the assistant said. 'Trust me—these are right.'

Oh, Lydia didn't trust her.

But she bought them anyway.

For *him*.

Or rather to one day dress up alone to the memory of him.

As she arrived back at the hotel Lydia looked at the restaurant across the street, to the roped-off section and the table he had reserved for them.

Of course he wasn't there yet.

Yet.

Knowing he would be—knowing she *could* be—made tonight somehow worse.

Her mother called, but she let it go to voicemail.

A pep talk wasn't required.

Lydia didn't need to be told that everything hinged on tonight. That the castle was at the very end of the line and that it would come down to her actions tonight to save it.

She had a shallow bath, so as not to mess up her new curls, and as she washed she tried to remind herself how good-looking Bastiano was.

Even his scar did not mar his good looks.

He had been attending a wedding when they'd first met.

Maybe this time when he kissed her she would know better how to respond.

Try as she might, though, she couldn't keep her focus on Bastiano. Her thoughts strayed to Raul.

With a sob of frustration Lydia hauled herself out of the bath and dried herself.

In a last-ditch attempt, Lydia rang Arabella. Searching for an excuse—any excuse—to get out of this meeting tonight.

'Lydia!' Arabella was brusque. 'I meant to call you. You didn't say it was *this* weekend you were in Rome.'

Of course Lydia had.

'I've actually got a party on tonight,' Arabella said.

'Sounds good.'

'Invitation only.'

And of course Lydia was not invited.

And there she sat again, like a beggar beside the table, waiting for Arabella's crumbs.

'That's fine.'

Lydia rang off.

Maurice was right. She had no friends.

Arabella was her only contact from her first school, but

she kept her at arm's length, and there hadn't even been a semblance of friendship at the other school.

Lydia could remember the howls of laughter from the other students when she had shaken hands and made a small curtsey for the teacher at the end of her first day.

It was what she had been taught, but of course *her* norms weren't the norms of her new school.

She didn't fit in anywhere.

Yet this morning Lydia had felt she did.

Oh, Raul had been far too forward and suggestive, but when they had spoken she had felt as if she were confiding in a friend—had felt a little as if she belonged in the world.

But all Raul wanted was sex.

Lydia had hoped for a little more.

Not a whole lot, but, yes, perhaps a little romance would be a nice side dish for her first time.

Wrong dress, Lydia thought as she looked in the mirror.

Wrong shoes, Lydia thought as she strapped on her neutral heels.

Wrong man, Lydia knew as she walked into the bar and saw Bastiano waiting.

Oh, he was terribly good-looking—even with that scar—and yet he did not move her. But perhaps *this* was romance, Lydia thought sadly, for he was charming as he ordered champagne. He was the perfect gentleman, and on the surface it was all terribly polite.

As was her life.

She thanked him for his generous hospitality. 'It's so lovely to be here. We've been looked after so well.'

'It is my pleasure,' Bastiano said. 'Are you enjoying Rome?'

'Absolutely.' Lydia smiled and thought of her far more honest response this morning with Raul.

It was after six, and she knew—just knew—that Raul wouldn't wait for very long.

And that she would regret it for ever if she missed out on tonight.

'I was thinking,' Bastiano said, 'that for dinner we might—'

'Actually…' Maurice interrupted, and put his fingers to his temples.

Lydia knew he was going to plead a headache and excuse himself from dinner. Leaving her alone with Bastiano.

It was seven minutes past six and she made her choice.

'Oh, didn't Maurice tell you?' Lydia spoke over Maurice, before he could make his excuses and leave.

Out of the corner of her eye she saw Maurice clench the glass he was holding, and she could feel his eyes shoot a stern warning, and yet Lydia spoke on.

'I'm catching up with a friend tonight—we're heading off to dinner soon. I wanted to stop by and say thank you, though.' She gave Bastiano her best false smile, but it wasn't returned. 'I don't want to get in the way of your business talk.'

'I don't think you could ever be in the way.' Bastiano's response was smooth.

'Oh, you're far too polite!' Lydia offered a small laugh to a less than impressed audience.

It sank like a stone.

'I'll leave you two to talk castles.'

She placed her unfinished drink on the table and said her farewells, and simply ignored the fury in Maurice's eyes and the muscle flickering in Bastiano's scarred cheek.

Oh, there would be consequences, Lydia knew.

But she was prepared to bear them.

For now she was free.

She wanted the red dress and the lipstick to match. She had, Lydia acknowledged, bought them for this moment, after all.

But there just wasn't time.

He could be gone already, Lydia thought in mild panic as she swept out through the revolving door.

When she glanced across the street she felt the crush of disappointment when she saw that Raul wasn't there.

But then she heard him.

'You're late.'

Lydia turned and there he was, tie loosened, tall and gorgeous, and, yes, she had made her choice.

'For the first time in my life.'

He was going to kiss her, she was sure, but she walked on ahead.

'Come on,' Lydia said quickly, worried that Maurice might follow her out.

They walked briskly, or rather Lydia did, for his stride beside her seemed slow and more measured. She felt fuelled by elation as they turned into a side street.

'Where to now?' Raul asked, and they stopped walking and she turned.

'You're the expert.'

Oh, he was—because somehow she was back against the wall with his hands on either side of her head.

She put her hands up to his chest and felt him solid beneath her palms, just felt him there for a moment, and then she looked up to his eyes.

His mouth moved in close, and as it did so she stared deeper.

She could feel heat hovering between their mouths in a slow tease before they met.

Then they met.

And all that had been missing was suddenly there.

The gentle pressure his mouth exerted, though blissful, caused a mire of sensations—until the gentleness was no longer enough.

Even before the thought was formed, he delivered.

His mouth moved more insistently and seemed to stir her from within.

Raul wanted her tongue, and yet he did not prise—he never forced a door open.

No need to.

There it was.

A slight inhalation, a hitch in her breath, and her lips parted just a little and he slipped his tongue in.

The moan she made went straight to his groin.

At first taste she was his and he knew it, for her hands moved to the back of his head, and he kissed her as hard as her fingers demanded.

More so, even.

His tongue was wicked, and her fingers tightened in his thick hair, and she could feel the wall cold and hard against her shoulders.

It was the middle of the city, just after six, and even down a side street there was no real hiding from the crowds.

Lydia didn't care.

He slid one arm around her waist to move her body away from the wall and closer to his, so that her head could fall backwards.

If there'd been a bed she would have been on it.

If there'd been a room they would have closed the door.

Yet there wasn't, and so he halted them—but only their lips.

Their bodies were heated and close and he looked her right in the eye. His mouth was wet from hers and his hair a little mussed from her fingers.

'What do you want to do?' Raul asked, knowing it was a no-brainer.

It was a very early bedtime and that suited him fine.

But the thought of waltzing her past Bastiano and Maurice no longer appealed.

A side entrance, perhaps, Raul thought, and went for her neck.

She had never thought that a kiss beneath her ear could make it impossible to breathe, let alone think.

'What do you want to do?' he whispered to her skin, and then blew on her neck, damp from his kisses. He raised his head and met her eye. 'Tonight I can give you anything you want.'

'Anything?' Lydia checked.

'Oh, yes.'

And if he was offering perfection, then she would take it.

'I want to see Rome at night—with you.'

'It's not dark yet.'

He could suggest a guided tour of his body—a very luxurious one, of course—but then he looked into her china-blue eyes.

'I want some romance with my one-night stand.'

'But I don't *do* romance.'

'Try it,' Lydia said. She didn't want some bauble in the morning and so she named her price. 'For one night.'

And Raul, who was usually *very* open to experiments, found himself reluctant to try.

Yet he had cancelled his flight for this.

And she had had the most terrible time here on her last visit, Raul knew.

The bed would always be there.

And he *had* invited her to state her wants.

He had known from the start that Lydia would make him work for his reward.

'I know just the place to start,' Raul said. 'While it's still light.'

CHAPTER FOUR

THIS WAS ROME.

He would have called for a car, but she hadn't wanted to go to the front of the hotel and risk seeing Maurice.

And so Raul found himself in his first taxi for a very long time.

He would not be repeating it!

Still, it was worth it for the result.

He took her to Aventine Hill. 'Rome's seventh hill,' he told her.

'I know that,' Lydia said. 'We came past it on a bus tour.'

'Who were you sitting with?' Raul nudged her as they walked.

'The teacher.'

'They really hated you, didn't they?'

But he put his arm around her shoulders as he said it, and it was something in the way he spoke that made her smile as she answered.

'They did.'

And then they stopped walking.

'This is the headquarters of the Order of the Knights of Malta,' he told her. 'Usually it is busy.' But tonight the stars had aligned, for there was a small group just leaving. 'Go on, then.'

'What?'

And she waited—for what, she didn't know. For him to open the door and go through?

They did neither.

'Look through the keyhole.'

Lydia bent down and did as she was told, but there was nothing to see at first—just an arch of greenery.

And then her eye grew accustomed to the view and she looked past the greenery, and there, perfectly framed in the centre, was the dome of St Peter's.

He knew the moment she saw it, for she let out a gasp.

It was a view to die for.

The soft green edging framed the eternal city and she bent there for a while, just taking it in.

It was a memory.

A magical one because it made Rome a secret garden.

Her secret garden.

By the time she stood there were others lined up, all waiting for their glimpse of heaven, and her smile told them it would be worth the wait.

Raul refused to be rushed.

'Don't you want a photo?' he asked. Assuming, of course, that she would.

'No.'

She didn't need one to remember it.

Even if Raul took her back to the hotel now, it would still be the best night ever.

In fact if Raul were to suggest taking her back to the hotel she would wave the taxi down herself, for he was kissing her again—a nice one, a not-going-anywhere one, just sharing in her excitement.

He did not take her back yet.

They walked down the hill, just talking, and he showed her the tiny streets she would never have found. He took her past the Bocca della Verità sculpture—the Mouth of Truth—though he did not tell her the legend that the old man would bite off the hand of liars.

For perhaps she might test him.

Though Raul told himself he did not lie.

He just omitted certain information.

And he continued to do so, even when the opportunity arose to reveal it.

They were now sitting on a balcony, looking out to the Colosseum, and a waiter placed their drinks down on the table.

Cognac for Raul and a cocktail that was the same fiery orange as the sky for Lydia.

He didn't assume champagne, as Bastiano had.

Like this morning at breakfast, she let her eyes wander through the menu selections.

She chose hers—he knew his.

Raul gave her choice at every turn, and that was something terribly new to Lydia.

Finally she had good memories of Rome.

'Salute,' Raul said, and they clinked glasses.

Wonderful memories, really.

It wasn't the sight of the Colosseum that brought a lump to her throat but the fact that *now* there were candles and flowers on the table, and that at every turn Raul had surprised her with his ease and enjoyment.

He did not sulk, nor reluctantly trudge along and put up with things before taking her to bed.

Raul led.

But she must remember it could never—for her—be the City of Love.

Raul didn't do love.

'How did Bastiano take your leaving?' Raul asked, and his question caught her by surprise, for her mind had long moved on from the hotel.

Raul himself had only just remembered the real reason he was there.

'He was fine,' Lydia replied. 'Well, he was polite. I can't blame him for being fed up—anyone would be, stuck with Maurice for the night.'

He was about to say that he doubted Bastiano would hang around anywhere he didn't choose to be, but stopped himself.

For the first time since they had met Lydia looked truly relaxed. The conversation flowed easily, and quite simply he did not want to take the chance of ruining a very nice night.

But he did need to know more. And he did not need to delve, for a very at ease Lydia was now talking.

'I know he can't stand Maurice.'

'How do you know that?'

'Because Bastiano told me.'

She was stirring her drink and didn't see the sudden tension in his features. It dawned on Raul that Bastiano and Lydia might already be lovers for all he knew.

'There was a wedding at the castle one weekend,' Lydia explained. 'It was a very good one. Of course Maurice had been through the guest list, and he made a bit of a beeline for Bastiano. He'd found out that he'd converted an old convent into a retreat, and Maurice wanted to hear his thoughts on doing something similar with the castle.'

Raul gave a disparaging laugh, and Lydia assumed it was in reference to Maurice's gall at approaching a guest.

But Raul was mocking Maurice's ignorance—Bastiano would never part with his knowledge for free.

'Bastiano wasn't interested,' Lydia said.

'Maurice told you that?' Raul checked.

'No, Bastiano did.' Lydia gave a soft laugh and looked out onto the street as she recalled that night. 'I was serving drinks, and Bastiano made some comment about saving him from the most boring man... I laughed. I knew exactly who he was referring to. But then I felt guilty, as if I ought to defend my family, and so I told him that Maurice was my stepfather.'

And there was the difference between them. Raul felt no guilt in not admitting the truth.

Perhaps a slight niggle, but he easily pushed that aside.

'You told Bastiano that Maurice was your stepfather?' he asked.

'Yes.' Lydia nodded. 'Bastiano apologised and said he would speak with him again and pay attention this time.

'And that was it?' Raul checked.

'Sorry?' Lydia frowned.

'That was all that happened between you two?'

She went pink.

'Excuse me,' Raul said. 'That is none of my business.'

The thought, though, did not sit well with him.

But then she told him.

'Just a kiss.'

She screwed up her nose as Raul breathed out in relief that they had never been lovers.

Then the relief dissolved and he loathed the fact that they had even shared a kiss.

'Come on,' he said, confused by the jealousy that arose in him. 'It's dark now.'

Oh, it was.

And busy and noisy.

It was everything Rome should be.

The Trevi Fountain had kept its promise, because she had made a wish to be back under better circumstances and now she was.

They walked for miles, and though the cobbled streets weren't stiletto-friendly Lydia felt as if she were wearing ballet slippers—the world felt lighter tonight.

'Where are we now?' Lydia asked.

'Citta Universitaria—my home for four years.'

'I would have loved to have gone to university,' Lydia said. 'I wanted to study history.'

'Why didn't you?'

'I failed my exams.'

Another truth she rarely told.

She hadn't decided to go straight into the family business, as her mother often said.

Lydia had failed all her exams.

Spectacularly.

'I messed up,' Lydia admitted.

She offered no reason or excuse although there were so many.

He knew that.

'I had to repeat some subjects after my mother died,' Raul told her. He rarely revealed anything, and certainly not his failings, yet it seemed right to do so now. 'I hit the clubs for a while.'

His honesty elicited both a smile and an admission. 'I wish that I had.'

'I moved here from Sicily to study under great protest—my father wanted me to work for him. Filthy money,' he added. 'Anyway, after my mother died for a while I made it my mission to find out how wild Rome could be at night.'

'Where in Si—'

'I lived there,' he said, pointing across the street.

She had been about to ask whereabouts in Sicily, Raul knew, but she had mentioned the convent a couple of times and perhaps knew its location. Certainly he didn't want her knowing that he and Bastiano were from the same place. So he interrupted her and gave more information about himself than he usually would.

Raul pointed upwards and Lydia found herself looking at a hotel. It was far smaller than the one they were staying at, but it was beautifully lit and from the smart cars pulling up and the guests spilling out it seemed rather exclusive.

'How could a student afford to stay in that hotel?' Lydia asked.

'It was flats back then. In fact they were very seedy.'

'And then the developers came along?'

'That was me.'

And she stared at a hotel—in the centre of Rome, for goodness' sake—and found out that he owned it.

'How?'

But Raul did not want to revisit those times.

'Come on…'

It was late—after midnight—and he'd had enough of taxis to last a lifetime, and so, despite the hour, he texted Allegra and very soon a vehicle appeared.

It wasn't a taxi!

She sat in the back and he climbed in and sat so he faced her.

It was bliss to sink into the seats. 'My feet are killing me,' Lydia admitted. 'These shoes really weren't made for walking.'

'Take them off, then,' Raul said, and he leant over and lifted her foot and placed it in his lap.

Lydia could feel his solid thigh beneath her calf, and though she willed herself to relax her leg was trembling as he started to undo the strap.

He ran his hand along her calf and found the muscle was a knot of tension. He worked it with deft fingers.

The muscle did not relax.

In fact it tightened.

And when her toes curled to his touch he placed her foot so that she could feel his desire for her.

She ought to tell him she was a virgin.

But she rather guessed that Raul wouldn't find her innocence endearing.

His fingers continued to work on the tense muscle till it loosened. High in her thigh she contracted, and then he removed the sandal and lifted her naked foot.

'Please don't,' she choked as he lifted it towards his mouth. 'I've been walking…'

'Dirty girl.'

He kissed the arch of her foot, and she tried again to pull away, but only because the wicked sensation his tongue delivered shot straight between her legs.

'Raul…' She pronounced it correctly for the first time—it simply rolled off her tongue. 'Someone might see.'

'They can't see in.'

She could see, though.

For that moment Lydia felt as if she could see inside herself.

And she was…

The feeling was so unfamiliar it took a second for Lydia to recognise just what it was.

She was happy.

Just that.

'We're here,' Raul said, and released her foot, and that tiny glimpse of carefree happiness was over.

Just like that.

For she saw him—Maurice—standing outside the hotel.

He was smoking a cigar and on his phone—no doubt to her mother.

'We'll use the side entrance.'

Raul went to the intercom to inform the driver, but her hand stopped him.

'No.'

It was over.

The windows were dark and she knew that Maurice couldn't see in—neither would he be expecting her to return in such a luxurious vehicle.

'I need to face things.'

'Tomorrow,' Raul said.

And she looked at this man who chose not to get close enough to anyone to remember a birthday.

A man who did not live by the rules.

She did.

'I think it would be better dealt with tonight. It might be a little more difficult to take the moral high road about Bastiano with my knickers in my purse.'

'Lydia…' Raul started, but then halted. He had no qualms

over a one-night stand, but he conceded with a nod that she made a valid point.

'Go and tell him to get the hell out of your life, and then come to my suite.' He gave her the floor and the number, while knowing the night *he* had planned was gone. 'Will you be okay?'

'Of course I will.' Lydia gave a scoffing laugh. 'I'm twenty-four—he can hardly put me on curfew.'

'Will you be okay?' Raul asked again.

'Yes.' Lydia nodded. 'This needs to be dealt with.'

It did.

He asked his driver to move a little way down the street, and in that space of time Raul did something he rarely did. He took out a card.

Not the one he generally gave out.

'This is my number—you'll get straight through to me. If there is any problem…'

'There won't be,' Lydia said, but he opened her purse and put in the card.

This was it—both knew.

Though both hoped otherwise.

'Remember what I told you this morning,' Raul said, and she nodded.

He went to kiss her, but she moved her head to the side. It really wasn't a turn-on, knowing that Maurice waited.

And she should never have let Raul take her shoe off, because now there was all the hassle of getting it back on.

And happiness seemed determined to elude her as she climbed out of the vehicle.

'Where the hell have you been?' Maurice asked as she approached.

'Out,' Lydia snapped.

'Your mother is worried sick,' Maurice said as they walked briskly through the foyer, though he waited until they were in the elevator to say any more. 'I'm trying to save *your* family's business and you walk out on the one person who could help do just that.'

'I came for a drink.'

'He wanted to take us both to dinner. I've said to Bastiano that you'll be there tomorrow.'

'Well, you shouldn't have,' Lydia retorted.

They got out of the elevator and Lydia headed for her suite. 'I'm going to bed.'

'Don't you walk away from me,' Maurice told her. 'You'll be there tomorrow night, with a smile on, and—'

'Maurice, *why* do I need to be there?' She pointed out what Raul had this morning. 'I don't hold the deeds to the castle—my mother does. And I don't actually *like* the idea of turning it into a retreat. There's absolutely no reason for me to be there.'

'You know there is.'

'But *why*?'

Say it, Maurice, Lydia thought. *Have the guts to voice it out loud.*

'Because Bastiano wants you.'

'Then you need to tell him that I'm not part of the deal.' Her voice was shaky. The truth, even if deep down she'd already known it, was actually very difficult to hear said out loud. 'In fact you can tell Bastiano that, as of now, I no longer live or work at the castle.'

'Lydia, he's a charming man, he's extremely wealthy, and he's very interested in you.'

'Well, I'm not for sale! I've told you—I'm leaving.'

'And where are you going to go? Lydia, you've got no qualifications, no savings…'

'Odd, that,' Lydia responded, 'when I've been living at home and working my backside off for the last six years.'

She was done, she was through, and she dug in her purse for her keycard and let herself into her suite.

Maurice knocked loudly.

Oh, my God.

She could not take even another night of this.

She didn't have to, Lydia realised as she recalled Raul's advice.

'You can walk away from anyone you choose to and you don't have to come up with a reason.'

She had *many* good reasons to walk, Lydia thought, and started throwing her possessions into her case.

'Your mother is going to be very upset…' Maurice called through the door, but he fell silent when it was opened and Lydia stood holding her case.

'I'm leaving.'

'What the hell…? Lydia…'

Lydia could see a bit of spittle at the side of his mouth, and she could feel his anger at her refusal to comply.

When she always had in the past.

For the sake of her mother Lydia would generally back down when things got heated—but for the sake of herself she now stood her ground.

It was as if the blinkers had been lifted, and she could now see the control and the pressure he exerted.

And she would play the game no more.

No, she could not save the castle and, no, she would not meekly comply just to keep his mood tolerable. She could almost feel the eggshells she had walked on dissolving beneath her feet.

She marched to the elevators and he followed. He reached for her as she reached the doors and suddenly she was scared.

Raul had been right to be concerned.

She *was* scared of Maurice and his temper.

Oh, she wasn't running to Raul—she was running away from hell.

Maurice slapped her.

He delivered a stinging slap to her cheek and pulled at her hair, raised his other hand—but somehow she freed herself.

Lydia ducked into the elevator and wrenched the doors closed on his hand.

'Thank you,' she said. With the gate safely between them she spoke in a withering tone. 'Now I know for a fact what an utter bastard you are.'

She did not crumple.

Lydia refused to.

And she refused to waste even a single tear.

She was scared, though.

Scared and alone.

And she would have run into the night.

Without Raul, absolutely she would have run.

But instead of going down Lydia pressed the elevator button that would take her to his floor.

CHAPTER FIVE

RAUL STEPPED INTO his suite, unexpectedly alone.

Allegra had, of course, rung ahead, and everything had been prepared for Raul to return with a female guest.

The suite was dimly lit, but Raul saw champagne chilling in a bucket. He bypassed it. Throwing his jacket on a chair, he poured a large cognac and downed half in one gulp, then kicked off his socks and shoes, wrenched off his tie and removed his shirt.

In the bathroom Raul rolled his eyes, for the sight that greeted him seemed to mock. Candles had been lit and the deep bath was filled with fragrant water. But Raul would be bypassing that too—perhaps a cold shower might be more fitting.

He soon gave up prowling the penthouse suite dressed for two and lay on the bed. He took another belt of his drink and considered extending his stay for another night in Rome.

Unlike before, when he had actually wanted to flaunt Lydia under Bastiano's nose, Raul suddenly had a sense of foreboding.

Yes, Lydia might have stood up to her stepfather tonight, but for how long would that last? She was strong—Raul had seen that—but her family clearly saw Lydia as their ticket out of whatever mess they were in. And Bastiano, Raul knew, didn't care *what* methods he used to get his own way.

It wasn't his problem.

Over and over Raul told himself that.

He was angry with Bastiano rather than concerned about Lydia, Raul decided.

Only that didn't sit quite right.

Tomorrow he would be out of here.

Raul had rescheduled the jet for midday tomorrow. He would soon be back in Venice and this trip would be forgotten.

Raul didn't even want the hotel now—Sultan Alim's words had hit home. The Grande Lucia was far too much responsibility. He wanted investments he could manage from a distance. Raul wanted no labour of love.

In any area of his life.

Raul managed to convince himself that he was relieved with tonight's outcome.

Well, not relieved.

Far from it.

He was aching and hard, and was just sliding down his zipper, when he heard knocking at the door.

Good things, Raul realised as he made his way to the door, did come to those who waited. For just when he had thought the night was over, it would seem it had just begun!

He didn't bother to turn on the lounge light—just opened the door and Lydia tumbled in.

She had a suitcase beside her, which would usually be enough to perturb him, but there were other concerns right now.

She was shaking while trying to appear calm.

'Sorry to disturb you…'

Her voice was trembling.

'What happened?'

'We had a row,' Lydia said. 'A long overdue one. Anyway, I don't want to talk about that now.'

Oh, it wasn't just that she knew the price for a night in his room—Lydia wanted to go back to feeling happy.

Preferably now, please.

She wanted the oblivion his mouth offered, not to think of the turbulent times ahead.

He was naked from the waist up and her demand was sudden. 'Where were we?'

And her mouth found his and her kiss was urgent.

He tasted of liquor, and he was obviously aroused when she pressed into him.

Yet for once Raul was the one slowing things down.

His body demanded he kiss her back with fervour, that he take her now, up against the wall, and give her what she craved.

Yet there was more to this, he knew.

'Lydia…'

He peeled her off him and it was a feat indeed, for between his attempts to halt her he was resisting going back in for a kiss. He was hard and primed, and she was desperate and willing.

An obvious match.

Yet somehow not.

'Slow down…' he told her. 'Angry sex we can do later.'

Raul never thought of 'later' with women and was surprised by his own thought process, but his overriding feeling was concern.

'I'm not angry,' Lydia said.

She could feel his arms holding her back as he somehow read her exactly and told her how she felt.

'Oh, baby, you are!'

She was.

Lydia was a ball of fury that he held at arm's length.

She was trying to go for his zipper. She was actually wild.

'Lydia?'

He guided her to a chair, and it was like folding wood trying to get her to sit down, but finally he did.

Lydia could hear her own rapid breathing as Raul went over and flicked on a light, and she knew he was right.

She was angry.

He saw her pale face and the red hand mark, and Raul's

own anger coiled his gut tight. But he kept his voice even. 'What happened?'

'I told Maurice that I shan't be his puppet and neither shall I be returning home.'

He came to her and knelt down, and his hand went to her swollen cheek.

'Did he hit you anywhere else?'

'No.' She shook her head. 'I'm fine. Really I am.'

Raul frowned, because there were no tears—it was suppressed rage that glittered in her eyes.

'Do you want me to go and sort him out?'

'I would hate that.'

He rather guessed that she would.

'Please?' he said, and saw that she gave a small smile.

'No.'

He would do so later.

Right now, though, Raul's concern was Lydia. He stood and looked around. There was a woman in his hotel suite, and for the first time Raul didn't know what to do with her.

Lydia too looked around, and she was starting to calm.

She saw the champagne and the flowers, and the room that had been prepared for them, and cringed at her own behaviour. She had asked for romance and he had delivered, and then she'd thrust herself on him.

'Can we pretend the last fifteen minutes never happened?' Lydia asked.

'You want me to go back to licking your feet?'

Lydia laughed.

Not a lot, but on a night when laughter should be an impossible task somehow she did.

She felt calmer.

Though she was shaken, and embarrassed at foisting herself upon Raul, now that she had stood up to Maurice she felt clearer in the head than she had in years.

'Do you want a drink?'

She nodded.

'What would you like?'

And she could see his amber drink and still taste it on her tongue.

'The same as you.'

'So, what happened?' Raul asked, and she answered as he crossed the suite.

'A necessary confrontation, and one that's been a long time coming,' she admitted. 'I've hated him since the day my mother first brought him home.'

'How long after your father died?'

'Eighteen months. Maurice had all these lavish ideas for the castle—decided to use it for weddings.'

'I hate weddings,' Raul said, taking the stopper off the bottle and pouring her a drink. 'Imagine having to deal with one every week.'

'They're not every week—unfortunately. Sometimes in the summer…' Her voice trailed off mid-sentence and Raul knew why. He was minus his shirt, and with his back to her, therefore Lydia must have seen his scar.

She had.

It was the sort of scar that at first glance could stop a conversation.

A jagged fault line on a perfect landscape, for he was muscled and defined, but then she frowned as she focused on the thinner lines.

A not so perfect landscape.

Oh, so badly she wanted to know more about this man.

But Lydia remembered her manners and cleared her throat and resumed talking.

'In the summer they used to be weekly, but the numbers have been dwindling.'

'Why?' Raul asked, and handed her the drink. He was grateful that she had said nothing about the scars. He loathed it when women asked about them, as if one night with him meant access to his past.

And it was always just one night.

Lydia took a sip. In truth it had tasted better on his tongue, but it was warming and pleasant and she focused on that for a moment. But then Raul asked the question again.

'Why are the numbers dwindling?'

'Because when people book a luxury venue they expect luxury at every turn, but Maurice cuts corners.'

He had heard that so many times.

In fact Raul had made his fortune from just that. He generally bought hotels on their last legs and turned them into palaces.

The Grande Lucia was a different venture—this hotel was a palace already, and that was why he was no longer considering making the purchase.

'Maurice is always after the quick fix,' Lydia said, and then stilled when she heard the buzzing of her phone.

'It's him,' Lydia said.

'I'll speak to him for you,' Raul said, and went to pick it up.

'Please don't.' Her voice was very clear. 'You would only make things worse.'

'How?'

'You won't be the one dealing with the fallout.'

And, yes, he *could* deal with Maurice tonight, but who would that really help? Oh, it might make Raul feel better, and Maurice certainly deserved it, but Lydia was right—it wouldn't actually help things in the long run, given he wouldn't be around.

'Turn your phone off,' Raul suggested, but she shook her head.

'I can't—he'll call my mother and she'll be worried.'

Raul wasn't so sure about that. He rather guessed that

Lydia's mother would more likely be annoyed that Lydia hadn't meekly gone along with their plans.

He watched as her phone rang again, but when she looked at it this time, instead of being angry she screwed her eyes closed.

'Maurice?'

'No, it's my mother.'

'Ignore it.'

'I can't,' Lydia said. 'He must have told her I've run off.' Her phone fell silent, but Lydia knew it wouldn't stay like that for very long. 'I'll ring her and tell her I'm safe. I shan't tell her where I am—just that I'm fine. Can I…?' She gestured to the double doors and it was clear that Lydia wanted some privacy to make the call.

'Of course.'

It was a bedroom.

Her first time in a man's bedroom, and it was so far from the circumstances she had hoped for that it was almost laughable.

It had been an almost perfect night, yet it was ruined now. Lydia sat on the bed and cringed as she recalled her entrance into his suite.

Lydia was very used to hiding her true feelings, yet Raul seemed to bring them bubbling up to the surface.

Right now, though, she needed somehow to snap back to efficient mode—though it was hard when she heard her mother's accusatory voice.

'What the hell are you playing at, Lydia?'

'I'm not playing at anything.'

'You know damn well how important this trip is!'

A part of Lydia had hoped for her mother to take her side. To agree that Maurice's behaviour tonight had been preposterous and tell her that of *course* Lydia didn't have to agree to anything she didn't want to do.

It had been foolish to hope.

Instead Lydia sat there as her mother told her how charming Bastiano was, how he'd been nothing but a gentleman to date, and asked how she dared embarrass the family like this.

And then, finally, her mother was honest.

'It's time you stepped up…'

'Bastiano doesn't even know me,' Lydia pointed out. 'We've spoken, at best, a couple of times.'

'Lydia, it's time to get your head out of the clouds. I've done everything I can to keep us from going under. For whatever reason, Bastiano has taken an interest in you…'

Lydia didn't hear much of the rest.

For whatever reason…

As if it was unfathomable that someone might simply want her for no other reason than they simply did.

It was Lydia who ended the call, and after sitting for a few minutes in silence she looked up when there was a knock at the door.

'Come in,' Lydia said, and then gave a wry smile as Raul entered—it was *his* bedroom, after all.

'How did it go with your mother?'

'Not very well,' Lydia admitted. 'I'm being overly dramatic, apparently.'

'Why don't you have a bath?'

'A bath!' A laugh shot out of her pale lips at his odd suggestion.

'It might relax you. There's one already run.'

'I'm guessing I wouldn't have been bathing alone, had I come up the first time.'

'Plans change,' Raul said. 'Give me your phone and go and wind down.'

'You won't answer it?' Lydia checked.

'No,' Raul said.

Her family was persistent.

Raul, though, was stubborn.

The phone continued to buzz, but rather than turn it off Raul went back to lying on the bed, as he had been when Lydia had arrived.

And that was how she found him.

The bath *had* been soothing. Lydia had lain in the fragrant water, terribly glad of his suggestion to leave her phone.

It had given her a chance to calm down and to regroup.

'They've been calling,' Raul told her by way of greeting.

'I thought that they might.' Lydia sighed. 'I doubt they'll give up if Bastiano hasn't. Apparently Maurice has said he'll meet him tomorrow and I'm supposed to be there.'

'And what did you say?'

'No, of course—but it's not just about dinner with Bastiano…'

'Of course it's not,' Raul agreed.

'I think he wants sex.'

'He wants more than sex, Lydia. He wants to marry you. He thinks you'd make a very nice trophy wife. Bastiano wants to be King of your castle.'

He watched for her reaction and as always she surprised him, because Lydia just gave a shrug.

'I wouldn't be the first to marry for money.'

And though the thought appalled her it did not surprise her.

'I doubt my mother married Maurice for his sparkling personality,' Lydia said, and Raul gave a small nod that told her he agreed. 'Would *you* marry for money?' Lydia asked.

'No,' Raul said, 'but that's not from any moral standpoint—I just would never marry.'

'Why?'

'I've generally run out of conversation by the morning. I can't imagine keeping one going with the same person for the rest of my life.'

He did make her smile.

And he put her at ease.

No, that wasn't the word, because *ease* wasn't what she felt around him.

She felt like herself.

Whoever that was.

Lydia had never really been allowed to find out.

'You'd have to remember her birthday,' Lydia said, and sat next to him when he patted the bed.

'And our anniversary.' Raul rolled his eyes. 'And married people become obsessed with what's for dinner.'

'They do!' Lydia agreed.

'I had a perfectly normal PA—Allegra. Now, every day, her husband rings and they talk about what they are going to have for dinner. I pay her more than enough that she could eat out every night…'

Yes, he made her smile.

'Do you believe in love?' Lydia asked.

'No.'

She actually liked how abruptly he dismissed the very notion.

It was so peaceful in his room, and though common sense told her she should be nervous Lydia wasn't. It was nice to talk with someone who was so matter-of-fact about something she had wrestled with for so long.

'Would you marry if it meant you might save your family from going under?'

'My family is gone.' Raul shrugged. 'Anyway, you can't save anyone from going under. Whatever you try and do.'

The sudden pensive note to his voice had her turning to face him.

'I wanted my mother to leave my father. I did everything I could to get her to leave, but she wouldn't. I knew I had to get out. I was working a part-time job in Rome and studying, and I had found a flat for her.' He looked over at Lydia briefly. 'Next to the one I told you about. But she wouldn't leave. She said that she could not afford to, and that aside from that she took her wedding vows seriously.'

'I would too,' Lydia told him.

'Well, my mother said the same—but then she had an affair.' It was surprisingly easy to tell her, given what Lydia had shared with him. 'She died in a car accident just after the affair was exposed. I doubt her mind was on the road. After she died I found out that she'd had access to more than enough money to start a new life. I think her lover had found that out too.'

He wanted to tell her that his mother's lover had been Bastiano, but that wasn't the point he was trying to make, and he did not want to make things worse for her tonight.

'Lydia, what I'm trying to say is you can't prevent anyone from going under.'

'I don't believe that.'

'Even if you marry him, do you really think Bastiano is going to take advice from Maurice? Do you think he will want to keep your mother and her husband in residence?'

He took out all her dark thoughts, the fears that had kept her awake at night, and forced her to examine them.

'No.'

'Take it from me—the only person you can ever save is yourself.'

Strong words, but clearly she didn't take them in, because when her phone buzzed Lydia went to pick it up.

'Leave it,' Raul said.

'I can't do that,' Lydia admitted. 'I might turn it off.'

'Then they'll know you're avoiding them. Just ignore it.'

'I can't.'

'Yes, you can—because I shan't let you hear it.'

She had thought Raul meant he would turn the ring down, but instead as the phone started to ring again he reached for her and drew her face towards him.

Nothing, Lydia was sure, could take her mind from her family tonight.

She was wrong.

His kiss was softer than the others he had delivered.

So light, in fact, that as she closed her eyes in anticipation all he gave was a light graze to her lips that had her hungry for more as his hand slid into her hair.

Kiss by soft kiss he took care of every pin, and Lydia found her lips had parted, but still he made her wait for his tongue.

She had tasted him already, and her body was hungry for more.

Yet he was cruel in attack for he gave so little.

He undid the knot of her robe with the same measured pace he had taken in dealing with her hair and then pushed it down over her arms so that she sat naked.

Lydia felt something akin to panic as contact ceased and he ran his gaze down her body. It *wasn't* panic, though, she thought. It was far nicer—because as the phone buzzed by the bed she was staring down at him, watching his mouth near her breast, and she would have died rather than answer it.

'Do you want to get that?' Raul asked, and she could feel his breath on her breast.

'No…' Her voice had gone—it came out like a husk.

'I can't hear you,' he said, and then he delivered his tongue in a motion too light, for she bunched the sheet with her fingers and fought not to grab his head.

'No,' she said, and when his mouth paused in delivering its magic, she added, 'I don't want to answer.'

'Good.'

He sucked hard now, and she knew he bruised.

Raul gave one breast the deep attention that her mouth had craved, and she fought not to swear or, worse, to plead.

She should tell him that he was her first, Lydia thought

as he guided her hand to his crotch and she felt his thick, hard length through the fabric.

But then her phone buzzed again and the teasing resumed, for he stood.

'Do you want me to get that?'

'Turn it off,' Lydia said.

'Oh, no.'

He slid down his zipper and the buzz of the phone dimmed in her ears when she saw him naked.

Yes, that would hurt.

Oh, she really should tell him, Lydia thought as she reached out to hold him. But then she closed her eyes at the bliss of energy beneath her fingers and the low moan that came from him as his hand closed around hers.

He moved her slender fingers more roughly than she would have. She opened her eyes at the feel of him.

She could hear their breathing, rapid and shallow, and then his free hand took her head and pushed it down, and she tasted him just a little as her tongue caressed him.

And for Raul, what should have been too slow, the touch of her tongue too light, somehow she owned the night.

The slight choking in her throat closing around him brought him close to release, so that he was grateful for the sudden buzzing and it was Raul who was briefly distracted.

Lydia wasn't.

She was lost in the taste of him when for the second time that night—but for a very different reason—she felt a tug on her hair and looked up.

Now when she licked her lips it was to savour the taste of him.

And Raul, who did not want this to be over, put her to bed.

On top of it.

Raul was decisive in his positioning of Lydia, and her loose limbs were his to place.

He knelt astride her and put her arms above her head, held them one-handed as the other hand played with the breast he wasn't sucking.

'Raul…' She was about to tell him about her virginal status, but her phone buzzed again and he thought that was her complaint.

'Shush…'

And then he moved so that he knelt between her legs, and reached to the bedside drawer for a condom, and she lay there watching as he rolled it on.

'Raul…' Her voice was breathless, but she should say it now—she was trying to.

'You talk too much.'

She had said two words and both had been his name. She went to point that out but lost her thought processes as his head went down between her legs and she lay holding her breath and nervously awaiting his intimate touch.

He kissed her exactly as he had the first time.

Raul's mouth lightly pressed *there*, and then there was the tease of his tongue. Slowly at first, as Lydia had been slow, for he thought she had been teasing him at the time.

'Please…' Lydia said, not sure if she was asking to speak, asking him to slow down or asking for more.

His jaw was rough, his mouth soft and his tongue probing. It was sublime.

His mouth worked on and she started to moan.

His tongue urged her on.

Lydia's thighs were shaking and she fought to stay silent. And then she gave in, and he moaned in pleasure as she orgasmed. He kissed her and swallowed as she pulsed against his lips.

And then he left them.

She was heated and twitching, breathless and giddy and perfectly done as he moved over her and crushed her tense lips with his moist ones. His thigh moved between her legs and splayed her, and even coming down from a high, with the feel of him nudging and the energy of him, Lydia knew this would hurt.

'Slowly,' she said, but her words were muffled, so she turned her head. 'I've never—'

He was about to aim for hard, fast and deep, when he heard those two words that were so unexpected.

'Slowly,' she said again.

He could do that.

An unseen smile stretched his lips at the thought of taking her first, practically beneath Bastiano's nose. And then the thought of taking her first made his ardour grow.

But then, just when bliss appeared on the menu, the stars seemed to collect and become one that shone too bright. And, like a headmaster grabbing an errant student by the shoulder, he suddenly hauled himself back from the edge.

Everything went still.

All the delicious sensations, gathering tight, slowly loosened as his weight came down on her rather than within her.

And then he rolled off and onto his back and lay breathless, unsated, both turned on and angry.

He told her why. 'I don't do virgins.'

There was so much she could protest at about that statement.

Do?

And her response was tart, to cover up her disappointment and, yes, her embarrassment that he had brought things to a very shuddering halt.

'What, only experienced applicants need apply?'

'Don't you get it?' He ripped off the condom and tossed it aside, and ached to finish the job. 'There's nothing to apply *for*, Lydia. I like one-night stands. I like to get up in the morning and have coffee and then go about my day. It's sex. That's it. There are no vacant positions waiting to be filled in my life.'

'I wasn't expecting anything more.'

'You say that *now*.'

And *now* Raul sulked.

He had heard it so many times before.

Raul didn't *do* virgins, and with good reason—because even the most seasoned of his lovers tended to ask for more than he was prepared to give.

'I mean it,' Lydia insisted.

'Do you know what, Lydia? If you've waited till you're twenty-four I'm guessing there's a reason.'

There was—she'd hardly had men beating down the door.

But a small voice was telling her that Raul, as arrogant as his words were, was actually right—making love *would* change things for her.

Then again, since she had met Raul everything had already changed.

'Go to sleep,' he said.

'I can't.'

'Yes, Lydia, *you* can.'

His voice was sulky, and she didn't know what he meant, but as she lay there Lydia started to understand.

She felt a little as if she was floating.

All the events of the night were dancing before her eyes, and she could watch them unfold without feeling—except for one.

'What happened to your back?'

Her voice came from that place just before she fell asleep. Raul knew that.

Yet he wished she had not asked.

Lydia had not asked about one scar but about his whole back.

He did not want to think about that.

But now he was starting to.

CHAPTER SIX

'IT'S YOUR MOTHER'S FUNERAL,' the priest admonished, but only once Raul had been safely cuffed and led away.

Raul and Bastiano, the police decided, should not be in the same building, so Raul was taken to the jailhouse to cool down and Bastiano was cuffed to a stretcher and taken to the valley's small hospital.

A towel covered Raul's injury, and he sat in a cell until a doctor came to check on him.

Raul loathed anyone seeing his back, due to the scars his father had put there, but thankfully the doctor didn't comment on them. He took one look at the gaping wound and shook his head.

'This is too big to repair under a local,' the doctor informed him. 'I'll tell the guards to arrange your transfer to the hospital.'

'Is Bastiano still there?' Raul asked, and the doctor nodded. 'Then you'll do it here.'

The thought of being in the same building as Bastiano tonight was not one he relished, and a hospital was no place for his current mood.

'It's going to hurt,' the doctor warned.

But Raul already did.

The closure of the wound took ages.

He felt the fizz and sear of the peroxide as it bubbled its way through raw flesh, and then came the jab of the doctor's fingers as he explored it.

'I really think…' the doctor started, but Raul did not change his stance.

'Just close it.'

Deep catgut sutures closed the muscles and then thick silk finally drew together the skin.

He was written up for some painkillers to be taken throughout the night when required, but he did not bother to ask the guards for them.

Nothing could dim the pain.

It was not the wounds of the flesh that caused agony, more the memories and regret.

He should have known what was going on.

His mother's more cheerful disposition on his last visit was because she'd had a lover. Raul knew that now.

And there was guilt too—tangible guilt—because she had called him on the morning she had died and Raul had not picked up.

Instead he had been deep in oblivion with some no-name woman and had chosen not to take the call.

Raul lay on the hard, narrow bed and stared at the ceiling through the longest night of his life.

There would be many more to come.

Light came in through the barred windows and he heard a drunk who had sung the night through being processed and released.

And then another.

Raul was in no rush for his turn.

'Hey.'

The heavy door opened and a police officer brought him coffee. He was familiar.

Marco.

They had been at school together.

'For what it's worth, I'm on your side,' Marco told Raul as he handed him a coffee. 'Bastiano's a snake. I wish they had let you finish the job.'

Raul said nothing—just accepted the coffee.

God, but he hated the valley. There was corruption at every turn. If memory served him correctly, and it usually did, Bastiano had slept with the young woman who was now Marco's fiancée.

Just after nine Raul signed the papers for his release and Marco handed him his tie and belt, which Raul pocketed.

'Smarten up,' Marco warned him. 'You are to be at the courthouse by ten.'

Raul put on his belt and tucked in his shirt somewhat but gave up by the time he got to his tie. One look in the small washroom mirror and he knew it was pointless. His eyes were bruised purple, his lips swollen, his hair matted with blood and he needed to shave.

Groggy, his head pounding, Raul stepped out onto the street into a cruelly bright day and walked the short distance to the courthouse. Raul assumed he was there to be formally charged, but instead he found out it was for the reading of Maria Di Savo's last will and testament.

His father, Gino, was there for that, of course. And he sat gloating, because he knew that apart from the very few trinkets he had given her in earlier years everything Maria had had was his.

Raul just wanted it over and done with, and then he would get the hell out.

He was done with Casta for good.

But then, for the second time in less than twenty-four hours, the man he hated most in the world appeared—again at the most inappropriate time.

'What the hell is *he* doing here?'

It was Gino who rose in angry response as an equally battered Bastiano took a seat on a bench. His face had been sutured and a jagged scar ran the length of his now purple cheek. Clearly he had just come from the hospital, for he was still wearing yesterday's suit.

And then the judge commenced the reading of the will.

This was a mere formality, and Raul simply hoped he might get the crucifix Maria had always worn.

That wish came true, for he was handed a slim envelope and the simple cross and chain fell onto his palm.

But then out slid a ring.

It was exquisite—far more elaborate than anything his mother had owned—rose gold with an emerald stone, it was dotted with tiny seed pearls and it felt heavy in his palm. Raul picked it up between finger and thumb and tried to place it, yet he could not remember his mother wearing it.

He was distracted from examining the ring when the judge spoke again.

'*Testamona Segreto.*'

Even the rather bored court personnel stood to attention, as suddenly there was an unexpected turn in the formalities.

Raul stopped looking at the ring and Gino frowned and leant forward as all present learnt that his mother had made a secret will.

More intriguing was the news that it been amended just a few short weeks ago.

A considerable sum had been left to Maria on the death of her brother, Luigi, on condition that it did not in any way benefit Maria's husband.

Luigi had loathed Gino.

But Luigi had died some ten years ago.

Most shocking for Raul was the realisation that his mother had had the means to leave.

Raul had been working his butt off, trying to save to provide for her, when she could have walked away at any time.

It made no sense.

Nothing in his life made sense any more.

And then Raul felt a pulse beat a tattoo in his temples as the judge read out his mother's directions.

'The sum is to be divided equally between my son Raul Di Savo and Bastiano Conti. My hope is that they use it wisely. My prayer is that they have a wonderful life.'

Raul sat silent as pandemonium broke out in the courthouse. Money was Gino's god, and *this* betrayal hit harder than the other. He started cursing, and as he moved to finish off Raul's work on Bastiano, Security were called.

'He gets nothing!' Gino sneered, and jabbed his finger towards Bastiano. 'Maria was sick in the head—she would not have known what she was doing when she made that will.'

'The testimonial is clear,' the judge responded calmly as Gino was led out.

'Bastiano used her. Tell him that we will fight…' Gino roared over his shoulder.

Raul said nothing in response—just sat silent as his mother's final wishes sank in.

She had chosen Bastiano as the second benefactor and had asked that her money be divided equally…

Oh, that stung.

He looked over at Bastiano, who stared ahead and refused to meet his gaze.

Why the hell had she left it to *him*? Had Bastiano known about the money and engineered the entire thing? Had he sweet-talked her into changing her will and then deliberately exposed their affair, knowing that the fragile Maria could never survive the fallout?

Gino was still shouting from the corridor. 'I stood by her all these years!'

Raul sat thinking. He knew he could contest this in court—or he could wait till he and Bastiano were outside and fight. This time to the bloody end.

He chose the latter.

Outside, the sun seemed to chip at his skull and he felt like throwing up—and then Bastiano stepped out, also wincing at the bright afternoon sun.

'So,' Raul said by way of greeting, 'the gossip in the valley was wrong.' He watched as Bastiano's brow creased in confusion, and then he better explained. 'As it turns out— *you* were the whore.'

The court attendees spilled out onto the street, the guards hovered, and a police vehicle drove slowly past. Raul saw that Marco was at the wheel.

As it slid out of sight Raul knew that if Marco was summoned to a fight outside the courthouse the response time would be slow.

They stared at each other.

Raul's black eyes met Bastiano's silver-grey and they shared their mutual loathing.

'Your mother...' Bastiano started, and then, perhaps wisely, chose not to continue—though that did not stop Raul.

'Are you going to tell me to respect her wishes?' Raul sneered. 'You knew she had this money—you knew...' He halted, but only because his voice was close to faltering and he would not allow Bastiano to glimpse weakness.

He would beat Bastiano with more than his fists.

Raul cleared his throat and delivered his threat, low but strong, and for Bastiano's ears only. 'Collect promptly... pay slowly.'

It was an old Italian saying, but it came with different meaning on this day.

Bastiano might have collected promptly today, but he would pay.

And slowly.

Their eyes met, and though nothing further was said it was as if Raul had repeated those words and he watched as his threat sank in.

Raul would keep his word—the vow he had made by his mother's grave.

Every day he would fight Bastiano—not with fists but with action, and so, to the chagrin of the gathered crowd, who wanted the day to end in blood, Raul walked away.

Bastiano might have got a payout today, but Raul would take his mother's inheritance and build a life from it far away from here.

And in the process he would destroy Bastiano at every opportunity.

Revenge would be his motivator now.

CHAPTER SEVEN

LYDIA KNEW EXACTLY where she was even before her eyes had opened.

There was constant awareness of him, even in sleep. Hearing his deep breathing and feeling his warm, sleeping body beside her, Lydia thought it was the nicest awakening she had ever had.

She chose not to stretch, or pull herself out of this slumberous lull. The mattress felt like a cloud, and the room was the perfect temperature, because even with the bedding around her waist she was warm.

Raul's back did not make pleasant viewing.

Oh, it was muscled, and his shoulders were wide, and his black hair narrowed neatly into the nape of his neck. All was perfect except for the scars.

And there were a lot of them.

There was the ugly, thick vertical one that was untidy and jagged and ran from mid-shoulder to waist.

But there were others that ran across his back.

Thin white lines…row upon row.

She had asked him about his back last night.

Lydia lay there trying to recall his answer.

There hadn't been one.

And she did not ask with words this time—instead with touch, for while she had been looking at his back her fingers had inadvertently gone there.

Raul felt the question in her touch and loathed the fact that he had fallen to sleep on his side, and he rolled onto his back.

'I'm sorry I asked,' Lydia said.

'Then why did you?'

'Because when I'm with you I seem to forget to be polite.'

A phone rang, and this time it wasn't Lydia's. The battery had finally given out.

Raul reached over and swore, even before he had answered the call and then he spoke for a few minutes and lay back down—but this time he faced her.

'We overslept.'

'What time is it?'

'Midday.'

Lydia's eyes widened in surprise. 'Did you miss your plane?'

'No, it is missing me. That's why Allegra rang. She's going to reschedule.'

He stared at her and Lydia found out then why she had thrown herself at him last night.

It was the correct response to those black eyes, Lydia realised, because her desire was still the same.

'Sorry I didn't tell you I was a virgin.'

'It's a miracle you still are.'

She didn't want to be, though.

How heavenly to be made love to by him, Lydia thought, though she said not a word.

He reached out a hand and moved her hair back from her face, and still nothing was said. Lydia liked sharing this silent space with him.

No demands—just silence.

He thought again of all she'd told him—how she had sat at breakfast yesterday and given him that dark piece of her past.

And they were back in that place, together again, only this time it was Raul who spoke.

'I got into a fight at my mother's funeral. At the cemetery.'

'Oh, dear.'

She smiled—not a happy one, just a little smile at their differences.

And he gave a thin smile too.

'With whom?' Lydia asked.

'Her lover.'

And it was at that moment, when he didn't name Bastiano, that Raul, for the first time, properly lied.

Oh, last night it had technically been a lie by omission. She had been angry and confused and there had been good reason for him not to disclose. But now they were in bed together, facing each other and talking as if they were lovers, and Raul knew at his base that he should at that moment have told her.

Yet he did not want her to turn away.

Which she would.

Of course she would.

'When did you find out that your mother was having an affair?' Lydia asked.

'Right after she died,' Raul said. 'I didn't believe it at first. My mother was very religious—when she was a girl, growing up she had hoped to be a nun...'

'Why didn't she?'

'She got pregnant at sixteen.'

'With you? By your father?'

'Of course.' Raul gave a nod. 'It wasn't a happy marriage, I knew that, but I was still surprised...' He didn't finish.

'To find that she cheated?' Lydia asked, and watched his eyes narrow at her choice of words.

'I think my mother was the one who was cheated.' He thought of Bastiano's slick charm and the inheritance that he had ensured was signed over to his name.

'Or,' Lydia pondered out loud, 'maybe she fell in love.'

'Please!' Raul's voice was derisive, but more at Lydia's suggestion than at her. And then he told her something. 'She was used. I hate that man.'

'Do you ever see him?' Lydia asked. 'Her lover?'

'On occasion,' Raul admitted. 'I have made it my mission to take from him, to get there first, to beat him at everything…' It was the reason he was here at the Hotel Grande Lucia. Usually he would be ringing Allegra, drafting an offer to put to Alim.

Yet he had slept until midday.

And that need to conquer had been the real reason for pulling back last night.

Lydia deserved far better than that.

And it was there again—the chance to tell her just who Bastiano was, here and now, in bed, during the most intimate conversation of his life—for Raul never usually discussed such things.

But he didn't tell.

There was no need for that.

And anyway she would be gone soon. So Raul kissed her instead.

It was a different kiss from last night—they knew more about each other now than then—but it did not last for long.

Raul knew his own reputation, and that it wouldn't be changing any time soon, and so he pulled back.

She was dismissed.

Yet still they lingered in bed.

'What are you going to do with the rest of your day?' he asked her.

'I'm going to head home while I've still got one. I'll see if I can transfer my flight to today,' Lydia said. 'I want to tell my mother—away from Maurice—that I'm moving out.'

'Good,' Raul said. 'You need to…' He halted. It was not his place to tell her what to do.

'I know what I need to do, Raul.'

She closed her eyes for a moment and thought of the mountain in front of her that she was about to climb—walking out on the family business, forging a career of her own, finding somewhere to live with nothing.

Yet there was excitement there too.

It was time.

And that made her smile.

'What will *you* do today?' Lydia asked.

Raul thought for a moment—the weekend spread out before him, and really he could take his pick.

Allegra was waiting for Raul to call with his amended schedule.

There were parties and invitations galore—particularly as he was known to be in Rome. And yet whatever he chose Raul knew it could not top last night.

'I'll go home,' Raul said.

'And where's that?' Lydia asked.

'Venezia.'

Venice.

Lydia gave a wistful sigh, but then, so contrary were her memories from there, she screwed up her nose just a fraction—and he saw that she did.

To cover herself, and because she could not take him delving deep this morning, she quickly chose laughter and gave him a dig in his ribs.

'You never told me that you lived there.'

'Why would I?'

'When I was talking about it you never let on…' And then she halted, remembering that Raul owed her no explanations—they danced on the edge of the other, revealing only what they chose. 'I'm not very good at being a one-night stand.'

'No,' he agreed with a wry smile, 'you're not.' And then his smile dimmed, but still his eyes held hers and Raul asked a question. 'Would you have regretted it if we had slept together?'

'No.' Lydia shook her head. 'Raul, you seem to have

decided that just because I haven't slept with anyone I'm looking for something permanent. By all accounts I could have had that with Bastiano, but I chose not to. He's not...' Lydia faltered and then, rather than finishing, swallowed her words down. Raul didn't need to hear them. The truth was she had no feelings for Bastiano.

None.

Yet she did for Raul.

'Not what?' Raul asked.

He's not you would be her honest response.

But rather than say that Lydia was far more evasive. 'He's not what I want.'

'What *do* you want?'

'I wanted what every woman wants, a bit of romance while I was here. I'm not shopping for a husband.' She gave a shrug and pulled one of the tangled sheets from the bed to cover herself. 'I'm going to have a shower.'

And it was in the shower, with space between them, that Lydia pondered what she had been about to say.

He's not you.

With Bastiano there was no attraction. Had it been Raul whom her family were trying to match-make her with she'd have been embarrassed, yes, and annoyed, perhaps, and yet there would have been excitement and trepidation too.

She liked Raul far more than it was safe to let on.

And Raul liked Lydia.

A lot.

That feeling was rare.

Mornings were never his strong point—generally he preferred women who dressed in the dark and were gone. He wasn't proud of that fact, just honest, as he examined his usual wants. Yet this morning he was lying listening to Lydia in the shower and trying to resist joining her.

And again she had surprised him.

Lydia was tough.

There had been no tears, no pleas for help or for him to get involved. In fact she had actively discouraged it when he had offered to step in and deal with Maurice.

There was a level of independence to her that he had seen in few and he did not want her to be gone.

And, more honestly, he wanted to be her first.

It had nothing to do with Bastiano.

In fact Raul wanted her well away from here.

He was wondering if he could give Lydia what she wanted.

The romantic trip to Italy she craved.

He could do that for a day, surely?

Raul didn't look over at her when Lydia came out from the bathroom and went through to the lounge. There she found her case and pulled out an outfit.

Lydia chose the nice cream dress she had brought for sightseeing and some flat sandals.

Her hair was a bit of a disaster, but she had left her adaptor in her hotel room, so there was no point dragging out her straighteners.

Lydia made do and smoothed it as best she could. She could hear Raul making some calls on his phone and commencing his day.

She had been but a brief interlude, Lydia knew. And so she checked that her sunglasses were in her purse and then walked back into the bedroom—and there he lay. He was even more beautiful now than when she had met him.

Then Raul had been in a suit and clean-shaven.

A mystery.

Now he lay in bed with his hands behind his head, thinking. She knew, because she had lain beside him all night, that he was naked save the sheet that barely covered him. He was unshaven and his eyes seemed heavy from sleep as he turned and looked at her.

And the more that she knew, the more of a mystery he was.

This was regret, Lydia thought.

That he could so easily let her go.

And how did she walk away? Lydia wondered.

How did she go over and kiss that sulky mouth and say goodbye when really she wanted to climb back into bed?

How did she accept that she would never know how it felt to be made love to by him?

But rather than reveal her thoughts she flicked that internal default switch which had been permanently set to 'polite'.

'Thank you so much for last night.'

'I haven't finished being your tour guide yet.'

He stretched out his arm and held out his hand, but Lydia didn't go over. She did not want to let in hope, so she just stood there as Raul spoke.

'It would be remiss of me to let you go home without seeing Venice as it should be seen.'

'Venice?'

Oh, she repeated his offer only because she was mystified. She'd been preparing to leave with her head held high, but then, when she had least expected it, he'd offered more.

So much more.

'I like to call it by its other name—La Serenissima,' Raul said. 'It means the Most Serene.'

'That's not how I remember my time there.'

'Then you have a chance to change that. I'm heading there today. Why don't you come with me? Fly out of Marco Polo tomorrow instead.'

There was another night between now and then, and Lydia knew that even while he offered her an extension he made it clear there was a cut-off.

Time added on for good behaviour.

And Raul's version of 'good behaviour' was that there

would be no tears or drama as she walked away. Lydia knew that. If she were to accept his offer, then she had to remember that.

'I'd like that.' The calm of her voice belied the trembling she felt inside. 'It sounds wonderful.'

'Only if you're sure,' Raul added.

'Of course.'

But how could she be sure of anything now she had set foot in Raul's world?

He made her dizzy.

Disorientated.

Not just her head, but every cell in her body seemed to be spinning as he hauled himself from the bed and unlike Lydia, with her sheet-covered dash to the bathroom, his body was hers to view.

And that blasted default switch was stuck, because Lydia did the right thing and averted her eyes.

Yet he didn't walk past. Instead Raul walked right over to her and stood in front of her.

She could feel the heat—not just from his naked body but her own—and it felt as if her dress might disintegrate.

He put his fingers on her chin, tilted her head so that she met his eyes, and it killed that he did not kiss her, nor drag her back to his bed. Instead he checked again. 'Are you sure?'

'Of course,' Lydia said, and tried to make light of it. 'I never say no to a free trip.'

It was a joke—a teeny reference to the very reason she was here in Rome—but it put her in an unflattering light. She was about to correct herself, to say that it hadn't come out as she had meant, but then she saw his slight smile and it spelt approval.

A gold-digger he could handle, Lydia realised.

Her emerging feelings for him—perhaps not.

At every turn her world changed, and she fought for a

semblance of control. Fought to convince not just Raul but herself that she could handle this.

They were driven right up to his jet, and his pilot and crew were waiting on the runway to greet them.

'Do you always have a jet on standby?' Lydia asked.

'Always.'

'What's wrong with first class?' Lydia asked, refusing to appear too impressed.

'When children are banned from first class, then I'll consider commercial flights.'

He wouldn't!

Raul liked his privacy, as well as his own staff.

Inside the plane was just as luxurious as the hotel they had come from, and very soon there was take-off and she looked out of the window and watched Rome disappear beneath them.

Lydia felt free.

Excited, nervous, but finally free.

'I travel a lot.' Raul explained the real reason for his plane. 'And, as you saw this morning, my schedule is prone to change. Having my own jet shaves hours off my working week.'

'How did you do all this?' Lydia asked.

'I received an inheritance when my mother died.'

'Your family was rich?'

'No.'

He thought back to Casta. They had been comfortable financially, compared to some, but it had been dirty money and always quickly spent.

Neither the Di Savo nor the Conti wineries had ever really taken off.

And then he thought of him and Bastiano, drinking the wine together and laughing at how disgusting it tasted.

They had been such good friends.

In the anger and hate that had fuelled him for years, Raul had forgotten that part.

It would serve him better not to remember it now.

Bastiano was the enemy, and he reminded himself of that when he spoke next.

'My mother had some money from her brother. She left half to her lover and half to me. It was enough for me to buy the flat I was renting. Then I took out a mortgage on one across the floor and rented it out. I kept going like that. You were right—developers did come in, and they made me an offer that I should not have been able to refuse.'

'But you did?'

'Yes. If they could see the potential, then so could I. One of the owners upstairs had done some refurbishing, and I watched and learnt. By then I had four studio apartments, and I turned them into two more luxurious ones… It had always been an amazing location, but now it was a desirable address. A few years later the other owner and I got the backing to turn it into a hotel. I bought him out in the end. I wanted it for myself. That was always the end game.'

'You used him?'

'Of course,' Raul said. 'That's what I do.'

He didn't care if that put him in an unflattering light.

Better that she know.

'Do you go back often?' Lydia asked. 'To Sicily?'

Raul shook his head. 'I haven't been back since my mother's funeral.

'Don't you miss it?' Lydia pushed.

'There is nothing there for me to miss.'

'You didn't go back for your father's funeral?' Lydia checked.

'No. He was already dead to me.'

'But even so—'

'Should I pretend to care?' Raul interrupted.

Lydia didn't know how to answer that. In her family ap-

pearances were everything, and there was a constant demand to be seen to do the right thing.

Raul lived by rules of his own.

'No,' she answered finally.

Her response was the truth—she could think of nothing worse than Raul pretending to care and her believing
in his lies.

Better to know from the start that this was just tempo-
rary, for when he removed her from his life she really would
be gone for good.

'Do you want to change for dinner?'

'Dinner?' Lydia checked, and then she looked at the sun,
too low in the sky. The day was running away from them
already.

And soon, Lydia knew, it would be her turn to be the
one left behind.

CHAPTER EIGHT

LYDIA HAD BEEN in two different bedrooms belonging to Raul.

One at the hotel.

The other on his plane.

Tonight would make it three.

Raul was wearing black pants and a white shirt—dressed for anything, she guessed.

Lydia opened her case, and there was the red dress she had bought with Raul on her mind.

It was too much, surely?

Yet she would never get the chance again. She thought of where she'd be tomorrow—rowing with her mother and no doubt packing a lifetime of stuff into trunks and preparing to move out of the castle.

A bell buzzed, and Lydia knew she had to move a little more quickly.

Simple, yet elegant, there was nothing that should scream 'warning' in the dress, and yet it hugged her curves, and the slight ruching of the fabric over her stomach seemed to indicate the shiver she felt inside.

On sight he had triggered something.

Those dark eyes seemed to see far beyond the rather brittle façade she wore.

She didn't know how to be sexy, yet around him she was.

More than that—she wanted to be.

She added lipstick and wished she'd worn the neutral shoes.

Except Lydia felt far from neutral about tonight.

It was too much.

Far, far too much.

She would quickly change, Lydia decided.

But then there was a gentle rap on the door and she was informed that it was time to be seated.

'I'll just be a few moments,' Lydia said, and dismissed the steward. But what she did not understand about private jets was the fact that there were not two hundred passengers to get strapped in.

'Now.' The steward smiled. 'We're about to come in to land.'

There was no chance to change and so, shy, reluctant, but trying not to show it, Lydia stepped out.

'Sit down,' Raul said.

He offered no compliment—really, he gave no reaction. In fact he took out his phone and sent a text.

Oddly, it helped.

She had a moment to sit with her new self, away from his gaze, and Lydia looked out of the window and willed her breathing to calm.

Venice was always beautiful, and yet today it was even more so.

As they flew over on their final descent she rose out of the Adriatic in full midsummer splendour, and Lydia knew she would remember this moment for ever. The last time she had felt as if she were sitting alone, even though she had been surrounded by school friends.

Now, as the wheels hit the runway, Lydia came down to earth as her spirit soared high.

And as they stood to leave he told her.

'You look amazing.'

'Is it too much?'

'Too much?' Raul frowned. 'It's still summer.'

'No, I meant…' She wasn't talking about the amount of skin on show, but she gave up trying to explain what she meant.

But Raul hadn't been lost in translation—he had deliberately played vague.

He had heard Maurice's reprimand yesterday morning and knew colour was not a feature in her life.

Till today.

And so he had played it down.

He had told her to sit, as if blonde beauties in sexy red dresses wearing red high heels regularly walked out of the bedroom of his plane.

Actually, they did.

But they had never had him reaching for his phone and calling in a favour from Silvio, a friend.

Raul had been toying with the idea all afternoon…wondering if it would be too much.

But then he had seen her. Stunning in red. Shy but brave. And if Lydia had let loose for tonight, then so too would he.

'Where are we going?' Lydia asked.

'Just leave all that to me.'

Last time she'd been in Venice there had been strict itineraries and meeting points, but this time around there was no water taxi to board. Instead their luggage was loaded onto a waiting speedboat, and while Raul spoke with the driver Lydia took a seat and drank in the gorgeous view.

Then she became impatient to know more, because the island they were approaching looked familiar.

'Tell me where we're going.'

'To Murano.'

'Oh.' Just for a second her smile faltered. Last time Lydia had been there she had felt so wretched.

'Sometimes it is good to go back.'

'*You* don't, though,' Lydia pointed out, because from everything she knew about Raul he did all he could not to revisit the past.

'No, I don't.'

She should leave it, Lydia knew, and for the moment she did.

There was barely a breeze as their boat sliced through the lagoon. Venice could never disappoint. Raul had been right. It heightened the emotions, and today Lydia's happiness was turning to elation.

In a place of which she had only dark memories suddenly everything was bright, and so she looked over to him and offered a suggestion.

'Maybe you should go back, Raul.'

He did not respond.

They docked in Murano, the Island of Bridges, and Raul took her hand to help Lydia off the boat. The same way as he had last night in Rome, he didn't let her hand go.

And in a sea of shorts and summer tops and dresses Lydia *was* overdressed.

For once she cared not.

They walked past all the showrooms and turned down a small cobbled street. Away from the tourists there was space to slow down and just revel in the feel of the sun on her shoulders.

'I know someone who has a studio here,' Raul said.

He did not explain that often in the mornings Silvio was at Raul's favourite café, and they would speak a little at times. And neither did he explain that he had taken Silvio up on a long-standing offer—'If you ever want to bring a friend…'

Raul had never envisaged that he might.

Oh, he admired Silvio's work—in fact his work had been one of the features that had drawn Raul to buy his home.

He had never thought he might bring someone, though, and yet she was so thrilled to be here, so lacking in being spoilt…

'Silvio is a master glassmaker,' Raul explained. 'He comes from a long line of them. His work is commissioned years in advance and it's exquisite. There will be no three-legged ponies to tempt you.'

And Lydia had never thought she could smile at that memory, yet she did today.

'In fact there is nothing to buy—there is a waiting list so long that he could never complete it in his lifetime. People say that to see him work is to watch the sun being painted in the sky. All we have to do this evening is enjoy.'

'You've never seen him work?'

'No.'

But that changed today.

It was the great man himself who opened a large wooden door and let them in. The place was rather nondescript, with high ceilings and a stained cement floor, and in the middle was a large furnace.

Silvio wore filthy old jeans and a creased shirt and he was unshaven, yet there was an air of magnificence about him.

'This is Lydia,' Raul introduced her.

'Welcome to Murano.'

'She has been here before,' Raul said. 'Though the last time it was on a school trip.'

The old man smiled. 'And did you bring home a souvenir?'

'A vase.' Lydia nodded. 'It was for my mother.'

'Did she like it?'

Lydia was about to give her usual smile and nod, but then she stood there remembering her mother's air of disdain as she had opened the present.

'She didn't seem to appreciate it,' Lydia admitted.

It had hurt a lot at the time.

All her savings and so much pain had gone into the purchase, and yet Valerie had turned up her nose.

But Silvio was looking out of the windows.

'I had better get started. The light is getting low,' he explained.

'Too low to work?' Lydia asked.

'No, no...' He smiled. 'I do very few pieces in a fading light. They are my best, though. I will get some coffee.'

Silvio headed to a small kitchenette and Lydia wandered, her heels noisy on the concrete floor.

There was nothing to see, really, nor to indicate brilliance—nothing to pull her focus back from the past.

'My mother hated that vase,' Lydia told Raul as she wandered. 'She ended up giving it to one of the staff as a gift.' God, that had hurt at the time, but rather than bring down the mood Lydia shrugged. 'At least it went to practical use rather than gathering dust.'

The coffee Silvio had made was not for his guests, Lydia quickly found out. He returned and placed a huge mug on the floor beside a large glass of water, and then she and Raul had the privilege of watching him work.

Molten glass was stretched and shaped and, with a combination of the most basic of tools and impossible skill, a human form emerged.

And then another.

It was mesmerising to watch—as if the rather drab surroundings had turned into a cathedral. The sun streamed in from the westerly windows and caught the thick ribbons of glass. And Lydia watched the alchemy as somehow Silvio formed two bodies, and then limbs emerged.

It was like witnessing creation.

Over and over Silvio twisted and drew out tiny slivers of glass—spinning hair, eyes, and shaping a slender waist. It was erotic too, watching as Silvio formed breasts and then shaped the curve of a buttock.

Nothing was held back. The male form was made with nothing left to the imagination, and the heat in her cheeks had little to do with the furnace that Silvio used to fire his tools and keep the statue fluid.

It was sensual, creative and simply art at its best. Faces formed and pliable heads were carefully moved, and the kiss that emerged was open-mouthed and so erotic that Lydia found her own tongue running over her lips as she remembered the blistering kisses she and Raul had shared.

It was like tasting Raul all over again and feeling the weight of his mouth on hers.

Lydia fought not to step closer, because she didn't want to get in the way or distract Silvio, yet every minuscule detail that he drew from the liquid glass deserved attention. She watched the male form place a hand on the female form's buttock and flushed as if Raul had just touched her there.

Raul was trying not to touch her.

It was such an intimate piece, and personal too, for it felt as if the energy that hummed between them had somehow been tapped.

And then Silvio merged the couple, pulling the feminine thigh around the male loin, arching the neck backwards, and Lydia was aware of the sound of her own pulse whooshing in her ears.

The erotic beauty was more subtle now, the anatomical details conjoined for ever and captured in glass. And then Silvio rolled another layer of molten glass over them, covering the conjoined beauty with a silken glass sheet.

Yet they all knew what lay beneath.

'Now my signature...' Silvio said, and Lydia felt as if she had been snapped from a trance.

He seared his name into the base, and smoothed it till it was embedded, and then it was for Raul and Lydia to admire the finished piece.

'I've never seen anything like it,' Lydia admitted as she examined the statue.

How could glass be sexy? Yet this was a kiss, in solid form, and the intimate anatomical work that had seemed wasted when the forms had been merged was now revealed—she could see the density at the base of the woman's spine that spoke of the man deep within her.

'It's an amazing piece,' Raul said, and Lydia couldn't believe that his voice sounded normal when she felt as if she had only just returned from being spirited away.

'There are more…' Silvio said, and he took them through to another area and showed them several other pieces.

As stunning as they all were, for Lydia they didn't quite live up to the lovers' statue. Perhaps it was because she had witnessed it being made, Lydia mused as they stepped back out into the street.

It was disorientating.

Lydia went to head left, but Raul took her hand and they went right and he led her back to the speedboat.

The driver had gone, on Raul's instruction, and it was he who drove them to San Marco.

Raul took great pride in showing her around this most seductive of cities.

They wandered through ghostly back streets and over bridges.

'It's so wonderful to be here,' Lydia said. 'It was all so rushed last time, and it felt as if we were just ticking things off a list.'

'And the obligatory gondola ride?' Raul said, but her response surprised him.

'No.' Lydia shook her head. 'Some of the girls did, but…' She stopped.

'But?'

'Sitting on the bus with the teacher was bad enough. I think a gondola ride with her would have been worse somehow.'

She tried to keep it light, as Raul had managed to when

they had been talking about her lonely school trip in Rome.
She didn't quite manage it, though.

Raul, who had been starting to think about their dinner
reservation, steered her towards the canal.

'Come on,' he said. 'You cannot do Venice without a
gondola ride.'

Till this point Raul had, though.

Raul's usual mode of transport was a speedboat.

But there was nothing like Venice at sunset from a gondola, as both found out together.

The low boat sliced gently through the water and the
Grand Canal blushed pink as the sun dipped down. He
looked over as she sighed, and saw Lydia smiling softly as
she drank it all in.

'You don't take photos?' Raul observed.

'My phone's flat,' Lydia said, but then admitted more.
'I'm not one for taking photos.'

'Why not?'

He was ever-curious about her—something Raul had
never really been before.

'Because when it's gone it's gone,' Lydia said. 'Best to
move on.'

The gondolier took them through the interior canals that
were so atmospheric that silence was the best option.

It was cool on the water, and there were blankets they
could put over their knees, but she accepted Raul's jacket.

The silk was warm from him, and as she put it on he
helped her. The only reason he had not kissed her before
was because he'd thought it might prove impossible to stop.

But Raul was beyond common sense thinking now—
and so was she.

He took her face in his hands and he looked at her
mouth—the lipstick was long gone.

'I want you,' he told her.

'And you know I want you.'

Lydia did.

His mouth told her just how much he wanted her. She watched his eyelids shutter, and then he tasted her. Lydia did the same. She felt the soft weight of him and her mouth opened just a little as they flirted with their tongues. There was tenderness, promise and building passion in every stroke and beat. Yet even as they kissed she cared for the view, and now and then opened her eyes just for a glimpse, because it was like spinning circles in a blazing sky.

His hand slipped inside the jacket. First just the pad of his thumb caressed her breast, and then—she had been right— the dress drew his attention down.

His hand was on her stomach, just lingering, and Lydia felt his warm palm through the fabric. Her breathing stilled and he felt the change and pulled her closer, to taste and feel more.

They sailed under ancient bridges and he kissed her knowingly. So attuned were they no one would guess they weren't lovers yet.

There was just the sound of the gondolier's paddle and the taste of passion.

She was on fire, and yet he made her shiver.

Soon Raul knew the gondolier would turn them around, for the canal ended soon. They were about to pass under the Bridge of Sighs and the bells of St Mark's Campanile were tolling.

Which meant, according to legend, that if they kissed they would be granted eternal love and bliss.

Which Raul did not want.

But their mouths made a fever—a fever neither wanted to break—and anyway he didn't believe in legends.

They pulled their mouths apart as the gondolier turned them around, but their foreheads were still touching.

Lydia was breathless and flushed, and though Raul had

made so many plans for her perfect Venetian night he could wait no more.

They should be stopping soon for champagne, and then a canalside dinner at his favourite restaurant. Except his hand was back between them, stroking her nipple through velvet, and her tongue was more knowing.

His best-laid plans were fading.

Lydia pulled her mouth back, but he kissed her cheek and moved his lips towards her ear, and his jaw was rough and delicious, and his hand on her breast had her suddenly desperate.

'Raul…' Lydia said.

Oh, she said his name so easily now.

And he knew her so much more, because there was a slight plea in her voice and it matched the way he felt.

He pulled back his own mouth, only enough to deliver the gondolier an instruction.

The sky was darker as they kissed through the night, and soon they were gliding back towards the Grand Canal, and now Raul wished for an engine and the speed of his own boat.

The gondolier came to a stop at a water door and said something. It took a moment for Lydia to register that they had stopped and so had the kiss. Realising that she was being spoken to, she looked around breathlessly, staring up at yet another *palazzo* and trying to take in her surroundings.

'It's beautiful!' Lydia said, trying to be a good tourist while wishing they could get back to kissing.

Raul smiled at her attempt to be polite when she was throbbing between the legs.

'It's even more beautiful inside,' Raul told her. 'This is my home.'

Lydia almost wept in relief.

He got out first and took her by the hand, and then pushed open the dark door.

She entered his home an innocent.

Lydia would not be leaving it the same.

CHAPTER NINE

THROUGH THE ENTRANCE and into an internal elevator they went, but Lydia prayed there would be no fire in the night, for she did not take in her surroundings at all—their kisses were frantic and urgent now.

His body was hard against hers, and his hands were a little rough as Raul fought with himself not to hitch up her dress.

The jolt of the old elevator was barely noted—there was just relief that they could get out.

They almost ran.

Raul took her hand and led her with haste through a long corridor lined with ancient mirrors and lit with white pillar candles.

And at the end, as if she were looking through a keyhole, there was the reward of open wooden doors that revealed a vast bed.

She would wake up soon, Lydia was sure.

She would wake up from this sensual dream.

Yet she did not.

There were colours that rained on the walls and the bed, yet she was too into Raul to look for their source.

And was she scared?

No.

Shy?

Not a bit.

Raul stripped, and then no words were needed, no instruction required, as naked, erect, he dealt with her dress.

Lydia held up her hair as he unzipped her.

She shook as he removed the dress, then her bra.

And she moaned as he knelt to remove first her shoes and then the final garment between them.

Raul slid the silk down and probed her with his tongue. Lydia stood and knotted her fingers in his hair, and as Raul gently eased in two fingers, though it hurt, it was bliss.

She parted her legs as he licked and stretched her, and ensured she was oiled at the same time.

He turned away from her then, reaching for the bed-side table.

'You're on the Pill?'

Lydia nodded, a touch frantic. She wanted no pause for she needed him inside her.

Lydia had the rest of her life to be sensible and behave.

Just this night.

He took her to his bed and they knelt upon it, kissing and caressing each other. Gliding their hands over each other's body. His muscled and taut...hers softer. They recreated the scene from earlier, at the glassblower's, because it had felt at the time as if they were watching themselves.

'Since we met...' Raul said, and kissed her arched neck.

And her breasts ached for him, but not as much as be-tween her legs.

His erection was pressed against her stomach, nudging, promising, and he wanted to take her kneeling but was aware that it was her first time, and he had felt how tight she was with his fingers.

Raul tried to kiss her into lying down so that he could take things slowly.

She resisted.

And he was glad that she did.

He raised her higher, hooked her leg around him and held himself. And she rested her arms over his shoulders and then lowered herself.

A little.

It hurt, but it was the best hurt.

Raul's eyes were open, and they were both barely breathing, just focused on the bliss they felt.

'Since we met…' he said again, and his voice was low, rich and smoky.

And she lowered herself a little more, and he felt her, tight and hot.

She wanted him so badly but could not see that last bit through. 'Raul…'

There was a plea in her voice again, and he heeded it and took control and thrust hard.

Lydia sobbed as he seared into her. Everything went black, and not just because she'd screwed her eyes closed. She thought she might faint, but he took her hips and held her still and waited as best he could for her to open her eyes.

They opened, and she thought she would never get used to it—ever—but then her breathing evened. And when she opened her eyes again, as she had on the canal, this time they met his.

Raul's hand went to the very base of her spine. His touch was sensual and she moved a little, slowly, acclimatising to the feel of him within her.

She was sweaty and hot as his hands moved to her buttocks and he started to thrust.

'Raul…'

She wanted him to slow down, yet he *was* moving slowly.

And then Lydia wanted him never to stop.

Pain had left and in its place was a craving, an intense desire for more of what built within.

His hands had guided her into rhythm, but now she found her own. And it was slower than they could account for, for their bodies were frantic, but they relished the intense pleasure. Raul felt the oiled and yet tight grip of her, and each thrust brought him deeper into the mire, to savour or release. Lydia was lost to sensation. His breath in her ear was like music as it combined with the energies concentrated within her.

Her calf ached, but she did not have the will to move it, and then her inner thighs tensed as she parted around him.

The centre of her felt pulled so tight it was almost a spasm, and then she was lost for control and he held her still. And then, when she had thought he could fill her no more, Raul swelled and thrust—rapid and fast.

Lydia screamed, just a little, but it was a sound she had never made before and it came from a place she had never been.

Her legs coiled tight around him, her body hot and pulsing as he filled her.

'Since we met,' he said as she rested her head on his shoulder and felt the last flickers of their union fade, 'I've wanted you.'

'And I you,' Lydia said, for it was the truth.

And then he kissed her down from what felt like the ceiling.

'Res…' Raul said, and then halted and changed what he had been about to say. 'Rest.'

And she lay there in his arms, silent.

Lydia knew there could be no going back from what had just taken place.

And it had nothing to do with innocence lost.

How the hell did she go back to her life without him?

CHAPTER TEN

A GORGEOUS CHANDELIER, creating prisms of light in every shade of spring, was the first thing Lydia saw when she awoke.

There was a long peal of bells ringing out in the distance, but it was a closer, more occasional, deep, sonorous chime that held her attention. It rang low, soft and yet clear, till the sound slowly faded. When it struck again she remembered gliding underneath the Bridge of Sighs with his kiss.

Lydia knew the legend.

She had stood by the bridge with one of her school friends and struck it from her study sheet.

Eternal love and bliss had not applied to her then and it could not now, Lydia knew.

And so she stared up instead and remembered her vow to not show the hurt when it ended.

Pinks, lemons and minty greens dotted the ceiling, and she saw that the beads were actually flowers that threw little prisms of light across the room.

He was awake.

Stretching languorously beside her.

Lydia relished the moment.

His hand slid to her hips and pulled her closer, and rather than ponder over the fact that soon she would be gone, Lydia chose to keep things light.

'I never pictured you as a man who might have a chandelier in the bedroom.'

Raul gave a low laugh.

He was a mystery, but not hers to solve, and so she did her best to maintain a stiff upper lip.

'A floral chandelier at that,' Lydia added. Her eyes could

not stop following the beams of light. 'Though I have to say it's amazing.'

'It drives me crazy,' Raul admitted. 'When I first moved in I considered having it taken down, or changing the master bedroom, but the view of the canal is the best from here.'

'Oh, you can't have it taken down,' Lydia said.

'Easy for you to say. I feel like I am having laser surgery on my eyes some mornings.'

Lydia smiled and carried on watching the light show.

She never wanted to move.

Or rather she did, but only to the beat of their lovemaking.

His hand was making circles on her stomach and he was hard against her thigh.

Lydia didn't want to check the time just to find out how little time they had left.

'I love your home.'

'You haven't really seen it.'

And she was about to throw him a line about how she could live in just his bedroom for ever, but it would come out wrong, she knew.

He watched the lips he had been about to kiss press together.

Raul saw that.

Then he thought of what he'd been about to say last night. *Restare.*

Stay.

He should be congratulating himself for not making such a foolish mistake by uttering that word last night.

Yet the feeling was still there.

And so Raul, far safer than making love to her, as he wanted to, told her how he had come by his home.

'There is a café nearby that I go to. I sometimes see Silvio there, and we chat. On one occasion he told me that this *palazzo* had come on the market. He was not interested in purchasing it but had been to view it as some of his early work was inside.'

I don't care, Lydia wanted to say. *I want to be kissed.*

Yet she did care.

And she did want to know about his home and how he had come by it.

She wanted more information to add to the file marked 'Raul Di Savo' that her heart would soon have to close.

And his voice was as deep as that occasional bell and it resonated in every cell of her body.

She wanted to turn her mouth to feel his, but she lay listening instead.

'Half a century ago it underwent major refurbishment. Silvio made all the internal door handles with his grandfather. But it was the chandelier in the master bedroom that he really wanted to see.'

And now they both lay bathed in the dancing sunbeams of the chandelier as he told its tale.

'It was created by three generations of Silvio's family, long before he was born. I knew that I had to see it, so I called Allegra to arrange a viewing, and then, when I saw it, I had to own it.'

'I can see why.' Lydia sighed. 'I'm back in love with Venice.'

And then she said it.

'I never want to leave.'

It was just what people said at the end of a good trip, Raul knew, but silence hung in the air now, the bells were quiet, and it felt as if even the sky awaited his response.

He needed to think—away from Lydia. For the temptation was still there to say it, to roll into her and make love to her and ask her to remain.

It was unfamiliar and confusing enough for Raul to deal with, let alone her. And so he tried to dismiss the thought in his head that refused to leave.

And Raul knew that Lydia needed her heart that was starting to soar to be reined in.

'People love their holidays,' Raul said. 'I know that. I study it a lot in my line of work. But there is one thing I have consistently found—no matter how luxurious the surroundings, or how fine the cognac, no matter how much my staff do everything they can to ensure the very best stay…' he could see tears sparkle in her eyes and he had never once seen her even close to crying before '…at the end of even the most perfect stay most are ready to go back to their lives.'

'Not always.' Lydia fought him just a little.

And they *both* fought to keep the conversation from getting too heavy, but they were not discussing holidays—they both knew that.

'I know,' Lydia persisted, 'that when I've had a really good holiday I want more of it…even just a few more days…' She lied, and they both knew it, because Lydia had never had a really good holiday, but he kept to the theme.

'Then that means it was an exceptional trip—a once-in-a-lifetime experience. A guest should always leave wanting more.'

He saw her lips turn white at this relegation and tempered it just a little as he told her they could never be. 'I'll tell you something else I have found—if people do return to that treasured memory it is never quite the same.'

'No.' Lydia shook her head.

'True,' Raul insisted. 'We have couples come back for their anniversary and they complain that the hotel has changed, or that the waterways are too busy, or that the restaurant they once loved is no longer any good… And I know they are wrong, that my hotel has got better since they were there and that the restaurant retains its standard. I know that the waterways of Venice are ever beautiful. It is the couple who have changed.'

'How arrogant of you to assume your guests have no cause for complaint.'

'They don't.'

And as she fought for her belief that all things might be possible, that their slice of time might lead to more, his words thwarted her.

'Why risk spoiling something wonderful?' Raul asked, but when Lydia didn't answer he lay there asking himself the same thing.

Why would he even risk suggesting that she stay?

But didn't guests extend their stays all the time?

Only Lydia wasn't a guest.

He climbed from the bed and attempted to get life back to normal.

'I'm going out for a little while,' Raul told her. 'I'll bring back breakfast.'

Only 'normal' seemed to have left—for Raul never brought back breakfast, and he certainly didn't eat it in bed.

But he had made plans yesterday when she had walked out in that dress. He had sworn to give her the best of Venice, and now it was time to execute that plan.

Then things could get back to normal—once she had gone his head would surely clear.

Lydia, he decided, *wasn't* a guest—she was in fact a squatter who had taken over his long-abandoned heart.

'You'd better call soon to transfer your flight.'

'I will,' Lydia said, glad that he was going out for breakfast. She just needed the space, for the air between them had changed. And she was cross with Raul that he should be able to see her off on a plane after the time they had shared.

And he was cross that he was considering otherwise—that he was *still* considering asking her to stay.

Raul shot her an angry glance as she watched him dress, but she didn't see it. Lydia was too busy watching as he pulled on black jeans over his nakedness.

He looked seedy and unshaven, and he was on the edge of hardening again, and she fought not to pull up her knees as lust punched low in her stomach.

He pulled on black boots, although it was summer, and then turned to reach for his top. She saw the nail marks on his scarred back and the injury toll from yesterday started to surface.

She was starting to feel sore.

Deliciously so.

'Go back to sleep,' Raul suggested.

He went to walk out, but his resident squatter did what she always did and niggled at his conscience. And so, rather than stalk out, he went over and bent down and gave her a kiss.

They were arguing, Lydia knew.

And she *liked* it.

His jaw scratched as he fought with himself to remove his mouth and get out, and then her tongue was the one to part his lips.

And that perfunctory kiss was no more.

Hellcat.

She made him *want*.

He was dressed and kneeling on the bed, kissing her hard, and she was arching into him.

His hand was rough through the sheet, squeezing her breast hard, and she wanted him to whip the sheet off.

Her hand told the back of his head that.

Lydia wanted him to unzip himself and to feel rough denim.

And so he stopped kissing her and stood.

Raul liked her endless wanting.

And he liked it that he wanted to go back to bed.

And *that* was very concerning to him.

Yes, he needed to think.

'Why don't you go back to sleep?' Raul suggested again, his voice even and calm, with nothing to indicate the passion he was walking away from.

Apart from the bulge in his jeans.

She gave a slightly derisive laugh at the suggestion that she might find it possible to sleep as he walked to the door.

Raul took the elevator down and, as he always did on a Sunday, drove the speedboat himself. He took it slowly. The sky was a riot of pink and orange, and there was the delicious scent of impending rain hanging heavily in the air.

Her gift would be arriving soon, and Raul badly needed some time alone to think.

Restare.

Stay.

He had almost said it out loud last night but had held back, worried that he might regret it in the light of day. Yet the light was here and the word was still there, on the tip of his tongue and at the front of his thoughts.

Usually he would take breakfast at his favourite café and sit watching the world go by, or on occasion chat with a local such as Silvio.

Not this morning.

He wanted to be home.

On a personal level Raul had never really understood the pleasure of breakfast in bed. He always rose early and, whether home or away, was dressed for the first coffee of the day and checking emails before it had even been poured.

On a business level Raul had both examined and profited from it. There was a lovers' breakfast served at his hotel here in Venice, and a favourite on the menu was the *baci in gondola*—sweet white pastry melded with dark chocolate.

Raul was at his favourite café and ordering them now—only this time he was asking them to be placed in one of their trademark boxes and tied with a red velvet ribbon.

It was to be a true lovers' breakfast, because he did not want maids intruding, and he wanted his coffee stronger and sweeter than usual today.

Raul wore the barista's eye-roll when he also asked for English Breakfast Tea.

'Cinque minute, Raul,' the waitress told him.

Five minutes turned into seven, and he was grateful for the extra two, but even when they had passed still the thought remained.

Restare.

He wanted a chance for them.

Lydia lay, half listening to the sounds of Venice on a Sunday morning, and thought of their lovemaking.

It was still too close to be called a memory.

Yet it would be soon.

Unless she changed her flight times.

What if she told him she couldn't get a flight out of Venice until tomorrow?

Lydia got out of bed and pulled on a robe and found her phone. Even as she plugged it in to charge it Lydia knew she was breaking the deal they had made—simply to walk away.

Only it wasn't that simple.

This felt like love.

It was infatuation, Lydia scolded herself.

He was the first person who had shown an interest...

Only that wasn't so.

There had been others, but she had chosen to let no one in.

'Signorina...'

There was a knock at the door and Lydia opened it and smiled at the friendly face of a maid, who said her name was Loretta.

'You have a delivery.'

'Me?' Lydia checked. 'But no one knows that...' And

then her voice trailed off, because the name on the box was indeed hers, and as she took it Lydia felt its weight.

There were stickers saying 'Fragile' all over the box and Lydia was trying to reel herself in.

The word was the same in both Italian and English, and she wanted to peel the stickers off and place them on herself.

She was too fragile for this much hope.

Lydia took the box out to the balcony to open it.

It didn't matter that it had started to rain. She needed air, she truly did, because as she peeled back layers of tape and padding, the hopes she had been trying not to get up soared, for there, nestled in velvet, was the art they had seen made.

It was exquisite.

Dark gold it was shot through with colour, red and crimson, and she ran her fingers along the cool glass and recalled the way Raul had held her last night.

It was more than a gift, and far more than the once-promised morning-after present, surely—it felt like a diary of *them*.

The kisses and caresses…the oblivion they had found… the melding of two bodies. It was the most beautiful thing she had ever seen, let alone been given.

How could she even hope to hold on to her heart? Lydia thought, and then she looked out on the canal and there he was, steering the boat with ease, the man she loved.

Loved.

Her own admission scared her.

Raul didn't want her love.

She felt that if he so much as looked up he might read her, so Lydia gathered the box and the statue and went back into the room and attempted to reel herself in.

It was a gift.

An exceptionally generous gift.

It didn't necessarily mean that he felt the same and she had to remember that.

She was trying to hold on to that thought so hard that when her phone rang, unthinkingly Lydia took the call.

'You fool.'

That was how Maurice greeted her, and Lydia pulled the phone back from her ear, about to turn it off, because she refused to let him ruin this day.

But, having called her a fool, Maurice then asked her a question.

'What the hell are you doing with Raul Di Savo?' Maurice asked.

'That's not your concern.'

He'd never told her his surname, though she had seen it on the business card he had given her.

More concerning was how Maurice had known. But, unasked, he told her. 'There are pictures of the two of you all over the Net.'

'Us?'

'Have you *any* idea of the fire you're playing with? He's using you, Lydia.'

That much she knew wasn't true.

Lydia looked at the statue he had bought her, the most beautiful gift ever given, and she recalled not just Raul's touch but how even without words he made her feel good about herself.

Even if their time was to be fleeting, for once in her life someone had truly liked her.

That was the real gift.

'He isn't *using* me,' Lydia sneered, utterly confident in that statement.

She had gone willingly, after all.

And then everything changed.

'He just wants to get at Bastiano.'

She was so sick of hearing that man's name. 'What the

hell does Bastiano—' And she stopped, for in that second Lydia answered her own question.

Even before Maurice told her outright, Lydia already knew.

'They were friends until Bastiano had an affair with his mother. Raul has sworn to make him pay slowly... Screwing you was mere revenge.'

Hope died silently, Lydia found out as she stood there.

No protest.

No flailing.

For Maurice's filthy term matched her thoughts.

She *had* been screwed.

It made sense.

Well, better sense than that she might ever be loved for herself.

She ended the call and looked for the photos Maurice had alluded to. Her heart was thumping...she knew that soon Raul would be back.

There was only one photo she could find—they were in that Rome café, drenched in the morning sun, and he was holding her hand.

She had been innocent then.

And Lydia wasn't thinking about sex.

She had been innocent of the level of hurt he might cause, for she had sworn she would let no one close ever again.

Oh, she was a fool—for she had.

So, *so* close.

Lydia wanted to retch as she thought of their lovemaking, and she held in a sob as she had a sudden vision of herself coming undone under his expert ministrations.

Had he been laughing on the inside?

Everything was tainted black.

Her phone rang again, and Lydia saw that it was Arabella.

She must have seen the photos.

Lydia was no doubt popular now.

'Hey…' Arabella said. 'When are we going to catch up? How about tonight?'

'I can't make it.'

'Well, soon?'

'No, thank you.'

'When, then?'

'I've got to go.'

Lydia gave no reason.

Raul had taught her that much at least.

She ended the call and ran to the balcony and stood there dragging in air and trying to fathom how to face the man who had destroyed her.

Would he be like Arabella and barely flinch when he found he'd been caught out?

All her confidence was shredded.

She was no butterfly emerging, Lydia knew, but a dragonfly.

Didn't they spread their wings for just one day?

Her wings were gone now, torn and stripped, and it hurt to be bare.

She stood clutching the stone balcony in the rain and wondered if she had time to pack and get out. But it was too late. She looked down and saw the empty speedboat and knew he must be on his way up.

Leaving without tears, leaving with pride, wasn't just a wish but an imperative now—Raul must *never* know the hurt he had caused her, Lydia vowed.

Not one tear would she give him.

She would have been better off with Bastiano!

At least there she had known the score.

A whore, albeit with a ring on her finger.

And then it came to her—Lydia knew how to hurt Raul now.

CHAPTER ELEVEN

'HEY…'

She turned and saw him. His hair was wet, and had she not found out, Lydia knew they would have been naked soon.

Why did he have to be so beautiful?

How she wished there had been just another day till she'd found out.

'Why are you standing in the rain?' Raul asked.

'I was just taking in the view before I go.'

'About that…'

'I called and they can transfer my flight, but I have to leave soon.'

'You don't.' Raul shook his head. He had a jet on call, after all, but more than that he wanted to say it.

Stay.

'Come and have breakfast and we can talk.'

'No, thanks,' Lydia said, and she wondered herself how she did it, because she actually managed to smile.

She had at her father's funeral as she had thanked the guests for coming.

And she had smiled at Arabella that awful day in Murano as she had purchased the vase.

No one knew her, and now she would make sure no one ever did.

Yes, her innocence was gone.

In every sense.

'I have a lot to sort out, Raul. I need to get home and face things.'

'I know that, but it can wait a few days. Come inside— I brought breakfast.'

And Lydia knew she wasn't that good an actress. She could not lie in bed and eat. And so she shook her head. 'I need to go, Raul.'

He kissed her to change her mind.

And she let him.

Desperate for the taste of him just one more time.

He nudged with his hips, he cajoled with his tongue, and he nearly won.

'Come on.'

He led her inside, but instead of going to bed Lydia reached for her case and placed it on the bed and started to pack.

'I don't get why you're leaving,' Raul said. He did not understand her mood.

'Wasn't it you who said I don't need to give an excuse or a reason?'

Indeed it had been.

And so he watched as she put the red shoes into the case, and the underwear he had peeled off last night, and selected fresh for today.

Her robe was clinging and her nipples were thick, and Lydia, as she went and unplugged her phone, did not understand how she could both hate and want.

'Can we talk?' Raul said.

'And say what?' Lydia asked, and there was strain to her voice.

'I don't want you to leave yet.'

A few moments ago she would have knelt at his feet for those words, now she turned angrily.

'Oh, sorry—were you hoping for a morning shag because you bought me a statue?'

Oh, it wasn't her wings growing back—it was nails. Thick steel nails that shot out like armour.

'Raul, thank you so much for your hospitality. I had a wonderful time.'

'That's it?'

And she did know how to hurt him!

'I think we both know I was never going to be leaving Italy a virgin. It was you or Bastiano. I chose you.'

He stood there silent, Raul did not ask why, yet Lydia answered as if he had.

'Bastiano isn't what I want.'

'And what is?'

'Money.'

'He has that.'

She screwed up her nose. 'I want old money.'

'I see.'

'If I'm to marry for money I'd at least like a title.'

'You're a snob.'

'I have every right to be.'

'And a gold-digger,' Raul said.

'Yes!' Lydia smiled a black smile. 'I'm a snob *and* a gold-digger, and some Sicilian who just made good doesn't really do it for me.'

'You make no sense, given the way you screamed last night.'

'We're talking about Bastiano,' Lydia said. 'As you pointed out—he wanted marriage and a nice trophy wife. I, on the other hand, wanted sex.' She ran a finger along his jaw and taunted him and it felt so good. 'For a one-night stand, you were the far better option. What I *really* want is a gentleman.'

'Well.' He gave a black smile and removed her hand from his face. 'I don't qualify, then.'

'No.'

He dropped all contact, and as she turned and walked away suddenly Lydia wasn't so brave.

As she bent to retrieve her red dress and picked it up from the floor, it felt as if she was waving a flag to a very angry bull, though Raul did not move.

His hackles were up. Raul could fight dirty when he chose—and he was starting to choose to now.

He looked at her slender legs and her hair falling forward and knew she could feel his eyes on her body as she pretended to concentrate on folding the dress as she bent over the open case.

She was pink in the cheeks and her ears were red, and as his eyes took in the curve of her bottom he knew she was as turned on as he was.

Tension crackled between them and she could almost picture his hands pulling up her robe.

It was bizarre.

He made filthy thoughts mandatory, gave anger a new outlet, and she recalled his promise that angry sex could wait.

'You know,' he said, 'once you leave, you're gone. I don't play games, and I don't pursue…'

'I'm not asking you to.'

He walked over—she heard him but did not turn around. She must have folded that dress twenty times when his hand came to her hip. Just a small gesture, almost indicating that she should turn to him, but Lydia resisted.

'Hey, Lydia,' he said, and he bent over her and spoke in that low, calm voice, while hard against her bottom. 'When you find your suitably titled Englishman, don't think of me.'

'I shan't.'

'It would not be fair to him.'

'You really—' She stopped, and she dared not turn around, for now one hand moved to her waist and the other to her shoulder, and there was a desire in Lydia for the sound of his zip, but it never came.

'When you're in bed,' Raul said, and she held on to the bed with cheeks flaming, 'and he says, "Is that nice, darling?" or "Do you like it like that?"' He put on an affected tone. 'Try not to remember that I never needed to enquire.

And,' he added cruelly, 'when you lie there beside him, unsated, and you *do* think of me...'

'I told you—I shan't.'

'Liar.'

He pressed into her one more time and then pulled back and let her go and she straightened up.

She was a bit breathless.

Oh, and still angry.

She pulled off her robe and he did not avert his eyes. He watched as she pulled on knickers, and watched as she put on her bra.

And he watched as she pulled on the taupe dress—the one with the buttons.

Bloody things!

As she struggled to dress he walked over—but not to her. This time he picked up the statue and tossed it into her case.

'I don't want your stupid statue.'

'I thought you were a gold-digger,' he pointed out. 'Sell it.' Raul shrugged. 'Or hurl it out of the window of your turret in frustration when your fingers can't deliver.'

'Oh, *please*,' Lydia sneered. 'You think you're *so* good.'

'No,' Raul said. 'I *know* that we were.'

He did.

For he had never experienced it before—that absolute connection and the erotic bliss they had found last night.

She snapped her case closed and, rather annoyingly, set the security code on the lock.

As she bumped it from the bed he kicked off his boots and got on. Raul lay on the rumpled sheets and reached for his cake box and took out his phone.

She could see herself out, Raul decided.

The private jet was closed.

Lydia stood there for a moment. It was hard making a dignified exit when you didn't know the way out.

'Is there a street entrance?' Lydia asked, and watched as he barely glanced up from his phone.

'Yep.'

Raul opened the box of pastries and selected one, took a bite as he got back to his phone.

Lydia could find it herself.

'You can see yourself out.'

CHAPTER TWELVE

ALL ROADS LED to Rome.

But today Raul hoped that Rome would lead him to Lydia.

Raul could not get her out of his mind.

Disquiet gnawed and unfinished business reared up and he simply could not let it go.

Summer was gone.

As he walked past the café where they had shared breakfast Raul looked up to the dark clouds above and it looked as if the sky had been hung too low.

It had felt like that since Lydia had gone.

Autumn had arrived, and usually it was Raul's favourite time of the year.

Not this one.

He missed her, and Raul had never missed anyone, and he just could not shake off the feeling.

It was something he could not define.

Even if the tourists never really thinned out in Venice, La Serenissima had felt empty rather than serene. Here in Rome the locals were enjoying the slight lull that came with the change. Back in Sicily the vines that threaded the valley would be turning to russet...

Raul never went back.

Not even in his head.

Yet he was starting to now.

Lydia had been right—perhaps he should go back.

If this visit to the Grande Lucia did not work out as he hoped, then Raul would be making his first trip back to Casta since the will had been read.

The doorman nodded as Raul went through the brass

revolving door, and he stood for a moment remembering their brief time there.

But that was not right. It didn't *feel* brief—if anything it was the most examined part of his life.

Lydia was the most contrary person he knew.

Cold and guarded...warm and intense.

And, although they had both agreed to a one-night stand, he still could not make sense of that morning.

That kiss before he had left to get breakfast had held promise, but Raul had returned to a stranger and he *had* to know why.

But he didn't even know her surname.

Raul knew some of the darkest most intimate parts of Lydia, and yet her full name he did not know.

Nor where she lived.

Usually those details did not matter to him.

Oh, but they did now.

He had searched, and so had Allegra.

There were a surprising number of castles in England, and there were many that were used for weddings.

They had got nowhere.

Allegra was working her way through them all and had flown over to England three times.

And now Raul was in Rome.

Back at the Grande Lucia, where it had all started.

Now that Raul was showing no interest in purchasing the hotel he was having trouble getting through to Sultan Alim.

And so he was here in person.

But trouble remained in the shape of the young receptionist.

'Sultan Alim is only available by appointment.'

'Call and tell him that Raul Di Savo is here.'

'As I said, he only sees people by appointment. We don't disturb him with phone calls.'

She was as snooty and as immutable as he demanded that Allegra should be if someone—anyone—tried to invade Raul's time.

'Is he even in the country?' Raul asked, but that information was off-limits.

'He would prefer that we do not discuss his movements. I shall let him know you were here.'

Now what?

Did he sit in the foyer and wait for a royal sultan who might already be back in the Middle East? Or warn the poor receptionist that if she valued her job she should let Alim know…

And then Raul saw someone who might be able to help.

She was walking through the foyer carrying a huge display of roses.

Gabi.

The indiscreet wedding planner!

'Hey,' Raul said.

'Hi.'

He had forgotten how to flirt—even for gain.

'Gabi?'

'Oh!' She stopped. 'You were in the ballroom when Alim…' Her voice trailed off.

There had been something going on that afternoon. Raul knew it. He hadn't given it much thought until now.

'I'm hoping to meet with him.'

'Good luck!' Gabi rolled her eyes. 'He's back home.'

'Oh!'

'For his wedding.'

'I see.'

'I'm planning it, actually.'

She looked as if she were about to cry.

'Can you let him know I need to speak with him?'

'I'm a wedding planner,' Gabi said. 'I don't get access to the Royal Sultan.'

And neither would he, Raul thought as Gabi flounced off.

So that left Bastiano—and Raul already knew where *he* was.

Casta.

His jet landed at Cosimo airport, and though it was warmer the sky still seemed to be hung too low. Raul put on his shades and transferred to the helicopter he had arranged to take him to the old convent.

To afford the nuns seclusion it had been made accessible only by horse or helicopter.

Of course Raul chose the latter.

The convent was an ancient sprawling building that no one could get to, set on the crest of the valley overlooking the wild Sicilian Strait.

Its inaccessibility made it the perfect retreat, and Raul had to hand it to Bastiano for his foresight.

Not that he would admit that.

Raul boarded the helicopter and saw his orders had been followed. There was a bunch of lilies there, which, after meeting with Bastiano, he would take to Maria's grave.

He would arrive unannounced.

Raul had sworn never to return.

Only for Lydia he did.

It would be kinder, perhaps, not to look out of the helicopter window and at first he chose not to. The last time he had been home it had been on a commercial flight and then a frantic taxi ride to the valley.

Raul had been eighteen then, and he recalled the taxi driver asking him to pay the fare in advance before agreeing to take him.

Different times.

Same place.

He looked, and the view was starting to become familiar. Even if he had never seen it from this vantage point, the lie of this land was etched on the dark side of his soul.

There were the fields that the Contis and Di Savos had fought over for generations, and yet the wine had never made either family their fortune—and Raul's palate now knew it never would.

His stomach turned in on itself, and it had nothing to do with the sudden banking of the chopper, more the view of the schoolyard, and beyond it to what had been his family home.

He could hear his childish lies to his father.

'Mamma has been here all day.'

Or...

'I think she went to breakfast with Loretta.'

And now perhaps he understood why Lydia did not take photos, for there were memories you did not want to see.

Raul hadn't lied just to save himself.

He had lied to cover for his mother.

Over and over and over.

And then he recalled her more cheerful dispositions. When she would sing and start to go out more, and Raul's lies to his father would have to begin again.

There was the church, and to the side the tombstones.

Raul's history stretched beneath him and there was nothing he wanted to see.

But he made himself look.

The ocean was wild and choppy, crashing onto jagged rocks, and then he saw it.

Far from falling into disrepair the old convent now stood proud, and he remembered his mother's tears when it had closed down.

Had it really been her dream?

The chopper landed and Raul climbed out.

He thought Security might halt him, but he walked

across the lush lawn and towards the gateway without confrontation.

There was a sign for Reception and Raul headed towards it. He walked past a fountain and then ignored the bell and pushed open a heavy arched door.

There were downlights—a modern touch that softened the stone walls—and at a desk sat a young woman wearing what looked like a dental nurse's uniform.

'*Posso aiutarla?*'

With a smile she asked Raul if she could help him.

'*Sì.*' Raul nodded. 'I am here to speak with Bastiano.'

No frown marred her Botoxed brow, but Raul could see the worry in her eyes as she checked the computer, even though her smile stayed in place.

'May I have your name?'

'Raul Di Savo...'

She must be just about due to have her anti-wrinkle injections topped up, for now a line formed between her brow and the smile faded.

Oh, that name—even now—was known in the valley.

'Do you have an appointment?'

'No,' Raul responded. 'He isn't expecting me...'

'On the contrary.'

Bastiano's voice arrived before he did, and Raul looked up as he emerged from the shadows of the archway. A glint of sun captured the scar on his cheek, and Raul thought he looked like the devil himself appearing.

'Bastiano.' Raul didn't even attempt to keep the ice from his voice. 'I would like to speak with you.'

'I rather thought that you might,' Bastiano said, his response equally cool. His indubitable charm would never be wasted on Raul. 'Come this way.'

Raul followed him through the arch and they walked along a cloister that looked down on a quadrangle where a small group were sitting in the afternoon sun, talking. They glanced up at the two dark-suited men, for there was a foreboding energy about them that drew attention.

Even the receptionist had followed, and stood watching as they disappeared into the old refectory.

The darkness was welcome, and the windows were like photo frames, setting off a view of the Sicilian Strait that roared in the distance.

'Take a seat,' Bastiano offered.

It would be churlish to stand, Raul knew, when he was here for a favour, so as Bastiano moved behind his desk Raul sat at the other side.

'There is something I need from you,' Raul said. 'I would have preferred not to just land on you, but you refused to take my calls.'

Bastiano didn't say anything, but Raul saw the smile of triumph that he attempted to contain. Of course he would not take Raul's calls—he would far prefer to witness him beg.

'I didn't return your calls because I don't think I can help you, Raul,' Bastiano answered, and his manicured hand gestured to some papers on the desk before him. 'Alim said you have been trying to reach him. I know how badly you wanted the hotel, but a deal has been reached—the contracts are awaiting my signature.'

Bastiano thought he was here about the Grande Lucia, Raul realised.

But then why *wouldn't* he think that?

A few weeks ago that had been all that had mattered to Raul—acquisitions, pipping Bastiano to the post and amassing the biggest fortune.

'I'm not here about the hotel,' Raul said, and he watched as Bastiano's contained features briefly showed his confusion.

But he righted himself quickly.

'So what is it that you want?'

'You were considering investing in a property in the UK.' Raul attempted to be vague, but it did not work.

'I have many investments there.'

'It was a castle.'

Raul knew the exact second that Bastiano understood the reason for his visit, for now he made no effort to contain his black smile as he spoke. 'I don't recall.'

'Of course you do.' Raul refused to play games. 'If you could give me the details I would be grateful.'

'I don't require your gratitude, though.'

He had been mad to come, Raul realised.

But then mad was how he *had* been of late.

And now he sat in front of his nemesis, asking him for help.

Worse, though, there were other questions he wanted to ask him. Bastiano held some of the keys to his past.

A past Raul did not want to examine.

Yes, this was madness, Raul decided.

No more.

He stood to leave and did not even bother making the right noises, for there was nothing even to pretend to thank Bastiano for.

But as he reached the door Bastiano's voice halted him.

'There is something I want.'

Raul did not turn around and Bastiano continued.

'If you return the ring I'll give you the information.'

Still Raul did not turn around, though he halted. He actually fought not to lean on the door, for he felt as if the air had been sucked out of the room. He was back in the courtroom, staring at that emerald and seed pearl ring and wondering from where it had come.

Gino had given his mother nothing other than a thin gold band that might just as well have been a ball and chain, for in Maria's eyes it had held her to him for life…

Not quite.

She had been unfaithful, after all.

Then Bastiano spoke. 'I gave it to your mother the week before she died. It belongs in my family...'

'Why did you give her the ring?' Raul turned.

'She said that she wanted to leave Casta and be with me. The ring secured our plans.'

'You expect me to believe that you two were in *love*?' Raul sneered.

'I thought so for a while.' Bastiano shrugged. 'It was really just sex.'

Raul was across the room in an instant, and he reached out to upend the table just to get to Bastiano, but somehow the bastard had him halting, for he held out a pen as if it were a knife.

'I want my ring,' Bastiano said.

And the pen in his hand was the only thing preventing Raul from slamming him against the stone wall and exacting his final revenge.

'You'll get it.'

Bastiano wrote down the details, but, as he did, he said something that a few years ago would have had Raul reaching again for his throat.

Now it made Raul feel sick.

'Don't make her a saint, Raul,' Bastiano said. 'She was far from that.'

Raul felt as if his head was exploding as he walked out.

The helicopter's rotors started at the pilot's sight of him and Raul ran across the ground.

It took minutes.

Barely minutes,

And he was standing at his mother's grave.

It should feel peaceful—there was just the sound of birds and the buzzing of his phone—but the roar in his ears remained.

It had never left.

Or rather it had dimmed in the brief time he and Lydia had shared.

Now he turned off his phone, and it felt as if even the birds were silent as he faced the truth.

Bastiano had not been the first affair.

He had been the last.

And there had been many.

Raul had been taught to lie—not just to save himself but to cover for his mother.

He looked back to the convent and remembered her tears when it had closed and her misery. Then he recalled her being more cheerful, when her mood would lift for a while. And while it would make most children happy to see their mother smile, Raul had known that if he were to keep her safe, then the lies had to start again.

Maria Di Savo.

Unhinged, some had called her.

'Fragile' was perhaps a more appropriate word.

At least it was the one Raul chose.

But with more open eyes than the last time he had stood here.

'Rest now,' he said to the stone, and he went to lay the lilies.

But then he divided them into two.

And he turned to the grave of Gino Di Savo.

There was someone he had never considered forgiving— it had been so far from his mind as to be deemed irrelevant.

It was more than relevant now.

Was Gino even his father?

Sixteen and pregnant in the valley would have been a shameful place to be.

Had the younger Gino been kinder?

Had he lived with the knowledge of constant infidelity?

Perhaps Raul would never know.

He understood the beatings more, though.

And maybe there were some respects to be paid.

'Rest now,' Raul said again, and he put the remaining lilies on Gino Di Savo's grave.

CHAPTER THIRTEEN

'IT'S A VERY recent piece.'

The valuation manager had called in the director. And Lydia was starting to get a glimpse of just how valuable the statue was.

'Three months,' Lydia said, but they didn't look over at her.

For the first morning in a very long time Lydia had held down some toast and decided it was time to be practical and deal with things.

Lydia had returned to the castle expecting anger and re-crimination, and had been ready to get the hell out.

Instead she'd returned to her mother's devastation.

It wasn't only Lydia who hadn't cried on her father's death.

Valerie too had held it in, and finally the dam had broken.

'I'm sorry!' She had just slumped in a chair and cried. 'I've told him he's never to come back.'

Of all the hurts in Lydia's heart, Maurice didn't rank, and so instead of fighting back or getting out Lydia had done what Raul had done. She'd poured her mother a drink and stayed calm.

She'd been her practical self, in fact, and had put her own hurts aside.

Lydia pulled the castle as a wedding venue and then dealt as best as she could with what was.

There was no money and very little left to sell.

Last week she had suggested that Valerie go and spend some time with her sister.

Lydia needed to be alone.

She was pregnant.

But she did have her mother's practical nature and had decided to find out what the statue was worth.

Not to save the castle.

Raul was right—it would require a constant infusion.

The proceeds of the sale of the statue might at least go towards a deposit on a house.

But then the valuation manager had called for the director and numbers had started to be discussed between the men.

Lydia realised she had far more than a deposit.

In fact she could buy a home.

It was worth that much and very possibly more.

She could provide for her baby and Raul didn't even need to know.

'Are you thinking of the New York auction?' the manager was asking his senior.

'That's a few months off.'

He glanced over to Lydia and offered her an option.

'I have several collectors who would be extremely interested—we could run a private auction. This piece is exquisite.'

And she loved it so.

It was just a piece of glass, Lydia told herself.

There was a reason she didn't take photos—going over old memories hurt too much.

She would be better rid of it, Lydia knew, and yet it was the only thing she had ever loved.

Apart from Raul.

He wasn't a thing—he was a person.

An utter bastard, in fact.

But the statue spoke of a different time, before it had all fallen apart, and Lydia could not stand the thought of letting it go.

Over and over she dissected each moment with him.

At every minute her mind was back there, peeping through the keyhole he had once shown her and seeing them.

Every moment was captured, and yet she had no photos, bar the one of them holding hands that was smeared all over the internet.

Apparently the great Raul did not usually stoop to holding hands, so the press had been interested.

She'd been telling him about her father then.

Confiding in him.

And he had been playing her all along.

All she had of him was this statue.

No, Lydia corrected, in six months' time she would have his baby.

And Raul needed to know.

The director finally addressed her. 'With your permission I'm going to make a few phone calls, and then perhaps we'll be able to see more where we're at.'

'Of course,' Lydia agreed.

And so must she make some calls.

Lydia was shown to a comfortable waiting room that was more like a lounge and offered tea.

'No, thank you,' Lydia said as she took a seat. 'Could you please close the door?'

The door was closed and from her purse Lydia took out the business card he had given her.

It had been three months since Lydia had heard his voice.

The business card had had many outings, but always she'd bailed before completing his number.

Today Lydia held her breath as she was finally put through.

He didn't answer.

It was just a recording—telling her to leave a message. *'Lasciate un messagio...'*

An anti-climax, really, and yet the sound of his voice had her folded over in the chair.

Not because of what she had to say to him, but because of what she wanted to.

That even while she was so terribly angry with him, it was the hurt of not seeing him, not hearing him, not touching him that refused to heal.

She didn't know what to do.

How did you tell a man who would have a baby removed from a restaurant for crying that you were pregnant with his child?

Raul would think she was calling for money.

How could he not, given she had looked him in the eye and *told* him she was a gold-digger?

And a snob.

Oh, she had to play the part now. But she couldn't and so rang off.

Straighten up, she told herself, and reminded herself of the terrible things he had done.

Raul had used her so badly.

He had sunk to such depraved lows and she must always remember that.

Always.

Panic was starting to build, but Lydia took a deep breath and told herself to be practical and deal with things.

So she straightened up in the chair and repeated the call.

'Lasciate un messagio...'

'Raul, this is Lydia.'

She refused to cheapen herself by giving him dates and further details. If Raul was such a playboy that he didn't remember her, then she wasn't going to make things easier for him.

'I'm pregnant.'

She had said it too fast and too soon, Lydia knew that, but better that than to break down.

'I've had a few weeks to get used to the idea, and I'm actually...' She let out her first calm breath—maybe because she'd told him now...maybe because she was speaking the truth. 'I'm fine with it. We'll be fine. The baby and I, I mean.'

And she knew that had sounded too brusque.

'What I'm trying to say is that I'm not calling for support, neither on an emotional nor financial front. We both know you don't do the former, and I've had the statue valued and it covers the latter...'

Not quite.

Yes, no doubt she could squeeze him for half of his billions, but it was not the route she wanted to take. The thought of lawyers and acrimony, of whether or not he believed her, were the last things she wanted.

'If you need to discuss things, then give me a call back.'

Lydia ended the call and sat staring at her phone for a very long time.

His reaction she could not fathom, and, for the first time since arriving back in England, Lydia felt grateful for the distance between them.

He knew now.

CHAPTER FOURTEEN

SHE WAS IN a holding pattern now of her own making.

Awaiting his response.

Once home, Lydia had replaced the statue by her bed.

She had decided that it was not for sale.

Some things *were* more important.

For now.

She did not want to be like her mother, holding on to a castle she could not afford to keep, but she was not going to rush into selling it.

Lydia checked her phone for the hundredth time, but of course it hadn't rung.

So she checked her email to see if anyone had responded to her many job applications.

She'd had one interview at a museum, but there were four other applicants—no doubt all with qualifications.

And she had an interview next week to work at one of their rival wedding venues.

Joy.

Not.

The pregnancy would start to show soon.

Who would want to take her on then?

Lydia opened a window and leant out and looked over the land her mother's family had owned for ever.

The hills to the left and the fields to the right had been sold off some time ago, but if she looked ahead it was still theirs—for now.

And she understood her mother a little better, for she knew it hurt so much to let go.

Lydia heard the low buzz of a helicopter and looked to the sky.

It was a familiar sound in these parts—the well-heeled left for London in the morning and returned in the evening, but usually later than now.

Occasionally there was an air ambulance or a tourist.

Except this helicopter hovered over the castle and the buzzing sound grew louder.

She could see the grass in the meadow moving in the swirl the rotors created.

It was Raul who was descending, Lydia knew.

Not for *her*.

He'd had weeks and months to find *her*.

No, she had dropped the baby bombshell and he had responded immediately.

He was here about their child.

Her breath quickened as he climbed out. He was wearing a dark suit and tie and shades. He looked completely together as he strode across the land with purpose and she watched him.

There was no instinct to hide.

If anything her instinct was to descend the stairs and run towards him, but that would show just how much she had missed him.

Raul didn't need to know that.

And neither would she tell him that she knew about his long-running feud with Bastiano.

Yes, Lydia was far from innocent now.

Knowledge was power, and she would use it wisely.

And she would never reveal how deeply she had loved.

So she did not check her reflection, nor bother to don lip gloss. Instead she descended the circular stairs of the turret and walked through to the main entrance.

Neither did she go through the palaver of making him knock.

The door was heavy, but she opened it with practised

ease. The days of having staff to attend to such things were long since gone.

'Raul…' She hesitated, because unlike her earlier summation she saw he *wasn't* quite so together. There was a grey pallor to his face and his jaw was tense. His eyes remained hidden behind dark shades. 'I wasn't expecting you.'

'Then you don't know me.'

Those words sent a shiver of warning down her spine.

No, she didn't know him—but those words told her the news she had so recently broken to him was being taken very seriously indeed.

'Were you already in England?'

'No.'

Raul had been walking away from the cemetery when he had heard her message.

'Oh…' The speed of his arrival was rapid, but then she had only been privy to his casual use of his private jet but once.

'I'm sorry for the shock.'

'Nobody has died, Lydia.'

Raul was right. It was a pregnancy they were dealing with, after all, not a sudden death, and yet it was surely a shock to a man like him—a confirmed bachelor, a reprobate playboy.

Or maybe not, Lydia mused.

Perhaps he had illegitimate children dotted all over the world, for certainly he seemed to be taking rapid control.

'We need to talk.'

'Of course we do,' Lydia said. 'That's why I called. Come through and I'll make some tea.'

She would take him to the receiving room, Lydia decided. It was a little faded and empty, but it was certainly the smartest room. There she would ask him to take a seat, and then go and make some tea, and then they could calmly discuss…

Fool.

'I don't drink tea, Lydia.'

As she went to walk away his hand closed around the top of her arm, and Lydia actually kicked herself for thinking she could so easily dictate this.

'Coffee, then?'

She received a black smile in response.

'The helicopter is waiting to take us to my jet—we shall discuss this in Venice.'

'Venice?' She shook her head, her attempt to deal with him calmly, disintegrating. 'Absolutely not. We can talk here. My mother is at her sister's and Maurice is gone.'

His features did not soften.

'We can go out for tea if you prefer. If that makes you feel…'

She did not get to finish.

'You think we are going to sit in some quaint café and discuss the future of our child?'

'We could!'

'And what time does this café close?' He watched her jaw clench and then continued. 'We have a lot to sort out, dear Lydia.' The term was without endearment. 'Did you really think you could drop a message like that on my phone and expect us to go out for *afternoon tea*?'

'I thought we could calmly discuss—'

'I am calm.'

He didn't sound it to Lydia.

Oh, his words were calm, but there was an undercurrent, an energy that danced in the grand entrance hall and not even these ancient walls could contain it.

'We shall speak at my home.'

'No!'

'Okay, we'll talk at my office.'

'In Venice?'

'Of course.'

'No.'

'Lydia, what time to you have to be at work tomorrow?' Raul asked, guessing she probably hadn't bothered to get a job.

'That wasn't kind.'

'I'm not here to be kind.'

She glimpsed again his power and knew this man did not fight fair.

He proved it now.

'I thought you said you were leaving home and getting a job…' He gave a black laugh as he looked around. 'But you're still here, and of course you don't need to work now.'

'Raul…' She wanted to take back that gold-digger comment, but it was way, way too late. 'Please listen—it was an accident.'

'Of course it was!'

She could almost taste his sarcasm.

'Lydia, unlike you, I *do* have to work—however, I have set aside an hour tomorrow at eleven for us to start to go through things. If you don't want to fly with me, fine, but can you get yourself there, at least?'

'I'm not going to be there, Raul.'

'Then we do this through lawyers. Text me the name of yours.'

He was done.

Raul was not going to stand there and plead.

His head was throbbing.

The events of today—Bastiano, the revelations about his mother, his father, if Gino had even been his father, and now the fact that he himself was going to be a father…

Hell, Raul wanted a drink.

He did not want to be standing in some draughty old castle, rowing with a woman he wanted—even after the way she had left—to have all over again.

Lydia turned him on.

And, titled or not, he turned *her* on too.

Raul could feel it.

This day might end not in bed but on the floor, two minutes from now.

But sex had got them into this hot mess and it was time for him to get out.

'Lawyer up!' he said, and turned and left.

He was leaving, Lydia knew.

Leaving their baby in the hands of lawyers.

She ran out and grabbed his arm.

'I'll talk to you.'

He looked down at her hand and shook it off, because even minimal contact he could not keep to for long.

'Then go and pack,' Raul told her. 'If you're not ready in five minutes we leave it to the professionals to sort out.'

She packed—though five minutes didn't give her much time. Especially when she wasted two of them by sitting on her bed and wondering what she should do.

She could not bear to go back to Venice.

Yet Lydia knew she had to.

Somehow she had to get past the raw hurt and sort out the future of their child.

He had hurt her so deeply, though.

And he didn't even know.

Just like the jagged wound that ran down Raul's back, just like the savage scar on Bastiano's cheek, her pain ran deep.

She had been used for revenge.

It was a wound that could never properly heal.

And yet Lydia knew she had to be adult and somehow work out terms with this difficult and complex man.

There was the baby to focus on, and she would not be weakened by his undeniably seductive charms. The sexual energy between them had unnerved her—Lydia was still aware of her palm where she had grabbed his arm.

But she dusted her hands together and brushed it off.

No way!

Worried that her mother might return and sell the statue, Lydia wrapped it in a thick jumper and packed it. Trying as she did so to not remember the night when it had been the two of *them* melded and heated. She swore she would not allow herself to lose her head to him again.

No, she would not weaken.

Lydia walked down the steps and he didn't rush to relieve her of her case. Instead he stood impatient at the door.

'Hold on,' she said, and bent down. 'I forgot to lock it.'

'For God's sake!' he said, and went over and took it. 'Come on.'

'Raul…' Lydia stalled. She wanted to make things very clear. 'I'm going to Venice only to discuss the baby.'

'What else would I be bringing you there for?' he asked. 'Lydia, you've had what you wanted from me in the bedroom department.'

'I just want to make it perfectly clear. I don't want—'

'Lydia, let me stop you there,' Raul interrupted her. 'This isn't about your wants—we're going to be discussing our child.'

'Well, let's keep things civil.'

'Civil?' Raul checked. 'I thought you didn't consider me capable.'

'I meant businesslike.'

'That,' Raul responded as they walked to the waiting helicopter, 'I can clearly be.'

'Good.'

He might just as well have painted her gold and handed her a spade as he stalked ahead with her case.

And the last word was his.

'But then, you knew that right from the start.'

CHAPTER FIFTEEN

THERE WAS NO worse place to be lonely than Venice.

And for Lydia that theory was proved again.

Loretta, his housekeeper, walked her along the lovely mirrored hallway, but instead of going straight ahead, Lydia was shown to the right.

She walked along another hallway and through to an apartment within his home. Loretta brought her dinner, and it was served at a polished table on beautiful china, but though her surroundings were gorgeous Lydia ate alone.

Raul, of course, ate out.

Naturally she didn't sleep, and in the morning she spent ages trying to work out what to wear.

It wasn't just that she had no idea what she should wear to a meeting to discuss their child's future. Nothing was a comfortable fit.

Lydia had no choice but to settle for the taupe dress— the one with the buttons. Only now it strained across her breasts.

Instead of undoing a couple of buttons she put on a little cardigan.

It would have to do.

She loathed it that she had been pencilled in as some sixty-minute item on his to-do list.

And she certainly hadn't expected an audience to be in attendance!

But as she walked into the drawing room Raul sat relaxed and chatting with a very beautiful woman.

'This is Allegra,' Raul told her. 'My assistant.'

Lydia, with her hackles already up and perhaps a little

too used to her mother's handling of staff, gave Allegra a cursory nod and then ignored her.

Raul could see that Lydia was uncomfortable and he didn't blame her for that.

He had resisted discussing this at her home and was aware that he had the advantage, so he moved to the first point on his list.

'Would you be more comfortable in a hotel?'

'I don't intend to be staying very long,' Lydia replied coolly. 'The apartment is sufficient.'

Sufficient?

She had a six-room apartment within his home.

But Raul said nothing—just moved to the next point.

'There is a property less than a mile from here that has come onto the market. Allegra has arranged a viewing for you at two today.'

'Why would I need to see a property here?' Lydia asked. 'The baby will be raised in England.'

'But I shall be seeing my baby regularly. I assume you will want to be close when I do? Especially at first.'

'You assume correctly. However…'

But Raul had moved on.

'Allegra is going to look into the hiring of a nanny. It would appear good ones need to be secured early.'

That was an easy one, and Lydia dismissed it with a shake of her head. 'I shan't be hiring a nanny.'

It really annoyed her when Allegra wrote something down, and then she asked Lydia a question in a rich Italian purr.

'Will you want to sit in on the preliminary interviews, or would you prefer I do that and then we discuss the shortlist?'

'I just *said*…' Lydia was responding to Allegra as if she was speaking to a three-year-old with a hearing problem '…that I don't require a nanny.'

'We heard you the first time,' Raul said. 'But *I* need a nanny for the times when the baby is to be with me.'

Lydia, who had been glaring at Allegra, snapped her gaze back to Raul. 'Could we speak alone, please?'

'Of course.'

Allegra stood and walked out. Lydia sat with her back ramrod-straight and said nothing until the door behind her had closed.

Oh, but when it closed!

'You've been busy.'

'Yes,' Raul agreed.

And as she sat there she gleaned the fact that while she'd been eating alone last night Raul had been out to dinner, with Allegra, discussing her baby's future.

Of course he had.

Raul's time was heavily in demand, and a lot of his day-to-day stuff was delegated.

'Do you really think I have time to be wandering around looking at apartments for someone I spent a weekend with three months ago?'

Lydia opened her mouth to respond, but then closed it.

'You wanted businesslike, and you have made it clear you don't want to be in Venice for long, so I discussed things with my assistant…'

'Over *dinner*,' Lydia sneered. 'Have you slept with her?'

Oh, she hated it that she'd asked that—she really did.

'What the hell does that have to do with anything?'

And she hated his exasperated inevitable answer.

'Yes, but that was ages ago.'

And then he asked Lydia again.

'What the hell does that have to do with this?'

And she still couldn't answer, because really it should have *nothing* to do with this—yet it did.

'Lydia, I have a past—quite a colourful one. You really should choose your one-night stands more carefully.'

'I just don't like the fact…'

'Go on,' Raul said when she faltered, and he leant back in his chair to hear what she had to say.

'I don't like the fact that someone you've been intimate with is discussing my future and my baby.'

'*Our* baby.'

'Yes, but…' She tried to get back to the nanny point, because she was starting to sound jealous.

Which she was.

And irrational.

Which she wasn't.

Was she?

'Lydia, Allegra is very happily married.' He was annoyingly patient in his explanation. 'In fact I've already told you that. If you really think she's making bedroom eyes at me and we're still at it, then that's your issue. But we're not. I don't like cheats. Now, can we bring it back to business?'

'*It* is a baby.'

'*Che cazzo!*' he cursed.

'Don't swear.'

'The baby can't hear me!' Raul said.

'You discuss it so clinically.'

'You told me yourself to keep it businesslike. Come on, Lydia, tell me what you want. You've had three months to get used to the idea. I've had less than twenty-four hours. Tell me what you've decided and we can work from there.'

And she tried to tell him just that.

'There's no need for me to have an apartment here. Of course we'll visit often…'

A smile—a black smile—played on his lips, and she sat back as Raul chose his words.

'And where would you stay?' Raul asked. 'The guest wing?'

As she nodded that dark smile faded.

'Lydia, I don't want my ex, or rather one of my one-night

stands, as a regular guest in my home. I don't want someone who has already said that she disapproves of me dictating the relationship I have with my child.'

'And I don't want my baby to be raised by a nanny.'

'Tough.' Raul shrugged. 'Do you *really* see me getting up at night to feed it and...' He pulled a face.

And, no, she could *not* see it.

'Raul, I haven't made any plans...'

'Oh, I would say you set your plans in motion a long time ago,' Raul said. 'And I would suggest that when you "forgot" to take your Pill you thought you'd chosen carefully indeed.'

She frowned.

He enlightened her.

'I said I don't like children, and you decided I'd make a very good absentee father...'

'No!' she shouted.

'Correct,' Raul said. 'Because I shan't just be a cheque-book father—I'm going to be very hands-on.'

He dismissed her then—she knew it from the wave of his hand.

'We're getting nowhere. We can try again tomorrow if you would like?'

'You're going to schedule me in again?' Lydia asked in a sarcastic tone.

Raul ignored it but answered her question. 'If you want me to.'

And that was how they would be, Lydia was starting to realise.

Parents, but apart.

So, so far apart that she could not see across the void.

'Do you want to see the apartment?' Raul checked before he closed this disaster of a meeting. 'We should try to get as much as possible done while you're still here.'

'Fine.'

Raul heard the resignation in her voice and loathed it.

They had ended up fighting, and he knew he tended to win fights.

'I think perhaps we should do this through lawyers,' Raul admitted.

He didn't want to fight Lydia. He just wanted the details sorted. He would leave it to them and then sign.

'Raul, I can't afford a lawyer.'

It was a very difficult admission for someone like Lydia to make.

But he just sat there and leant back in his chair, and wondered just who she took him for.

'We both know that's not true.'

'Seriously, Raul. I know I live in a castle...'

'Lydia,' he told her as he sat there, and let her know himself how to nail him to the wall. 'Call a lawyer—the best you can find—and tell him my surname.'

'I can't afford to.'

'Try it,' he said. 'Tell them whose baby you're having and I guarantee they won't give a damn as to the current state of your finances. They'll probably offer to hold your hand in the delivery room.'

She stood.

'For their cut, of course,' Raul added.

He watched as she walked out, and usually he would be feeling delighted that a meeting had concluded early and he could get on to the next thing.

Yet she *was* the next thing.

When there was so much he should be getting on with Raul sat there thinking. Not even about the baby, but about her.

All roads did *not* lead to Rome.

But to Lydia.

Instead of thinking about the baby, which surely she should be, all Lydia could think about was Raul.

He was trying to get this sorted for both of them as best he could, Lydia thought as the realtor let both herself and Allegra into the apartment.

It was stunning, with crimson walls and drapes and a view of the canal.

In fact from one of the bedrooms she could see the balcony of his home.

'I missed that when I came this morning,' Allegra said when she looked to where Lydia's gaze fell, and again she wrote something down.

'Sorry?' Lydia checked.

'I'm sure you don't need a view of Daddy's home from yours! You'll want your own life…'

Allegra was trying too, Lydia realised.

Lydia was so used to everyone being the enemy.

No one really was here.

They were trying to do this without lawyers, and she was fighting them at every point, and Lydia knew why.

It wasn't the Venice apartment she wanted, nor the monthly payment dump in her account, or flights on his jet for time with Daddy.

It was Raul.

And for a tiny moment she had considered that desire attainable.

That was why she still held on to the statue—because when she'd opened up that box and looked down from the balcony for a second she'd thought it was possible that someone might actually *love* her.

Allegra was talking with the realtor, and then she excused herself to take a call on her phone.

From her affectionate tone, it was her husband, and from what Lydia could glean they were discussing what they would have tonight for dinner.

She almost smiled as she recalled for the millionth time one of her and Raul's conversations.

Only she couldn't smile.

Because if they were a couple she'd be texting him now, or telling him tonight, and they'd be laughing at their own private joke.

But they weren't a couple.

And in that same conversation he'd told her he never wanted marriage.

She looked out to the canal. She was back where she had longed to be, but she ached at the coolness between them.

Lydia didn't just want the parenting side of things to be sorted.

There was a reason she was resisting everything he suggested and she faced the lonely truth—

Lydia wanted Raul, herself and the baby to be a family.

CHAPTER SIXTEEN

'HERE.'

Loretta set down Lydia's dinner. Homemade fettuccini and a creamy sauce that smelt delicious. Finally Lydia's appetite was back.

'It looks lovely.'

'It is nice to have someone to cook for.' Loretta accepted the compliment. 'This is a recipe from Casta. I haven't made it for years.'

'You're from Casta?'

'I worked for Raul's father, and now for him. I know who I prefer.'

Lydia didn't respond at first. She assumed from that that Raul worked her too hard.

'I guess Raul must be demanding.'

'Raul?' Loretta laughed. 'No. I love working for him. It's been nearly ten years now, and I still pinch myself to make sure that it's true. I worked in his father's bar for more years than I care to count. Then Raul brought me to Rome and I used to take care of the apartments, and then I ran the housekeeping side of his first hotel.' She gave Lydia a smile. 'I'll leave you to eat.'

'Thank you,' Lydia said. Only she didn't want to be left to eat—she wanted to chat with Loretta, and she wanted to know more about Raul, but it wasn't her place to ask.

What *was* her place?

Lydia didn't know.

And so she ate her dinner and had a bath, and then pulled on summer pyjamas which were short and a bit too tight, then lay in her bed in the guest room while no doubt Raul headed out.

Perhaps for another dinner to discuss her and the baby.

His latest set of problems.

And all because he wanted to get back at Bastiano!

Lydia didn't have the energy to think about that right now.

She was hurting.

They had to talk.

And, no, she didn't care if she was running outside his schedule and it wasn't her appointed hour.

They were *going* to discuss this.

Properly.

Even the difficult things, like nannies and visiting times.

She had no idea where in the house he was.

But she'd find him.

And if he wasn't at home…

She would wait.

Raul was actually in his office.

He looked up as Allegra stopped by on her way home and told him what she had organised.

'I've arranged two other apartments for Lydia to look at tomorrow, and there's a courier coming tomorrow at nine.'

'A courier?'

'You said you had a package you wanted hand-delivered to Casta?'

'Oh, yes.'

'How did you find her in the end?' Allegra asked as she pulled on her coat. 'I think I visited maybe fifty castles and rang a hundred more.'

'She found me,' Raul replied.

Only that wasn't quite true. But he didn't run everything by Allegra, and he certainly wasn't going to discuss the meeting he'd had with Bastiano with her.

With anyone.

'Anything else?' Allegra checked.

'I don't think so.'

She was gone.

And Raul didn't blame her a bit.

Last night she had worked till close to midnight, trying to have things as prepared as possible for today.

And tonight he had kept her again past ten.

'Raul?'

He looked up and there was Allegra, still hovering at the door.

'Yes?'

'I just thought I should let you know I'm also looking for a nanny.'

'Maybe hold back on that till Lydia has got more used to the idea.'

'I meant for me.'

'Oh,' Raul said, though what he really wanted to say was *merda*.

What the hell was going on with everyone?

'You're supposed to say congratulations.'

Raul rolled his eyes.

'I'm going to be running a crèche—I can see it now. Go home.'

'I am going. Seriously, though, it's going to be difficult finding a nanny who works to your hours. I don't want Lydia to explode in temper, but we really do need to start making some enquiries.'

'Leave it for now,' he said, and as Allegra walked off he wearily remembered his manners and congratulated her on the news of her baby. *'Complimenti!'*

Allegra just laughed as she walked out.

She knew he didn't mean it!

And her care factor?

Zero.

She really was a most brilliant PA.

But Allegra was wrong about one thing, Raul thought—Lydia didn't explode.

She imploded rather than let out the rage she held on to.

He'd seen it himself.

Whereas *he*...

Raul poured cognac and it was well earned—especially when he recalled how he had held on to his temper when Bastiano had insulted his mother.

But, no, that wasn't right.

It had been the truth that had held him back.

Bastiano had thought it was love between them.

Yet he had been just seventeen.

His mother had been in her mid-thirties.

What a mess!

Raul went into his drawer and took out the ring and went to package it for the courier.

Usually, of course, his parcels and such were left for others to deal with.

Not on this occasion.

This was beyond personal, Raul thought as he looked at the ring.

It was like holding a ghost—and one he didn't even know.

Bastiano was an orphan.

Had this been his mother's ring?

What the hell had his mother been doing, taking such a ring from a teenager?

A kid, really.

They had been children then.

Sure, they had thought they were adults, but what the hell...?

His mind leapt to the defence of the seventeen-year-old Lydia.

He was furious at how she'd been treated by adults who should have known better.

And now he sat trying to do the hardest thing in his life—afford Bastiano the same feelings.

'Raul!'

This time it wasn't Allegra.

Instead a very pale Lydia stood in the doorway, in short pyjamas.

He could see all the tiny changes in her. Her hips were rounder, her breasts fuller, but he wasn't really noticing them in reference to her being pregnant.

Her hips were round and her breasts were full and she would never, *ever*, not turn him on.

And how the hell did he keep his distance?

How did he keep removing himself from want?

He saw her gaze descend to the ring he held.

'Don't worry.' He did his best to keep things level and dropped the ring back in the drawer. 'I wasn't planning a surprise. It isn't for you.'

And to her shame, to the detriment of her stupid heart, for a second she had hoped that she might have found someone who would never leave.

Fool!

And when Lydia was angry, when she was hurting, she was ice.

'Of course it isn't,' Lydia said in her most crisp and affected tone, but then it cracked, just a little, and she could hold it in no more. 'You never cared about me—not for a moment. You were too busy working out how to get to Bastiano...'

'Merda.'

This time he said it out loud as he realised that she knew.

'Lydia!' Raul stood—not in defence, more in horror.

'Don't!' she warned him. 'Don't you *dare* try to justify it.'

'I'm not. How long have you known?'

'*I* get to ask the questions—did you follow me out of that

dining room because you were interested in me or because you wanted to find out more about Bastiano?'

Before he could react, she took away the safe answer.

'And please don't say *both*, Raul—at least give me the truth.'

He owed her that.

'Bastiano.'

Absolutely the truth hurt, but she forced herself to speak on. 'And when you invited me for dinner was it to get to him? When you told me to choose…?'

She wanted to spit as she recalled it.

'Were you hoping to flaunt me in front of him?'

'Yes,' Raul answered, and he knew that the absolute truth was needed now. 'Because that's how I've always operated—that's how I have run my life. I lie to get by. I say what I have to. However—'

'I *hate* you!' Lydia shouted.

Oh, the ice hadn't cracked—it had split wide open. And fury was pouring out—years of it.

And it terrified her.

'You're the cheat, Raul! You say you hate them, but you're actually the cheat. You were lying all along.'

'Not all along.'

'Yes! You screwed me to get back at him!'

She walked out, and then she ran.

Back to her room.

The bed was turned down and the light was on and she wondered how it could look just as it had before, now he had told her himself the truth—he had pursued her to get back at Bastiano.

'Lydia.' He didn't knock, he just came in, and he was very calm.

'Get out.'

'No. We're going to talk about this.'

His head was actually racing—everything looked different now.

'When did you find out?'

'Does it even matter?'

Of course it did—and of course he knew when she had found out.

When everything between them had changed.

'You were right,' Lydia said, her temper rising. 'We'll do this through lawyers.' She meant it. 'I'm going to screw *you* now, Raul. I am going to make your life hell.'

'You couldn't.'

He took her arms and tried to calm her, but she was crying now—seriously crying.

'You couldn't make my life hell.'

Lydia took his words as a threat—that he was mightier, richer—but he meant it otherwise.

Hell was *not* having her in his life.

An angry Lydia he could deal with—was what he had waited for, in fact.

Because her fury was private and deep and finally she shared it.

Loudly.

'You lied.'

'I did,' Raul agreed. 'That's what my life was like until you came along.'

'You were using me.'

'At first,' Raul said, but then reconsidered. 'Actually, I wanted you on sight. I remember your buttons.'

'I don't take that as a compliment.'

'Take it any way you like. The floor is yours.'

His calm enraged her.

That he could just *stand* there when she'd exposed what he had done.

'I should never have told you about the baby.' She picked

up the statue. 'I should have just sold this and you'd never have known.'

'I thought you already had sold it.'

And it had hurt him that she had.

Like her blasted mother—taking heirlooms and passing them on to get through another week.

He loved that statue too, and now she was holding it in her hand and about to toss it.

Raul stood there, a little conflicted.

He could stop her, because he knew she'd regret it later.

But she was angry.

Not just at him—that much he knew.

And, hell, she deserved to show it.

Lydia did.

She threw it.

Not at him.

She threw it against the wall and heard it shatter and she did the same.

Because she loved it, and she had destroyed the nicest thing she had ever had.

Except for Raul.

Yet she had never really had him at all.

And she wanted him so much.

But he didn't want her.

So why was he kissing her? Why was he telling her he'd better lock up the china or they were going to have very expensive rows?

Why, when she was crying and kicking and, oh, so angry, did he contain her, yet let her be, and seem to want her at the same time?

They were frantic—tearing buttons and shredding clothes with their lips locked, because Raul wanted to be out of his head too.

Today had been hell.

Yesterday too.

And all the weeks before that.

He wanted her badly.

Raul kissed her hard, pushed her to the wall, and her bottom was bare in his hands, and her swaying breasts were stilled by his chest.

Lydia climbed him.

Even as Raul was preparing himself she was wrapping around him, and then she was safe in strong arms and being taken away.

It was rough and intense, and her face was hot and wet as he kissed her cheek on his way to finding her mouth.

And there was not a scream left within her as she climaxed—there wasn't even air in her lungs left to come out. Because he took everything she had and gave her more.

Everything raced to her centre as he thrust in deep and filled her. Her orgasm was so tight as he joined her in a climax that went on as hers faded.

She was calmed and coming down, watching the tension of his features and revelling in the feel of his final rapid thrusts.

And then thought returned, but the hurt did not.

At least not in the way it had been there before.

They were still kissing as he let her down. Standing in a war zone and yet safe and kissing.

And then she peeled back and peeked out and saw the glass on the floor.

'I broke our statue...'

Because that was what it was.

Theirs.

A diary of them.

And she had destroyed it.

'Why didn't you sell it?'

'I couldn't.'

And that meant so much to Raul.

She hadn't taken a single photo—Lydia, he knew, held on to nothing—yet she had been unable to let this go.

'And now I've destroyed it,' Lydia said, looking at all the shattered glass.

'No.' He picked it up from the floor and showed her that the beautiful couple were somehow intact, just minus the sheet.

'I hated that sheet,' Raul said. 'I didn't like to say so to Silvio. It's his art and all that, but I think he made a mistake.'

'He's a master of his craft!'

'Well, I think it looks better now.' Raul shrugged. 'Though the valuers might disagree.' He smiled at her. 'But you don't need them now, and we don't need lawyers.'

Lydia wasn't so sure.

She could not deal with Raul with her head.

One tryst and she craved more—one more night in his bed and she would be putty.

And she was scared to try to forgive him.

Lydia was scared of his lies—in that he was the master.

'Come to bed.'

She knew he meant his.

'Come on.'

And it scared her, not that she would take his crumbs…

But that she did.

CHAPTER SEVENTEEN

WRAPPED IN A sheet on Lydia's command, so as not to scare Loretta, they headed down the mirrored hall.

'She won't be here,' Raul said as they shuffled along with him holding the statue.

'Well, I'm not walking naked through your house.'

'*Our* house.'

Lydia ignored that. Instead she asked about Loretta.

'How come she works for you?'

'Because she was always good to me, and when my father died I knew she would be without work.'

'So you *do* have friends?'

'I guess.'

They were at his bedroom—back to where she had promised never to be.

It was even more beautiful the second time around.

'It's so gorgeous.'

'It's your room now.'

He saw her shoulders stiffen.

'I mean it.'

'Raul, can we talk about this tomorrow? There's still a lot to sort out.'

'It's sorted.'

'Raul, I'm here because you found out I was pregnant. I don't think that's an awful lot to base a relationship on.'

'Nor do I,' Raul agreed. 'I lived with my parents, after all. It's not just the baby.'

'Please don't just say the right thing. You're a liar, Raul.' She thought back to the plane, the first time they had flown here. 'I can't bear the thought of you *pretending* to care. That's what you've been doing all along…'

'Never.'

'You stand there and tell me you're speaking the truth and then straight away you lie.'

'When I held your hand I wasn't lying. When we took a taxi rather than my car I was caring for you then. And when we didn't have sex that first time…'

He thought back.

'For a second I considered how good it would feel to get back at him.'

And she let out a sob and a laugh, because he was being too painfully honest now.

'But then I stopped,' Raul reminded her. 'And by morning I could not let you leave.'

'You should have told me you knew Bastiano.'

'I know that,' Raul admitted. 'But I knew that if I did you'd leave. And you did.'

'Had you *told* me…' Lydia said, and then halted. He was right. Whichever way she might have found out, she'd have gone.

'I missed you so much.' Raul said.

Now she knew he was lying.

'So much that you did nothing to try to contact me until I called and told you I was pregnant?'

'Lydia, I didn't even know your surname. I've had Allegra scouring all the castles in England.

She didn't believe him and he knew it.

'Ask her.'

'She'll say what you tell her to.'

'I think,' Raul said, 'that I've finally found someone as mistrusting as me.'

'You had three months to find me, and yet on the same day I call you to say I'm pregnant suddenly you appear.'

'I was already on my way when I heard your message,' Raul told her. 'Here…'

He placed the now naked statue on the bedside table and

then went to his drawer and took out a piece of paper with her name and address written on it.

'That's Bastiano's handwriting. I went to Casta to ask him.'

He handed it to her and Lydia looked at the paper. And she thought she would keep it for ever, because it told her that she *had* been missed.

'You went to Bastiano just for this?'

'Well, it wasn't for his company.'

'Did the two of you fight?'

'No,' Raul said. 'Nearly. He said he wanted a ring that had been left to me by my mother.'

'The ring you were looking at before?'

Raul nodded and got into bed, patted the space beside him for her to lie down with him.

'Hasn't he had enough from you?' Lydia asked as she climbed in. She really could not fathom his mother leaving half her legacy to a very young lover rather than leaving it all to her only son.

'It was a ring that he gave to her, apparently.'

'Oh.'

'He wanted it back in return for your address. I think it might have belonged to his mother. He's an orphan.' He made himself say it. 'He wasn't my mother's first affair.'

'How do you know?'

'Because I had been lying to my father to save her since I was a small child.'

And he had been lying to himself to save her memory since she'd died.

'Bastiano was just seventeen—half her age. Back then I thought we were men, and I hated him as such, but now...'

It felt very different, looking back.

'We were good friends growing up.'

'Could you be again?'

Raul was about to give a derisive laugh, but then he thought for a moment. 'I don't know...'

And it was nice to lie in bed talking with another person, rather than trying to make sense of things by himself.

'I think that my mother had problems for a very long time. Perhaps even before she was married. I don't even know if I'm my father's son.'

'Does it matter?'

'I think it did to him.'

'Is that why he beat you?'

He had never told her that Gino had given him those scars on his back, but it was clear now and Raul nodded.

And when he examined those times without hate and with her by his side things were easier to see.

His hand was on her stomach, and he could feel the little bump. It was starting to sink in properly that he would be a father.

She felt his hand there and wondered at his thoughts. 'I'm not a gold-digger, Raul.'

'I know. I had to put that statue in your case, remember?' He had gone over and over that time.

'I don't think I took the Pill every day, even though my mother had insisted I should be on it. I had no intention of sleeping with Bastiano, and maybe I should have known I wasn't covered. I didn't think.'

'Lydia, you could have been wearing a chastity belt that night and I'd have rung for wire cutters. I could have insisted we use a condom. Have you told your mother about the baby?' he added.

'No.'

'When will you?'

'When I'm ready to.'

'I'm glad you told me first,' Raul said.

'She was a mess when I got back. I think losing my father finally caught up with her. She kicked Maurice out. She's staying at her sister's now. She's agreed the castle should go on the market.'

'Lydia. I'll look after your mother, but not *him*.'

Maurice he could never forgive.

Lydia lay in his arms and gave a soft laugh at the way he'd spoken of Maurice, but then she thought about what he'd just said about her mother.

'You don't have to do that.'

'Of course I do.'

'No, Raul, you don't.'

'We're going to be a family, Lydia. Marry me?'

She lay silent. She could feel his hand on her stomach and put her hand over his. Lydia knew how she felt about Raul. But she also meant what she'd said—a baby wouldn't save them.

'You don't even *like* children.'

'No, I don't,' Raul agreed. 'I'll like ours, though. Please believe that I'm not asking you to marry me because of the baby.'

'I know that.'

She *almost* did.

But by his own admission Raul was a manipulative liar, and there was still the tiniest niggle that he was simply saying the right things to appease her.

But then she thought of his look of horror when she had exposed him. So unlike Arabella, who hadn't even flinched at being caught.

He seemed so loath to hurt her.

She was scared, though, to believe.

And as her mind flicked around, trying to find fault with this love, Raul lay sinking into his first glimpse of peace.

That feeling—not quite foreboding, but almost—was fading. His constant wondering as to how she was had been answered. He thought of that first surge of jealousy when he'd thought that she and Bastiano might be lovers.

And now they lay there together and he looked at her. 'Were you jealous at the thought of Allegra and me?'

'Of course I was.'

'Are you now?'

'No.' She shook her head.

'She really was looking for you for weeks. And,' he added, 'I've just found out she's pregnant too.'

And then she knew she wasn't jealous any more, or suspicious of Allegra, because he answered a question she wasn't even thinking.

'It's not mine.'

'I would *really* hope not.'

And he smiled, and when he did, for Lydia it was easy to smile too, but he could see the little sparkle of tears in her eyes on what should be their happiest night.

'Marry me?' he said again.

'Raul…'

Oh, she knew he cared—and deeply. And she knew how she felt. But there was still a tiny part of her that was scared that he'd asked in haste.

That without a baby there wouldn't be any 'them'.

She would just have to deal with it, Lydia knew. She would just have to accept never quite fully knowing if they were only together for the sake of their child. Because in every other way it felt perfect.

Stiff upper lip and all that.

'I hated being without you,' Raul said.

'And me.'

'No,' Raul said, 'I mean it. I felt as if there was something wrong. The sky seemed hung too low.'

He had been trying to work out what was wrong for months, and now suddenly, just like that, he knew exactly what had been wrong.

Raul had never felt it before.

Lydia lay looking at the chandelier struck by moonlight.

The shutters were open and there was the sound of a gondolier singing beneath them on the canal.

And then she heard something.

Not a bell.

But something as clear as one.

And it struck right at her soul and she turned her face to the sound.

'I love you,' Raul told her.

It can be said many ways, but when it is said right it strikes so clear and so pure. And the sound and the feeling vibrates and lingers and lasts even when it must surely be gone.

It's never gone.

She had heard his truth.

This really was love.

EPILOGUE

THERE HAD BEEN one more lie that Raul had told her.

Raul *did* get up at night for his baby.

And he fed and changed her.

Serena had come into their lives four weeks ago, and so far it had proved the perfect name.

Yes, she was from Venice—or La Serenissima—but it was more for her nature that the name had been chosen.

They had been rewarded with such a calm baby.

Of course she cried—but she calmed easily when held.

And they loved her so much.

From her one blonde tufty curl to her ten perfect toes.

It was seven on a Sunday—Lydia knew that without opening her eyes because her favourite bell rang its occasional deep note and the others would join in soon.

Raul was speaking to Serena as they stood on the balcony, telling her she should go back to sleep.

It made Lydia's heart melt to watch the gentle way he held his daughter.

He was naked from the waist up and she could see his scars. She was grateful for them.

Sometimes she needed their reminder, because life felt perfect and the scars told her how far they had come.

Lydia closed her eyes as he turned around, pretending to be asleep.

'Shh…' Raul said as Serena let out a protest when he returned her to her crib.

Serena hushed, and after a moment of watching her sleep Raul got dressed.

Lydia wanted to protest and insist that he come back to bed.

Sunday was her favourite day.

Raul would go out from their room and return with the breakfast Loretta had prepared. They loved Sunday breakfast in bed.

Where was he going?

Lydia heard the elevator taking him down and then the engine of his speedboat.

Perhaps he had gone for coffee?

Raul did that now and then.

She had hoped he would not this morning.

She lay there listening to the bells and then rolled on her back and looked at the lights. Wherever he had gone she was happy.

So happy that she fell back to sleep and then awoke to his voice.

'Happy Birthday.'

He *had* remembered.

Lydia had dropped no clues and given no reminders.

She hadn't met a stranger that morning. Lydia knew she had met the love of her life. A man who had told her that there was no one in his life whose birthday he remembered.

Now he had two.

Raul held out a cardboard box tied with a red velvet ribbon which was vaguely familiar.

And then he told her where he had been.

'Baci in gondola,' Raul told her. 'Had you not chosen to walk out that morning you would have had these.'

He handed her the box and she opened it up.

'I was coming back to ask you to stay.'

'I know that now.'

And then she asked him something that she had not before.

'Would you have told me about Bastiano then?'

'No,' he said. 'Maybe later that night, but that morning I was definitely coming home to go back to bed with you.'

'Here.' He handed her the other box he was carrying. 'Your present.'

Lydia opened it up and she was reminded of just how much she was loved.

It was an album filled with stunning photos of the castle. Exterior shots and also interior.

And as she turned the pages it was like stepping into each room and seeing it as it had once been when she was a child.

The castle would be opened to the public today.

With Raul's help, things had been turned around.

Valerie lived in a cottage on the grounds, and this afternoon would be taking the first visitors in a very long time through the glorious building.

But that wasn't all of Lydia's presents.

'We fly at ten,' Raul told her. 'Then we are having afternoon tea in the garden. You'll make a gentleman of me yet.'

He *was* one.

A thousand times over and Lydia still cringed a bit when she thought of the words she had said, right here in this bedroom, that awful day.

They had survived it.

Better than that, they had thrived.

Raul came into the bed and they lay there, listening to the bells and to the contented sounds of their baby.

'When are we getting married?' Raul asked.

It hadn't yet happened.

'Soon.' Lydia smiled.

'You keep saying that,' Raul grumbled.

The last six months had been wonderful, but crazy. Their love had hit like lightning, and Lydia kept waiting to come down from the dizzy high and get organised.

She was starting to accept that there was no come-down when Raul was close.

Their kiss was slow, and he kept telling her he loved her,

and then Raul rolled on top of her and told her that he was tired of waiting.

She felt him *there* and he smiled.

'I didn't mean for that.'

'I know you didn't,' Lydia said.

But it had been four weeks and she was ready now.

'You're sure?'

He was very slow and tender, and that was a side of Raul that even he was only starting to find out existed.

It was the best birthday she could have known. They made slow Sunday love and afterwards he stayed leaning over her and told her that there was another thing she did not know.

'Raul?'

'We get married today,' Raul said.

Lydia frowned.

They both wanted a small wedding and had thought about having it here in Venice.

Or Rome, where they had first met, perhaps?

Even Sicily, for together they had been back there.

'At the castle,' Raul said.

That had been but a dream, for it had been falling down around them when they'd first met.

It was beautiful now.

'Yes?' he checked.

'Yes!' Lydia said.

'Per favore?' Raul said, and took her right back to the day they had met.

'Yes, please!' Lydia said, and together they smiled.

She *had* chosen wisely, for Raul was the love of her life.

And he would be King.

* * * * *

*If you enjoyed this story,
look out for more scandalous tales of*
BILLIONAIRES & ONE-NIGHT HEIRS
coming soon!

*In the meantime,
why not explore these other great reads
from Carol Marinelli?*

*THE SHEIKH'S BABY SCANDAL
DI SIONE'S INNOCENT CONQUEST
RETURN OF THE UNTAMED BILLIONAIRE
BILLIONAIRE WITHOUT A PAST
THE COST OF THE FORBIDDEN*

Available now!

Angelique knew she should release him and step back, but she was quite blown away by the masculine interest that flared to life in Kasim's gaze.

She wasn't falsely modest. She knew she was beautiful. It was one of the reasons camera lenses so often turned on her. Men looked at her with desire all the time. There was no reason she should react to this man's naked hunger. But she did.

A very animalistic sexual reaction pierced deep in her loins, flooding her with heat. And, yes…it was reciprocal desire. He was looking at her as if he found her appealing, and she certainly found him as attractive as they came. There might even be something chemical here, because her gaze dropped involuntarily to his mouth. Longing rose within her.

His lips quirked.

She knew he was reading her reaction and was amused. It stung. She felt raw and gauche. It was the bane of her existence that she couldn't always stop whatever feelings were overtaking her. But this was so intense it was unprecedented, touching her at all levels. Physical, mental, emotional… He held her entire being enthralled.

"We are finished talking," he said, while his arm bent against her grip. His hand arrived at her waist, hot and sure. His other hand tightened slightly on her arm, drawing her forward a half step, commanding, but not forcing. "If you would like to start something new, however…"

Don't, she ordered herself, but it was too late. His mouth was coming down to hers and she was parting her lips in eager reception.

The Sauveterre Siblings

Meet the world's most renowned family...

Angelique, Henri, Ramon and Trella—two sets of twins born to a wealthy French tycoon and his Spanish aristocrat wife. Fame, notoriety and an excess of bodyguards is the price of being part of their illustrious dynasty. And wherever the Sauveterre twins go, scandal is sure to follow!

They're protected by the best security money can buy—no one can break through their barriers... But what happens when each of these Sauveterre siblings meets the one person who can breach their heart...?

Meet the heirs to the Sauveterre fortune in Dani Collins's fabulous new quartet:

Pursued by the Desert Prince
March 2017

His Mistress with Two Secrets
April 2017

Ramon and Isadora's story
Coming soon!

Trella and Prince Xavier's story
Coming soon!

PURSUED BY THE DESERT PRINCE

BY
DANI COLLINS

First Published in Great Britain 2017
By Mills & Boon, an imprint of HarperCollins*Publishers*
1 London Bridge Street, London, SE1 9GF

© 2017 Dani Collins

ISBN: 978-0-263-92513-5

Our policy is to use papers that are natural, renewable and recyclable
products and made from wood grown in sustainable forests. The logging
and manufacturing processes conform to the legal environmental
regulations of the country of origin.

Printed and bound in Spain
by CPI, Barcelona

Canadian **Dani Collins** knew in high school that she
wanted to write romance for a living. Twenty-five years
later, after marrying her high school sweetheart, having
two kids with him, working at several generic office jobs
and submitting countless manuscripts, she got 'The Call'.
Her first Mills & Boon novel won the Reviewers' Choice
Award for Best First in Series from *RT Book Reviews*. She
now works in her own office, writing romance.

Books by Dani Collins

Mills & Boon Modern Romance

The Secret Beneath the Veil
Bought by Her Italian Boss
Vows of Revenge
Seduced into the Greek's World
The Russian's Acquisition
An Heir to Bind Them
A Debt Paid in Passion
More than a Convenient Marriage?
No Longer Forbidden?

The Wrong Heirs

The Marriage He Must Keep
The Consequence He Must Claim

Seven Sexy Sins

The Sheikh's Sinful Seduction

The 21st Century Gentleman's Club

The Ultimate Seduction

One Night With Consequences

Proof of Their Sin

Visit the Author Profile page
at millsandboon.co.uk for more titles.

Dear Reader,

I've always found the idea of being a twin fascinating. I especially love the stories you sometimes hear of a particular pair having a subliminal connection, even when distance separates them. Or the smaller, simpler things—like a pair inventing their own language or dressing the same without consulting the other.

I brought all this to my new quartet, The Sauveterre Siblings. They're a wealthy family who have been blessed with identical twin boys and then a pair of identical twin girls. The press are mad for them. They followed the children's every move, and only grew worse after the youngest was kidnapped when she was nine. Trella was returned to them, but they all wear the scars.

In this first story Angelique is still trying to find who she might have been if her sister had never been torn from her. Kasim has his own demons created by a lost sibling. Their worlds are very different, but they're drawn inexorably into an affair that is only meant to last one night.

I hope you enjoy watching the Sauveterre twins find that special someone who will help each of them heal from their past.

Dani

To my sisters, who often live far away,
but remain close, close, close in my heart.
Love yous. xoxo

CHAPTER ONE

ANGELIQUE SAUVETERRE PICKED up a call from her exterior guards informing her that Kasim ibn Nour, Crown Prince of Zhamair, had arrived to see her.

She slumped back in her chair with a sigh, really not up to meeting someone new. Not after today.

"Of course. Please show him up to my office," she said. Because she had to.

Hasna had said her brother would drop by while he was in Paris.

Angelique didn't know why the brother of the bride wanted to meet the designer of the bride's wedding gown, but she assumed he wanted to arrange a surprise gift. So she didn't expect this meeting to be long or awful. Her *day* with Princess Hasna and the bridal party hadn't been awful. It had actually been quite pleasant.

It was just a lot of people and noise and Angelique was an introvert. When she told people that, they always said, *But you're not shy!* She had been horribly shy as a child, though, and brutally forced to get over it. Now she could work a room with the best of them, but it fried her down to a crisp.

She yearned for the day when her sister, Trella, would be ready to be the face of Maison des Jumeaux. An ironic thought, since her twin wore the same face.

As she freshened "their" lipstick, Angelique acknowledged that she really longed for Trella to be the one to talk to new clients and meet with brothers of the bride and put on fetes like the one she'd hosted today.

She wanted Trella to be all better.

But she wouldn't press. Trella had made such progress getting over her phobias, especially in the past year. She was determined to attend Hasna and Sadiq's wedding and was showing promise in getting there.

It will happen, Angelique reassured herself.

In the meantime… She rolled her neck, trying to massage away the tension that had gathered over hours of soothing every last wedding nerve.

At least she didn't look too much worse for wear. This silk blend she and Trella had been working on hadn't creased much at all.

Angelique stood to give a quick turn this way and that in the freestanding mirror in the corner of her office. Her black pants fell flawlessly and the light jacket with its embroidered edges fluttered with her movement while her silver cami reflected light into her face. Her makeup was holding up and only her chignon was coming apart.

She quickly pulled the pins out of her hair and gave it a quick finger-comb so her brunette tresses fell in loose waves around her shoulders. *Too* casual?

Her door guard knocked and she didn't have time to redo her hair. She moved to open the door herself.

And felt the impact like she'd stepped under a midnight sky, but one lit by stars and northern lights and the glow of a moon bigger and hotter than the sun could ever hope to be.

Angelique was dazzled and had to work not to show it, but honestly, the prince was utterly spectacular. Dark, liquid eyes that seemed almost black they were such a deep brown. Flawless bone structure with his straight nose and perfectly balanced jawline. His mouth— That bottom lip was positively erotic.

The rest of him was cool and diamond sharp. His country was renowned for being ultraconservative, but his head was uncovered, his black hair shorn into a neat business cut. He wore a perfectly tailored Western suit over what her practiced eye gauged to be an athletically balanced physique.

She swallowed. *Find a brain, Angelique.*

"Your Highness. Angelique Sauveterre. Welcome. Please come in."

She didn't offer to shake, which would have been a faux pas for a woman in Zhamair.

He did hold out his hand, which was a slight overstep for a man to demand of a woman here in Paris.

She acquiesced and felt a tiny jolt run through her as he closed his strong hand over her narrow one. Heat bloomed under her cheekbones, something his quick gaze seemed to note—which only increased her warmth. She hated being obvious.

"Hello." Not *Thank you for seeing me*, or *Call me Kasim*.

"Thank you, Maurice," she murmured to dismiss her guard, and had to clear her throat. "We'll be fine."

She was exceedingly cautious about being alone with men, or women for that matter, whom she didn't know, but the connection through Hasna and Sadiq made the prince a fairly safe bet. If a man in the prince's position was planning something nefarious, then the whole world was on its ear and she didn't stand a chance anyway.

Plus, she always had the panic button on her pendant. She almost felt like she was panicking now. Her heart rate had elevated and her stomach was in knots. Her entire body was on all-stations alert. She'd been feeling drained a few seconds ago, but one profound handshake later she was feeling energized yet oddly defenseless.

She was nervous as a schoolgirl, really, which wasn't like her at all. With two very headstrong brothers, she had learned how to hold her own against strong masculine energy.

She'd never encountered anything like this, though. Closing herself into her office with him felt dangerous. Not the type of danger she'd been trained to avoid, but inner peril. Like when she poured her soul into a piece then held her breath as it was paraded down the catwalk for judgment.

"Please have a seat," she invited, indicating the conversation area below the mural. There were no pretty views of actual Paris in this windowless room, but the office was still one of her favorite places for its ability to lock out the world. She spent a lot of time on her side of its twin desks and drafting tables.

Trella's side was empty. She was home in Spain, but they often worked here in companionable silence.

"I just made fresh coffee. Would you like a cup?"

"I won't stay long."

That ought to be good news. She was reacting way too strongly to him, but she found herself disappointed. So strange! She took such care to put mental distance between herself and others. The entire world would have this effect on her if she didn't, but he only had to glance around her private space and she felt naked and exposed. *Seen.* And she found herself longing for his approval.

He didn't seem to want to sit, so she pressed flat hands that tremored on the back of the chair she usually used when visiting with clients. "Was there something particular about the wedding arrangements you wanted to discuss?"

"Just that you should send your bill to me." He moved to set a card on the edge of Trella's desk.

She turned to follow his movement behind her. So economical and fascinating. And who was his tailor? That suit was pure artistry, the man so obviously yang to her yin.

He caught her staring.

She tucked her hair behind her ear to disguise her blush.

"Her Majesty made the same offer and you needn't have troubled yourself. It's a wedding gift for Sadiq and the princess."

He noted the familiarity of her using Sadiq's first name with a small shift of his head. "So Hasna said. I would prefer to pay."

His gaze was direct enough to feel confrontational, instantly amplifying this conversation into one of conflict. Her pulse gave a reflexive zing.

Why would he be so adamant—?

Oh, dear God! He didn't think she and Sadiq were involved, did he?

Why wouldn't he? According to the headlines, she'd slept with half of Europe. When she wasn't doing drugs or having catfights with her models, of course.

"Sadiq is a longtime friend of the family." She retreated behind the cool mask she showed the world, ridiculously crushed that he would believe those awful summations of her character. "This is something we want to do for him."

"We." His gaze narrowed.

"Yes." She didn't bring up her sister or what her family owed Sadiq for Trella's return to them. The fact that Sadiq had never once sought any glory for his heroism was exactly why he was such a cherished friend. "If that was all…" She deliberately presumed she'd had the last word on the topic. "I should get back to the final arrangements for your sister's things."

Kasim had to applaud his future brother-in-law's taste. Angelique Sauveterre had grown from a very sweet-looking girl into a stunning young woman. In person, she had an even more compelling glow of beauty.

Her long brunette hair glimmered and shifted in a rippling curtain and what had seemed like unremarkable gray eyes online were actually a mesmerizing greenish hazel. She was tall and slender, built like a model despite being the one to dress them, and her skin held a golden tone that must be her mother's Spanish ancestry.

Cameras rarely caught her with a smile on her face and when they did, it was a faint Mona Lisa slant that allowed her to live up to the reputation of her father's French blood: aloof and indifferent.

She wore that look now, but when she had first greeted him, she had smiled openly. Her beauty was so appealing, Kasim had forgotten for a moment why he was here and had been overcome with a desire to pursue her.

Perhaps this captivating quality was the reason Sadiq was so smitten?

"About those arrangements… Today went well?" He had understood it to be the final fitting of his sister's wedding gown and the bridesmaids' dresses as well as a private showing of other clothes made for Hasna, all taking place on the runway level of this building. Once the last nips and tucks were completed, the entire works would be packaged up and shipped to Zhamair for the wedding next month.

"You would have to check with the women who were here, but they all seemed pleased by the time they left." So haughty and quick to keep the focus on his sister.

From what he'd heard around his penthouse, the consensus had been a high level of ecstasy with everything from the clothes to the imported cordial to the finger sandwiches and pastries.

"Hasna doesn't seem to have any complaints," he downplayed. "Which is why I'm willing to spare her the nuisance of replacing all that you've promised her."

Angelique was tall in her heels. Not as tall as him, but taller than most women he knew, and she grew taller at his words, spine stiffening while her eyelashes batted once, twice, three times. Like she was filtering through various responses.

"All that we've *made* for her," she corrected, using a light tone, but it was the lightness of a rapier. Pointed and dangerous. "Why on earth would you refuse to let her have it?"

"You can drop the indignation," he advised. "I'm not judging. I've had mistresses. There is a time to let them go and yours has arrived."

"You think I'm Sadiq's mistress. And that as his *mistress*, I offered to make his bride's gown and trousseau. That's a rather generous act for a *mistress*, isn't it?"

She repeatedly spat the word as if she was deeply offended.

He pushed his hands into his pants pockets, rocking back on his heels.

"It's a generous act to arrange a private showing for such a large party at a world-famous and highly exclusive Paris design house." It hadn't been only his mother and sister, but Sadiq's mother and sisters, along with cousins and friends from both sides.

The cost of something like today wasn't so high as to imperil his riches, of course. The groom's family could equally afford it and given the extent of the Sauveterre wealth, and the rumors that the family corporation had underwritten this folly of an art project in the first place, he imagined Angelique wouldn't be too far out of pocket, either.

"Had this afternoon been the only line item offered at no charge, I wouldn't have batted an eye," he said. "But the gown? I know my sister's taste." He imagined it had easily run to six figures. "And to throw in wedding costumes for the rest of the party? Including mothers of the bride *and* groom?"

"Sadiq's parents and sisters are also friends of the family."

"Plus a full wardrobe for Hasna to begin her married life," he completed with disbelief. "All at no cost? This is more than a 'gift' from a 'family friend.' If I had learned of it sooner, I would have taken steps long before today."

Hasna had been chattering nonstop about her big day, but what did he care about the finer details? He was glad she was marrying for love, he wanted everything to go well for her, but the minutia of decor and food and colors to be worn had meant nothing to him. It wasn't until he had noted she was grossly under budget—not like her at all—that he had quizzed her on when to expect an invoice for the dress.

"If I'm Sadiq's mistress, then I should want the fat commission off this! I would have told him to *make* his bride come to us as a payoff for losing his support—

which I don't need, by the way." The hiss in her tone sliced the air like a blade. "That is *not* the way it went at all. Hasna didn't even know Sadiq knew us. She said we were her dream designer and he arranged it secretly, to surprise her. *We're* the ones who decided not to charge him."

"Yes, funny that he would have kept this tremendously close 'friendship'—" he let her hear his disdain "—such a secret from the woman he had been courting for a year and professed to love. I might have understood if he *was* paying you off." He wouldn't have condoned it, not when Hasna had fought so hard for a love match and had managed to convince him that Sadiq returned her feelings, but at least he would have seen the why of this ridiculous arrangement.

"Have you discussed this with Sadiq?" she demanded frostily, arms crossed. "Because I am as insulted on his behalf as I am on my own."

"Sadiq is plainly not capable of doing what is needed. I will advise him after the fact."

"I am not sleeping with Sadiq! I don't sleep with married men, or engaged ones, either."

"I'm fairly confident you stopped sleeping with him once the engagement was announced. I can account for his whereabouts since then."

"He knows you're watching him like that? With these awful suspicions about him?"

"I don't judge him for having lovers prior to settling down. We all do it."

Although it annoyed him that his brother-in-law had slept with this particular woman. Kasim didn't examine too closely why that grated. Or wonder too much about how such a soft-spoken man had managed to seduce her. Sadiq had always struck Kasim as being more book-smart than street-smart, earnest and studious and almost as naive as Hasna.

This woman was surprisingly spirited. She would dominate someone like Sadiq.

Which more than explained why Sadiq hadn't been able to end things as definitively as he should.

"And I'm...what?" she prodded. "Trying to coax him back by outfitting his wife? Your logic is flawed, Your Highness."

Her impertinence took him aback, it was so uncommon in his life. The most sass he heard from anyone was from his sister and she typically confined it to light teasing, never anything with this much bite.

He found Angelique's impudence both stimulating and trying. She obviously didn't understand who she was dealing with.

"Why are you arguing? I'm offering to *pay* you for the work you've done. The more you resist admitting the truth and promising not to see him again, the more likely I am to lose patience and pull the plug on this entire arrangement, Hasna's tears be damned."

"You would do that?" Her jaw slacked with disbelief. "To your sister?"

She had no idea to what lengths he would go—had gone—to protect his family.

He wouldn't allow himself to be drawn into yet another inner debate about his actions on that score. It still wrenched his heart, especially when Hasna still cried so often, but he had done what he had to. Ruthlessly.

And would do it again.

But he would not see his sister's heart broken again. She loved Sadiq and Sadiq would be the faithful husband she desired him to be. If that meant fast-tracking a new wedding gown, so be it.

He let Angelique read his resolve in his silence.

She stood there with her chin lifted in confrontation, trying very hard to look down her nose at him. "All I have to do is say that I'm Sadiq's mistress and this goes away?"

"Plus send me the bill and never contact Sadiq again."

"I can give your money to charity," she pointed out.

"You can. The important thing is that you will not be able to hold the debt over Sadiq's head."

"Ah, finally I learn my real motivation." Her arms came out in amazement. "I was beginning to think I was the stupidest mistress alive."

"Oh, I'm quite in admiration of your cleverness, Angelique."

His use of her name made her heart, which was already racing at this altercation, take a jump and spin before landing hard.

"Have we arrived at first names, Kasim?" It was a deliberate lob back, not unlike when she played tennis with her siblings and she was so well matched she had to throw everything she had into each swing of her racket.

This man! She had spent years developing a shield against the world and he brushed it aside like it was a cobweb, making her react from a subterranean level. It was completely unnerving.

His lashes flinched at her use of his given name. *Good.*

"Your insolence toward me is unprecedented. Take extreme care, *Angelique*."

Her fingernails were digging into her own upper arms, she was so beside herself. She used the sharp sting to keep a cool head. She had training for this type of negotiation, she reminded herself. He thought he was holding a small fortune in seed pearls and silk hostage, but he was actually holding a knife to the throat of her sister's happiness along with the debt their family owed to Sadiq.

Given that, there was no way Angelique wanted to jeopardize the wedding arrangements or cause a long-term rift.

Listen. That was the first step, she reminded herself as her ears pounded with her racing pulse. Apparently Kasim felt he wasn't being heard.

"To be clear," she said with forced calm, "you believe I've orchestrated this to put Sadiq into my debt?"

"Perhaps not financially. His family is wealthy in resources and political standing as well as actual gold. You've managed to neutralize yourself in my sister's eyes, so she couldn't possibly see you as a threat if you were to move in at a later date for whatever Sadiq was deemed useful for."

"Can I ask how you concluded that I'm so cold-blooded? Because even the online trolls don't accuse me of this sort of thing." She was nice! Her family regularly told her she was *too* nice.

"If your heart was involved, you would have refused this commission altogether. If you wanted to retaliate for a broken heart, you wouldn't be trying so hard to please Hasna. No. I've told you, I've had mistresses. I understand exceedingly practical women. This is an investment in your future. I accept that on a philosophical level, but not when it risks my sister's happiness. That I cannot allow. So." He nodded decisively at the card he'd left on the desk. "Send me the bill. Do not contact him again."

He made as if to leave.

"Wait!" She leaped forward and grabbed his arm.

He froze, gaze locking onto her hand on his sleeve for one powerful heartbeat before he lifted his eyes. His face was filled outrage and something else, something glittering and fiercely masculine.

"Have we arrived at *that* level of familiarity, Angelique?" He pivoted in a swift move to face her, taking her own arm in his opposite grip.

It was the sudden dive and snatch of a predatory bird catching prey in its talons.

They stood like that in what seemed like a slowdown in time. Her heart pounded so hard her lungs could barely inflate against it.

"We're not finished t-talking." Her voice came out painfully thin. She knew she should release him and step back, but she was quite blown away by the masculine interest that flared to life in his gaze.

She wasn't falsely modest. She knew she was beautiful. It was one of the reasons camera lenses so often turned on her. Men looked at her with desire all the time.

There was no reason she should react to *this* man's naked hunger. But she did.

A very animalistic sexual reaction pierced deep in her loins, flooding her with heat and... Yes, it was reciprocal desire. He was looking at her as if he found her appealing and she certainly found him as attractive as they came. There might even be something chemical here because her gaze dropped involuntarily to his mouth. Longing rose within her.

His lips quirked.

She knew he was reading her reaction and was amused. It stung. She felt raw and gauche. It was the bane of her existence that she couldn't always stop whatever feelings were overtaking her. This was so intense it was unprecedented, touching her at all levels. Physical, mental, emotional… He held her entire being enthralled.

"We are finished talking," he said, while his arm bent against her grip. His hand arrived at her waist, hot and sure. His other hand tightened slightly on her arm, drawing her forward a half step, commanding, but not forcing. "If you would like to start something new, however…"

Don't, she ordered herself, but it was too late. His mouth was coming down to hers and she was parting her lips in eager reception.

CHAPTER TWO

He knew how to use that sexually explicit mouth of his, firmly capturing her lips in a hot, hard kiss. He slid a hand to the back of her head, rocked his damp mouth across hers, and damn well made love to her mouth like he had the absolute right!

She knew immediately that he was punishing her, but not in a violent way. He wanted her response, wanted to make her melt and succumb to him, to prove his mastery of her and this situation.

And he was doing it, sliding right past her resistance, ready to make her his conquest.

Hard-learned shreds of self-protection rallied. She had trained to meet any attack with an attack of her own.

She kissed him back with all the incensed outrage he had provoked in her, all the frustration that he affected her this powerfully.

She didn't accept his kiss. She matched it. She stepped into his space so the heat off his body penetrated the silk she wore, branding her skin through it. Then she scraped her teeth in a threat across his bottom lip and stabbed her own fingers into his hair. It was completely unlike her to be sexually aggressive, but how dare he come in here with his accusations and intimidations?

Did this feel like she was daunted? Did it?

She felt the surprise in him, and the hardening as he grew excited.

His reaction fed hers. The quickening of arousal in her swelled, rising like a tide that picked her off her feet, washing her in heat, sensitizing her skin and making her hyperaware of her erogenous zones. Her back arched to crush her breasts against his hard chest. Her pelvis nudged into the shape behind his fly, inciting both of them.

His arms tightened around her and he kissed her harder. Not taking control so much as pressing his foot to the accelerator so they burned hotter and faster down the track they were on. His hand slid down to her backside, possessively claiming a plump cheek through silk.

The sensation was so acutely good, the moment rushing so fast beyond her control, Angelique pulled back to release a small moan and gasp for air.

He growled and ran his mouth down her throat, now angling her hips into his so he ground himself against her with blatant intention.

She let him, completely overcome by the moment. She was used to being treated somewhere between a trophy and a revered goddess on a pedestal. No man had ever kissed her like a woman who was not just wanted, but *craved*. This was *real*.

It felt earthy and elemental.

Pure.

She let her head hang back, hair falling freely, and maybe, yes, she was succumbing, but not to him. To this. *Them*. What they were creating together.

He muttered something that sounded like an incantation and his lips moved from her collarbone to the line of her camisole.

She gasped, "Yes," aching for him to bare her breasts to his mouth, she felt so full and tight. When his hand moved up to her chest to caress along the edge—

Wait.

"Don't—" she tried to say, but he had already picked up the silver disk of her pendant to move it over her shoulder.

One second, Kasim was sunk deep in arousal, well on his way to making love with a woman of exceptional passion.

Then the door crashed open and men burst in with guns drawn.

His heart exploded.

He instinctively tried to shove Angelique behind him, but she resisted, shouting, "I'm fine! Orchid, orchid! Stand down. Orchid!"

She held out a splayed hand like it could deflect bullets and tried to scramble in front of *him*, as if she could protect him with that soft, slender figure, but Kasim was pumped with as much adrenaline as the invaders. He locked his arms protectively around her while his brain belatedly caught up to recognize that these were guards he'd seen on his way in.

"I'm fine," Angelique insisted in a shaken tone. "Stand down. Seriously," she said with a look up at Kasim that was naked and mortified. "Let me go so I can defuse this." Her hand pressed his shoulder.

Kasim's arms were banded so firmly around her, he had to consciously force himself to relax his muscles.

"I'm fine," she assured her guards as she slid away from him. She was visibly shaking. "Honestly. This was my fault. He was looking at my necklace. I should have warned him to be careful."

Looking at her necklace? Her lipstick was smudged and she was bright red from her forehead to the line of her top. Her guards weren't stupid.

They were professionals, however. One said, "Second level?"

"Water lily, and did you really?" She went across to a panel and reset something, then sighed and crossed to her desk to pick up her smartphone with a hand that still trembled. "Thank you. Please resume your stations."

The guards holstered their weapons and retreated, closing the door behind them.

While her phone rang with the video call she'd placed, she plucked a tissue and leaned into a small desk mirror to hurriedly wipe her mouth. "This will only take a sec, but if I don't—"

A male voice barked a gruff *"Oui."*

"Bonjour, Henri." Angelique tilted the phone so she could see the screen. She still looked somewhere between dumbfounded and grossly embarrassed, but was trying to paste a brave smile over it.

Kasim was utterly poleaxed. That kiss had been so intensely pleasurable, all he could think about was continuing from where they'd left off. *Get off the phone.*

"Je m'excuse. Totally my fault," Angelique continued. "False alarm. Orchid, orchid. It was only a drill."

"Qu'est ce qui c'est passé?"

"Long story and I'm in the middle of something. Can I call you later?"

"I'm looking at the security records."

Angelique closed her eyes in a small wince. "Yes," she said in a beleaguered tone, as though answering an unasked question. "The prince is still here. May I *please* call you later?"

"One hour," he directed and they ended the call.

Angelique dropped the phone onto her desktop and let out an exasperated breath.

"Ramon will be next. My other brother," she provided, nodding as her phone dinged. "There he is. Spanish Inquisition." She clasped her hands and looked to the ceiling with mock delight. "So fun! *Thanks.*"

"You're blaming me?" He hadn't thought he could be more astonished by all that had just happened.

She shrugged as she acknowledged the text, then dropped the phone again.

Moving to the shelf in the corner, she said, "How about that coffee?"

Angelique moved to where the French press had been sitting so long it bordered on tepid. She shakily pushed down the plunger and poured two short cups, needing something to calm her nerves.

Yes, let's not cause a rift with the wedding, Angelique, by having the Prince of Zhamair shot dead in your office.

What had happened to her that she'd let him kiss her like that? From the moment he'd walked in here, he'd been tapping a chisel into her. Now she was fully cracked open, all of her usual defenses and tricks of misdirection useless. It took everything she had not to let him see how thoroughly he'd thrown her off her game.

"Cream and sugar?" she asked, buying time before she had to turn around.

"Black."

She finished pouring and made herself face him.

He paused in using his handkerchief to check for traces of her lipstick against his mouth and tucked it away. He looked positively unruffled as he took one cup and saucer from her, his steady grip cutting the clatter of china down by half.

She quickly picked her own cup off its saucer and took a bolstering sip of the one she'd doctored into a syrupy milk shake.

The silence thickened.

She tried to think of something to say, but her mind raced to make sense of their kiss. What had he meant about starting something new? What did he even think of her now? Her level of security on its best days had suitors running for the hills.

He wasn't a suitor, she reminded herself. He was an arrogant dictator who had his wires crossed. That's why she'd grabbed his arm. She hadn't been able to let him leave thinking the worst. *Demanding* the worst.

"I wondered about the gauntlet of security I had to run in order to get in here," he said, eyeing her thoughtfully. "I didn't realize this was still such an issue for your family."

Yes, let's talk about my sister's kidnapping and how it continues to affect all of us. Her favorite topic.

"We're very vigilant about keeping it a nonissue. As you witnessed." She was trying to forget how horrifying it had been to have her guards interrupt the best kiss of her life because she'd been too dazed by it to prevent a rookie error with the panic button.

But she supposed the kidnapping was the reason this meeting had come about, ever rippling from the past into the future, so… Very well. There were days they revisited that dark time and this was one of them.

As she made that decision, she was able to move behind her desk and set her coffee aside with a modicum of control. Flicking her gaze, she invited him to take a chair.

"I'll stand."

"Suit yourself. Either way I know I've captured your full attention." She clasped her hands on her desktop, trying to steady herself. "I mean that literally. You won't be allowed to leave until I say you may."

He snorted, but she could see she did, indeed, have his full attention. She felt the heat of his gaze like the sun at the equator.

She swallowed. Good thing she was still wearing her pendant. Too bad he knew about it. She resisted the urge to grasp it for reassurance.

"The advantage that you continue to possess," she said, trying to mollify him, "is that you're willing to refuse the clothes we've made for your sister. I've heard all you said about wanting to protect her. I feel the same toward my own sister."

Empathy. Step two of a hostage negotiation. This was good practice, she told herself. Another drill.

"You're obviously aware of the general details of Trella's kidnapping." She had to swallow to ease how quickly those words tightened her throat. Her knuckles gleamed like polished bone buttons, but she couldn't make her hands relax.

"I know what was on the news at the time, yes."

She glanced at him, not sure what she expected to see. Avarice, maybe. People always wanted gruesome details beyond the basics of a nine-year-old girl being set up by a math tutor as boarding school was letting out, held for five days and found by police before money changed hands. There'd been more than one probing question today from different women in Hasna's bridal party.

Angelique was adept at dodging those inquiries, but they rubbed like salt in a cut every single time.

Kasim was next to impossible to read, but there was

an air of patience in him, like he understood this wasn't easy for her and was willing to wait.

Great. Now her eyes began to sting. She was a crier, unfortunately. She already knew there would be tears later, when she spoke to her brothers. It wasn't because she was upset by the false alarm, just that when a roller coaster like today happened, she tended to fall apart at some point as a sort of release.

She pushed the Remind Me Later button on her breakdown and strained her back to a posture she thought might snap her in two, but was enough to keep her composure in place.

"What's never been made public is Sadiq's part in helping us retrieve Trella."

Kasim set his cup into its saucer and placed it on the corner of her desk. Folded his arms. "Go on."

"You can't simply accept that this is the reason we feel a debt to him?"

"Your brother could give him shares in Sauveterre International, if that was the case. Your other one, the one who races, could buy him a car. Why this?"

"Sadiq is very modest. He has refused all the different times we've tried to offer any sort of compensation. He doesn't brag about his connection to our family. In every way he can, he protects our privacy. That's why we love him."

She took another brief sip of her overly sweetened coffee, trying to find the right words.

"As you've pointed out, his family has plenty of money. Gifting him shares would be…a gesture, not something meaningful. He's not the least bit into cars the way Ramon is, but when your sister mentioned she was going to approach us about making her gown, Sadiq was excited that he had an in."

Maison des Jumeaux wasn't exclusive because it was expensive—although it was obscenely so. No, their clothes were coveted because she and Trella were extremely selective about the clients they took on, always protecting their own privacy first. Gossipy socialites didn't even get an appointment, let alone an original ball gown with a hand-sewn signature label.

"Sadiq only prevailed on our friendship to ask that we accept her as a client, but of course we wanted to do it and of course we wouldn't charge him. He *wanted* to pay. I think the only reason he's letting us get away with not charging is because it's really Hasna who benefits, not him. For Trella, it's a way to repay Sadiq *herself*. It's very important to all of us, for her sake, that she be allowed to do that."

It was part of her sister's healing process. Attending the wedding had become a goal Trella was determined to achieve, come hell or high water.

"Is your sister having an affair with him?"

"That's what you got from everything I just said? No! And neither is my mother, before you go *there*. Family money paid for the materials and Trella and I are doing the work. This isn't a buy off or an attempt to hold something over Sadiq. We're contributing to his special day in the way that makes him happiest. That's *all*."

He pondered that with a raspy scrape of his bent fingers beneath his jaw.

"You still don't believe me?" What on earth would it *take*?

"How did he help solve the kidnapping? How old was he? Fifteen? Sixteen?" His voice was thick with skepticism. "How well did he even know your family? I understood he only went to Switzerland when he began prepping for university."

"I trust this conversation won't leave this room? Because the police asked us to keep it confidential and we always have. We never speak publicly about the kidnapping because there are many details we wish to keep private."

"Of course," he muttered testily, as though he was insulted she would question his integrity.

"You know Sadiq is a bit of a computer whiz? Well, the internet was quite young and few tools had been developed for online sleuthing. It probably wouldn't even be legal now, the kind of hacking he'd done, but who cares? We have him to thank for Trella's return. And you're right that he only knew *of* us. We weren't friends yet. He was in a few classes with my brothers, but when Trella was taken, he was on the steps beside Ramon. He saw it happen and was horrified. He wanted to help and used his own time, hours and hours I might add, to create software code that produced a lead that panned out for the police. If you want more information, you can take it up with Sadiq."

The truth was, Sadiq was a security specialist. He'd merely been a nerd with a passion at that time, but now it was his private business—literally his confidential side job that she only knew about because her family had introduced him to the man who had the contract for their own security. She didn't know if even Hasna was aware that Sadiq wrote code for Tec-Sec Industries.

"There aren't many people we trust unequivocally, but Sadiq is one of them. He didn't do us a *favor*. He saved my sister's *life*. So if he wants me to make dresses for your sister for the rest of my life, I will. Happily. Without checking with *you* first."

CHAPTER THREE

KASIM HADN'T EXPECTED her to admit outright that she had had an affair with Sadiq, but he hadn't expected an explanation like this, either. It shed an entirely different light on things. He couldn't help but believe her.

Of course, she had done her best to scramble his brain with that kiss, so he forced himself to proceed cautiously.

"I'll allow that Sadiq is what the Americans call a 'geek.' He *is* very modest and I've seen that do-good streak. He always seems sincere in his kindness toward Hasna. I can believe he would take it upon himself to help a stranger's family. But I will check this with him," he warned.

"Be my guest!"

Sadiq would back her story regardless. It was a far more tasteful explanation than admitting he'd had an affair with her. It was more tasteful to *him*, Kasim acknowledged darkly.

"I may have to relay some of this to my parents." He was sorry now that his mother knew anything about this. She had already used the waiving of payment to stir up his father, basking in the importance of being the one to inform the king that there might be a scandal attached to their daughter's wedding. She could easily have put the wedding itself in jeopardy in her quest for her husband's attention, ever in competition with the king's consort, Fatina.

It was exhausting and, given his father's blood pressure and enlarged heart, Kasim expected his mother to show more sense. It was almost as if she was *trying* to provoke a heart attack. Maybe she was. Hell hath no fury, as the saying went, but at least he could defuse her latest damage with this information.

"If that's what it takes to keep both our sisters from suffering profound disappointment, fine," Angelique said stiffly, rising. "I trust they will also keep that information confidential."

"They will," he promised, brushing aside politics at home as he realized she was trying to kick him out.

He wasn't ready to leave.

His mind had barely left their kiss. The way she had responded like a boxer coming into a ring had been exhilarating.

"Have dinner with me," he said.

"Pah! Are you serious?" She blinked her mossy eyes at him. *"Why?"*

It was a completely singular reaction. Women cozied up to him and *begged* for an invitation to dine with him.

"We have more to talk about."

"Like?"

He dropped his gaze to the pink-stained tissue crumpled on her desk.

She blushed, but it wasn't all embarrassment. There was memory there, too. One that made her flush into her chest. The knowledge she was growing aroused again stimulated all the latent signals of his own desire.

Angelique looked away. "That was a mistake."

"It was an effective distraction," he allowed.

Her gaze flashed back to his. "That was *not* what I was trying to do."

He shrugged. "Nevertheless, it put certain possibilities on the table." He was already imagining that same explosive passion colliding on silk sheets. Or this desk she stood behind.

"I can't," she dismissed crisply.

"Why not?" A thought struck. "Are you in a relationship?" He tensed, dismayed.

"I wouldn't have kissed you if I was, would I?"

"I don't know." He relaxed, starting to enjoy that pique of hers. It put a pretty glow in her eyes and revealed the intoxicating passion he'd tasted on her lips. "This is why we should have dinner. So we can get to know one another."

"Are *you* in a relationship?" she shot back.

"No." He scowled, not used to anyone asking questions so direct and personal.

She relaxed slightly, but her brow quickly crinkled in consternation. "Do you want to talk more about Sadiq? You still don't believe me?"

"I want to go on a date, Angelique. I would think that was obvious."

"A *date.*"

How could that take her aback? She actually retreated a half step. Her brows gave a surprised twitch, then, oddly, she looked uncertain. She dropped her gaze to her desktop. Bashful?

"I rarely date."

"Then it should be a treat to have dinner with me."

She laughed, which might have been offensive if she didn't have such a pretty, engaging laugh. Her enjoyment was genuine and thorough. At his expense.

"I won't apologize." She held up a hand as she noted the way he folded his arms and set his teeth. "It wasn't your conceit that got to me so much as the painful truth of that remark. You have no idea."

Conceit? He'd been stating a fact.

She ran a fingertip beneath her eye, smile lingering.

"In gratitude for that exceptionally good chuckle, I'll spare you some pain. I attract a lot of attention. I'm really not worth the trouble to take out. I know this because I've been told so more than once." Her amusement faded to something more sincere. Resigned. Maybe even a tad wistful and hurt.

He started to say they could dine alone at his penthouse, then recalled his Paris residence was overrun by his mother and sisters and assorted female relatives.

"Your place then," he said.

She shook her head, but there seemed to be some regret there. "Trella counts on certain spaces being kept private and our flat here is one of them."

That devotion to her sister kept getting to him. The second nature of it. He understood it very well and had to like her for it.

"Dining in public it is, then."

She grew very grave. "I'm serious, Kasim. My sort of notoriety is a punishment. You would be tarred as my lover overnight."

"Since I intend to spend the night with you, where is the harm?"

"Do you?" she scoffed, flushing with indignation. And stirred sensuality.

He saw the deepening of her color and the swirl of speculation behind her gaze. The way she swallowed and licked her lips. Her nipples rose against the light silk of her top and filmy jacket.

He smiled with anticipation.

"That's rather overconfident, isn't it?" she said snippily.

"Don't act surprised, Angelique." He flicked his gaze down to the breasts that had flattened against his chest, the pelvis that had pressed into the thrust of his. "We're very well matched and both intrigued to see where this could go. If you're so eager you don't want to go to dinner first, we can progress to that discovery right here and now. Provided you remove your necklace first."

Her chin was not so narrow as to be pointed, but not so round as to be girlish. It was as perfect as the rest of her. She set it into a stubborn angle and said, "Punishment it is."

She marched past him to the door.

"Maurice," she said as she swung the door open. "A card, please. I'll be dining with the prince later. Would you be kind enough to send someone to scout the restaurant of his choosing?"

She relayed the card to Kasim as he came up behind her. If he wished to be so forward, her glare spat at him, he could suffer the wrath of her *celebrité*.

He wasn't scared. His worst family secret had been painstakingly—and yes, agonizingly—buried. Reports that he had affairs with beautiful women only aided that particular cause.

"Your men can call that number with the details," Angelique said.

He pocketed the card thoughtfully. "I'll pick you up at seven."

"No need. My security will deliver me."

"So cautious." He felt the seeds of irritation forming. Perhaps he didn't care about the notoriety she provoked, but the triple-A level of security could become tiresome. "It's a test?" he guessed. If the arrangements for a simple dinner were too much for him, he was not prepared for the rest of the way she lived, she seemed to be conveying.

"It's my reality," she said with a flat smile.

He annoyed me.

That was the only reason Angelique had agreed to dinner.

Or so she told herself.

And repeated to Trella, when her sister rang through on the tablet before she'd got round to calling Henri.

"What's going on with you?" Trella demanded with a troubled frown. "I'm feeling… I don't know. Restless. Keyed up. Henri texted that your blip was a false alarm, but was it more serious?"

She and her sister didn't keep much from one another. There was no point. They read each other too well.

Not that they were psychic. Angelique never feared Trella could peer into her private moments, but they had an uncanny connection. Despite whatever distance might separate them, they were eerily aware of the other's emotional temperature. They *knew* if the other was happy or sad, angry or scared.

It was one of the reasons Angelique was encouraged to believe Trella was actually getting better this time. The Sauveterres were all paranoid to a point, but for Trella, terror had become her constant companion and a very debilitating one. She didn't *want* to fall apart with anxiety attacks, but for years they had struck without mercy and Angelique had always been aware when they did. It hadn't helped her own sensitive nature one little bit.

Living a cloistered life had leveled out the worst of Trella's episodes, but now she was trying to overcome her fear of being in public so she could go to Sadiq's wedding. It wasn't so much fear of actually being around people or in the public eye that held her back, but fear that any change in her routine would trigger fresh attacks. So it was proving to be a "two steps forward, one back" process, but she was getting there.

Angelique was just as worried that anything could cause Trella to backslide, so she was very firm in stating, "Today was me being an idiot. That's *all*."

She didn't go into detail about the kiss, but gave Trella a good laugh describing the scene as Kasim set off her panic button.

"He said it would be a treat to have dinner with him. I'll show him a treat," she muttered.

"It's been a long time since you went on a date. Even longer since it was someone you were genuinely attracted to," Trella noted.

There went any attempt at disguising from her sister how deeply Kasim affected her.

"I don't know why I am! He's not my usual type at all."

"You don't have a type. You go out with men who make you feel guilty if you turn them down, or sorry for them."

"Well, there's no feeling sorry for this one. He's…" *Indescribable.* She was reacting to him from a completely different place than she'd ever experienced. He didn't pluck her heartstrings as Trella suggested, or tweak her conscience. It was a way deeper reaction than that. He drew her to him.

And made her feel too transparent just thinking about him. She quickly mentioned she still owed Henri a call, but lingered to ask Trella, "Have you noticed… Is something going on with Henri and Cinnia?"

Trella tilted her head in consideration. "He hasn't said anything to me, but now that you say it…"

Henri didn't peep a word about anything unless he wanted it known, but if he did confide a secret, it was to Trella first. They were all close, but they each had their own special relationship with each other. It went all the way back to the day Angelique and Trella were born. Their twin brothers had been allowed to name their sisters and it had created a sense of responsibility in each boy for "his" baby sister.

Ownership, Trella and Angelique had often called it in a mutter to each other. Half the time the boys acted like their sisters were kittens picked up from the animal shelter, but it was a dynamic that had colored their entire lives. They all loved each other equally, but when it had come to holding a sister's hand or pushing her on a swing, they had naturally divided into Henri and Trella, Ramon and Angelique. Oldest with youngest, middle with middle.

Which wasn't to say that Henri was any less protective of Angelique than he was of Trella, or that Ramon was more. Trella's kidnapping had sent the boys' instincts off the scale. Their father's death six years later, when the men were barely twenty-one, had added yet another layer to their self-imposed yokes of responsibility.

Thus both men would insist on an explanation for today's false alarm.

Angelique hung up on her sister and placed the call to both brothers at once, opening with, "I can't talk long. I have a date."

Their identical faces stared back at her, Henri in the

London flat that he often shared with Cinnia, Ramon in the corporate office in Madrid. They both gave her their full attention, but Henri's expression was marginally more severe, Ramon's a shade amused.

"Do you really expect us to believe the 'looking at your necklace' story?" Ramon asked.

"Do you really want a different one?" she challenged.

"Soyez prudent, Gili," Henri said. "He doesn't keep his women long and he has publicly stated that his father will choose his bride—a traditional virgin from Zhamair, no doubt. I wouldn't recommend a romance."

"Hear that, Ramon? Don't get your hopes up."

No smile out of Henri. He really was a grump these days. Angelique scanned behind him for Cinnia. She usually dipped into the screen for at least a quick hello.

"I have to go to Beijing for a week, but I'll be back in Paris after that. You can explain properly then," Henri stated.

Good luck, she thought, suppressing a snort, and took note of how permanent that sounded. *Back in Paris after that.* Henri usually divided his time between Paris and London with occasional popovers to New York and Montreal. More often than not he said "we," meaning him and his companion of two years, Cinnia.

Ramon only introduced his lovers to the family if they happened to bump into each other at a public event. Women were a catch and release sport for him and he was forever on the run anyway, covering Spain, Portugal and all of South America for Sauveterre International. The men were actively working on acquisitions in Asia and Australia, but as Ramon sometimes joked, "We're only one person."

"Trella told me not to bring her tomorrow," Ramon

said abruptly, dark brows pulling into a frown. "Did she tell you that?"

"What? No!" Angelique was taken aback. "I just spoke to her. She said, 'See you tomorrow.' We're going to finish Hasna's gown and start packing everything." Had she blocked her sister from airing some misgivings, too focused on herself and her date with Kasim?

"No, I mean she said she wants to travel to Paris alone. With guards, of course, but she doesn't want me to come with her." Ramon scratched his eyebrow. "It started because I said I was heading to Rio right after and that I had to be there until Sadiq's wedding. She said I shouldn't have to double back and she would go to Paris alone."

"Go with her anyway," Henri ordered. "I'll change my schedule and come get her, if you don't have time. Where is Mama?"

"No!" Angelique interjected. "Boys." They were thirty, but sometimes calling them that was the only way to pull them out of their patriarchal tailspins. "We've always said that Trella has to be allowed to do things in her own time. That meant not pushing before she was ready, but it also means not holding her back when she *is* ready. You know how hard she's trying."

"Exactly why she shouldn't push herself and trigger something. No. I don't like it," Henri said flatly.

"Neither do I," Ramon said.

"Too. *Bad*," Angelique said, even though her own heart was skipping and fluttering with concern for her sister. "I'll be here," she reminded. "It's a couple of hours on the private jet. I do the trip all the time."

"It's different," Ramon grumbled. "You know that."

"Let her do this," Angelique insisted, ignoring the sweat in her palms as she clutched her tight fists. "I'll text her so she knows I can come get her if she changes her mind."

She signed off with warm regards to both her brothers and finished getting ready for her date.

Angelique had to give Kasim credit. He did his homework—or his people did.

He chose a restaurant she and her family frequented for its excellent food and location atop the Makricosta, one of Paris's most luxurious hotels. The staff was also adept at protecting her privacy, not forcing her to walk through the lobby, but willing to arrange an escort from the underground parking through the service elevator.

It always amused her that the most exclusive guests of fine establishments wound up seeing plain Jane lifts and overly bright hallways cluttered with linen carts and racks of dirty food trays.

To her surprise, Kasim was in the elevator when it opened. That instantly sent its ambiance skyrocketing. He was casually elegant in a tailored jacket over a black shirt that was open at the throat.

Her blood surged, filling her with heat. What *was* it about this man?

"I didn't realize you were staying here," she said, trying not to betray his effect on her as she and Maurice stepped in.

"I wasn't. Until I had a date with you." His gaze snared hers and held it.

A jolt of excitement went through her as the suggestiveness in his comment penetrated. *Don't act surprised. We're very well matched...*

She'd never progressed so fast with a man that she'd contemplated sex on a first date. In fact, her advancement to the stage of sharing a bed was so slow, she had only got there a couple of times. Each time she had arrived with great expectation and left with marginal levels of satisfaction.

Now her mind couldn't help straying into sensual curiosity. What would it be like to sleep with Kasim? Their kiss had been very promising. She grew edgy just thinking of it.

"In case you wished to dine unseen," he added almost as an afterthought, with an idle glance at the ever stone-faced Maurice, but with a hint of droll humor deepening the corners of his sex god mouth, like he knew where her mind had gone and was laughing at her for it.

Wicked, impossible man. He had *made* her think about sleeping with him. Deliberately.

She didn't let on that his trick had worked, although her pink cheeks probably gave her away. "The restaurant is fine. I'm rarely bothered there."

The maître d' greeted her warmly by name and assured Kasim it was an honor to serve him. He showed them to a table at a window where a decorative screen had been erected prior to their arrival, enclosing them in a semiprivate alcove.

Kasim held her chair and glanced at the screen as he seated himself. "Apparently we dine unseen regardless."

"Did you want to be seen with me? You wouldn't be the first."

"I wouldn't be ashamed," he said drily. "You're very beautiful. But if you're more comfortable like this, by all means."

Angelique tried not to bask in the compliment as their drink orders were taken. She had freshened her makeup and vetted her outfit over the tablet with Trella, settling on an ivory cocktail dress with a drop waist that ended above her knees in a light flare. The sleeves were overlong and held a belled cuff while the entire concoction was embellished with some of Trella's best work in seed pearls and silver beads.

Public appearances were always this fine balancing act between avoiding being noticed but wanting to show Maison des Jumeaux in its best light if she happened to be photographed, all while trying not to look over-or underdressed for the actual event.

"Judging by what you said today, I didn't think there'd been recent threats. Is this just the vigilance against them that you spoke of?" He nodded at the screen.

"That's me trying to maintain some level of mystery," she joked, but her voice was flat. "Yet another reason I don't bother dating," she expanded. "You already know far more about me than I do about you…not that whatever you've read online is true." She *so* hoped he knew that and wondered why it mattered so much.

"You haven't stalked me?" His brows angled with skepticism. "Asked Hasna about me?"

"I rarely surf at all. Too much chance of running into myself. And no. I'm too protective of my own privacy to invade someone else's." She didn't bring up that Henri had been more than happy to check him out on her behalf. "In my months of working with your sister, she only volunteered the information that you insisted she finish school in exchange for supporting her desire for a love marriage and that you refuse to sing at the wedding, even though your voice is quite good."

He snorted. "It's not. And she's lucky our father is allowing any music at all, let alone a handful of Western tunes. That's it?"

She debated briefly, then admitted quietly, "She told

me you lost your brother a few years ago. I'm very sorry." At least her sister was alive. She was grateful for that every single day.

Kasim looked away to the window as though absorbing a slap.

"I shouldn't have brought it up," she murmured.

"It's public knowledge," he dismissed, bringing his attention back to her with his thoughts and feelings well hidden.

She instantly felt like a hypocrite for claiming she didn't invade others' privacy. She desperately wanted to know what he was thinking behind that stony mask. He fascinated her. That was why she had come to dinner. There. She'd admitted it to herself. She wanted to know more about him.

"It seems I do have the advantage." He shot his cuff as he leaned back to regard her. "In my defense, even the weather and financial pages have click-bait links with your name in them. I can't help but see whichever headline is making the rounds."

"Which is why I look out the window to see if I need an umbrella and ask my doorman for the news. Thank you," she murmured as their wine was poured.

When they were alone, he said, "The story was very compelling. I was about your brothers' age. Hasna was yours. I couldn't help feeling invested in the outcome. I suppose the entire world presumed it gave them a stake in your lives."

The world had presumed a stake in their lives long before her sister was kidnapped. It was one of the reasons her family had been targeted.

She didn't bother lamenting it aloud. Her family had learned to accept what couldn't be changed. Identical twin boys born to a French tycoon and his Spanish aristocrat wife had been fairly unremarkable, but when a pair of identical girls had come along six years later, and the four together had won the genetic lottery on good looks, well, the children had become media darlings without being consulted. She had never been Angelique. She was "one of The Sauveterre Twins."

Which she would never for a moment wish to change. She adored her siblings and wore the designation with pride. It was the attention they relentlessly attracted that exhausted her.

"It's been fifteen years. I would have thought the fascination would have died down," she said with a self-deprecating smile.

"With your sister living in seclusion? It only adds to the mystery." He eyed her as though he wondered if it was a ploy to keep the attention at a fever pitch. "The free exposure can't be hard on business."

"You're wrong," she said bluntly, amused by the way his expression stiffened at being accused of such a thing. "Discretion is one of the most valuable services we offer our clients. The planning of a maternity gown for the red carpet, for instance, when the pregnancy won't be announced until closer to the event. Or a wedding gown when the engagement is still confidential. Sometimes the wedding itself is a secret affair. Trella and I live under such tight security it's fairly easy to extend that amenity to clients."

She sent a pithy look at the screen beside them.

"Until a tourist wants a selfie with me like I'm a historic fountain. Or a shopkeeper wants instant publicity and posts the brand of toothpaste I prefer. And yes, I know I can stay in and buy online. That's what Trella does. But I like to be human and walk in the sun, browse shops for housewares and books. Being followed and photographed while doing it is far more nuisance than benefit and just makes poor Maurice's job harder."

Kasim flicked his gaze beyond her to where she knew Maurice would have been seated at a table with a sight line on her. He was likely sipping a coffee while awaiting a light meal, gaze monitoring the restaurant's employees and patrons.

"It's the reason I don't date," she said, noting where he was looking. "Men don't care to be watched while they attempt to romance a woman."

"It would be a special predilection, wouldn't it? One I don't possess, I'll admit."

She had to chuckle at that, relieved he had a sense of humor about it.

"And if I were merely attempting something that had little chance of success, I might be self-conscious," he added, gaze clashing into hers. "But I'm not."

Oh.

"You're a very confident man." She allowed herself to lean into the fire, to let the heat of his interest warm her cheeks and glow in her eyes. "You come on very strong."

"I didn't expect to find you so intriguing." He held her gaze without actually looking into her eyes. Instead he visually caressed her face, touching her loose hair with his dark gaze. She couldn't look away as he studied her like she was a painting. "A meeting in your office would have sufficed if you'd been less… impassioned. You're not like anyone I've ever encountered."

She had expected another compliment on her looks. This was far more disarming. It made her feel like he saw within her, to the real woman inside, the one few noticed or understood. Plus it was an acknowledgment of something she'd had to work on most of her life: being unique from her sister and being comfortable with her own powerful emotions.

If she wasn't careful, she would be seduced without realizing it. He was very good at it.

"I like your sister, you know. I wouldn't want to hurt her. She's delightful." She waited a beat, deliberate with her timing as she added, "Not much like you at all."

His mouth twitched and he took a thoughtful sip of his wine. His lashes were so thick and long, they were almost pretty, but he was undeniably masculine as he lifted them to regard her. There was nothing soft in the dangerous air he projected.

She held her breath.

"Feel privileged, Angelique. I'm letting you get away with a lot."

She bit the inside of her lip, wondering if she should apologize. Was she ruining this little bit of rapport they'd arrived at?

"Hasna is a lovely person," he agreed. "And you're right. She and I are opposites. Women lead different lives in our country so they grow up with gentler personalities." Something about that statement made him briefly pensive. "At least that's what I've always thought made her so tenderhearted and me more practical and assertive."

"Now you're not so sure?" She tried to read his inscrutable expression. "Supporting her desire for a love marriage sounds rather sentimental, if you ask me."

His cheeks hollowed as though he considered his words carefully.

"She was very upset about losing Jamal. I'm not incapable of compassion. I want her to be happy in her marriage and we've established that we both wish to protect our sisters from heartache, have we not? Is that how you came to open a fashion house with yours?"

She heard that as the shift in topic it was, which intrigued her because something about the way he was trying to compensate Hasna for their brother's loss struck her as guilt. Or responsibility, maybe.

Because she was the sensitive, intuitive one. In some ways it was her burden, but she couldn't deny that she often picked up on things others missed.

"Trella started making her own clothes," she began, then recalled why. Those early years of recovery had been so brutal. As if the kidnapping hadn't been traumatic enough, the press had crucified Trella, dubbing her The Fat One among other things.

"It's not that interesting a story, actually. Just something that both of us enjoyed. We have an artistic flare and work well together so we gave it a shot."

Trella was actually The Smart One. Her business plan had been excellent. The boys would have underwritten anything she'd proposed, to spoil her and give her something she could control and succeed at, but she had been determined to make her mark on the world in a very specific way. Feminine strength imbued every aspect of Maison des Jumeaux. Angelique was deeply proud to be part of it.

"The press makes a lot of the fact that family money gave us our start, but we've paid back the initial loan. I don't know why it's important to me that you know that."

"So I don't think you're chasing Sadiq's money, presumably."

"No." She couldn't help smirking at the way he stiffened every time she contradicted him. "I think it's because I know you respect women who are ambitious and independent. Isn't that why you were so adamant Hasna finish school?"

"No." He waited out the delivery of their appetizers before expanding on his reply. "The more accurate reason is that I didn't want to give my support too quickly or easily because, in order to broker that deal with my father, I promised that my own marriage would be an arranged one. With a suitable bride from my own country, one he could choose. You understand why I'm telling you that."

CHAPTER FOUR

"That's quite a sacrifice." Angelique's eyelids shimmered with golden tones, shielding her thoughts.

"It's duty. My father is not what anyone would call progressive. I have visions of a modern Zhamair. It would be good for our people, but I will never be given the chance to steer it that way if I don't play by his rules. My uncle would be more than happy to accept the crown if my father decided I was too liberal. My uncle is even more of a throwback than my father. So I have agreed to my father's condition. But I'm not in a hurry to give up my freedom."

He let himself admire her smooth skin with its warm glow, her mouth gently pouted in thought. Their kiss was still branding a permanent pattern into his memories—exactly the sort of freedom he was loathe to relinquish by tying himself down.

"You intend to be faithful to your wife, then, once you're married?"

"Certainly until heirs have been established. After that..." He scratched beneath his chin. "My father has two wives. I have not observed having more than one woman coming to your bed to be as idyllic as it sounds."

Her lashes came up, gaze curious as all Westerners were when he mentioned it. "Jealousy?" she guessed.

"How did you know?" Kasim said drily.

He privately thought the polygamy was the reason his father was so ferociously implacable, refusing to evolve with the times or even hold a rational conversation. He consistently asserted his will and slammed doors on further discussion. If he didn't control every aspect of his life with an iron fist, his wives might tear him in two.

That emotional turmoil bleeding all over his childhood was the reason Kasim had grown such a thick shield of detachment. How else could he have withstood the helpless agony of witnessing his brother's struggle? How else could he have been ruthless enough to end it? Taken altogether, it was the reason he was just as happy to marry a stranger. Love provoked madness and pain of every variety.

"Was your father's marriage to the queen an arranged one?"

"It was." He knew where she was going with that. "And it was a contented one until he brought Fatina into it. Which is why I don't intend to do anything similar."

"Because you want to rule," she murmured, gaze narrowed as she weighed that.

"That concern you feel for your sister's well-being? That's how I feel for my entire nation," he explained quietly.

He had never put it in so many words. As her lashes widened at the magnitude of what he was saying, he experienced a lurch in his heart. He had always thought of it as a goal, not a sacrifice. Suddenly he saw it differently.

"None of us are in a hurry to marry," Angelique mused, dropping her gaze again. "We're a tight bunch, my siblings and I. Letting someone into my life means opening all our lives. That demands a lot of trust and we've all been stung at least once, so we're all wary. It's why I don't even bother with affairs anymore, contrary to reports online." She flashed him an admonishing look. "Don't you dare say that if I don't have affairs, it should be a treat to spend a night with you."

"Oh, I'm starting to see the honor will be all mine." He meant it. Everything she had shared pointed to a woman who lived within her own restrictions. No wonder she had exploded in his arms. She was a powder keg of suppressed passion.

She sputtered with laughter, shaking her head. "You are an incredibly arrogant man."

"There is an expression, isn't there? About a kettle and a pot?"

"I'm not arrogant." She dismissed that with a shake of her loose hair and a haughty elevation of her chin.

"You are," he assured her. It was as captivating as the rest of her.

"No." She looked him right in the eye. "My sister is the brash one. Deep down." Her irises reflected the candlelight between them, mesmerizing as the glow of a fire in the blackest night in the desert. Tears gathered to brim her lashes. "I pretend to be."

She blinked to clear the wetness and her eyes widened with forced lightness.

"I am her and she is me. At least, that's how it feels sometimes. Can we talk about something else?"

"I wasn't talking about her. I was talking you into my bed," he pointed out, made cautious by that moment of acute vulnerability. Was it concern for her sister? Or an indication of a deeper sensitivity in her personality?

He recoiled inwardly from that. He had enough emotional drama in his life. He needed her to come to this with as light a heart as he had.

"I want *you*," he stressed. "What will that take, Angelique? Reassurances about your security? I see you've changed your necklace. Is that one rigged?" He winced as he recalled her talk of suitors having to tolerate being constantly under observation. "We're not being recorded, are we?"

"No. This one requires two hands to twist and set it off." She ran the teardrop pearl back and forth on its chain. "So I rarely wear it. In terms of physical safety, I have no concerns about being alone with you. I'm not even worried you would write a tell-all afterward."

"The sting you mentioned? A man did that to you?"

"One did. You can find him living under a false name in whichever Eastern European slum men use to hide when they've been financially ruined by defamation litigation and threatened with castration."

"Your brothers went after him?"

"*I* went after him," she said crossly. "Give me credit."

"Is that a warning? I would never do such a thing," he promised her. "I may be nonchalant about spending the night with a woman, but I don't degrade myself or my partner. You can be assured of my discretion."

Her shoulder hitched in acceptance, but she wore her Mona Lisa expression.

"You're resisting temptation. Why?"

He reached across to take her hand in his, cradling her knuckles in his palm. He used his thumb to catch at hers, pressing her hand open so he held the heel of her palm gently arched open to his touch. He smoothed his thumb to the inside of her wrist, pleased to find her pulse unsteady and fast.

"Is it because it's only one night?"

"No," she said softly. "That's actually a plus. Like I said, I don't fit others into my life very well."

"If you weren't reacting to me, I would finish our meal and send you home, but I can see your struggle against your own feelings. What's holding you back then? You clearly want to."

He caressed that sensitive area at the base of her hand, where a former lover had once told him life and fate lines had their root. *That's why it's such a sensitive place on a woman's body,* she'd said.

Angelique caught her breath.

He didn't believe in the supernatural, but he did believe in nature's ability to create sexual compatibility. That sort of gift should be relished when it was offered.

"My room is just down the hall. Anyone who sees us leave the restaurant will think we're going to the elevators."

He lifted her hand and pressed his lips into her life, into her fate, as he tasted and grew drunk with anticipation.

Oh, he was good.

Her pulse went mad under the brush of his lips and she had to concentrate to draw a breath.

"I told myself I was only coming out to prove to you I wasn't worth the trouble."

"To scare me off? I don't scare."

I do, she wanted to say. She wanted to go to his room so badly it terrified her. And she didn't understand why this want sat like a hook in the middle of her chest, pulling her toward him with a painful sting behind her breastbone. She didn't know how to handle any of this because she wasn't the bold, confident one.

What would Trella do?

It was a habitual thought, one that harked way back to her earliest years when her sister had been the one to stride eagerly forward while Angelique hung back.

She brushed aside thoughts of Trella. She shared almost everything with her twin, but not this. Not him.

That was what scared her. Who was she if not Trella's other half?

An internal tearing sensation made her touch her chest. She immediately felt the beading on her dress and wondered why she had worn Trella's creation. Armor, she supposed, but this wasn't about Trella. That was what made this situation so starkly unique and put her at such a loss.

In this moment she was only Angelique. Except she didn't know what Angelique would do in a situation like this. Her other lovers had wanted one of The Sauveterre Twins and the fame or influence or bragging rights that came with it. She had gone with them hoping for a feeling of fulfillment, but had never found it.

Kasim wanted *her*. That's what made him so irresistible.

And she had a feeling this would be more than fulfilling. Profound. Maybe life-altering.

Which was terrifying in its own way, seeing as it was only for one night, but if she refused him out of fear, she knew she would regret it for the rest of her life.

The lights were set low in the opulent suite. Champagne chilled in a bucket next to an intimately set table overlooking the Eiffel Tower. The muted notes of a French jazz trio coated the air with a sexy moan of a saxophone, subtle bass strings and a brush on a drum.

Angelique was walking into a setup and wasn't even sure how she had arrived here. It felt like she had floated. There had been a conversation with Maurice, who had escorted them down the hall. She had instructed him to go back and finish his own meal and put theirs on hold. Charles, her second guard, stood post at the door of the suite. He had assured her as she entered that he had inspected and secured these rooms prior to her arriving at the restaurant and had been at this door ever since.

They were very mundane details that were decidedly *un*romantic, but they had each been one of the many tiny steps that had carried her toward this moment.

"I am fascinated with this dress," Kasim said, picking up her hand and carrying it over her head, urging her to twirl very slowly before him. "It is a work of art. I'm afraid to touch it." He lowered her hand, but kept it in his, so they were facing one another. "But I want to touch you."

His words made her heart stutter. She tugged free of his grip and walked to an end table where she set down her pocketbook.

"I'm not used to being touched."

"I'm not going to chase you through these rooms, Angelique. If you've changed your mind, say so."

She turned to face him. "I haven't. I'm just nervous."

"Don't be. I won't rush you."

He didn't have to. She was rushing herself, not ignoring misgivings so much as refusing to give in to the natural hesitation that had held her back one way or another most of her life. If her sister hadn't pressed her toward this fashion house idea, she never would have had the nerve.

So part of her was saying, *Don't be impulsive*. But the truth was, this moment had been brewing since their kiss this afternoon.

This was why she had come to dinner with him. She was a person of deep feeling and what he made her feel was too strong to resist. She had never felt so much like herself as she did with this man.

But she wanted to be herself. She wanted him to want Angelique.

She lowered the zip on the back of her dress, slowly drawing the shoulders down her arms and very carefully stepping out of it without letting the skirt brush the floor.

Kasim's inhale was audible over the quiet music, sounding as a long, sharp hiss.

"You, however..." he said in a rasp. "Seem in a big hurry."

"You said you were afraid to touch it." Avoiding looking at him, she took great care with folding the dress in half lengthwise, then gently set it on the arm of the wingback chair.

She was naked except for her high silver shoes and a pair of lavender cheekies that cut a wide swath of lace across her hips and the top half of her buttocks. She had done enough quick changes backstage alongside half-naked models that she wasn't particularly self-conscious.

Nevertheless, it was intimidating to turn and face him. At the same time, it was a rebirth of sorts, standing there naked and vulnerable. Tears flew into her eyes at the significance of shedding the shield of her sister and being only Angelique.

Would he like her?

"What's this?" Kasim murmured, coming forward to cup her face and make her meet his gaze with her wet one.

"I don't often let myself *be*." Life was far easier when

she kept her thoughts on the future or her sister or a piece of fabric. Allowing the moment to coalesce around her, so she experienced the full spectrum of emotions he provoked—impatience and sexual yearning, uncertainty and deep attraction—it was huge and scary.

She smoothed her hand down the lapel of his suit jacket, then warily looked up at him, fearful of what she might find in his gaze.

What she saw made the ground fall away beneath her feet.

His eyes were hungry and fierce, but there was something tender there, too.

"I'll take care of you," he promised in a low growl, then dipped his head to kiss her.

She started slightly as his arms went around her and a jolt of such acute pleasure went through her it was almost like a shock of electricity.

He paused briefly, gentled his kiss. Then, as she pressed into him, encouraging him to continue, he deepened it, sweet yet powerful, making her knees weaken.

They quietly consumed one another. She speared her fingers into his hair and met his tongue with her own and let herself flow wholly into the kiss.

Releasing a jagged noise, he pulled away and threw off his jacket. Yanked at the buttons on his shirt. "Damn you for being so far ahead of me. You do this."

He left his shirt open but tucked in and set his hands on her bare waist, capturing her lips with his as he ran his hands around to her lower back, making her shiver then melt as he molded her closer. They were chest to chest, hot dry skin to hot hairy chest.

A sob of broken pleasure escaped her. More. She needed more of him, and pushed at his shirt, smoothing her hands over the powerful shape of his shoulders.

With a brief pull back, she yanked his shirt free of his pants, then they were embracing again, her hands free to steal beneath the hanging tails of his shirt to caress the warmth of his flexing back.

Skin. Lips. A cold belt buckle against her bare stomach and a hard shape behind his fly that made her both nervous and excited. She had never abandoned herself to desire, had never allowed herself to be so vulnerable, but she didn't have a choice. Time stopped. All she knew was the feel of him stroking her skin, pressing her closer, fondling her breast then looking at where her nipple stabbed at his palm.

He bent and covered the tight bead with his hot mouth, tongue playing in a way that had her shuddering as ripples of pure delight went straight down her middle to pool in her loins. When he moved to the other one, she ran her hands through his hair, loving the feel of the soft spiky strands between her fingers, and spoke his name like an endearment.

A moment later, he dropped to his knees, taking her underpants as he went and leaving them twisted on her shoes as he stroked his hands up and down her thighs, gaze so hot on the flesh he had bared that she felt it. Her inner muscles tightened and a press of moisture wet her lower lips in anticipation.

She closed her eyes, blocking out anything but the sensation of his light touch, so delicate she barely felt the caress at first, but she was so sensitive it took nothing but the graze of a fingertip to make her throb.

Her breath rasped over the music. He stole one taste and she fisted her hand in his hair. Her stomach muscles knotted with excited need.

His caress deepened and she sobbed as glittering sensations poured through her. Her knees wanted to collapse, but she held very still as his lovemaking intensified and her arousal doubled upon itself until she was saying his name over and over, pushing her hips in an erotic rhythm and she was dying, *dying*, because it was so good.

Climax arrived as a wave of pleasure that had her tipping back her head to release her cry of joy toward the ceiling, body shuddering, hard hands on her hips the only way she remained standing.

"Your guards might have heard that," he said with smug lust, rising before her.

Her heart lurched.

His command of her and the moment stung. Not so much the guards hearing, although that was hideously embarrassing. No, it bothered her more that Kasim was significantly less affected by what had just happened than she was. She ought to be feeling like the selfish one, but it felt quite a bit like he had benefited from her giving up her self-control so thoroughly.

He guided her backward onto the sofa. She was so weak she fairly wilted onto it, body still shaking with aftershocks, but she was clearheaded enough to know she wanted him as carried away as she was.

He opened his belt, unzipped his fly and brought a condom from his pocket, all the while studying her like he had every right.

He covered himself and knelt between her knees, drawing her hips to the edge of the cushions and moving a pillow to the small of her back.

"That's very pretty," he said in a lust-filled voice.

The pillow arched her back so her breasts came up a few inches and he bent to suck her nipples again. It was proving to be her greatest weakness, making her close her thighs on his hips and urge him to soothe the ache he incited.

"Do you want me, Angelique?" He kissed her throat. "I want to hear it. Tell me."

"I do," she admitted on a helpless sob, not caring about propriety or modesty. But she did care that she not be alone in her abandonment to passion. She grasped the hot shape of him, feeling the muscle leap under her cautious caress, so hard and promising.

With a determination to make him as wild as she felt, she guided him to where she wanted him and caressed her folds with his tip.

He reared back, stole a look into her I-dare-you expression, and something untamed flashed in his gaze. He hooked his arms beneath her knees and nudged her for entry, pretty much daring her right back. *Take me, then,* he seemed to challenge.

She was very aroused and arched to accept him, but the press of him stretching her made her instinctively flinch. It had been a long time.

His grip on her legs prevented her from closing them, but he felt her reaction. He paused. "What's wrong?"

"Don't stop," she gasped, grabbing at his neck and pulling herself upward against him, angling her hips to take him in and releasing a stifled groan as he filled her.

He made a feral noise and shuddered.

"Gently," he ordered, moving in small, abbreviated strokes, testing her body's arousal and willingness to accept his intrusion.

She lolled back on the cushion, smiling at him in a way she had never imagined smiling at any man, inviting him to have his way with her. Thoroughly. Completely.

"Let them hear both of us this time," she taunted,

and ran her hands over her breasts, cupping them, letting her nipples poke from between her splayed fingers. "Unless you can't wait for me."

He muttered something that was probably an accusation of insolence, but he began moving with powerful strokes, deliberate and measured, watching her to ensure she liked it. She did, unable to help moaning and arching, hands stroking up his arms. She caught at his shoulders and pulled him down while bringing herself up, so they were chest to chest. She lifted her mouth to catch at his in soft, biting kisses.

Soon it became uninhibited and wild. Sweaty and earthy and abandoned. It was incredible. She would have laughed in triumph, but her breaths were nothing but jagged gasps and cries of pleasure. She received him with joy, basked in being his vessel, and told him how good he made her feel.

"Don't stop. Don't ever stop."

The tension built to impossible levels, both of them digging fingernails into the other as they mated, the enjoyment of the act no longer enough. They sought the culmination. It was coming. They were almost there. So close. Tense. Tight.

The world exploded and he covered her mouth with his own, so they were the only two who heard the sounds of ecstasy they made together.

CHAPTER FIVE

KASIM SHOULD HAVE been fast asleep. He was utterly relaxed. Sexually replete. He certainly didn't want to move. The bedsheets were smooth beneath his back, the warmth of Angelique draped over him the only blanket he needed. Her hair felt pleasantly extravagant, spilled across his chest and neck in cool ribbons.

She was falling asleep, twitching lightly as she drifted into slumber, growing heavier against him. Equally sated.

The things they had done to one another. He closed his eyes and a banquet of remembered sensation washed over him. Smooth, soft hands. A wet, lavish mouth. Legs like silk slithering against his own. Her ripples of climax squeezing him again and again.

Not that they'd been particularly adventurous. He generally left the level of exploit to his lover, never needing fancy positions or toys to enjoy himself so long as he had an eager partner. But the sofa hadn't been enough. They had come in here to the bedroom and consumed one another all over again.

It hadn't been mere enthusiasm between them. It had been immersion. For a woman who "didn't do this," Angelique was tremendously willing to throw herself into the fire of passion. He couldn't help but burn right alongside her.

Which was such a disturbing loss of self-governance, part of him was thinking he should rise and take her home right now.

His body reacted to the thought with an involuntary tightening of his arm around her. A fierce urge rocked through him to roll atop her and have her again.

One night was *not* enough.

Sleep, he ordered himself. *Sleep and think clearly in the morning.*

His eyes wouldn't stay closed, preferring to stare at the decorative ceiling tiles, textured with shadows in the mellow light slanting like sunset from the lounge.

He likened his sleeplessness to those few times in his life when a day had been so perfect, he couldn't make himself go to bed and end it. A day in the desert with his father as a child, when the king relaxed and they only concerned themselves with basic needs. Or his last day with his brother, *knowing* he would never see him again…

His heart gave a wrenching twist and he tensed, restraining himself from rolling into Angelique and seeking more than escape into physical pleasure. Comfort?

No. He refused to be that needy.

She drew a long inhale, disturbed by the tension that kept taking a grip on him. She repositioned herself, sighed and relaxed, but he could tell she was awake. He could feel her lashes blinking against his skin.

"I'm thirsty, but I don't want to move," she said in a husk of a voice.

He was starving, but only moved his hand to her head and caressed her scalp through the thick waves of her silky hair.

With a beleaguered sigh, she pulled away and climbed from the bed to go into the bathroom.

Kasim tucked his arm behind his head, listening to the tap run. When she came out of the bathroom in a robe, he rose onto his elbow.

"Come back to bed," he ordered, voice graveled by sexual excess.

"It's already been a very long dinner," she said wryly. "I don't want to give the press more fodder than they might already have." She walked out to the lounge.

Angelique was trembling on the inside, reacting to something so intense it had left her dismantled and exposed.

She gathered her few pieces of clothing and dressed, aware of Kasim coming into the lounge behind her, but she didn't turn to look at him. If she met his gaze, if he was naked, she feared she would find herself back in his bed in a matter of seconds.

With a practiced wriggle, she got the zip fastened up her back, then swept her loose hair back and behind her shoulders. The silk liner on the dress was cool and the beadwork made it feel heavy and stiff. Her sensitive, sensual soul was firmly tucked away behind walls and guards again.

Searching out her pocketbook, she glanced at her phone and saw her brother wanted her to text when she arrived home safely. She rolled her eyes and plucked her lipstick from the velvet interior of her purse. She had already tidied the rest of her face in the bathroom and was determined to look like she had *not* been rolling around with the prince all evening if she happened to be photographed leaving the hotel.

"You don't have to go."

"I should let you sleep," she said, sending him a sly look in the mirror near the door. "You've worked hard."

"That tongue," he said on a breath of laughter, stalking close to catch at her and turn her, drawing her in front of his naked frame. "If you hadn't used it to pleasure every inch of me, I would curse it completely."

Oh, he did not just say that. She blushed. Hard. And she would *not* look to see if he was laughing. Or hardening. She stared at the flex of tendons in his neck.

He chuckled and bent his head to nuzzle against her mouth with his own, murmuring, "I'm rather fond of it, now. Let me say hello again."

He meant "good night," didn't he?

Their lips parted and sealed in a mutual coming together, like polar opposites aligning and locking. His tongue found hers and caressed, making showers of pleasure tingle down her front. She hummed a pleasured noise and pressed into him, trying to assuage the instant rush of greedy desire.

She found him hard and famished. He clutched her with increasing passion, threatening Trella's beautiful beadwork.

She drew back as far as he would let her and had to stifle a pant of pure need. His eyes were like midnight, his desire for her undisguised, from the flush of excitement across his cheekbones to the thrust of flesh pressing into her abdomen.

"Come back to bed." Implacable determination was stamped into his face.

Her heart turned over with helpless yearning.

Defensive, flippant remarks like, *I had a nice time*, threatened to come to her lips, but she found herself speaking more earnestly. Almost begging for clemency. Her stupid eyes grew wet with the conflict inside her.

"I would prefer to keep tonight private, if at all possible." Her voice reflected the arousal he incited and the powerlessness she felt in the face of it. If he pressed, she would stay the night. "If I get caught doing the walk of shame tomorrow morning, it will cheapen something that was actually very nice." She couldn't bear that. She really couldn't.

His eyes narrowed in a brief flinch. His mouth tightened and she thought he was about to demand she stay anyway.

"I'm going to London tomorrow. Come with me."

She blinked, thrown. She had geared herself up for this to be one night. A rush of hope flooded her. *Yes. More.*

Just as quickly, she thought, *No. How?*

Her mind splintered at the complexity of it. Obligation to Trella rushed in to make anything but these few hours impossible.

"I thought… You seemed pretty clear about there being no future." She searched his gaze.

His expression grew shuttered. "One more night, that's all I'm talking about."

Ouch. Right. She smiled her regret, hoping he'd take it as regret at refusing, not the very real regret that this was such a dead-end road.

"The more we see each other, the more likely we are to become a sensation."

"Still trying to scare me off? It is unrealistic to think we won't be found out, that's true. So what? If that's the only obstacle, there is none."

"It's not," she murmured with genuine reluctance, and tried to step away. Maybe when she went to Berlin next week? She would have to think about it. She was never impetuous, least of all about men and allowing them to impact her life.

He locked his arms, not holding her more tightly, but

turning his muscles to steel so she was forced to stand quietly and look up at him. She did *not* hide her disapproval at being manhandled.

"What then?" he queried.

"Trella is coming to Paris."

"So?"

"We have to finish your sister's trousseau."

"Hasna will not be wearing everything you're giving her on her first day of marriage. I will personally take responsibility for anything that arrives late."

"That's not the point." She tried again to pivot away from him.

He kept her in place, not allowing her to screen her emotions or remove herself from his thought-scattering touch. *Infuriating.*

"I never leave Trella alone when she's here." She'd never even considered it because she'd never been tempted. She set her hands on his wrists where he gripped her hips, trying to extricate herself from the lure of him. "Most especially not overnight."

"How old are you?"

"Twenty-four. And don't pass judgment." She could see opinions forming behind his eyes and it was true that they all babied Trella, but there were *reasons*.

Trella was traveling on her own tomorrow, though. Did that mean she was ready for other acts of independence?

Angelique found herself standing acquiescent in Kasim's embrace, considering her own arguments to her brothers about allowing Trella room to find her own confidence.

What if she had a rebound crash as a result, though? She was trying to justify deserting her sister. What was wrong with her?

Berlin, she thought again, because it was further into the future and gave her time to think. This man moved way too fast for her.

"Is security the issue? Your detail can travel with us," he said.

"No. I mean, yes, they would have to. And Henri keeps a flat in London that is completely secure. No, it's Trella. I could ask her..."

"I do not ask permission from strangers to go away with my lover."

"That's not— You don't understand." *Lover.* Her heart pounded with excitement at the sound of that.

"Enlighten me."

"No," she said bluntly. She never talked about Trella's experience. It was hers and nearly killed Angelique every time she revisited it. Her nostrils stung with unshed tears just thinking about it.

His fingertips dug in just a little against the soft flesh of her hips, insisting on possessing her full attention.

"Am I sleeping with you or your sister, Angelique?"

"That's the problem, Kasim. That is exactly the problem," she said as her eyes filled.

Kasim had begun to think she was playing coy, attempting a manipulation as some women were inclined, but the anguish in her beautiful features was real. It caused such a twist of protectiveness in him, he instinctively tightened his arms to draw her nearer.

The old habit of standing between Jamal and the constant threat of harm rose in him, mentally pushing him between Angelique and her sister, making him even more determined to separate her from something that was obviously harming her in some way.

She resisted his attempt to enfold her, bottom lip caught in her teeth, brow pulled into a wrinkle of angst.

With a flex of agitation at the stiffness of her, he pulled away and sought out his pants from the floor where he'd shed them.

"Explain," he commanded as he stepped into them and zipped. He reached for his shirt, slipping it on but leaving it unbuttoned.

"It's hard," she said in a small voice, one hand lifting helplessly. "It doesn't even make sense, really. But it's how I feel." She sighed heavily. "And I am the sensitive one, ruled by my emotions."

She sounded so forlorn.

He folded his arms, trying not to let that niggle at him. He had learned to shield himself against expressions of deep emotion. Too many times in his childhood he'd been bombarded by the pain of others—his mother and Fatina, the king's warring wives, trying to draw him to their side. Jamal's inner torture then Hasna's unrelenting grief...

There was no way to fix the emotional pain of others. He could only protect himself from becoming wound up in it.

Seeing Angelique had demons warned him to cut short whatever this was, but he found himself rooted, willing her to speak. He wanted to understand why she was resisting him. He wanted to help her.

"It was supposed to be me," she said, gaze naked and filled with guilty torment. "The kidnapping. I was the quiet one. The shy one. The one who was bad at math and needed a tutor. It was end of semester and our chauffeur was coming. Trella was already outside. She was the extrovert who wanted to say goodbye to everyone. My tutor called out to her. He thought she was me.

She went over to tell him I would be out soon and he grabbed her." She snapped her fingers. "Just like that. Ramon came out in time to see it happen and chased the van as far as he could, but they'd plotted their getaway very well…"

Her lips were white. Her hand shook as she tucked her hair behind her ear.

"Was she…?" He didn't want to finish the question. What kind of person assaulted a nine-year-old child?

"What happened in those five days is Trella's to tell or not," Angelique said in a voice that quavered. She knew, though. The answer was in her eyes. *Hell*. Whatever it was, it had been hell.

Kasim moved to take her cold hands in his, trying to rub warmth into them.

"You're suffering survivor's guilt," he said quietly. "I understand that." He did. Jamal should be living the life Kasim enjoyed. They were both sons of the king. There was no difference between them except those small characteristics that made every person unique unto themselves.

"The guilt is only part of it. We were already legendary, not that we ever wanted that sort of notoriety, but that's why we were targeted. The Sauveterre Twins, one of Europe's treasures, right? Of course payment would be made for Trella's return. Of course the press went mad at the sensationalism of it."

She cleared her throat, obviously struggling.

"My father had to use that circus to our advantage. I looked just like Trella so they used me as Trella's face, to plea for her return. Any tiny thing could have been the key to getting her back. It was horrible exploitation. He hated himself for doing it to me, but when you're desperate…"

Her eyes filled and she pulled her hand out of his to press the knot of her fist between her breasts.

"All the while… The connection between twins is a real thing, Kasim. It is for Trella and me. I knew she was terrified and suffering. It was unbearable. And then she came back to us so broken and I felt that, too." Her lips quivered.

He had to enfold her in his arms. Had to.

She shook like a tiny animal that had barely escaped certain death.

"She's safe now, hmm?" he coaxed gently into her hair. "Come back, Angelique. That was a long time ago and she's safe. You're both safe now."

She nodded and sniffed once, but he could feel the shudders of dark memory running through her. Her arms went around his waist, beneath his open shirt. The beadwork on her dress abraded his bare skin. He stroked her hair, imparting as much comfort as he could, rubbing his chin against her temple.

"You're afraid to leave her alone, in case something happens again," he surmised.

"I'm afraid all the time of everything." Her cheek was damp where she pressed it to his chest. "That's who I am, Kasim. I'm the worrier. I'm the introvert. But I had to become the strong one. The only way I've ever been able to do that— God, the only way I could find the courage to stand in front of cameras and beg for her return was to pretend I was her. I had to become her in some ways. How could I ever go back to being quiet, shy Angelique who leaned on her sister for confidence? My support was shattered. She needed *me* to be that person."

She wiped at her cheek and settled against him again.

"We should be two carefree young women, but she

was cheated. I know she would have risen to the challenge if it had been me so I have to do that for her. Everything I do is for both of us. Sometimes I feel like I am her and I don't know how to be just me."

Her odd comment at dinner about being each other, which he had thought was a bit of twin peculiarity, now made more sense. So did the one about her not letting herself "be."

"Who were you tonight?" he asked, cupping the side of her neck, invaded by a prickling tension as he urged her to look up at him.

She drew back, but her gaze stayed on her own fingertips as she smoothed the hairs down his breastbone in a petting caress that made shivers of delight travel up his spine.

"I stole tonight for myself."

"Good. That is the correct answer."

She tsked and gave him a little shove. He only settled her closer, pleased when she relaxed and rested her head against his shoulder again, arms looped around his waist.

"But I can't be selfish and take what I want. I can't do that to Trella. Do you understand?"

"You know you cannot live someone else's life for them, don't you?" How many times had he tried to solve Jamal's "problem" to no avail? "You cannot shelter someone forever. It's not fair to either of you. We are each responsible for our own lives."

"I know," she murmured. "Separating my life from my sister's has to happen. We both know that. But I can't force that on her and I certainly won't let you force it. And the truth is…" She tilted back her head to look up at him with a solemn expression. "I am not impulsive. I am a thinker. If you want Angelique to go anywhere with you, you have to give *Angelique* time to put it all together in her pretty little head."

He pondered that, distantly aware he didn't have much time. His father was already talking about finding him a bride as soon as Hasna's wedding was out of the way.

"How much time do you need? I was going to leave first thing in the morning and it's already…" He looked around and swore lightly. "There are no such things as clocks anymore."

Releasing her, he found his cell phone and clicked to see it was nearing midnight. He dropped the phone into his pocket, then left his hand there with it. He raised the other to pinch his bottom lip.

"I have meetings in the morning. Come later in the day. I'll make the arrangements."

"I can make my own arrangements," she informed him, but with a rueful purse of her lips. "Which I realize you just heard as agreement." She sighed and touched her brow. "I could call my mother, see if she feels like spending the night in Paris with Trella. Does anyone ever say no to you, Kasim?"

"They realize very quickly that it is a waste of both our time. You, apparently, are a slow learner."

"Don't," she said with a little flinch. "It's still a sore point for me. I can cut out a perfect square meter of fabric by sight, but ask me to add one half to three quarters and I just embarrass myself. Now I'm going to put on fresh lipstick." Her hand shook as she picked up the little golden tube and pointed it at him. "Keep your lips to yourself."

"Come here first," he commanded, compelled to reinforce the connection between them.

She paused in winding up the stick of color, sent

him a pert look. "Saying 'no' would just be a waste of a layer of lipstick, wouldn't it?"

"Look at you. You're actually very quick to learn."

She rolled her eyes, but she came across to kiss him.

CHAPTER SIX

IF I NEED YOU, I'll call.

Trella's words dogged Angelique as she stole off to London. They weren't telling any of the family that Angelique was leaving Trella for a night on her own in Paris. Better to let it be a fait accompli, they decided, given how reluctant their brothers had been to let Trella make the short flight alone.

Trella had passed her own test "with flying colors," she had excitedly said about her solitary flight, quite triumphant in her achievement.

Angelique had been so proud, she'd had a little cry about it, which had made Trella laugh and hug her and call her their sensitive little Gili.

Nevertheless, Angelique felt guilty for leaving. Trella was very safe. Situated on the top floor of the design house, the Paris flat was ultra-secure. Seamstresses and other staff came and went from the lower floors, working into the night if the mood took, but the flat had its own entrance, a panic room and a private passage to the office.

Trella had been very heartfelt in her plea for Angelique to do something for herself for a change.

I've held you back too long, Trella had insisted, then added with a sly look, *Besides, I'm curious about Henri and Cinnia. See what you can find out.*

Angelique had laughed at that, but if Trella had a setback, she would never forgive herself.

Deep down, however, she was anxious to see Kasim again. It was a foreign state of mind for her. After Trella's experience, she'd spent her adolescence wary of boys and sex. When she finally started to date, she had been hard-pressed to find men who measured up to the standards her father and brothers had set. When her suitors had fallen off because her life was too restrictive, or proved to be social climbers or other opportunists, she'd been annoyed and disappointed, but never truly hurt.

She had never been taken with any man. None had engaged her feelings very deeply and she had never, ever, allowed a man to come between her and her family.

In some ways, she was terrified of the influence Kasim was having on her. He fascinated her and thus had power over her. He was confident and secure in himself, almost brutally honest, but that lack of subterfuge was as seductive as the rest of him.

And oh, did he seduce! From a physical standpoint, she was completely infatuated. Her blood raced as she silently willed the driver into London after the family jet landed at the private airfield.

She hadn't given Trella many details about her evening with Kasim, but her sister had said with a sensual lift of her own hair, *I know you slept with him. Don't deny it. I'm kind of jealous, actually. In a good way. It makes me realize what I'm missing.*

That had made Angelique very self-conscious, but she knew Trella was interpreting her body language. They had the same expressions and mannerisms so even though Angelique could disguise her thoughts and feelings from many, her sister would read the indolent stretch or the warmed cheek and soft gaze of pleasant memory without effort.

Trella didn't tease her for it, and when Angelique studied Trella, she saw nothing but determination in her sister at being left alone this evening.

Kasim had been right about Angelique suffering survivor's guilt. She wondered if it was the reason she had given up so easily on her previous relationships. Being happy when her sister had been struggling had always felt incredibly disloyal.

She still felt disloyal, haring off to London to be with a man, but it was only one night, she told herself. Kasim hadn't promised anything else and neither had she for that matter, even though she felt a yearning for more.

Not that she'd defined exactly what "more" would be. The artist in her appreciated that whatever they had was too new and special for close examination. Deconstruction could kill it. Sometimes you had to go with instinct, then determine after the fact what you had.

Was this instinct? Or greed and selfishness? Or old-fashioned blindness to obvious facts?

Exactly the type of scrutiny she had to avoid, she thought with a stifled sigh.

Whatever it was, it drew her inexorably. Her pulse was racing over a single text from Kasim, promising to meet her at her brother's flat within the hour.

It was actually the family flat. Knowing Henri was in New York, Angelique assumed Cinnia was staying in her own flat, but texted her as a courtesy, mentioning that she was in town and asking if Cinnia wanted to get together for a meal.

Cinnia's reply came through as Angelique was letting herself in. It was a simple regret that she was stay-ing with her mother and was sorry she had missed the chance to visit.

Angelique put her bag in the room she and Trella used, checked that there was a decent bottle of wine in the fridge and moved restlessly into the lounge, won-dering if she and Kasim were going out for dinner and if so, where? What should she wear?

Paparazzi. Ugh, she thought with another sigh, but for once she wasn't filled with as much dread as usual. She would have hated to have her night with Kasim re-duced by the online trolls to a one-night stand, sullied and mocked, even though she'd gone to his room last night convinced it would be only that.

Having this affair extend into a second night made it feel— Well, it still felt so rare and precious she wanted to guard it jealously, but she was so thrilled to see him again, she was willing to pay the price.

"Oh, no," she murmured, jerked from introspection as she caught sight of the coffee table.

A courier envelope had been torn open and the con-tents spilled out. It was at least a hundred thousand euros in jewelry, probably more. It looked like the con-tents of Ali Baba's cave, glittering and sparkling inno-cently against the glass tabletop.

Angelique sat down hard on the sofa, chest tight. She thought about texting Trella, but Henri was the most private of all of them. He would kill her if he knew *she* had seen this. She couldn't share it like tawdry gossip, not even with Trella.

But what had gone wrong?

Henri was adamant in his decision never to marry, but he and Cinnia had seemed so good together. Angelique would have bet real money that Cinnia genuinely loved him. How had those tender feelings become something as harsh as throwing his gifts back in his face?

It was a cool, disturbing reminder that relationships fell into one of two categories: those with a future and those that ended. Her heart chilled, starkly confronted with the kind she had with Kasim.

There wouldn't be a moment of callous rejection between them, though. Not like this. She and Kasim were never going to spend two years together the way Henri had with Cinnia.

Upset for Henri and Cinnia—and disturbed on her own behalf—she pushed the jewelry into the envelope, but the artist in her was drawn to examine the tennis bracelet. She'd never taken a proper look at it. It was a string of alternating pink and white diamonds, one Cinnia had always seemed to be wearing. Angelique was really shocked she'd given it up, especially now that she saw how exquisite it really was. The craftsmanship in the setting was extraordinary. She searched it for an insignia that might tell her where it had come from.

When the door opened behind her, she stood with surprise, expecting Maurice, but it was Kasim. She had told Maurice to expect him, but had thought she'd have to ring him through the main doors downstairs before he would appear up here.

"How did you get in the building?" she asked as she moved to meet him, flushing uncontrollably with instant pleasure.

His mouth tilted with a hint of smugness, as if he read her infatuation and knew how slowly the minutes had passed for her before seeing him again. It was disconcerting, making her feel defenseless and obvious, but she still found herself crossing toward him, tugged by an invisible lasso around her middle.

He waited for the door to shut before he hooked his arm around her and kissed her.

It was proprietary and given how fleeting this affair was likely to be, she should be keeping better control over herself, but her heart soared. She quickly melted into him, instantly transported to the languorous memories of last night and anticipation for more of the same incredible pleasure he'd delivered.

"You missed me," he said when he drew back.

"You didn't miss me?" She tried to sound blasé, tried to pull away, but she was hyperaware of how needy that sounded. How completely easy she was being.

His hand slid to her tailbone and pressed her hips into his enough that she felt how he was reacting to her. "I've been thinking about you," he allowed.

Fluttery joy invaded her abdomen and she tried not to reveal how quickly and thoroughly he'd bowled her over.

"Good to know," she said lightly. "But I am genuinely curious how you got into the building. It's supposed to be locked down for residents only."

"It is. I was given the codes when I bought my flat this morning. Shall we go look at it?" He finally released her and stepped toward the door with a low wave for her to accompany him.

"You—you bought a unit in this building *this morning*?" She had grown up with wealth, but they only owned a flat here because her father had bought it during the design stage, just before his death. The address was obscenely exclusive with a wait list a mile long of international dignitaries and techno-billionaires trying to get in.

Perhaps she had underestimated *how* wealthy and

powerful Kasim was. The cost to jump queue must have been exorbitant.

"It's a good investment. My mother likes London," he said with a shrug. "She'll use it if I don't. Mostly I thought you'd appreciate the privacy. By some miracle, there is nothing online about us. I thought we'd celebrate our lack of infamy by staying in and extending our lucky streak. I've ordered dinner to be delivered in a couple of hours."

"We could have stayed here!" she pointed out.

He offered a pained frown. "I do not steal into a girl's bedroom at her parents' home."

No, he dropped a few million pounds on a suite he was only using for one night. *For her.*

She urged herself not to let that mean too much.

"Shall I change?" She was still wearing her travel clothes, a dark blue jersey skirt with a pale yellow top, both her own design. They were quietly feminine, breezy yet classic and a tiny bit waifish.

"You look beautiful." He skimmed his gaze down and back. "And whatever you wear is only for the elevator."

"You're not even going to pretend you're inviting me to look at etchings?" She planted her hands on her hips, only realizing as she did that she was still holding Cinnia's bracelet. Shoot. She was instantly self-conscious on her brother's behalf. "Um. I just have to put this down and grab my phone."

"What is it?" Kasim asked, catching at her wrist as the snaking sparkle caught his attention.

She opened her hand. "Something Henri bought for Cinnia," she prevaricated.

Her brother's long-term relationship was well documented in the press, but she wasn't going to be the one to start the rumors about its demise.

"I want to ask him where he got it because the work is outstanding. Look at the detail here. You can tell each of these claws has been crimped individually to create this effect all the way along. I'm in awe at how painstaking that would be. Have you ever seen anything like it?"

Kasim's nostrils flared as he picked up the bracelet and gave it a thorough study, his expression pulling into a tension that bordered on agony. As if suddenly realizing how hard he was staring, and that she was watching him, he quickly straightened his features and handed her the bracelet.

"No," he answered belatedly and rather abruptly. "Let's go."

Her heart did a little thump. The mood had definitely shifted. "What's wrong?"

"Nothing."

She was hurt that he would lie so blatantly to her, but moved across to tuck the bracelet into the envelope and picked up her phone.

The silence in the elevator was not precisely thick, but it was significant.

Kasim's cheeks were hollow, his mouth flat.

Maurice was with them, so Angelique kept her own counsel. Her guard went through Kasim's new flat ahead of them, even though Kasim's team had been here all day, ensuring it was not only clean and secure, but furnished and well stocked.

The layout was similar to her family's suite with a lounge opening onto a balcony overlooking the Thames. She imagined the door next to the wet bar led to the kitchen, as it did in their own. Down the hall would be the bedrooms and baths.

This one smelled faintly of paint and was filled with contemporary furniture and a handful of decent art pieces. His decorator was competent, if unimaginative, having fallen back on the latest issue of *Colors of the Year* for lack of inspiration.

The moment Maurice left them alone, Kasim drew her into his arms again and kissed her quite passionately. Almost aggressively, questing for a response. It was as if he was trying to propel them into the mindless state they'd experienced last night in Paris.

It was breathlessly exciting, yet made her feel… She wasn't sure and, as her blood began to heat, started not to care.

"Do I not even get a chance to explore the place myself?" she gasped when his mouth traveled to the side of her neck. Arousal suffused her, but she had the sense she was being used as much as desired. It scraped her insides raw.

"If you like," he said, straightening and not looking pleased.

"Have you even seen it?" she asked, trying to recover and stung by the distance she sensed between them.

"I'm more interested in this." His lashes cut downward as he slid his gaze to her toes and came back to her lips.

His ravenous gaze made her skin tighten, but her heart squeezed at the same time. She *knew* he was sublimating something.

"Kasim." She cupped his jaw. "What has upset you?"

"I'm not upset." He pulled away from her touch and moved to the bar. "Children get upset. Do you want wine?"

He was speaking shortly. Irritably. Like he was upset, she thought drily.

"Something about the bracelet bothered you. Did you recognize it?" She was intuitive that way. She just was.

"You can tell me what it was, or I can make up stories of my own to explain your reaction."

"I've never seen it," he said flatly, setting out two wineglasses. "But the workmanship reminded me of Jamal's. He designed jewelry."

He wound the screw into the cork with a little squeaking noise and pulled it out with a pop, movements jerky, facial muscles still tense.

"My father hated it. He took it as a reflection against his own masculinity. An insult. He was ashamed to have a son who was…artistic," he pronounced with disdain. "My mother used that to her advantage."

"What do you mean?"

He poured, steadying the bottoms of each glass with two fingers as he did.

"Jamal is—was Fatina's son. My father's second wife. My mother…"

He set aside the bottle. For a moment he was a man on the verge of exploding, wrapped tightly, but packed to the eyebrows with dynamite, fuse burning in his eyes.

"Children should not be used as weapons, but my mother loved to find fault with him. To his face, to my father, in public. However she could humiliate him and Fatina, she did it. In sly ways, though. Small little stabs. Death by a thousand cuts," he said grimly.

"That's horrible."

"It was. And my father was determined to turn him into something he could be proud of. That was his way of countering my mother's attacks, by telling Jamal he was to blame for her criticisms. If he only changed, we would all have peace. I'm furious every time I'm reminded of how it was for him."

"You couldn't make your father see reason?"

He snorted. "This?" He lifted his glass and touched

it to the rim of hers. "I don't care one way or another for alcohol, but it is completely outlawed in Zhamair. It's not a religious restriction. We have as many citizens who are Christian or Jewish as we do Muslims in our country, but my father's word is rule. My father is a dictator in the way that political scientists define one."

"But you do what you want when you're away," she noted with a glance at his Western clothes. "Couldn't your brother have done that? I'm sorry, I know it's very easy to say that he should leave his country and turn his back on his father. It's not something anyone would do without deep struggle, but…"

"No," Kasim agreed in a hard, grim voice. "It's not. Especially since it meant leaving his mother and the rest of his siblings. Fatina has four younger children, as well. And he felt my father's rejection very deeply. He wanted desperately to earn his respect. It was an impossible situation for him."

"That's so awful." Her heart ached for not just his brother, but for Kasim. No wonder he wanted to take the reins from a man who possessed no hint of compassion or empathy. No wonder he had fought so hard for Hasna to have a love marriage.

"How did he die?" she asked softly, then clutched where the pang in her chest had intensified. She could see the anguish still fresh in Kasim's face. "It wasn't suicide, was it?"

Kasim didn't speak, only stared into his wine for a long moment. His fingernails were so white where he clutched the stem of his glass, she though he would snap the crystal. His gaze came up and she thought he looked about to say something.

In the next second, he shut down, mouth flattening into a sealed line before he finally said in a neutral, almost practiced, voice, "It was a car crash. We were in Morocco on business. He was out on his own along a stretch of road near the ocean. He wasn't reckless by nature, but he was under a lot of pressure from my father to give up the jewelry design, work with me full-time and marry suitably."

His expression was filled with perturbed memories.

"The car went through the guardrail into the rocks below. Calling my father with the news was hard, but facing Fatina and Hasna, and my younger brothers and sisters…"

The torment in his expression was too much to bear. So much guilt, but how could he have prevented it? It was just a terrible accident. He shouldn't blame himself.

She set aside her glass and came around the bar to slide her arms around his waist. "I'm sorry."

"Why? You had nothing to do with it." He continued to hold his glass, his other arm hanging at his side, stiff and unresponsive to her embrace. He looked down his nose at her.

"I shouldn't have forced you to revisit his loss."

She felt the flinch go through him. He sipped, stony as a column of marble that didn't give under the lean of her weight, only supported her with cold, indifferent strength. "The bracelet did that."

"And you wanted me to help you think of nicer things." She traced her fingertips up the line of his spine through the back of his shirt, trying to reach him through physical contact since he seemed to have shut her out emotionally. "Now I will. If you like."

"What about your great explore?" He didn't bend at all.

"I've seen a flat just like this one. But this…" She brought her hands around to climb his chest and brush his suit jacket open, nudging it to fall back off his shoulders. "This territory is still new to me."

She was trying to be bold, to find the affinity they had shared in Paris, but was highly unsure when he failed to respond. Self-doubt, her great nemesis, twisted through her.

"I plan to be very thorough in my mapping of it," she said, voice wavering as she became convinced he was about to reject her.

"You're liable to see nothing but this ceiling for the next hour," he warned, setting aside his glass and clasping her hips in heavy hands.

"Maybe that's all *you'll* see," she said with a tremble of relief. "Did you think of that?"

Kasim had almost told her the truth about Jamal. It was a stunning break in his normal vigilance against any woman's intrusion into his inner world.

Idly caressing from the back of her thigh over the curve of her buttock to the hollow in the small of her back, he wondered how this smooth golden skin had come to get so far under his own in such a short amount of time.

He didn't regard women as a Western indulgence he allowed himself when he traveled, but he did treat his sexual relationships much as he did his business ones. Some were brief transactions, some longer term, but they were exchanges and trades, always agreements with clear parameters. Paramours didn't cause him to rearrange his life and they rarely stimulated more than his libido.

This one, however... He had made a ridiculously large transfer this morning so he could protect their privacy, mindful of her request last night to keep the world from cheapening their association.

Why? What did he care if their association was known or in what context? He would eagerly show her off. The idea of staking a public claim held a great deal of pleasure for him, in fact.

He very carefully blocked the vision of any other man thumbing into the small dimples at the top of each of her firm, round cheeks, then he lightly traced the line that separated them, fingertips claiming Angelique's backside along with the rest of her, sweeping the back of her thigh and taking possession of her calf.

He had grown up watching his father deal with the fallout of indulging unfettered lust. Every person was susceptible to being attracted to the wrong person— or rather, an inconvenient person in relation to the life they led. Giving in to that desire was the root of whatever problems arose.

Kasim had always regarded himself as superior to his father and brother. *He* was capable of rising above the temptations that foretold complications.

Was he kidding himself, believing this thing with Angelique was a trouble-free dalliance that could end tomorrow morning with a light kiss and a "pleasant knowing you"?

An uncomfortable bolt of rejection shot through him, not just resisting the idea of walking away, but outright refusing to countenance it. His reaction was so visceral, his hand closed in a small squeeze where it rested above the back of her knee. He was literally holding on to her and he'd only *thought* about the inevitable parting that awaited them.

It was a sobering confrontation with his inner animal, the one he had always been so sure he governed without effort.

"I'm awake," she murmured on a contented sigh,

as if she took his grip to be a test of her level of consciousness.

She turned her head so she could blink dreamy eyes at him while keeping her face mostly buried in her folded arms and the fall of her magnificent hair. "Just thinking. Do you want to meet me in Berlin next weekend? I have a thing."

He had places to be, people to rise above.

"I thought we were staying out of the spotlight."

Her sleepy smile slowly warmed to something vulnerable yet elated. It made his heart swerve and swell.

"I was really asking if you wanted to see me again after tonight." The tone in her voice caused a pleasant-painful vibration through him.

He looked at where his hand was still firm on the back of her thigh. "I fear for our lives at the rate we're going, but I was going to ask you to stay the weekend. I have to escort my mother and sister back to Zhamair on Sunday, but I will arrange to take them back late." He would also cancel his lunch arrangements for tomorrow with his foreign secretary and the British counterpart.

"I wasn't planning to spend the weekend," she said, last night's troubled light coming into her eye. Her sister again.

"No?" He tensed and felt her hamstring flex against his light grip.

Guilt and longing fought for dominance in her gaze. She released a soft moan of struggle and gave a taut stretch beneath his touch.

"I will if I can arrange it." Her tone echoed with something like defeat.

He began to pet her again, blood tingling as he fondled her with more purpose. He wasn't used to a woman resisting him. It made him restless for her capitulation.

Not something forced. No, he needed her to give herself up to him.

Rolling her over, he began to kiss her, running his mouth to all the places that made her arch and moan under him, impressing on her the benefit of belonging to him. As he felt the tension in her, the clasp of nearing climax, he kissed his way back up the center of her torso.

"Tell me what you want."

"You know," she sobbed, moving against his hand, but he followed her undulations, keeping his penetration shallow and light.

"You want this?" he very slowly and gently deepened his caress, deliberately holding her on the plane of acute pleasure she occupied, not letting her tumble into orgasm. "Or this?"

He rolled atop her and loved the saw of her breath as she gasped in a sensual agony. Holding himself in a tight fist, fighting back from his own approaching peak, he rubbed his aching tip against her slick folds, nudging at her with promise.

She danced and angled her hips, trying to capture him.

He shook with want, barely able to see straight, but made himself hold off and only kiss her. "What will you do for me?"

"Anything," she gasped, but opened her eyes. They were shiny with helpless torture, a hint of resentment even. She knew what he was demanding. *Her.*

He cupped her head and slowly, slowly sank into her. Their breaths mingled as their bodies joined, both of them parting their lips to release jagged noises of intense pleasure.

How could she resent this? How?

He made love to her then, sending her over the edge, then keeping her aroused so they were damned near clawing each other when the next crest approached. He didn't think he could wait for her, but he wanted her with him. Demanded it with the hard thrust of his hips against her. *Needed it.*

She locked herself around him and released a keening noise, shuddering beneath him. The greedy clasp of her sheath triggered his own climax and he shouted in triumph as he joined her in the paroxysm.

Angelique was a little stunned by what she'd just experienced. Not just the ferocity of Kasim's lovemaking. She'd been so aroused, she had craved that intensity, but there'd been a loss of self in that joining. He had been the only thing important to her. It left her scrambling to recover her sense of autonomy, while he made it impossible by rolling back into her and running proprietary hands over her still-tingling skin.

The condom was gone along with his urgency. Now he was the tender man whose touch was soothing and reassuring. He almost lulled her back into thinking everything about him was safe, but it wasn't. He imperiled the very heart of her.

She put up an instinctive hand against his chest, resisting his effort to pull her into a sprawl across his sweat-damp body.

"What's wrong?" He picked up her hand and lightly bit her fingertip, then kissed the same spot. "I can't make promises about Berlin, but I will try. Good enough?"

He sounded languid and satisfied while she was completely dismantled.

"Is it because we might be found out?" She had been

trying to think how they could continue on the sly, but couldn't see a way, not unless he wanted to go broke buying private flats. He hadn't seemed particularly worried about exposure anyway. "Would it be complicated for you with Hasna if something wound up in the press?"

He snorted. "I don't consult *my* sister on how I conduct my private life."

There. *That* was the issue. He resented her sister. She stiffened and tried to pull away.

"That was a cheap shot," he allowed, arms clamping like a straitjacket around her. "I take it back."

"No!" She turned her face away. "You don't get to kiss me into forgetting you said it."

He sighed against her cheek.

"I'm spoiled," he stated without compunction. "Never second fiddle to anyone except my father and that is a finite situation, not that I wish his life away. I only mean that I am his heir and aside from him, I am autonomous."

"Yet I'm supposed to be content as a second fiddle in your life."

A long pause that was so loaded, she had to glance warily at him, fearful she'd truly angered him.

Maybe she hadn't angered him, but she'd scored a point. She could see echoes of his mood earlier when he'd talked about his mother's brutal treatment of his father's second wife and his half brother.

"I have meetings all next week," he said in a cool tone. "Roundtable discussions with a dozen of our region's most powerful leaders. You must have an idea of our political and economic landscape? The stakes are always high. I go so my father won't or he'll send us back to the Stone Age. The conference could easily go into next weekend. That is the only reason I am avoiding saying yes to Berlin."

"Fine." Now she felt like she'd pressured a concession of sorts from him, but it was a hollow victory. "It was just a thought."

"What are you doing there?" His tone wasn't patronizing, but she read his question as an attempt to mollify her and move past their conflict.

"A fashion awards night." She glossed over it. "There's a white tie and champagne thing after. I'm presenting so I can't skip it. You'd probably find it boring anyway."

"Do you do a lot of these things? Who do you usually go with?"

She would not kid herself that he sounded jealous.

"Colleagues. Sometimes one of my brothers. Honestly, it's fine. I'm supposed to be at a thing tonight and—" She'd forgotten to cancel, she realized. She had decided not to go once she realized Trella would be in town, but had paid the plate fee because it was a charity she liked to support. It wasn't a big deal that she was a no-show. She shouldn't be experiencing this stab of guilt.

All part of Kasim's magnifying effect on her emotions, she supposed. She frowned, aware of a cloud of traitorousness blanketing her too, along with a niggling desire to rebel. She put it all down to letting him extract that surrender to his seduction at the expense of thinking of—

She scrambled out of his arms to sit up. *Trella.*

"What—?" Kasim made a noise.

She kicked away the covers as she scooted off the bed. "I have to check in with Trella."

"Why?"

"I just do," she muttered and quickly shrugged into his robe, tying it tight then leaving to scour the lounge for her cell phone.

Angelique had put down the agitation in her belly to the sound of an invisible clock ticking down on her time with Kasim and all the things that she was doing that were out of character: engaging in an affair, leaving her sister, shunning work responsibilities.

But there was that other plane of awareness that her sister occupied in her unconscious...

Kasim came into the lounge, pants pulled on, but wearing nothing else, blanking her mind. Lord, he was beautiful, moving with economy, sculpted muscles rippling under smooth, swarthy skin. For a moment she forgot to breathe, she was so captivated.

He prowled to where the food had been received and abandoned on the dining table an hour ago. They had been too busy with each other when it arrived to do more than set it aside and get back to bed.

He opened the wicker basket and said, "We should eat before this is stone cold."

When he glanced at her, he caught her ogling. A light smirk touched his gorgeous mouth. He hooked his thumbs in his waistband, so sexy her mouth watered.

"Unless you're hungry for something else?"

She swallowed and ignored the fact her blood turned to lava. It was better that he wouldn't be in Berlin. He had way too much power over her as it was.

"I could eat." She hid her reaction by gathering their still-full wineglasses and bringing them across to the table under his watchful eye.

"Your sister?" he prompted.

"Fine." She bit her lip, flashing him an uncertain look. "She told me not to hurry back."

Take advantage of flying under the radar as long as you can, Trella had texted, but Angelique was still aware of her sister in that peripheral way. Trella wasn't frightened precisely, but she was disturbed.

They had used their authentication codes, though. She knew it was definitely Trella telling her to stay in London, coming across like an adolescent pushing for independence, insisting she was *completely fine*.

Angelique hadn't tried a video call, too embarrassed at how much she would betray, especially wearing Kasim's robe.

"So you'll stay the weekend." Kasim looped his arm around her.

"Do I have a choice?" she challenged tartly.

He stroked the back of his bent finger along her jaw, perhaps looking apologetic, but all he said was "Not if I have anything to do with it, no."

Then he kissed her until she was leaning into him, utterly spellbound.

CHAPTER SEVEN

ASIDE FROM THE odd time when she had become tipsy from having too little to eat before having a glass of wine, Angelique had never been drunk or stoned. Kasim, however, provoked a feeling in her that she imagined one felt when ingesting party pills.

She walked around in a fog of euphoria after London, mood swinging wildly. One minute she was lost in recalling how they had essentially spent two solid days in bed, rising only to eat and make love elsewhere in the flat: the sofa, the kitchen chair, the shower. It made her too blissed out to care about the lost shipment of linen or the hundreds of euros in hand-made bobbin lace that wound up attached to the wrong gown.

The next minute she plummeted into a withdrawal depression, certain she'd never hear from him again. With his hand buried in her hair, he had kissed her deeply late Sunday afternoon, both of them aware cars and planes were waiting for them. He had finally released her, saying, "You won't hear from me. I'll be tied up in meetings. I'll try to meet you in Berlin. If I can't, we'll figure out something for the following week."

Would they, though? She wished they'd made a clean break of it. She could have handled that. This veering between hope and despair was too much!

If Trella noticed Angelique's distraction, she didn't say anything. She was immersed in finishing Hasna's wardrobe, almost obsessing over each piece, working late and rising early to ensure everything was perfect. She seemed really wound up about it when she was usually the coolheaded one about deadlines and never lacked confidence that their work would be received with great enthusiasm.

Angelique had a fleeting thought that her sister was burying herself in work to avoid her, but they *were* behind, thanks to Angelique staying in London an extra day. It was probably her own distraction making it seem like her sister was off. She was grateful to Trella for picking up the slack and tried to set her own nose to the grindstone so they could ship everything as planned.

Then, even though time passed at a glacial pace, she suddenly found herself rattling around her hotel room in Berlin, phone in hand as she compulsively checked her messages for word from Kasim, behaving exactly like an addict needing a fix. She had sent him her agenda yesterday, mildly panicked at the lack of word from him. She absolutely refused to let herself text again.

Tonight's event was taking place here in this brand-new hotel. Her suite was airy and ultra-contemporary, run by a firm out of Dubai that understood the meaning of luxury. She promised herself a soak in the private whirlpool tub when she returned later. It was already filled and warmed. Tiny whorls of steam wisped from the edge of its rollback cover and candles were at hand, awaiting a match.

She would need to drown some sorrows since it looked like Kasim wouldn't turn up. She was devastated.

That shouldn't surprise her. Right from the beginning he had pulled a formidable response from her.

She fought tears as she set out her gown and did her hair, then her makeup, saying a private *Thanks, Trella*, as her sister's face appeared in the mirror to bolster her.

She wished now she had brought one of Trella's designs. Her sister's confections tended to have a self-assured cheekiness whereas Angelique's evoked more introspective moods. Hers tonight was wistful and damned if it wasn't *blue*.

A powder blue in silk, sleeveless, but abundant enough in the skirt to move like quicksilver. The bodice was overlaid with mist-like lace that split apart at her naval and fell into a divided overskirt that became a small train. She pinned her hair back from her face, but let it fall in loose waves behind her naked shoulders and painted her lips a meditative pink.

Her earrings were simple drop crystals that caught the light. A velvet choker with a matching stone collared her throat. A panic switch was sewn on the underside. She and her sister often joked about starting their own line of high-end security wear, but they didn't want to tip off anyone that they wore it themselves.

Just for a moment, as she took in her reflection, she wondered what it would be like to live without so much vigilance. In a prince's harem, for instance.

This lipstick really emphasized the pout she couldn't seem to shake. *Ugh*.

She gathered her composure before facing the masses. It was better that Kasim wasn't with her, she consoled herself. Events like this, when her presence was advertised ahead of time, were always particularly rabid attention-wise. Maurice wore special sunglasses to deal with the glare off the flashbulbs it was so bad.

Maurice was reading something on his phone when she came out the door. He tucked it away promptly, but

took it out again when they were in the elevator, since
they were alone.

"Je m'excuse," he said. "It's a report about some
photos that have surfaced. I'm sending instructions to
question their authenticity."

She dismissed his concern with a flick of her brows.
"Of me with the prince?"

"It says 'prince,' yes, but—"

"I don't care," she insisted, even though she cared
a great deal.

The elevator stopped, the doors opened and some
models joined them. One was beyond thrilled to be
sharing an elevator with One of The Sauveterre Twins.
Maurice put his phone away and remained alert while
Angelique exchanged a few remarks with the strangers
and consented to a selfie.

Moments later, the doors opened onto the ballroom
floor. The paparazzi went mad as soon as they saw she
had arrived.

Maurice guided Angelique down the narrow path-
way toward the VIP entrance where greeters would be
waiting to check off her name on a tablet and handlers
would hand her a swag bag that she invariably gave to
her mother.

As she approached, a man in a tuxedo turned to
look at her.

Kasim.

He was asking if she'd already entered the ballroom
when the madness behind him made him turn.

She was stunning. Like an ethereal creature surrounded by fireflies as a million flashbulbs went off
behind her.

Even more riveting than her beauty, however, was

the way her composed features softened with surprise, then dawned into warm recognition. Her eyes sparkled and a joyous glow suffused her. Her breasts rose as he moved toward her.

He caught his own breath. Him. The man who had decided this affair was too inconsequential to mention to his father, merely stating he had, indeed, resolved the situation with Sadiq's "friend." While he'd been so far away from her, he'd been able to convince himself their time together had been merely a pleasant diversion.

Nevertheless, he'd found himself bulldozing his way through his meetings, working late to negotiate agreements and pushing hard for resolution, a mental clock urging him to leave on time to be here with her. He had worked nonstop on the plane, barely sparing a moment to put on his tuxedo before finalizing a few last details over the phone in his car, arriving at the perfect moment to watch her emerge from the gauntlet.

Bulbs were still flashing as she unconsciously posed, awaiting his approach with that beautiful, reverent look on her face. He wondered what his looked like. Irritated and possessive, he imagined, since he wanted to steal her away from this madhouse. *Now.*

Mindful of her flawless appearance, he held back on crushing her even though he ached to feel her against him. Instead, he took her hand and detoured past her lips to press a light kiss to her cheekbone.

Her lashes fluttered closed and she breathed, "I'm so glad you're here."

He almost didn't hear her, but the blush that stained her cheeks told him she'd said it and was adorably self-conscious for having revealed herself like that.

"Are you?" He straightened to bask in her look of adoration. "Because I think we've been found out."

Behind her, the paparazzi had moved to completely block the passage. They had become a wall of strobing light and a din of clicks and whirs and shouts of her name.

"Is there anyone else here?" Angelique blinked her green, green eyes, mouth quirking with irony. "I only see you."

"You're stealing my lines." Stealing something else if he wasn't very careful. "Let's get this evening over with so I can have you to myself."

They created a huge stir and for once she didn't care. She was proud, so delighted and proud, to stand beside this man. He was *here*. It wasn't the most important occasion of her life, but it was important to her that he had made an effort.

He *wanted* to be with her.

Although, that could change if the attention didn't lighten up. Kasim might not be as infamous as she was, but with those features, the camera had to love him. His air of detachment meant eyes followed him with a yearning for scraps of his notice.

"You weren't exaggerating about the attention," he said when she returned to her seat after her presentation and he rose to help her with her chair.

"No," she agreed, then had to tease, "Scared?"

"Pah!" he dismissed.

They were an "it" couple before the final speeches had wrapped. "Kasimelique," one of her colleagues teased her in a whisper as the trays of champagne began circulating and the networking portion of the evening began.

"I'm so glad to have that over with," Angelique said to Kasim once they had the first rush of introductions over with and were able to move into a quieter corner for a moment alone. "Did I sound all right when I was onstage?"

"Perfect. You weren't nervous, were you? You didn't look it."

"I told you, my trick is to pretend I'm Trella. Do you know that man?" She tried not to sound so keyed up as she flicked her glance to the right, but this crush of people was wearing on her. "The blond one with the sash," she clarified.

The stranger was tall and quite handsome with a regal bearing. He wore the red satin as a bold streak across his chest beneath his jacket.

"He keeps looking this way. Maybe he's related to a client, but I can't place him. I'm going to be so embarrassed if he comes over and I don't know his name." The Champagne probably wasn't a good idea, but she took a sip anyway. This was still her first glass.

"I don't know who he is, but I recognize the look." Kasim seemed to stand taller and more alert. He took a half step closer to her.

"What do you mean? Like, Nordic heritage? Or do you mean you know the sash?" She lowered her glass, smile fading as she read the suspicion in the way he looked down his nose at her.

"I mean possessive. He's resentful of my place beside you. *Jealous*."

"Are you serious?" She tried a laugh, but realized very quickly that Kasim was more than serious. He was trying to see inside her head.

"Kasim." She was deeply offended. "I swear to you, I don't know him." But she could see the reel of her online exploits playing behind his eyes.

"Believe what you want," she said frostily. *Don't*

you dare, she silently railed, heart clutched in a vise. He didn't trust her? After all they'd shared?

Well, honestly, what *had* they shared? A weekend of sex and not even some long-distance afterplay via text.

She looked at him with new eyes, thinking of how much she had anticipated his meeting her here, but now she had to wonder if she wasn't simply a convenient booty call. It was so lowering, she had to remind herself to breathe.

"Excuse me." He walked away into the throng, leaving her staring at his disappearing back, confounded and trying not to panic. That was *it*? He had just broken off their affair because a stranger looked at her in a way he didn't like?

Before she could fully absorb that and succumb to fury or despondency or both, the stark white of a truly beautiful tuxedo parked itself before her. It was cut by the slash of red and there was a star-shaped pin at his shoulder with a shield inside it.

The man could have come out of a fairy tale, he was so patrician and perfectly hewn.

She hated him on sight and wanted to throw her champagne in his face, but he spoke with an exotic accent and impeccable manners.

"Your lost item, Cinderella." He offered her a cupped hand.

Inside it was a gold hoop earring with a line of diamonds down the front. It looked exactly like a pair she owned. They'd been a gift from her father for her fifteenth birthday—not something run-of-the-mill that showed up in every low-budget jewelry shop. Trella's were similar, but that one was definitely the match to her own.

She took it to examine it more closely, trying to recall when she'd worn them last.

"Where—?"

"Caught under the pill—" he started to say in a tone that was very throaty with latent passion, but he cut himself off. Something in his expression grew sharp and arrested as he studied her face. Whatever lightness might have been in his mood became something accusatory as his gaze moved restlessly over her like he was searching for something he couldn't find.

She knew that look, but refused to believe she was interpreting it correctly. It was far too outrageous to imagine—

"I knew if I walked away, he would approach you," Kasim said, reappearing beside her.

Angelique startled, not exactly guilty, but defensive. *No.* She needed time to figure out what was going on with this stranger. She searched his blue eyes, now distinctly frosted with hostility toward Kasim. *And* her.

Kasim's gaze cut to the earring in her hand, making her close her fist around it.

"Introduce us." Kasim's tone was lethal.

Angelique was distantly aware of people sidling by them, glancing their way.

Kasim's expression was positively murderous and this stranger was shifting his gaze from her to Kasim, contempt curling his lip.

"I told you," she insisted to Kasim in an undertone. "I don't know him."

Trella, you didn't.

"My timing is inconvenient," the stranger said, flicking a look to Kasim that was a silent warning. *Be careful with this one.*

It was so infuriatingly *male*, like they were lofty

equals who came across tarts like her all the time, she instantly wanted to smack him. Both of them. How dare he show up and throw her under the bus this way. How dare he touch her sister! Her heart began to race, trying to assimilate how it could possibly have happened.

Was she crazy? Could he have been with Trella? How? *When?*

At the same time she was trying to work it out, she could see she was dropping like a free fall elevator in Kasim's estimation. That *hurt*, damn it. How could he think this of her?

"If you're going to accuse me of being a slut, at least tell me who you are," she bit out.

"You picked that label," the stranger shot back derisively. "And I don't *care* that you've moved on, but those are real diamonds. I was going to send it by courier back to Paris, but I read that you were going to be here and I was in Berlin." He shrugged a dismissal, looking distinctly bored as he glanced away. "My mistake. Carry on."

But he stood there like he was waiting for Kasim to give up and leave, as if he wanted to continue talking to her.

"*Back* to Paris," she repeated, reclaiming the stranger's attention while hotly aware that Kasim was glancing away as though looking for an exit. "When exactly was I there with you? Wait. Let me guess," she insisted, because it finally hit her. It was completely impossible, but she *knew*. "Last Friday night? The charity dinner for the Brighter Days Children's Foundation?"

The stranger's cheeks went hollow. "You know it was."

"Kasim, where was I last weekend? *All* weekend?"

Finally she had his attention. His resentful, derisive attention.

"You *are* both aware I have a twin. *Aren't you?*"

Kasim couldn't say that he was relieved when Angelique cleared herself of cheating on him. He was still too gripped by residual possessiveness. Maybe his jealous rage had eased enough that he was capable of rational thought, maybe he'd ceased wanting to *kill* the other man acting so proprietarily toward Angelique, but he was still pulsing with adrenaline. The sheer force of emotion that had overtaken him as he identified a rival was paralyzing.

Unnerving.

"I'll need your name and contact details," Angelique said while signaling Maurice to approach.

"His Highness, Xavier Deunoro," Kasim supplied stiffly. "Prince of Elazar."

Angelique and the prince both turned raised-brow looks his way.

Kasim shrugged. "I asked when I walked away."

"Another prince. *Charming,*" Angelique said scathingly.

Upset that he'd been mistrustful? She should look at the facts before him: they hadn't been together all week, her sister was never seen in public and this man had brought her damned earring from what was no doubt his *bed*. Shared intimacy was the only reason he would want to return it personally.

"She said she was you," the prince said as he reached to an inside pocket of his tuxedo. "The resemblance is remarkable, but there is something…" He narrowed his eyes. "I can't put my finger on it, but the moment I saw you tonight, I knew something was different."

That made Angelique stiffen and flash a wary glance at the man, but she recovered quickly and took the prince's card, relaying it to her guard with a hand that shook.

"That explains the photos you were questioning," she said to Maurice. "My brothers will want that, but wait until I've spoken to Trella. I'll head upstairs to do that now." With a hard glance at her sister's lover, she said, "If you tell anyone it was her and not me, I will personally hunt you down and unman you." She looked as gloriously provocative as she had the day Kasim had met her.

"You can try," the prince drawled. "Give her my regards."

Angelique turned away only to be confronted by a Hollywood starlet.

"I'm sorry," Angelique said with tested graciousness, briefly clasping the actress's hand. "I've been called away. I'm looking forward to our appointment next month, though. We'll talk then."

"My people will need a copy of the press release before it's sent," Kasim said, taking out his phone as he fell into step with her, winding toward the nearest exit.

"What press release?"

"The one clarifying her identity."

"That won't happen."

He checked briefly, not faced with any physical obstructions, but walking into the wall of his own ego.

"You will," he informed her. "Or I will."

"Do not make threats in that direction, Kasim."

"It's not a threat. It's a statement. I can't allow people to have a wrong impression." His father would find Kasim's means of putting Sadiq's problem to bed rather crude as it was.

"After what you just thought about me, you might be surprised how little I care about how this reflects on *you*. I would rather the general public think the worst of me than know the truth, however."

"Why?" he demanded.

"Reasons."

They approached the melee of reporters. He was forced to table his questions as they pushed their way through the chaos to the elevators.

Her guard efficiently plowed them a way and barred anyone from coming into the car with them, but Angelique still had the gall to look at Kasim like he was a hitchhiker who had hopped on from the highway.

"I'm going to my room to call my sister. You're not invited," she said.

"It's my room," he stated.

She shot a look to Maurice who was instantly alarmed. "That shouldn't happen," her guard said, reaching for his phone. "I'll call—"

"I know the owners," Kasim said tightly. "I pulled strings to take over the reservation. It's *fine*."

"It really isn't." Angelique sailed out the doors as they opened, striding down the hall with her elegant dress trailing behind her like a visible whorl of her cloud of fury.

One of Kasim's own guards had joined Maurice's partner at the door to the suite, leaving Kasim's bag just inside on the floor. Angelique gave both a baleful look and walked straight through the lounge into the bedroom where she quickly shut the door. Seconds later Kasim heard the dull ring of her placing a call and a greeting in a muted voice that held a tone that sounded much like her own.

He took out his own phone and searched for the most

recent photos of Angelique Sauveterre. Most were from tonight, first the ones of them greeting each other outside the ballroom, then mingling within. A few showed her onstage, and one grainy snap across the restaurant last weekend was obviously a belated effort to pile on tonight's revelation that they were dating.

Then there were a handful of images that showed her—it damned well looked *exactly* like her—in a clinch with the Prince of Elazar in a ballroom in Paris.

And someone had managed to snap her very tense expression as she had defended herself against two-timing right before they'd come up here.

Kasim gritted his teeth as he weighed Sauveterre security protocols against his own reputation. He could spare Angelique an hour to address this scandal in her own way, he allowed generously. After that, he would turn down the heat on this particular conflagration himself.

Twenty minutes later, Angelique emerged from the bedroom, cheeks flushed, brows pulled into a distraught line. Opening the door, she said, "Maurice, can you send a snapshot of that card I gave you to Trella? *Merci*."

She closed the door firmly and turned to glare at Kasim.

"Does she do this often?" Kasim asked.

She pursed her lips as though deciding whether to answer. Then she huffed out a breath and crossed her arms defensively, but her shoulders fell a notch.

"It's something she's tried a few times in the last year, basically since she knew Sadiq was getting married. She wants to attend the wedding and is determined to get over…" She stopped herself. Sighed again. "It's a way for her to test the waters of moving in public again. If she appeared as herself, the press would go stark raving mad. If she poses as me, however, and goes to Ramon's race with Henri and Cinnia or something like that, it's run-of-the-mill attention."

Tonight was run-of-the-mill?

"Shouldn't she get it over with? Coming out at my sister's wedding is liable to take attention away from the bride and groom. Has she thought of that?"

"It will be a closed ceremony and don't judge how she's doing this."

"Her actions deserve to be judged. I look like a fool. If you had had an actual affair with that man last *year*, I wouldn't care." That was a small lie, but he would be able to convince himself he didn't care. "The fact you've been photographed with both of us in the same week makes all three of us look bad."

"We're all going to have to grin and bear it, aren't we?"

"No," he told her sternly. "You warned me about attention. You didn't say your sister would ridicule me. I will give her the chance to come clean. If she doesn't, I will make the completely true statement that you were with me in London all of last weekend."

"No!" Her fists hit the air next to her thighs, arms straight and angry. "Don't *do* that to her."

"I didn't take the photographs, Angelique. She's bringing this on herself!"

"It could do so much damage, you can't even comprehend." She paced with agitation across the lounge. "The press was horrible to her for years after the kidnapping, printing every lurid scrap, fact or fiction, on what happened while she was captive. True or not, those things assaulted her every time, victimizing her again and again. Then, as if that wasn't bad enough, they called her unstable and a drug addict and *fat*. She was barely a stone heavier than me, but there was this magnifying glass on her so she couldn't buy a stick of gum without it being a cry for help, or a sign she was suicidal... It drove her to go the other way, until she was underweight and we were scared she would disappear completely. I'll tell you, if anything is designed to break a person's spirit, it's that sort of relentless, vicious criticism."

She paused to take a few panting breaths. Her face contorted in a wince of distant memory.

"Then, after my father's funeral... I guess we finally looked like young women by then. It's not like we were dressed for clubbing, you know, but photos circulated of us at the service and men stalked both of us online after that, saying the most disgusting things. Sending us—" She waved a hand toward her crotch. "*Those* sorts of pics. It was even worse for Trella. She knew what men like that are capable of." Her voice broke on the last words, eyes haunted.

"Angelique," he breathed, and started toward her.

She bent to unfasten her shoes and kick them away, then kept moving, restless with heightened emotion, dress swirling like a cape each time she turned.

"She started having panic attacks because of it. That is *not* public knowledge." She pointed at him as though warning him not to speak of it. Then she whirled away again. "She was terrified all the time. It was horrible for her. For all of us. It was like watching someone who is depressed to the point of being suicidal, or in chronic pain, and listening to them scream. You can't do anything except sit there and watch. She spent, God, a good two years stoned on medications, trying to get it under control. Finally she left the public eye and it took a while, but she was able to stabilize. That was so hard-won, none of us rocks the boat. We don't want to throw her off again."

She hugged herself, gaze fixed on the past.

"For years, one of us has always been with her, never farther than the next room. We all know it's not healthy. We *want* a normal life for her. Our version of normal, anyway," she muttered, then waved with exasperation toward the guards in the hall.

"Even Trella is balking at how she lives. I just asked her how this happened and she told me she feels like she's been doing time on a prison sentence for a crime she didn't commit. What did she do wrong, Kasim? Are her kidnappers half so tortured? They might be in jail, but have they suffered one-tenth as much as she has? And even through all of what she has faced, she *tries*."

Her eyes were wet and gleaming. She was visibly shaking with intense emotion, making his heart feel pinched and tight.

"She's been trying so hard to get over all her mental blocks. She flew to Paris alone. You have no idea what a big deal that was for her. And then, when she realized you and I were keeping out of the spotlight and I was expected at that dinner, she stole the chance to go out as me. To see how she felt going out *alone*. It was a spur-of-the moment thing, which is exactly like her when she's at her best. In certain ways this is such thrilling news."

She began pacing again, her dress flaring around her as she pivoted, but halted to press a hand to her brow.

"Not the part where she went home with a stranger, of course. I asked her how *that* happened, but she didn't want to talk about it, only apologized for not telling him who she really was. My brothers are going to kill me for not being there to stop her."

Kasim folded his arms, observing drily, "She took acting like you to the highest level, didn't she?"

Angelique jerked her head up, eyes narrowed with antipathy. "I had dinner with you first!"

They hadn't even finished their drinks, let alone started on the appetizers, but *okay*.

"That has to be me in those photos, Kasim. If the press gets wind that it was her..." She pinched the bridge of her nose. "Trella is a tiny baby sea turtle making her way to the water. If we can just give her time to get there before unleashing the crabs and gulls..."

He snorted. "Laying it on pretty thick, aren't you?"

"What do you want me to say? That it's okay if you traumatize my sister by causing the hell of public attention to rain down on her again? It's not."

"What do you want *me* to say? That it's okay if the world thinks you've slept with both of us? It's *not*."

"Who cares so long as you're the one in this room with me tonight? Or, wait, am I invited to stay in the room I booked for myself?"

He scowled. "Don't get bent out of shape about that. I don't book weekends with women then ask them to foot the bill."

"I see. That's interesting." She gave a considering nod, shoulders setting in a stiff line. "You realize that by mentioning these legions of other women for whom you have paid hotel bills, you're saying it's okay that you have a past, but not me. Is that what you were doing this week, by the way? When you were not texting me? Paying for hotel rooms with other women? Just because no one returned a cuff link downstairs doesn't mean you weren't making a fool of *me*, but do you hear me complaining? No. Because I'm well aware we haven't made any commitments to each other—"

"Enough," he cut in. "I paid for the room because I will put up with your pain-in-the-ass security protocols, but you will stay in *my* room. I will not ask permission from *your* guards to enter. As for the photos, I don't want people to think that's you because I'm jealous. All right? Is that what you need to hear?"

Her shoulders went back, but he could see he had finally pulled her out of her own interests into *theirs*.

"Which I might have hesitated to admit if you weren't acting like a green-eyed shrew yourself. No, Angelique, I was not sleeping with other women. I was working. Nonstop. So I could come here and be with you. Future or not, we are damned well exclusive to one another until we're over. Is that clear? Now, go warn your sister I won't be so forgiving if she does this to me again."

The line of her mouth softened. "You're not going to expose her?"

"Do I look like someone who takes pleasure in feeding baby sea turtles to the gulls?"

She threw herself at him.

CHAPTER EIGHT

ANGELIQUE GLIMPSED THE velvet box on the romantically set table when she arrived at Kasim's Paris penthouse.

She was getting to know him very well, but wouldn't have pegged him as a man who celebrated a one-month anniversary. His sentimentalism touched her. It told her he valued what they had as deeply as she did.

"We're staying in tonight?" she asked as she kissed him without even taking off her jacket or setting down her purse.

He had already shed his suit jacket and tasted faintly of Scotch and…tension? He lingered over their kiss, drawing it out with a quest for her response, waiting until they were both breathless and hot before drawing back.

"Do you mind?"

"No." She tossed her purse toward the sofa then hugged her arms around his waist again. Nestled her mons into his hardness, pleased with the evidence his desire wasn't letting up any more than hers. "It's been a long week. I missed you. I'd rather have you all to myself."

"Me, too." His voice was sincere, but…off. He started to pull her into another kiss.

She hesitated. "Are you angry?"

A flash in his eyes, then, "Not at you."

He combed his fingers into her hair and gently pinned her head back, so her neck was arched, her chin tilted up for the press of his damp lips. The stamp of hot kisses went down her throat, making her skin tighten and tingle.

"And you can't talk about it so you want to forget it. Perhaps I can help with that," she allowed with another press of her hips into his groin. It was her cross to bear that she was the lover of a man with great responsibilities.

His breath hissed in and he straightened to his full height, seeming to wage an inner debate. He bit out a soft curse and his hands fell away from her.

"We will have to talk about it," he said, twirling his finger to indicate she should turn and let him help her with her coat. "Much as I'd rather make love to you first, you probably wouldn't forgive me if I did. Let's get it over with."

Wary now, she watched him drape her jacket over the back of the sofa and move to the chilled wine in the bucket.

"A votre santé," she said when he brought her a glass.

He only made a face of dismay and said bluntly, "You can't come to the wedding."

Angelique held the wine in her mouth until it was warm and sour. She swallowed.

"Sadiq and Hasna's wedding?" *Obviously,* but she couldn't process how he could say such a thing. "I know we can't…be together when I'm there. I wasn't expecting—" To stay in his room. Maybe she'd fantasized about it. "I mean, I thought I'd stay with my family and you and I could…" She shrugged. "Dance?" Steal time somewhere? They were very adept at that.

"My father is inviting the woman he would like me to marry. It would be awkward and disrespectful for my mistress to be there."

And the hits just kept on coming.

His marriage was supposed to be some far-off thing that would happen one day, but in the mists of a distant future, like death. Unavoidable, but not something the average person worried about as an immediate concern.

"Did you explain my family's relationship with Sadiq?" Her hand began to shake. She leaned to set her glass on the coffee table before she spilled wine all over his antique Persian rug.

"My father is still convinced you had a personal relationship with him. Bringing up the complimentary wardrobe does more harm than good."

"I'm not going to miss Sadiq's wedding, Kasim. He asked us to be there. It's a big deal for all of us, especially if Trella is going to be with us. I have to be there for *her*."

"I'm not happy about it either, but it's *one* day."

"Does Hasna know?"

"I'm not about to play those sorts of politics," he said, sharp and hard. "That is my mother's game, to stir up tears to manipulate my father. Hasna understands our father very well along with my promise to marry the wife he chooses for me."

"Why—?" Why had he ever agreed to such a thing? But she knew. So he could rule differently. Better.

That selflessness on his part ought to inspire her to make peace here and act in the greater good, but she was too appalled at how casually and callously he was brushing aside her feelings in this.

He set down his wine and grasped her arms. "Angelique, it's one day. Then we can carry on as normal."

"Normal being this." She broke away from his hold to wave at the room.

The impermanence of their association penetrated. What she had seen as a relationship, one where she could reveal her deepest thoughts and worries, was nothing more than a convenience for him.

She caught sight of the table and its narrow velvet box. Its significance struck like a bludgeon.

"Silly me, I thought that was for our anniversary," she said dumbly.

"Anni—?" He pinned his lips shut. Such a man. One hundred percent oblivious.

She walked around the far end of the sofa and moved to open the box.

The necklace was a stunning confection of thin chains and cushion-cut emeralds set in gold.

This was all she would be left with when their affair was over. Some token of his. It wasn't even affection, was it? Appreciation? For the orgasms she'd given him?

And this affair *would* end. She had managed to ignore that reality these past few weeks of meeting him in hotel rooms across Europe.

He was marrying. Sooner than later. And his chosen wife would be at the wedding.

It was absolutely true that she couldn't meet that woman then carry on with Kasim until… When? The day his engagement was announced? Days before he married? Her heart was pulsing like a raw wound just thinking of it.

Each breath she drew felt like a conscious effort and burned both directions. In and out. Her throat closed and her eyes swam. Her voice came out strained with insult.

"I'm not a woman you buy off, Kasim."

She looked up in time to see him flinch and avert his gaze.

"I know you're disappointed," he began. "That is not—"

She cut him off with a hoot of disbelief. "Is that what I am? *Disappointed?*" Her chest was caving in on itself. "Are *you?*"

"It's *one* day."

"It's you turning me into your mistress, then letting your father call me a whore who's not good enough to be seen in his palace. One who is paid well, I admit, but no thanks. I'm not interested." She gave the velvet box a thrust of rejection so it tipped off the table onto the floor.

"You're overreacting," he bit out, trying to catch the necklace.

"No, *you* should have told me this could happen before you took me to your bed! That is information I needed because you know what Sadiq means to us."

"And what? You would have passed on all of this so you could attend one damned wedding?"

"All of what?" she charged, waving at the necklace he now held. "You've just reduced our relationship to an exchange of sex for jewelry. Do you know what I've given up so I could be with you? The sacrifices I've made? I've pushed Trella *away* so I could be close to you. What have you given up? *Nothing.* And now I know why. Because I mean nothing to you. So, yes, the wedding is a deal breaker. Tell your father your mistress won't be there because you no longer have one."

She turned toward her coat.

He caught her arm. "Angelique—"

"Don't," she said in the deadly, assertive voice she'd been trained to use, free hand snatching up her pendant in warning.

His mouth tightened and he lifted his hand to splay it in the air, like she'd turned a gun on him.

"Really? You'll call in your guards rather than have a civilized conversation about this?"

"How do you see this conversation ending? In your bed? Yes, I will call in my guards rather than let you seduce me into accepting this kind of treatment. You had chances to end this before my—" *Don't say "heart."* "Before my emotions were involved." Her voice shook. "Did you really think, after all that I've shared with you, that I was only here for a *necklace*?"

The control that she had cultivated through a lifetime of having to buck up and be strong was never harder to find. She shot her arms into her coat and picked up her purse.

"You're as emotionally tone-deaf as your father."

If she had been trying to stab him in the heart, she had picked up the most efficient knife with which to do the job, then snapped it off against the bone for good measure.

As he gathered the necklace from the floor, he thought of Jamal showing it to him a decade ago. It was one of his brother's first efforts at a big piece, not perfect, designed with more passion than attention to the finer details, but it was genuinely beautiful. Jamal had been rightfully proud and Kasim sincerely impressed.

Kasim had bought it, wanting to be his brother's first patron, declaring, *Someday it will be worn by a queen, as it should be.*

But lately, as he regularly saw green and gold tones in the eyes of his lover when she woke beside him, he had decided to give it to Angelique. He had known she wouldn't like what he had to say today, but he had hoped to soften the blow by giving her something that was genuinely precious to him, that was hard to give up because it was one of the few remnants of his brother he had.

Of course she wasn't aware of that. There had been no point in trying to explain. He had let the door slam and the quiet set like concrete around him.

Because they had no future. His father was choosing him a wife. The goal today had been to keep her from attending the wedding and that task was definitely accomplished.

Sometimes hard choices had to be made. Jamal had been one of them and Angelique another.

It made him furious and sick, but it was done.

Angelique heard the door, but didn't get out of bed. She was too devastated. Her eyes were swollen and gritty, her throat raw, her nose congested and her heart sitting in a line of jagged pieces behind her breastbone.

She had tried to brave it out on her own, but sometime in the darkest hours of the night, when her sister had texted, asking if she was all right, her willpower had collapsed.

Please come, she had texted.

Trella hadn't asked why. She had only texted back that she would leave as soon as the family jet could be cleared for takeoff. Now her sister's shoulders fell as she walked into the bedroom and took in the shipwreck that was her twin.

"What happened?" Trella asked gently.

"We broke up," Angelique said in a voice rasped by hours of crying. "I've been so stupid."

"No." Trella came to the bed and swept away the crumpled tissues to lie down in front of her. "You fell in love. That's not stupid." She stroked Angelique's hair back from where it was stuck to her wet cheek.

"I didn't mean to." Fresh tears flooded her eyes. "I never let anyone in. You know I don't. It's too painful."

"You were always so full of my suffering there was no room for anyone else."

"No."

"Yes, Gili." Trella stroked her hair, petting and soothing. "I tried not to put it on you, but you carry it because that's who you are. I'm not surprised you fell for him when he was the first person who didn't lean on you emotionally. When you finally felt like I didn't need you every minute. That must have felt like such a relief."

"He didn't lean on me because he didn't love me!" Angelique pushed a fresh tissue under her nose and sniffed. "And I feel so pathetic, crying like this when a bruised heart is nothing compared to—"

"Shh…" Trella said, stroking her hair. "Don't ever compare, *bebé* angel."

Angelique closed her eyes and tried to level out her breathing. "I thought I had learned how to be strong and I'm so…" *Sad. Scorned. Heartbroken.*

"Do you know how I get through my worst moments?" Trella's fingers gently wove in and picked up Angelique's hair, combing to the ends. Her voice was pitched into the tone they had used as children, when telling each other secrets in the night. "Every time I've wanted to give up, I've always thought to myself, I have to be there when *she* needs *me*. You gave me a gift, asking me to come. You're telling me I'm strong enough to be your support. It was worth fighting through all that I have so I could be with you here, in your hour."

Angelique had seen her begging Trella to come as pure weakness, but wondered now if she had failed to see what a comeback her sister was really making—because she'd been so wrapped up in Kasim.

"You didn't hesitate, even though I've been letting him come between us." Her lips quivered and she looked at her twin through matted lashes. "That was wrong. I'm so sorry."

"No," Trella crooned. "Don't apologize for offering your heart to him. It's his loss that he didn't see how tender and precious it is. And no matter what happens, we will always be us. I *will* be here for you, Gili."

Angelique's smile wobbled and she let out a breath she'd been holding for years. "I love you, Trella *bella.*"

"I love you, too."

Angelique wasn't going to Zhamair. She wasn't buckling to Kasim's demand that she stay away, though. It was the other way. She couldn't bear to see him, fearing she would make a fool of herself at the first glance.

Or, at the very least, have to face what a fool she already was.

She had always seen easily through men who asked her out. They wanted to date her because she was beautiful, a prize. Some had wanted to get closer to her brothers, others had been so overcome in her presence it had been a burden to live up to what they imagined her to be. It had been fairly easy to maintain a certain distance.

Kasim had been different. He was strong, confident, *honest.* She had felt safe with him and it had allowed her to put her true self out to him. That inner soul of hers was as shy and hesitant as she'd ever been, only coming out when she trusted she wouldn't be hurt.

Yet he had treated her like one more mare in the stable and she should have seen it coming, which left her feeling like she'd set herself up for this heartache. She had failed herself.

Be the tough woman Trella is, she kept urging herself, but she had never managed to be that woman when it came to Kasim. That was her downfall.

So she finished drafting her email to Sadiq mentioning the "terrible flu" that had her deeply under the weather and hit Send.

She was fooling no one. Her family knew that things were over between her and Kasim. Hasna had to be aware of it, as well.

She sniffed and glanced at her red eyes in her desk mirror. She certainly looked like she was battling a serious ailment. Heartsickness took a toll.

Trella, bless her, was doing everything she could to support her.

It was the great reversal Angelique had longed for and it wasn't nearly as relieving or satisfying as she'd imagined. For starters, her brothers looked at her reliance on Trella as a small betrayal of their unspoken pact. They had all worn the mantle of protector for so long, they couldn't put it down long enough to see that Angelique's pulling back had actually been a good thing for their baby sister.

Trella was stepping up on her own volition now. She had planned to attend the wedding, but it was her suggestion that she take on the wedding day with Hasna so Angelique could skip going to Zhamair. This morning, Trella had even volunteered to make a quick run to London *by herself* to meet in private with a certain longtime client who belonged to the royal family and had a confidential occasion coming up.

Trella was also talking of doing more of the front end work once she returned from Zhamair, which was something to look forward to, but for now the task of greeting prospective clients still fell on Angelique.

Thus, when her guard rang from the front doors, stating that her eleven o'clock was here, she could only sigh and agree to come downstairs.

As she rose, she glanced at the appointment details. Girard Pascal. Something about a gift for a bride. Since she had no other reference on this prospective client, he would be shown into the small receiving room off the front foyer.

The room was a quaint little conversation area filled with Queen Anne furniture that served as a border crossing of sorts. Technically inside the building, it was still on the perimeter. Staff and accepted clients went through a second controlled door to enter the hallowed interior.

The reception room had two doors and a window onto the foyer, giving the illusion of a more spacious chamber, but the glass was really there to allow the guards to monitor her safety if the doors happened to be closed.

Girard Pascal looked Arabic, that was her first impression, but there were many Parisians with Middle Eastern heritage who had been here for generations. With that name, she assumed he was French.

He looked like Kasim, was her second thought, as he stood to a height that was very close to her former lover's. The resemblance was only in his coloring and ancestry, she told herself. Maybe something indefinable across his cheekbones. His eyes, too. That bottom lip. His build and the commanding way he held himself.

She ignored the leap of her heart and told herself she

was making more of the superficial similarities because she missed Kasim. That was all.

Then he opened his mouth and spoke with the same accent, almost the same tone and intonation. "Please call me Girard. Thank you for seeing me."

He smiled warmly, looking nervous in a way that she almost thought was male attraction, but it wasn't. Nor was it the fan-based giddiness some people showed in meeting a Sauveterre. It was affection and admiration and a searching of her expression for something she couldn't define.

"I'm Angelique. Please sit and tell me what sort of gift you had in mind. If I can't help you, I'm sure I'll be able to suggest someone who can." It was her stock greeting, something to give her an out if she decided not to take on a client.

She was already leaning toward not. She didn't feel threatened, precisely, but she did feel prevailed upon. He wanted something from her. Not just a spring ensemble, either.

He held up a finger and went to the door, waiting while one of her guards brought over a black pouch smaller than his palm.

"Nothing showed on the X-ray. It's fine," her guard told her.

"Do you mind?" Girard said as he stepped back into the room and started to close the door.

Angelique moved to close the second door, then joined him at the coffee table, sitting in the opposite armchair from his.

"My request is very..." He frowned, searching for words, then poured out the contents of the pouch onto the coffee table.

It was a necklace, the chain three delicate strands of

white gold, the pendant complex and simple at once. The stones were blue, set into a graceful sweep that almost looked like a cursive letter.

"Arabic?" she guessed, caught by both its whimsy and the suggestion of joy.

"It means 'with.'" His smile flashed.

"It's beautiful." She was instantly taken by it and moved to the settee so she could examine it more closely.

"May I?" She reached out, adding in a murmur, "You want me to design something to go with it?" She would love to. The well of her creativity began to burble just feeling the weight of the piece against her fingers. It had a certain magic that penetrated her skin right into her blood.

"I believe you already have."

"Pardon?" She dragged her stunned gaze off the crimping on the claws, experiencing a shiver as she recognized the workmanship. "Did you make something for my brother, Henri? A tennis bracelet with pink and white diamonds?"

"I don't discuss my clients." His mouth twitched as if he knew that she'd said that same thing more times than she could count. "But my work is carried by a jeweler here in Paris and one in London. And I did make something like that when I first moved to France. It's quite possible the bracelet is mine."

"I meant to ask him where he got it," she murmured, but her brother wasn't speaking to her, primarily because she had dared to invade the family flat and discovered that Cinnia had left him. "I would love to work together," she blurted. "I'm bowled over by your skill."

He smiled with shy pleasure, eyes gleaming. "That touches me. You can't imagine how much. But let me ask my favor first. Then we'll see what you think of working with me on something else."

"Yes, right. Did you see a piece of mine somewhere? You know it's just as likely designed by Trella?" She looked at the pendant again, trying to imagine how she could have inspired something so beautiful. She was utterly in love with it.

"I made this for my sister. I was hoping you could take it to her."

"Your— Oh, my God!" If she hadn't been so enthralled with the necklace, she would have put it together sooner. Now she quickly dropped the pendant on the table and jerked to her feet, backing away from a ghost. "Oh, my God!"

Charles shot in.

She held up her hand.

"I'm fine. Just a shock," she insisted to her guard. "What is today's word? I can't even remember. Daffodil?" She touched her forehead. "Honestly, I'm fine. I just need a moment with…"

She waved at *Kasim's dead brother*. Her hand trembled.

"I'm so sorry," Jamal said with a wince. "I thought you might know."

"How—? *No*." She had to be white as a sheet, but managed to shoo Charles out.

He continued to watch her closely through the glass.

"Oh, my God, Jamal," she breathed. "How on earth would I know? Your whole family thinks you're dead." She held her hand to her throat where she felt her own pulse thundering like a bullet train.

"Kasim didn't tell you? He helped arrange it. The death certificate and name change…"

"No he didn't tell me!" It caused her quite a pang to

admit it, but she had already processed that however much she had thought she meant to Kasim, she had actually meant a lot less.

"Good God, *why*?" She moved to the settee and sank down, wilting as the shock wore off and her mind jammed with questions. "I mean, he told me that your father didn't like that you were an artist, but—"

"Is that what he said?" His smile was crooked and poignant. "Our father couldn't accept that I was *gay*."

"Oh," she breathed. More secrets with which Kasim hadn't trusted her. She had been so open about her own family. It made her feel so callow to think of it. Where had her precious speech gone? The one from her first dinner with Kasim, when she had told him she was reticent out of respect for her siblings. But had he entrusted her with Jamal's story? *No*.

"You couldn't just…live in exile? Here?" she asked.

"My lover was already here and beaten to within an inch of his life for…leading me into that life."

"No! Oh, dear God. Your father couldn't have arranged that?"

"People in his government. There are those in Zhamair who are still very prejudiced. They said they were protecting the reputation of the crown, but my father did nothing to prevent or punish them." Deep emotion gripped him for a moment and he struggled to regain his composure, swallowing audibly before continuing. "Either way, I couldn't risk Bernard's life again. I feared for my own. Merely leaving wouldn't have been enough. I was afraid to even see Kasim again, in case it made things difficult for him, or exposed us."

He propped his elbows on his thighs, back bowed with the weight of the world, expression weary. He rubbed his hands over his face, then looked at her over his clasped fingers.

"My mother's life is not easy. The queen is very resentful of her. If my mother had had a gay son living flagrantly abroad…" He shook his head. "No. It was terribly cruel to tell her I was dead, but if the queen picks on her now, my father stands up for her out of respect for her grief."

"I can't imagine," she murmured, appalled anew at the ugly aggression Kasim had grown up in. "I'm so sorry, Jamal."

"Why?" he said, looking and sounding so much like Kasim, her throat tightened. "You had nothing to do with it."

"I wish I could do something, I guess." She realized immediately that she had backed herself into a corner.

His smile was sharp and amused. "Thank you. I would like that."

She shook her head. "You're so much like him it's unnerving. But I can't take that to Hasna and tell her it's from you. You think *I* was shocked!"

"No," he agreed. "She can't know I'm alive, but Kasim could tell her it was in my old collection and that he had been saving it for her wedding day. It would mean a lot to me for her to wear this. I know she would."

"We're not, um… Kasim and I aren't seeing each other anymore." The press hadn't quite caught on, so she wasn't surprised he didn't know. The words still abraded her throat. "I'm not going to Zhamair."

"Ah. I didn't realize." His expression fell. "I'm sorry. From the photos I saw, you both looked quite…" He didn't finish, only looked at the necklace, crestfallen.

She looked at it, too.

With. He wanted to be with his sister in the only way he could.

She couldn't tell this to Trella or one of her brothers. It was Kasim's secret. Jamal's *life.*

I am a sucker, she thought. Trella would have a far better sense of self-protection. Kasim didn't even want her there. She would be an embarrassment. He might even throw her out.

But Jamal looked so disconsolate. And Hasna missed her brother so much. It would mean the world to her to have this...

She closed her eyes, defeated. "I'll go. I'll go to Zhamair and give this to Kasim."

CHAPTER NINE

THERE HAD BEEN many times over the years that Kasim wondered how his father could be such a pitiless, dictatorial bastard. These days, he understood the liberation in such an attitude as he adopted the same demeanor, contemptuous of those around him for being ruled by their emotions. What did the desires of others' egos and libidos and hearts matter when his own had to be ignored? Everyone made sacrifices.

Don't think of her.

Were it not for his sister marrying in *two days*, he would ride into the desert and take some much needed time to regroup. Instead, he was part of a ceaseless revolving door of relatives and dignitaries. One branch of the royal family had no sooner arrived and joined him and his parents for coffee, when a foreign dignitary was in the next room awaiting a chance to express felicitations.

This morning the parade had begun with an ambush. The king had introduced him to the father of the woman he thought would make a fine queen someday—when she grew up. Did his father seriously expect him to marry a child of barely eighteen?

To his prospective father-in-law's credit, a concern for the age difference was expressed. Kasim smoothly stated he could wait until she completed her degree if that was preferred. It would serve the kingdom better if the future queen was well educated.

The king had correctly interpreted it as an effort to put things off and took him to task the minute they were alone.

"Did you give me your word or not?"

"I cleared the field for her, didn't I?" Kasim replied in a similar snarl. A glance over the guest list a few days ago had shown that Angelique had sent her regrets. "Surely we can get one wedding over with before we host the next?"

Sadiq's family were announced, cutting short the clash. Kasim sat down with Sadiq and their fathers to sign off on the marriage contracts, then they joined the queen and Sadiq's mother.

"Hasna isn't here?" Sadiq said, morose as he glanced around the room.

"The gown has arrived," the queen said with a nettled look toward the king. "Fatina has been pestering to see it. Such a nuisance when Hasna has guests. What if she ruins it?"

"The girls will not let that happen," Sadiq's mother soothed. "They have been ever so careful this week, watching the unpacking of Hasna's wardrobe."

"The Sauveterres were staying with you?" the queen asked in her most benign yet shrewd tone.

"Oh, yes," Sadiq's mother said with a smile of pleasure. "The men went into the desert for what the Westerners call…a stag? Is that correct, Sadiq? I had a nice visit with their mother. We are all friends for many years."

"And they all came with you here?" the king asked, gaze swinging like a scythe to Kasim. "Both girls?"

"Yes, Trella was the one we worried wouldn't make it, but then Angelique came down with the flu. She recovered, though, and…" Sadiq's mother lost some of her warm cheer as she sensed the growing tension. "Is there a problem?" She touched the draped folds of her hijab where it covered her throat. "I know we said she was not coming, but she shares a room with her sister so I didn't think it would be an imposition when she made it after all?"

"It's no problem," Kasim said firmly, aiming it at his father.

Get rid of her, he read in the flick of his father's imperious glance.

If she had left things as they'd been in Paris, Kasim brooded as he strode down the marbled hall of the palace, he would be resentful, but not furious.

This. This was unacceptable. Now he would be in for it with his father. Threats would be made. His uncle and several cousins were coming to the wedding. Tensions were high. Impulsive autocratic decisions could easily be made in a fit of temper.

Not only was he now courting *that* disastrous possibility, thanks to Angelique coming here against his orders, but he was raw all over again. Her rejection stung afresh and his intense feeling of being hemmed in by impossible circumstances was renewed.

He had resigned himself to never seeing her again, damn her! Now she was *in his home*.

He started to ask a passing servant which suite the Sauveterres had been given, but glimpsed a face he knew down near the end of the hall, standing outside the door to his sister's apartment.

His heart rate spiked as he approached the guard.

"Charles," he said, ears ringing. Angelique was behind this door.

"Your Highness."

Kasim knocked.

Female laughter cut off and his youngest half sister cracked the door to peer out at him. Her smile beamed as she recognized him.

"Kasim!"

"Is Hasna dressed? May I come in?" He fought for a level tone. Distempered as he was, he would never take out his bad mood on a six-year-old.

There was a murmur of female voices, then Hasna called, "Yes, come in."

He entered, picking up his baby sister as he did, kissing her cheek and using her small frame to cushion the rush of emotion that accosted him as he anticipated seeing Angelique.

Hasna's suite was half the size of his, yet still one of the most opulent in the palace, decorated in peacock blues and silver, with high ceilings and the same sort of delicate curlicue furniture his mother favored.

She was in her lounge and stood on something because she was a foot taller than normal. He couldn't see what it was because her wedding gown was belled over it, flaring a meter in each direction. A filmy veil was draped over her dark hair and all of it was covered in more seed pearls than there were in the ocean.

Fatina rose from her chair and came to kiss his hand, tsking as her older daughter charged at him, arms raised in a demand to be lifted and hugged.

Kasim concentrated on setting down his one sister and lifting the eight-year-old so she could squeeze his neck with her skinny little arms and press her lips to his cheek.

"You're growing too fast," he told her. "You'll be wearing one of these soon and then who will draw me pictures? You look very beautiful, Hasna."

He set down his sister and pretended he was taking in the extravagance of the gown when he was far more focused on the flash of movement behind the flare of her skirt.

The veil rippled slightly and Angelique rose, her attention remaining stubbornly fixed on her creation.

His heart skyrocketed as he took in the graceful drape of her pink dress and the way she'd covered her head in an ivory scarf so she looked like she was a part of his world—

She turned her head to meet his gaze.

The mercury shooting to the top of his head stalled and plummeted.

Trella.

He didn't know how he knew. The resemblance was remarkable and he couldn't say that her eyes were set closer or farther apart, or that her face seemed wider or thinner. He just knew this wasn't Angelique, even though her greenish-hazel eyes stared at him.

Given the antagonism he sensed coming off her in waves, the straight pins poking out of her mouth were unabashedly symbolic.

He knew how she felt. He was ready to spit nails himself. Where the hell was her sister?

"Angelique has done an amazing job, hasn't she?" Hasna said. He could hear the lilt of trickery in her voice, hoping to fool him.

"I understood this to be a collaboration between the twins. Hello, Trella. It's nice to meet you. Is your sister here?" He looked around the lounge, returning to a state of tense anticipation.

"Oh! You can't tell this is Trella!" Hasna accused. "I can't. I still think this is Angelique and she's tricking me."

Trella pinned a place on the veil that she had marked with her fingers, then removed the rest of the pins from her mouth to say lightly, "I showed you my passport."

Hasna chuckled and Trella glanced at Kasim, smile evaporating.

"She went back to our suite."

He couldn't stop staring, feeling as though he was looking at a film of Angelique. She was a faithful image of her sister, but there was a sense of being removed by time or space. She made him long to be in the presence of the real thing.

"Still recovering from her flu?" he said with false lightness. "Perhaps she should have stayed home after all."

"It was minor. She's over it." Trella's glance hit Kasim with pointed disparagement.

Did she recall that he had done her a favor, hiding her night with the Prince of Elazar? An attitude of deference wouldn't be amiss here, he told her with a hard look, but he didn't have time to teach her some manners.

He had to get her sister on the next plane back to Paris.

Angelique was normally at her most relaxed around her family, but not today. She was wound up about being here, feeling like she was smuggling drugs, that pouch of Jamal's was so heavy on her conscience.

Ramon was not helping. He was growing restless away from work and began badgering her to play tennis.

"I thought Henri said he would?" She was actually

dying to see more of the palace. As they had come in by helicopter with Sadiq's family, Angelique had been awestruck. And taken down a peg. What had made her think she had any place in Kasim's life when his home sprawled in opulent glory over more area than a dozen football fields against the stunning backdrop of the Persian Gulf?

She told herself that it was the heat of the desert sun that caused her to sweat as they were taken by golf cart along a palm-lined path overlooking a water feature. It was actually anxiety. Kasim was here. Somewhere behind those columns and tall windows, beneath the domes and flags, he was carrying on with his life, perhaps already having moved on to another lover, completely unaware she had defied him and come to Zhamair after all.

She searched across the gardens, noting small gatherings in gazebos and colorful tents, trying to see if he was among any of the groups. Guilty and eager at once for a glimpse of him.

Maybe she wouldn't see him until the wedding. She'd been trying to decide whether to contact him outright and request a meeting prior to the wedding—and probably be asked to leave—or just hope she came across him and was able to say her piece before he deported her.

Being special guests of the groom and traveling with the groom's parents, her family was given a luxurious suite of four rooms with a stunning stained glass window set high on the exterior wall of the lounge. It poured colored light onto the white tablecloth of the dining table, where fruit, cordial, sweets and flowers had been waiting on their arrival.

"Gili!" Ramon said. "Are you listening?"

"Are you? I said you and Henri should play. I have to

hem these for Hasna's sisters." She lifted the silk dresses she'd brought back from Hasna's suite.

Fatina had cried when Hasna revealed that her daughters hadn't been overlooked in the wedding preparations.

Now that Angelique had met Jamal and had an even broader understanding of the family's painful dynamic, she was thrilled to be part of including Fatina's children in the wedding. And, as much as it pained her, she had accepted payment from Fatina for them. Fatina had insisted, worried what the queen would say if she didn't. Angelique had kept it very nominal, doing what she could to keep the peace.

Ramon sighed.

"You have to come with us so we can talk to any women we meet." He spoke like he was explaining it to a child. "I don't know how Sadiq survived these restrictions," he muttered, resuming his pacing.

Ah. It wasn't work he was missing so much as his extracurricular activities.

"Ask Mama to go with you," she suggested drily.

"Siesta or I would," he shot back. "Desperate times."

She shook her head at him.

Henri emerged from his room. He had changed into light gray sweatpants and a white long-sleeved tunic. He made a small noise of disgust as he saw that was exactly what Ramon already wore. They didn't try to dress alike, but it happened constantly. Even their panama hats had been purchased on two different continents, but their tastes were so in sync, they had each brought one to Zhamair.

When they set them on their heads, they did so facing each other, moving like mirror images—because that's what they were. She and Trella were stamps, both right-handed, both wearing their hair parted on the left because that's where their crowns were.

The boys were left and right, but were still difficult to tell apart for most people. They wore their hair in the same short, spiked cut, favored the same clothes and had such even features they easily passed for the other, not that they played that game.

Well, Ramon had tried with Cinnia a couple of times, because he was a tease, but she had always caught him. Her ability to tell both sets of twins apart from the get-go was one of the reasons Angelique had been so sure Cinnia was right for Henri.

Her brothers left and she sat down to work.

A knock sounded a few minutes later.

Most of Trella's security detail were women so they'd been given much-deserved vacation time, rather than coming to work where they would have been hampered in performing their regular duties. When the family was together like this, in a secure location, they needed fewer guards anyway.

Maurice was outside this door and she paused to listen, expecting him to ask for identification.

Nothing.

Weird. Unless he already knew the person knocking?

Angelique faltered, suddenly paralyzed with nerves, then forced herself to rise and open the door.

She caught her breath.

He looked so exotic in his *bisht* and *gutra*.

She had studied menswear to design her brother's wedding cloaks, but even though she'd taken great care with them, Kasim's was obviously of royal quality and tailored by hands that were intimately familiar with the engineering of such garments. His robe fit his shoulders perfectly. It was stark black with its V opening trimmed in gold, his white *gutra* framing his face and secured with a cord of matching gold.

He had let his beard grow in, but it was trimmed to a sexy frame that accentuated his mouth and the hollows of his cheeks. The contrast of white and black and gold made his eyes look all the more like melted dark chocolate.

He stole her breath.

His expression flashed something that might have been exaltation as he looked at her, but it was quickly schooled into the stern, confrontational look he'd worn the day she had met him.

"You can't be here," he said.

She searched for the woman she'd been in her office that first day, the one who had stood up to this man, but it was far harder to find her backbone when he looked right through her and saw all her weaknesses.

Her weakness for him.

Somehow she managed to speak despite the earthquake gripping her.

"You'll feel differently when I tell you what brought me here."

Instantly alert, he stepped in, crowding her into stumbling backward. His expression was grave as he firmly closed the door behind him and left his hand flat on the carved panel. His lips barely moved as he said in an undertone, "Pregnant?"

"What? *No!*" Her heart fishtailed, then did it again as his mouth tightened.

Disappointment? *Don't be stupid, Angelique.*

He smoothed his expression into something aloof and pitiless, sweeping his gaze around the empty lounge. He tensed and swore under his breath.

"Are you alone?"

As his gaze slammed back into hers, practically knocking her onto her back, her skin tightened with anticipation and a rush of heat hit her loins.

"My m-m—" How was she supposed to speak when he looked at her like that? "Mama is asleep in her room," she blurted, pointing to the one closed door. "Trella will be back any minute." *Quit making me think you still want me.*

His nostrils flared and he swung away, moving into her lounge like he owned it, which he did. He cast a glance around to take in the litter of tablets and purses, her open mending kit and his young sisters' dresses in vivid green and yellow.

"Damn you for coming," he said, pitching his voice low, but it was still overflowing with restless emotion. "What do you think you're accomplishing?"

Angelique moved to her purse and dug for the velvet pouch, hand shaking as she offered it to him.

Kasim hadn't been able to stop thinking about how they'd ended things, the bitterness of it. He hated that the acrimony would be even deeper after this. He had lived in that sort of thorny forest all his life and knew how unpleasant it was.

That Angelique had forced his hand and was making him reject her outright, forcing her to leave his country, seemed cruel on her part—which was the last word he would use to describe her. He hadn't expected this of her and that made it doubly hard to accept and behave as he knew he must.

Yet there was only the anticipation of pain as he stood here. Duty and reputation hung like anvils and pianos over his head, but in this moment, the bleak anger that had consumed him had become radiant light in her presence.

Angelique turned, expression solemn, and stood where the stained glass poured colors over her golden skin and pale blue dress.

He drank in the picture she made. Memorizing it.

Then she offered something to him and her expression was so grave, so filled with deep compassion, it made his heart lurch. All the hairs on his body stood up as he took the pouch and poured its contents into his hands.

He recognized the workmanship if not the piece. New. Better than anything else he'd made yet. His brother had definitely found his calling in this.

The piano landed.

She knew.

"Your family knows this is why you came?" His mind raced while cold sweat lifted in his palms. He tried to imagine how he would contain this, but his mind was as empty as the shifting dunes in the desert. Old protectiveness warred with fresh, fierce aggression while betrayal washed through him.

"No," she dismissed, barely speaking above a whisper. Her eyes stayed that soft, mossy green. "They think I decided to brave the wedding. That's all."

"How did you find him?"

"He came to me. Asked me to bring that to you for Hasna."

Trella walked in, making both of them start guiltily. Kasim let his arm fall so his sleeve fell over his fist where he clutched the pendant. He slipped it into the side pocket of his robe.

Trella's gaze flicked between them, sticking upon her sister's pale face. "Shall I come back?"

"No," Kasim said on impulse, probably a self-destructive one. "You can tell your family that she's with me." He clasped Angelique's hand in an implacable grip.

"Kasim—"

"We have to talk." He had to ensure Jamal would stay dead. That's what he told himself, even though he knew at a cell-deep level that he could trust Angelique with this secret. She hadn't told her family, had she?

"Gili, your phone," Trella urged, handing it to Angelique as Kasim tugged her toward the door.

There's no point, he thought, as he decided on the fly where they were going.

CHAPTER TEN

A LIFETIME OF taking precautions and Angelique had been kidnapped anyway. Maurice had been left in the dust. Fat lot of good her panic switch would do a hundred miles into the middle of nowhere.

But they were *some*where. As the helicopter lowered into an oasis, tents fluttered under the wind they raised.

Kasim was in the copilot's seat and unhooked his headgear as they settled on the ground, glancing back to signal she could do the same. The whine of the rotors slowed and dwindled.

"No wonder you were so offended by my audacity that first day." She leaned to see more of what looked like a scene from an epic Hollywood tale of Arabia. "You are a future king, Kasim. I didn't fully appreciate that."

"I am aware," he said flatly, crouching to circle in front of her and push open the door. He leaped to the ground before holding up a hand to help her exit.

This strong hand had spirited her down a servant stairwell that had felt like a secret passageway. She had allowed it because she had expected to come out in a library or private lounge.

They had wound up in a break room of some kind where men watched TV and read the paper. One had been eating a rice dish. They had quickly stood to attention when Kasim appeared, all plainly shocked so she assumed he never went there and never with a woman whose head was uncovered!

They'd leaped to do whatever Kasim ordered in Arabic and moments later he had tugged her upstairs and out to the helicopter.

She had balked and he'd said, "Get in or I'll put you in."

What was she going to do? Set off her panic switch and an international incident? He wasn't going to hurt her. He didn't want to extort money from her family.

"Are you flying me out of Zhamair? At least let me get my passport."

A muscle had pulsed in his jaw. "We'll be in the desert."

We. For some reason that had been enough to make her climb into her seat. Minutes later, they'd been chasing their own shadow across the sand.

Now they were at their destination, a pocket of verdant green in an otherwise yellow landscape that was turning bronze with the setting sun. Palms loomed over the tents that showed not the tiniest ripple now the rotors were still. The water mirrored the scene, placid and inviting.

People moved, however, bustling out of one of the biggest tents to stand at the door, heads lowering with respect as Kasim drew her into it.

"This is..." There weren't words for the fantasy of draped silk and tasseled pillows that surrounded her. Candles had been lit and an erotic incense perfumed the air. A low table with cushions for chairs was set with what looked like gold plates and cutlery. In the distance, music from a lute began.

The bed was low and wide, draped with netting so

it was a tent within a tent, sumptuous in its bold colors and swirled patterns on silk sheets, luxurious in its multitude of pillows.

"Where will you sleep?" she asked pointedly.

He gave her the look that said, *Take care*.

"Well, you're taking a lot for granted, aren't you? You may be a future king, but I am not some harem girl you can order to your bed for the night."

Listen to her, talking so tough when she might as well be a concubine stolen by a barbarian for all the power she had here. And for all the strength she had when it came to resisting him. She was already reacting as she always did, hyperaware of his physique as he shrugged out of his *bisht* and tossed it aside.

He wore a light *thobe* beneath and peeled off his *gutra*, running a hand through his hair, letting go of his veneer the way she had often seen him do when they entered a private space. He was shedding the future king to reveal the man who captivated her.

"Have you ever *been* a harem girl?" he drawled. "If not, it should be a treat for you to try it. You can dance for me later."

She was standing near the door with her arms crossed, and did her best to dice and slice him with her stare, but found herself fighting a laugh. *The bastard.*

"Don't you dare act like this is funny. My brothers will be beside themselves."

"So will my father. What was that expression you used after your sister's antics? Ah yes. They can grin and bear it." He slouched into the only chair, one with wooden legs, sumptuously cushioned in blue velvet with matching pads on the arms.

Oh, this banter felt familiar and inviting. Poignant.

She wanted to let all the harsh edges between them soften.

She couldn't. He had hurt her and could again, so easily. She ducked her head, avoiding letting her gaze tangle with his.

"Why did you bring me here?"

"Because my father wanted you removed from the palace." He indicated she should move. She was in the way of the servants bringing food.

Forced to step deeper into the tent, she watched as dishes of fruit and bowls of something that smelled rich and spicy were set out for them. When they finished, they looked back at him for further instructions.

He sent them away with a flick of his wrist, as supremely arrogant as Angelique had ever seen him.

Tipping his head against his chair back, he watched her through eyes so narrow his lashes were a single black line.

She shifted her bare feet under the skirt of her dress. Her phone was still in her hand, showing zero bars of coverage. He hadn't let her pause for a scarf or sandals.

"I would make you my harem girl if I could. Keep you here. That's how my father started up with Fatina. This is her family."

"This is their tent?" She glanced at the bed, not sure how she felt about that.

"This is my mother's. She used it once when they were first married. She doesn't like the desert. I use it."

"Ah." Of course. She scratched beneath her hair where the back of her neck was damp from perspiration. At least the sun was setting. The heat was beginning to ease.

"After me, my mother was reluctant to have another child. I don't judge her for that. I watched Fatina go through several pregnancies and she carries like she's made for the process, but it still looks cumbersome."

Cumbersome. How enlightened he sounded. She bit her lip against interrupting with sarcasm. The way he was being so forthcoming had her staying wisely silent, curious to hear how much he would tell her.

"When Fatina became pregnant, my father married her. If it was a son, he wanted him born legitimate. An heir and a spare. Mother was incensed. She promptly got herself pregnant with Hasna. She and Jamal are only a year apart. That's why they were so close." He had his elbow propped on the arm of his chair and smoothed the side of his finger against his lips. "My father was ambivalent toward Hasna. Still is. He sees little value in females. They are expensive."

"She's so sweet," she was compelled to say. "It's his loss he doesn't appreciate her."

"It is. And I often think that for all the nightmare his having two wives has been, at least she had Fatina. Mother was quite content to shuffle her newborn onto Number Two. The messy years of wiping noses and offering affection. She enjoys Hasna's company now, but if mother had raised her, we would have had two shrews terrorizing the palace, I'm sure."

What a way to talk about his mother.

"If she was thrown over because she was afraid to go through childbirth again, can you blame her for her jealousy? Does he love Fatina? That must have been a blow to her, too."

"She didn't have to turn into what she did. After Jamal, she quietly fed Fatina birth control pills for years. My father was furious when he found out. He knew by then that Jamal would never—" Kasim's mouth flattened, face spasming with anguish.

"He told me," she said, pulled forward a few steps on the silken rug that covered the floor, then halted and curled her toes against the cool material. *Jamal wouldn't marry and produce an heir.* That's what he had been about to say. "It's terrible that your father couldn't accept him. Was his life really in danger?"

She didn't want to believe it. Who hated to such a magnitude?

"From my father's intolerance, my mother's jealousy, and latent bigotry in some of our countrymen, yes." His hand fisted on the arm of his chair. "Do you think I would have taken such extreme steps otherwise? Even I couldn't risk seeing him."

He was so impassioned and tortured, she was drawn forward another couple of steps. At the same time, she wondered if Jamal was still in danger and glanced toward the door.

"They have some French, but don't speak English. And they'll have given us our privacy by now."

Privacy? For what? She was here to talk. That's *all*. Wasn't she?

"How was he?" Kasim's voice was low and yearning, hopeful, yet worried. When she met his gaze, she saw that same search she had seen in Jamal's eyes. He longed for news of his family.

"Good. I think," she reassured, smiling with affection because she had been quite taken with his brother by the time they'd parted. "Homesick, maybe, but he seemed content. I gave him my private number and begged him to collaborate with me on something, but I realize it might be too risky. I won't tell a soul, Kasim. I swear."

He dismissed that with a flick of his hand.

"I know you won't, but it may not matter. If I give Hasna that necklace... His body wasn't found, obviously. She and Fatina have held out hope. I had to give them that much. But what now? Do you know how much it has weighed on me that I hurt them like that? My father is no dummy and neither is my mother. Do I come clean? Put his life in danger again? What the hell do I do, Angelique?"

There was so much torment in his expression, her insides twisted painfully and her eyes welled. She threw herself into his lap and slid her arms around his neck, hearing his breath rush in as his chest filled. He clamped hard arms around her and squeezed her into the space against his torso, allowing her to drape her legs over the arm of the chair, then snugging her even tighter into the hollow of his body.

The way he held her pressed more tears out of her so she sniffed and tucked her wet cheeks into his throat.

"Don't cry," he said. "It's not for you to weep over."

"I'm crying for you," she said as a little shudder racked through her.

"I am fine, Angelique. My life is not in danger. At worst my father could disown me. I'll survive."

She drew back, thinking that men were so obtuse at times. "I'm crying *for* you. Because you can't. Can you? Have you ever let go of any of this?"

His brow angled with great suffering and his mouth tightened. "No," he admitted, and pressed her head to his shoulder. "No, I never have."

Fresh agony rose in her, spilling from her eyes and releasing as soft, pained sobs.

He stroked his hands over her back and arms, throat swallowing against her forehead, tension easing as he held her and held her while she cried. She cried for him and for them. She cried because he was leaning his heart against hers and his was so heavy, so very heavy, and she wanted to brace it forever, but she knew he wouldn't let her.

He was strong and disciplined and had responsibilities to a *country*. She might have room inside her for him, but his life did not have room for her.

Which meant it was pure self-destruction to slide her hand from his neck down to where his heart beat. Setting her damp and salty lips against his throat was both a step out of the pain she'd nursed since their breakup and a willingness to go back to a deeper level of it.

"I missed you," she confessed, because if she didn't say that, she would say something else. *I love you*.

He brought his hand to the side of her head and tucked his chin to look into her eyes. "I missed you, too."

His face spasmed anew. "But I still can't make you any promises."

"I know." It was a knife, twisting in her heart, but she only said, "We're together now, though. Even if it's only for an hour, Kasim…"

He groaned and she tasted the longing in him as he covered her mouth with his.

Joy quivered through her, blocking out the future and fear of loss, brimming her with happiness at being in his arms again. Pain ceased and all was right in her world.

They kissed without hurry, breaking away to look into each other's eyes, caress a cheekbone or the shell of an ear, then returned to another kiss of homecoming. She couldn't get enough of him. There would never be enough.

He rose, keeping her in his arms, and moved to the bed where they stretched out alongside each other with a sigh of relief. Together again, at last.

He jerked back. "I don't have condoms. I don't bring women here. I'll have to ask—"

She touched the side of his face. "I'm on the pill. It's okay."

"You never told me that before." He frowned.

"PMS makes me really emotional. That's the only reason I take them."

She would have pointed out that she didn't have them *here* because she hadn't been given an opportunity to pack, but he smiled and kissed her again, which distracted her from anything but how wonderful it was to lie with him again.

When he drew her onto her side so he could unzip her dress, there was reverence in his touch. He took his time, took great care as he stripped her dress down to her waist and unhooked her bra. She tugged it away herself and tossed it aside, smiling as he gave her breasts the possessive, hungry look that tightened her skin all over her body.

Heat pooled between her legs and she had to press into his groin with her own, *had to*.

"You have missed me," he said with satisfaction, cupping a swell and lowering his head to capture her nipple.

She gloried in the sensation, unable to get close enough to him. As her dress rode up, so did his *thobe*. She scraped her legs against his hair-roughened ones and used her hand to climb the fabric higher. His thighs were hot steel, but she was seeking that other column of strength.

He abruptly pushed onto his knees and threw off his *thobe*, revealing his sculpted form, the dark tone of his skin seeming extra dark as the light faded.

"You were naked under there," she commented, a little dazed by the idea. Her gaze slid past his six-pack to the thrust of his erection, so aggressive and familiar.

She was compelled to reach out, claim and squeeze.

He was velvet over steel, smooth and damp at the tip. She wanted that turgid heat moving inside her, soothing and stoking.

"Ah!" He reacted with a clench of his abdominals and fisted his hand over hers, eyes glittering fiercely at her.

"I will have my way with my harem girl first," he told her, thrusting in her grip a few times before peeling her hand off him and leaning to press the back of her hand to the mattress above her head. Then he tugged to remove her dress and underwear. "So many wicked pleasures…"

He stroked his hand from her collarbone over her breast to her hip, arranging her to best please his eye.

"Kasim." She writhed, loins clenching and aching as he skimmed his touch past her sensitive folds. She tried to guide his touch back to where she wanted it. "Please."

He caught her hand and tucked it beneath the small of her back. Then he gathered the other and did the same as he rolled atop her, using his legs to part her own.

"Don't tease," she protested. Caged beneath him, she rubbed her inner thighs against his, lifting her moist center to invite the penetration she longed for.

He shifted down a few inches and stayed propped on his elbows, admiring the way her hands beneath her back arched her breasts to him.

"Better," he said, and cupped both, lifting them for his delectation. He licked and teased and sucked, moving back and forth between them until she hugged her knees to his ribcage, shamelessly offering herself, *begging*, "Kasim, *please*."

He laughed and smoothly slid down even farther, licking at her very lightly, just once. She was so aroused, she had to catch back a cry.

"Don't be shy," he ordered, drawing a circle with his fingertip. "No one is listening but me. Do you like this?"

He pressed a finger inside her and tasted her again as he did.

She groaned in encouragement.

"You do," he said with satisfaction, and pressed two fingers inside her, making her moan with intense pleasure as he set about lavishing such attention she quickly shuddered with climax. Oh, she had missed him so much.

"So beautiful," he told her as he kissed his way up her belly. "You please me very much, my little harem girl."

"Your harem girl is going to tell you to go to hell if you don't quit calling her that," she panted.

He chuckled and rolled to her side, allowing her to free her arms, caressing himself with two fingers as he looked at her sprawled next to him, slumberous from climax, but aroused and filled with desire for him.

"Do you want me to do that to you, My Prince?" She rolled into him so her breath was humid against his chin. She nipped lightly. "Would you like me to please you with my mouth until you can't even speak?"

"Yes." He gathered a fistful of her hair, holding her still for his kiss, pressing over her and parting her legs with his, thrusting in and shuddering, lifting to look into her eyes as they absorbed the feeling of being joined without a barrier between them. "Later," he breathed. "Later I want you all over me. I want you to ride me and give me your nipples and I want you on your knees in front of me. I want you every way I can have you."

"I'm yours," she vowed. "All yours."

For now.

CHAPTER ELEVEN

"I'VE NEVER SKINNY-DIPPED BEFORE."

"No?" Kasim wondered how she was swimming at all. He was worn right out, barely able to sit upright on the natural rock ledge that hung just below the waterline.

He was exhausted, but knew he wouldn't sleep even if they went back to the tent. And he didn't want to miss a moment of her slick form twisting in the inky black of the water, rippling the reflection of the moon and stars. His midnight mermaid. He would remember this forever.

He wanted this night to last forever.

"Tell me something else about yourself," he coaxed.

"Like what?"

"Something about your childhood. Before." Before her sister's kidnapping he meant, when she had been carefree.

"Um…" Her voice hummed across the water like a musical note. "Oh, this is something not many people know. My father spoke French and my mother spoke Spanish, even when they spoke to each other. The boys grew up thinking that if Mama spoke to them, they had to reply to her in French and Spanish with Papa. If they spoke to each other, Henri used French and Ramon used Spanish. Then we came along and did the same thing."

"That's ridiculous."

"I know. The boys knew better by then, but they thought it was funny. We girls grew out of it once we realized it wasn't normal for other families."

Thinking of herself only as a piece of the collective wasn't normal, either. He wondered if she realized *that*.

"Now tell me something that is just about you," he commanded.

A pause, then a dreamy, but rueful, "I like birds."

"Which ones?"

"All of them. I'm weirdly fascinated and have dozens of books about them. I listen to recordings of their songs and study the patterns of their feathers. I love that they fly and always know where they're going. I'm intrigued by how they build their nests and I always imagine that when I'm old, I'll be one of those odd people squatting behind a log with binoculars, excited because I can tick off red-throated warbler in my birding book. Are you laughing at me?"

"That would make me a hypocrite. I own falcons."

The water rippled as she let her feet sink and brought her head up, swirling around to look at him. "Really?"

He had to smile at her excitement. He suspected he had just won her over for all time. For good measure, he added, "My mother has an aviary."

"Can I see it?" She skimmed closer in her excitement, then paused to tread water. "Never mind. I'd probably cry because they're caged."

He held up a hand to warn her as he noticed a servant coming toward the shoreline.

The report didn't surprise him. Nor did the apologetic way it was delivered. Fortunately he was too relaxed to order a beheading of the messenger.

He responded with a flat "Thank you," and jerked his head to indicate they should be left alone again.

"What was that?" Angelique asked, turning to watch the retreat.

"My father is not grinning and your brothers are not bearing." And he was not interested in talking about reality. They had stepped beyond time, at least until morning. He wished to enjoy it.

"Relaying my safe word didn't reassure them?" She sounded genuinely surprised. Small wonder.

"I didn't relay it."

"Kasim! Don't do that to them." She swam a little closer.

He reached out his feet, but she was too far away to catch and drag close. "Your sister knows you came with me willingly. What do they think I'm going to do with you?"

"Just tell them I'm all right," she said impatiently, looking again to where the servant had disappeared.

"My father knows where I am. He can arrange to transport them here if they need proof of life so badly."

"Or you could send a message."

"I'm just as happy to let them pressure him into having you returned to the palace."

"You're using me," she said with a lilt of outrage. "Using *them* to back your father into a corner. I thought you didn't play those games." She made a V in the water as she headed away from him, toward shore. "What would that even accomplish? He can still disinherit you, can't he? Are you going to risk that so I can stay for the wedding? For *one* day?"

She was really asking if he was fighting for a broader future with her. And she was right that he would be disinherited for *that* sort of transgression. He was playing a dangerous game as it was, thinking he could steal this night with her.

"Why can't you just enjoy what we have?" he challenged. That's what he was doing.

"I *was*. Sex and skinny-dipping is great. But apparently I'm not here for that. You want to punish your father. You're using me to embarrass him because you're angry about Jamal." As she climbed from the water, her shoulders hunched, even though the air was still velvety and warm.

"Stop accusing me of only wanting sex from you." He pulled himself up and out, pushing to his feet so water sluiced off his naked body in a trickling rush. "I brought you here because this is where I'm happiest. I wanted you to see it."

He waded along the ledge until he reached the path on the shore, then he circled through the high grass to where she stood, towel wrapped around her middle, arms hugged over it.

"Will you take me back? Please?"

"To the palace? You're going to choose a night with your family over one with me? Live your own life, Angelique! Quit hiding behind your sister."

She recoiled like he'd taken a swing at her.

"This *is* me. I don't hurt the people I love."

"Meaning I do?" Now who was delivering the sucker punch?

She dropped her gaze so he only saw her pale eyelids, not whatever emotion might be glimmering in her eyes.

"You're better at holding yourself apart from things. I even understand why you had to become that way. But I feel things, Kasim. Do you think I came to Zhamair for a midnight swim in an oasis? No. I came because my heart was torn apart by a family so broken I

couldn't stand it. I came *despite* knowing I would probably wind up in your bed and be shattered at having to
leave it again."

"Then *don't*," he growled, hating to hear that he was
hurting her when it was the last thing he wanted to do.
He thought of her sitting in his lap, crying for him, and
his guts twisted.

"And what?" she challenged softly. "Become Wife
Number Two? Look how well that turns out!" Her profile was shadowed with despair as she gazed over the
moonlit water.

He sighed and pinched the bridge of his nose. The last
time they'd had this conversation, he had fought to ex-
clude one day from their lives. Now he saw the single day
they might steal—only a night, really—slipping away.

"You want me to call your brothers with your code
word, *fine*."

"Your father will still know I'm out here and resent
it. Do you really want to fuel the fire? I don't want to
be the reason you two went to war the day before your
sister's wedding. Kasim, I *love* you."

The words struck him with such a blast of heat and
light, he rocked back on his heels, speechless at how
powerful the statement was.

"I know you don't feel the same," Angelique rushed to
say, appalled that she had spilled her heart out at his
feet like that. Crushed that he only stood there looking
stunned. How could he not have expected this?

"I don't *want* to know how you feel," she added
quickly. "It would make this even more impossible to
deal with," she babbled on, drowning in yearning. "But
that's who I am. If you think I hide behind my sister, it's
because I don't know how else to protect myself from

feeling so much. You get past even that and it makes me feel so defenseless."

She wanted to look at him, but was afraid what she'd see. Pity? Weariness with yet another woman falling at his feet?

"You *could* talk me into being a second wife, and we'd both lose respect for each other for it," she said, feeling as though one of his falcons had taken her chest in its talons and was squeezing relentlessly. Her voice thinned. "So I'm asking you not to wield your power over me. Be the man I love and show respect for someone weaker than you. Don't use me in your fight with your father. Take me back and make peace with him for your sister's sake."

He let out a breath like she'd kicked it out of him.

"Don't be selfish like my parents," he summed up, voice as dry and gritty as a wind off a sandstorm. "You should give yourself more credit, Angelique. You're plenty brutal when you need to be."

He took her back to the palace and let her go without so much as a reluctant "goodbye." She didn't suppose she would ever forgive him for that, even though it was exactly what she had asked for. She had hoped for some kind of miracle though. Foolishly hoped.

Henri met her off the helicopter and escorted her wordlessly back to their suite where she half expected Ramon to be waiting up. He wasn't. They were all asleep.

"Is Trella okay?" she asked as Henri firmly closed the door behind them.

"*Bien*. She's your champion. You know that." He unstoppered a bottle, smelled the contents, and set it away with disgust. "Cordial. How do they survive without a decent brandy? Do you want to tell me what you were thinking, disappearing like that?"

She lifted a hand and huffed out a breath of despair. "Do you want to tell me what went wrong between you and Cinnia?"

He jerked his head back. *"Non."*

She tilted her head. He knew how she felt then. Sometimes things were far too painful to share.

He sighed and held out his arm. *"Je m'excuse, Gili.* Come here. I hate fighting with you. It just makes me feel like a bully."

She laughed faintly. "Because I don't fight back?"

"You just did. Most punishingly." He hugged her. "But it tells me how hurt you are when you hit below the belt like that."

"I'm sorry about you and Cinnia," she murmured as she hugged him back. "It's so hard to find people we can trust. Even harder to keep them," she added in a voice that thinned to a whisper.

He squeezed her and set her away. "You should get some sleep. We may be packing to leave first thing."

They didn't. Kasim pulled strings and Angelique was allowed to stay for the wedding. At least, she assumed Kasim had arranged it, until she and Trella caught up to the bride to help her dress.

Hasna had been crying, as most brides were wont to do, and was running late while her makeup was fixed. Her suite was being cleared, everyone leaving to take their seats. Angelique offered Fatina a smile as the woman hurried past her, but Fatina didn't even acknowledge her. She was ashen beneath her olive complexion. She looked both wispy and frail, yet had an incandescent glow behind the wetness in her eyes.

Angelique's blood chilled with premonition, but she was pulled back to Hasna's reflection as she spoke.

"I told Mama to tell Papa I want you both at the wedding. I realize there are politics, but…" She touched the pendant at her throat and Angelique wondered if there were other reasons for the smudged mascara and puffy eyes, the haunted shadows behind Hasna's somewhat shell-shocked expression.

Oh, Kasim. Angelique wished, illogically, that she could have been with them when he'd given Jamal's gift to his sister, to hold his hand and bolster him as he had made his explanation.

"That's fine," Hasna said with a flustered dismissal of the makeup artist, sounding very much the princess as she said, "*Go*. I just want to be married and live with my husband. Help me dress."

The woman left and Angelique and Trella helped Hasna into her gown. She was a vision, with a distinct line of maturity setting her shoulders and running like a line up her spine. Some might see it as her wedding causing this coming-of-age moment, but Angelique knew it was the necklace she kept touching. The memories of time lost with a cherished brother.

It was another tear in the fabric of Kasim's family and Angelique silently ached for all of them.

"I don't think I've ever been prouder," Trella said, linking her hand with Angelique's. "Oh, look at you, crying over how beautiful she is! Our tender little Gili. We used to call her Puddles. She hated it."

Her sister was being Trella, giving Angelique an excuse for the tears that were filling her eyes because yes, she was proud of their work, but she was bombarded by so much emotion in this moment. She hurt for Hasna and Fatina, Kasim and Jamal. At the same time, she saw the dress as a symbol of what had brought Kasim into her life. It was exactly what she would never wear when walking toward him. In fact, today especially, she couldn't go near him. In future, it would be far too painful to approach him, not that she expected to bump into him anywhere.

The wedding reception was the last time she would ever see him and she wanted to weep openly with her loss, until she collapsed in a heap.

Trella squeezed her hand in comfort, as though she felt the echo of agony that clenched Angelique's heart.

Hasna's bouquet dropped an inch and her come-and-go smile faded into misery.

"You have both worked so hard to make this day absolutely perfect and—" Her gaze briefly met Angelique's, but she quickly shielded her thoughts with a sweep of her lashes. "I can't believe I have to ask you for another favor. Sadiq will kill me if he knows, but my mother wants a picture of the three of us. She said it's about the dress, but I know it's because she's excited to have the first photos of you both together in public."

Hasna looked embarrassed and angry, but resigned.

Angelique glanced at Trella, worried the photo request was too high a price. If Trella wanted to refuse, she would back her up, even if it meant they were both expelled from the wedding, the palace and Zhamair.

Even though it would mean not catching a last glimpse of the man she loved.

Trella smiled even as her fingers tightened on Angelique's.

"Of course," Trella said. "I knew photos would wind up in the press and I'm only sorry it might overshadow your special day. But if you're not bothered by that, then I'm not. You, Gili?"

Angelique shook her head and tried to bolster Hasna by saying, "Anything for you, because you make Sadiq so very happy. You know how much we want that for him."

Hasna's smile returned, shakily, then beaming with anticipation. She blinked. "Yes. He's lucky to have such good friends. Me, too." She touched her pendant and nodded. "I'm ready."

When it came to levels of power, there were elected officials, religious leaders, authoritarian dictators and right at the very top of that heap: Mother of the Bride. When she also happened to be a queen, she accomplished great feats with a single sentence.

"You cannot expect Hasna to give up the prestige of hosting such rare guests for a woman who may or may not join this family." Her tone implied that she would veto Kasim's prospective bride completely if she impacted the illustriousness of Hasna's day.

His mother didn't know the reason Hasna had become so insistent on having *all* of The Sauveterre Twins at her wedding. Kasim had gone to see his sister last night, when he'd returned from the desert. She had known the moment she saw the pendant that Jamal was alive. "You would have shown this to me before, with all the rest."

As the truth had come out, she had railed at him, and cried bitterly, but she understood that it had been Jamal's choice, and the people truly at fault were their parents. He hoped she had managed a few hours of sleep after that. He hadn't, too aware that Angelique was close, but essentially gone from his life.

Then, just before the ceremony, he had held out his arm to escort Fatina to her place behind the king and queen. She had been trembling, her face a stiff mask, as she'd said, "I saw what you gave to the princess."

Her eyes had held a maelstrom of emotion, topmost resentment and betrayal, but underscored by a glittering return of hope.

He would owe her some explanations, too, he supposed. At least he was able to brood unnoticed as the attention through the reception was drawn in a completely different direction.

Watching the wedding guests behave like the twins were creatures in a zoo made Kasim sick. They had all been briefly introduced at the receiving line, Angelique removing her hand from his like the contact had burned. Her eyes had remained downcast and his heart had been a tortured knot from the moment he saw her coming to the moment she'd disappeared into the crowd.

Her brothers now bookended their sisters, Henri on Trella's right, Ramon on Angelique's left, all posed in a row like movie stars to allow photographs, the men wearing dark green, the women a lighter shade, so all their eyes flashed like emeralds. Their smiles were aloof and unbothered.

They *were* a sight, so very good-looking, tall and flawless and so startlingly the *same*. An old woman touched Ramon like she wasn't sure he was real. He said something that made her cover a titter and blush. Angelique sent her brother a reproving look and pinched his arm.

Kasim's lungs felt tight as he memorized the vision of her. His heart had echoed her voice through him with every pound since she'd said, *I love you.*

Respect someone weaker. Did she not know how weak she made him?

He fantasized about having a second wife. The wife he really wanted. He loved her, too.

And claiming her would make him just like his father.

He ran a hand down his face, ensuring none of this struggle was evident as he gritted his teeth and tried to get through the hours of this everlasting wedding.

A servant touched his arm. "You must come," he said. "The king."

What now? Kasim stalked after the man, taking a relieved breath as they went through a door and the worst of the noise was closed out behind them. "Where is he?"

"The doctor is with him in the Consort's Chamber."

"Doctor?" Kasim's heart lurched. He strode past the man up the stairs to more quickly reach Fatina's suite.

Her rooms were at the far end of the wing from the royal apartments, but it didn't surprise him that his father was there. It did shock him to find his mother coming toward the same door from the other direction, expression tense. Fatina's maid was trailing behind her, obviously having fetched her with the same urgency.

This was serious.

Kasim's mind raced. Should Hasna be called away from her guests? Was it that bad? He pushed into the lounge and found his father being loaded onto a stretcher, an oxygen mask over his gray face. He wasn't conscious.

"What happened? What have you done?" The queen was quick to accuse Fatina.

Not her. Me, Kasim thought.

Fatina was crying, tail end of her scarf bunched up to her mouth, shoulders shaking with sorrow.

"Why was he even here when he should be downstairs with his guests? *You*—"

"Mother," Kasim said through his teeth. He looked to the doctor.

The royal physician wore a very grave look. "We will do what we can. Perhaps the queen should accompany us in the helicopter."

For potentially his father's last moments. Kasim's insides clenched.

As they all looked to Kasim for direction, he thought about the guests downstairs. The woman he'd used to needle his father—not to score points, but because he loved her.

The end result was the same, however. He had given his father a heart attack.

Kasim felt not just the weight of decisions that would have to be made in the next five minutes, but the weight of a nation landsliding to rest with infinite weight upon his shoulders. Even if his father recovered, Kasim was the man in power until he did.

And he didn't deserve it.

He had thought his father's censure had hung heavily around his neck. His own self-contempt was worse.

"Mother," he prompted. The word stuck in his throat. "I will follow with Hasna as soon as we can." And Fatina. He wished he could give her the honor of flying with the man she loved. She was rocking in her chair, face buried in her scarf as she tried to stifle her sobs.

Turning to a servant, he ordered them to have Hasna and Sadiq wait for him in one of the anterooms downstairs. He would tell them first, then make the announcement.

And he would say an unspoken, but final goodbye to Angelique.

I don't want to be the reason you two went to war the day before your sister's wedding.

Nevertheless, she was. She would never see this differently and neither would he.

Do you need me? I will stay if you want me to.

Angelique had rather foolishly sent the text as the wedding fell apart and Kasim disappeared, presumably to have a police escort to the hospital where his father was struggling to hang on to his life.

He didn't respond. Not that day, not before she left Zhamair, not as his nation went into mourning at the news of their king's demise, and not after his father was laid to rest and Kasim was crowned king.

She followed all of it, doing exactly what she had told him once she would never do. She stalked him online and even read what was said about the two of them, reliving their various moments together, not caring about the inaccuracies and wild theories and outright lies.

As one week turned into two, then three and more, it became obvious that he didn't need her. He took his rightful place on the throne and seemed fully in control of all he surveyed. Infinitely resilient and autonomous.

Now she felt vulgar for having sent the text in the first place. All she had wanted was to reach out to him in that moment when he must have been so anguished, but who was she to think she had anything a *king* could need?

It hadn't struck her until afterward that her presence at the wedding might have been the catalyst for his father's heart attack. Kasim had been so remote as he'd made his announcement that the king had been taken to hospital, so very stately and contained, yet she had sensed his agony.

Now she wondered—did he blame himself? *Her?*

She wished she hadn't been so quick to climb on her high horse at the oasis. She should have stayed there with him. No, that was selfish. It might have made things worse with his father. Of course, how could the outcome have been any worse than death? Still, she had been so preachy when really, she had been doing what he had accused her of. She had hidden behind her family because she loved Kasim so deeply, it scared her.

And leaving without having spent a full night at the oasis didn't mean she hurt any less now.

She hurt for both of them, so much so she went online yet again and walked straight into a statement from a source "close to the king." A marriage was being arranged and an announcement would be forthcoming.

She couldn't tell if it was an older statement made by his father or something Kasim might have said recently.

Either way, it rattled her all over again and drove her away from looking at any kind of screen for days.

She had to get on with her life.

But she couldn't make herself go back to Paris. She had come to Spain from the wedding, to lick her wounds, allowing her mother to mollycoddle her now that Trella was so much better and spending the bulk of her time in Paris.

Trella had finally confided a few details about her night with the Prince of Elazar to Angelique and was dealing with the fallout from it—big fallout—but she was fiercely determined to handle things alone and not lean on her siblings again, particularly her twin. It was both admirable and worrying, but Angelique had to let Trella muddle through and just impress on her sister that she was here if she was needed.

Even though she felt as useful as a milquetoast.

Thank God they had Sus Brazos, the family compound. "Her arms," it meant, referring to the safety of their mother's arms. They had taken to calling it that when Trella had retreated here.

Trella might have come to see the family stronghold as a prison, but Angelique needed it rather desperately. The gated compound overlooked the Mediterranean, ever inspiring with its expansive view. The buildings were a gleaming white, the main villa obscenely luxurious and up-to-date even though it had been built when her parents first married. The staff were all such longtime employees they were a type of extended family.

It made her feel safe and cosseted in every way, which allowed Angelique to relax as she ate quiet meals with her mother, walked the gardens, sunbathed and sketched, turned in early and tried to heal her broken heart.

The days were very predictable here, which was part of its charm. And it was also why she was so stunned when she was interrupted while watching seabirds diving into a churning pool out on the water. She had a guest at the gate, she was told.

"The King of Zhamair."

CHAPTER TWELVE

ANGELIQUE WORE A summer dress in pale pink with tiny ivory polka dots. It had a high neck, but bared her golden shoulders and accented her slender waist and long legs, falling in layers of tall slits and sharp points. Her hair was in a high ponytail and she pressed her lips together over what he suspected was a fresh coat of lipstick. She seemed breathless as he was shown into their lounge.

"Welcome," she said, pressing her palms together. "My mother isn't here, I'm afraid. She had a luncheon with friends. She'll be sorry she missed you. Shall I order coffee? Your Highness?"

Kasim felt like it was their first meeting all over again. She was treating him like a stranger and was too beautiful for words, emptying his mind of all but base masculine thoughts. His perfectly tailored suit felt too tight.

Still, he found himself letting out his breath, relieved to finally see her, but exasperated by the fact he'd had to chase her down in Spain when he'd expected to find her in Paris.

"Excellency," he corrected absently. "And no to coffee."

Her mouth twitched, probably thinking he sounded

pretentious. She had never been particularly impressed by his station, which was part of her charm for him.

She sent a jerky nod to dismiss the maid and said, "Let me guess. You'd prefer to stand?"

"I would. Why is that funny?" he demanded as he heard the tiny noise she tried to stifle. "I've been sitting for hours, traveling to Paris then here."

"Paris?" The news arrested her.

"To take Fatina to see Jamal." It had been a bittersweet joy to embrace his brother again. As he'd met his brother's partner, and left Fatina to reunite with her son, Kasim had felt as though his last barrier to being with Angelique had been removed.

But now, as he entered the inner sanctum of her world, and recalled how she'd been treated like a museum exhibit at his sister's wedding, he wondered if he was taking too much for granted. The wife of a king was not exactly a low-key profile. Why would she want to take on such a position? He was struggling with the elevation in circumstance himself and it was only one notch.

"He does live in Paris, then? I wasn't sure," she said.

"Hmm? Oh. Jamal. No, he doesn't. It was complicated." A cloak of weariness fell over him. He wanted to throw off his *gutra* and shave his beard and be the man of lesser responsibilities he'd been when they'd first met.

But he was king now. And was expected to marry.

"It has been a very complicated, demanding few weeks."

"Of course. I'm so sorry about your father. I should have said—"

"Your mother's card was among the rest," he cut in. "My mother appreciated the gesture."

"She must be devastated. And poor Hasna, to lose her father on her wedding day. How is she?"

"Grieving. We all are. They curtailed their honeymoon." But he was glad his sister had such a stalwart support in her husband. It was one less weight on his own shoulders.

Angelique nodded, mouth pouted as though she wanted to say something, but knew there was nothing to say. As she looked at him, her eyes brimmed.

"Don't." He flinched, took a step toward her, then veered away, running a hand down his face in frustration. "I'm so tired of tears, Angelique."

She swallowed, trying to choke back the emotions swamping her. But she couldn't take it in! He was *here*, and so blindingly handsome. His eyes were dark and unreadable, but riveting. His mouth was stern, tension pulling at that sexy mouth of his.

He wore his beard, precision trimmed to frame his face, and also his *gutra*.

He had come to her world, but still had one foot in his.

Her heart panged because she felt firmly shut out of that side of his life. Shut out of all of it, really.

She drew a breath, but didn't know what to say.

He looked her over in the way he did sometimes, like he was taking in her hair or clothes or the set of her shoulders or the angle of her foot, but really, he was seeing what those things revealed. Like he was reading her. Seeing *her*.

It made her feel so transparent it was painful. She struggled to hold on to her composure. "This is just really…confusing. I'm not sure why you're here."

"After ignoring your text, you mean?"

She shrugged a shoulder, cheeks stinging with embarrassment all over again. "It wasn't appropriate of me to send it. I realized afterward that our going to the oasis may have contributed…" Her voice dried up. She didn't want to think she was to blame for his father's death.

"Maybe it did." His shoulders lifted and fell. "I certainly believed I'd killed him when I was being crowned."

"I'm so sorry," she whispered, hating herself for being his weakness, the thing that he'd gone after to the detriment of his father and his relationship with him.

"He had a heart condition. His heart had been failing for years." His mouth curled with irony. "But I didn't respond to your text because I blamed myself for his death. I blamed *us*."

Her worst nightmare. Her heart plummeted. There went the small dream she had formed at his arriving here, the one she hadn't really let form.

"I even blamed you for bringing that damned necklace from Jamal. I was not the man you asked me to be," he said with self-disgust.

And this was his punishment. The ultimate sacrifice, losing his father. He wasn't trying to dump that on her shoulders. She saw he carried it alone, but she felt awful all the same. Wanted to help him.

"What I didn't know, until he was dead and I was king, was that Fatina had fought with him that night herself. I was so busy in those first days after he passed away, it was two whole weeks before I could sit down and talk with her privately about her future. She fell apart, completely racked with guilt."

"They fought about Jamal?"

"She told him she wanted a divorce. I won't break her confidence by repeating all she told me, but… I do believe he loved her in whatever way he was able. Losing her, realizing he had lost her love by failing Jamal, was more than he could bear."

"But he had a heart condition," she hurried to repeat. "Please tell me you didn't make her live with that guilt."

He cast her a look that demanded some credit.

"I told her she was a generous wife and a good mother. I was unsurprised she would fight for the happiness of all my brothers and sisters, particularly Jamal. I told her she shouldn't blame herself and that I wanted to arrange for her to see Jamal as soon as possible."

"You're a good man, Kasim."

He made a dismissive noise. "I would have preferred to bring Jamal home, but I don't think that would be safe yet. I'm afraid to resurrect him. But I was able to reach him through the jeweler and we met him in Paris. He says hello and that he is still interested in working together if you are."

"That's why you're here? To deliver his message?"

"No." He gave her a look that suggested she was dense, then paced across to the windows that looked out on the sun-drenched sea. "I am here because I am under a great deal of pressure to go through on the promise I made to my dead father, to marry the woman he chose. But if I succumb to an arranged marriage, I know I would take you on the side and turn into him."

He slashed his hand through the air.

"I will not repeat history. I will not have you end up hating me as Fatina did my father. Not when I need your love so badly. I *will* need that love in the years to come, to keep me human. Ruling a country is not easy."

"Kasim…" This was heaven and hell wrapped up in one moment. She dropped her head so she wasn't looking at him. She was so tempted. "If you loved me—"

"Angelique. Look at me."

She lifted her head. The fierce determination in his features made her heart skip while the tenderness in his eyes stole her breath.

"What have I learned from my family? You love who you love. If you fight it, if you try to force it in another direction, there will be nothing but pain. You asked me once to give you up for the sake of my country. I'm coming *after* you for the sake of my country. Without you, the one I love, I will be as frustrated as my father. I'll become bitter and my heart will shrivel into a pitiless husk. Save my people from that. Save me from turning into that."

She let out a small laugh. "You're overstating, aren't you?"

"No. I watched it happen to him. He was much kinder in my youth, but his being trapped with my mother while wanting Fatina twisted him."

Her ridiculously tender heart pitied his father for the position he'd been in. Still, "Would your country have accepted her if he had married Fatina?" She'd seen Fatina's family. They were modest people of the desert. "I don't want to be a source of unrest in your country. I have a reputation, true or not. People will think you should have found someone more upstanding."

"In choosing my wife, I will be the authoritarian that my father was," he said with a point at the floor. "I will not compromise. I could engage myself to the woman he chose and tomcat through Europe for the next four years until I marry her, but I don't want that sort of freedom. I don't *want* other women. I don't want *her*. I want *you*. I will have you. My uncle and my advisors and anyone else who disapproves can…" He showed his teeth. "Grin and bear it."

She couldn't take it in, especially now she'd seen the scope of his life. If she had thought being a media darling was onerous, she couldn't imagine flouting his country's conservatives and becoming his wife.

"I'm not someone who thumbs their nose at the establishment. They'll tear me apart."

"They'll try." His mouth tightened. "But you'll win them over. God knows you'll be well protected until you do. I swear to keep you safe, Angelique."

"But you're overestimating what I'm capable of."

"Like hell," he said softly. "You think you're only brave if you pretend to be your sister. You are bravest when you're defending her because you *love* your sister. That love of yours is such a well of strength. I've seen it and I want it beside me, supporting me. I know that *my* love for *you* will make me a better man. Provided I can indulge it," he added with a look that was both sensual and tender.

Oh, he was such a seducer. Her heart fluttered like a caught bird and her eyes stung with moved tears. She cupped her hot cheeks.

"How could this be a surprise to you?" he chided, coming toward her and increasing her excited turmoil.

He took her wrists and drew them down so they stood face-to-face. She had no way to hide how overcome she was.

"I didn't think you loved me," she confessed in a daze. "I thought maybe if we had had more time you might have come to care…"

"I *care*," he admonished. "I always cared. And I am not someone who needs a lot of time to know my own mind." He shifted his grip and caressed the back of her knuckles with his thumbs. "But we will have to take things slow. Announcing an engagement this soon after my father's death— You're not pregnant, are you?" he asked with a sharpening of his expression.

"What? No! How could I be?"

"We didn't use anything at the oasis."

She huffed out a disbelieving laugh. "I'm on the pill, remember?"

His mouth twisted. "Shame. It would have given us a reason for shortening our timeline, but it's probably for the best if we do things in the right order." He sighed. "I want to make so many changes in my country, relax restrictions and change attitudes, but it has to be done carefully or there will be chaos. Is that the reassurance you need, Angelique? You will have time to put all these pieces together in your pretty head."

He was teasing her, reminding her of their first night together when he had tried to railroad her into extending their affair. She wanted to duck into him, maybe have a little cry because this was so much to take in. She was trying to smile, but her lips were trembling.

"I didn't bring a ring. I asked Jamal to make one for you."

She had to choke out a little laugh and pull one hand free to swipe at a tear that leaked down her cheek. "You don't have to *bribe* me."

"No? Well, I brought this anyway, hoping it would be an inducement." He released her other hand and reached inside his suit jacket, bringing out a velvet box she recognized.

Her heart did a little bump and roll as he flipped the lid to show her the emerald necklace he'd tried to give her in Paris.

"I should have explained that day that it was not a pay-off. Jamal made this years ago, before he left Zhamair. I told him that one day my queen would wear it."

"Queen!" Her knees wilted and Kasim quickly hooked his arm around her, catching her into him. Which didn't help at all because finally being back in his arms was such a relief she melted against him completely.

"What did you think?" He leaned to drop the necklace on the side table and scooped her under her knees, moving to sit on the sofa with her in his lap.

"I just wanted you to love me. Yes, I had fantasies we might marry, but because I want to be your *wife*. I want to see you every day and share my life with you."

"Finally she says yes."

She curled her arm around his neck and laugh-cried against his throat at his presumption. *So* like him.

But she loved him. So much.

Tipping back her head, she set her trembling hand against his bearded cheek, gazed into his beloved eyes and said, "I would be honored to be your wife."

"And my queen."

"Harem girl, if that's what you need me to be," she said, barely able to see him, her eyes were so full. She swiped at her silly leak of tears. "Good thing I had no time for makeup. I'm trying not to do this, you know. You said you were tired of tears, but I'm just so *moved*."

"The sad tears are killing me. The angry ones. I trust these are happy ones?"

"They are. Oh, Kasim." She lifted to press her mouth to his, unable to hold back her expansive feelings.

His arms tightened to gather her closer and he kissed her with deep passion and infinite tenderness. Love imbued the moment, sending a rush of joy and heat through her. Desire. That delicious, sharp desire that only he ignited in her awoke to make her burn.

He was reacting just as instantaneously. She felt his

hardness against her thigh and he slid to press her beneath him on the sofa.

As his mouth slid down her throat, he lifted his head and frowned at her bare neck. "No panic button."

"I wasn't going to put one on for *you*."

"Even though I intend to steal you from your family?"

"That part will be hard for me," she admitted. "It's good I'll have time to do that in stages. But there are times when I'm impatient, you know." She loved the feel of his stubble against her palm and absolutely had to trace his bottom lip with her thumb. "I don't want to go to a hotel," she whispered.

"No?" He was reading the hunger in her and answering with a growing heat in his own gaze. He shifted so he was between her legs, pressing his hardest flesh against her softest.

"It will take too long to drive there and have it scouted. I want to sneak you into my bedroom so you can ravish me there. *Now*."

He pulled away, drawing her up as he went. "See how good you are at encouraging me to compromise? Lead the way, my beautiful future wife."

EPILOGUE

Two months later...

ANGELIQUE WAS ALWAYS happiest when her whole family was together, but she felt a little guilty for being *so* happy today. It was her engagement party, however, so she was entitled to be elated.

And it wasn't a huge party, which made her even happier. Just those closest to them gathered at Sus Brazos for a weekend to celebrate what amounted to a secret engagement since they weren't officially announcing it for another few months.

She was making other people happy with this small party, too. Sadiq and Hasna were here and Jamal had just arrived with his partner. Kasim was sequestered with the four of them while his brother and sister took a few minutes to reunite in person after being in touch again since the wedding.

It gave Angelique a few minutes to study her sister, who was arguing heatedly with Ramon on the far side of the pool. Of the four of them, those two were the only combination to descend into yelling matches. They weren't there yet, but it was only a matter of time before one of them completely lost their temper and pushed the other into the water to cool off, evening clothes notwithstanding.

The way Henri was glaring at them, it might very well be both of them taking a swim—by his hand.

"What's going on?" Kasim asked, coming up behind her and wrapping his arms around her waist.

"They have Mama's hot Spanish blood." She leaned back into him. "Henri and I have our father's French temperament, you lucky duck. Our silence speaks volumes. Their volume does."

"What are they fighting about?"

"Unclear and probably not important," she said with a fatalistic sigh. She suspected Trella had picked this fight to let off steam. Her sister was troubled. Angelique had been feeling it, but couldn't do a thing about it. Trella was being that delightfully frustrating shade of her true self: stubborn and ferociously independent.

She had even come up with a plan to transition Angelique from the day-to-day operations at Maison des Jumeaux, while allowing her to keep her foot in the door, submitting designs and indulging her artistry around her duties as queen—oh, she would never fully grasp that!

Trella was determined for Angelique to move on with her life without feeling held back. It made Angelique wistful, even though she was also grateful. She loved Kasim so very much and wanted to be with him without guilt.

"How is Hasna?" She turned in his arms to ask the question.

"Good. They'll be out in a moment, but I couldn't wait to show you... Come here."

He pulled her a little farther along the veranda to a corner where the light was soft and the view was nothing but starry night and glittering sea. The fragrance off the early summer blooms came up from the garden below and the warm air caressed her bare shoulders and calves.

She had a feeling she knew what he wanted to show her, but was still overcome as her future husband caressed her arms before he went down on one knee.

"Angelique, my love."

"Oh! You don't have to do that." She instantly choked up and lost sight of him behind a film of emotive tears.

"Arrêtez," she heard Henri growl at her siblings, receiving instant silence. She suspected they were being watched.

She was never comfortable as the center of attention, but she looked into the face of the man she loved and knew he would keep her safe no matter what.

"Will you marry me?" He showed her the ring that Jamal had made, the one she had been holding her breath to see. Now, in this deeply moving moment, she couldn't make herself look away from the love in Kasim's eyes.

"You know I will. I love you with everything in me. Please." She waved for him to rise. He was a king after all.

He did, suddenly tall and close. He slid the ring on her shaking hand and handed her his handkerchief so she could clear her vision enough to fall in love with the hint of a feathered design cut into the band. Claws like talons held a stunning round diamond. It was simple and elegant, pretty, but imbued with the fierceness of her husband while conveying that he did know her very well and longed to please her.

"I *love* it."

"I love you." He cupped her chin and kissed her tenderly. "This time next year we will marry in Zhamair. It's far too long to wait, but this is a step in the right direction."

A small burst of applause made them both glance in that direction and she blushed to discover not just her mother and siblings, but Jamal and his partner, Hasna and Sadiq, all beaming at them.

They would marry in a ceremony that would be big and overwhelming, and her life would be equally huge and daunting, but she would have these cherished people to help her through it.

And this man. She looked up at Kasim, her other half. Not her reflection, but her complement. Curling her arms around his neck, she went up on tiptoes to kiss him.

* * * * *

If you enjoyed this story,
look out for more scandalous tales of
THE SAUVETERRE SIBLINGS
coming soon!

In the meantime, why not explore these other
great reads from Dani Collins?
THE SECRET BENEATH THE VEIL
BOUGHT BY HER ITALIAN BOSS
THE CONSEQUENCE HE MUST CLAIM
THE MARRIAGE HE MUST KEEP
VOWS OF REVENGE
Available now!

MILLS & BOON®

MODERN™

POWER, PASSION AND IRRESISTIBLE TEMPTATION

MILLS & BOON®

EXCLUSIVE EXTRACT

Stefano Moretti wants only revenge from his wife, Anna. When she reappears after leaving him, with no memory of their marriage, he realizes that this is his chance…for a red-hot private seduction, followed by a public humiliation! Until Stefano realizes there's something he wants more than vengeance — Anna, back in his bed for good!

Read on for a sneak preview of
ONCE A MORETTI WIFE

Stefano pressed his thumb to her chin and gently stroked it. 'When your memories come back you will know the truth. I will help you find them.'

Her heart thudding, her skin alive with the sensation of his touch, Anna swallowed the moisture that had filled her mouth.

When had she given in to the chemistry that had always been there between them, always pulling her to him? She'd fought against it right from the beginning, having no intention of joining the throng of women Stefano enjoyed such a legendary sex life with. To be fair, she didn't have any evidence of what he actually got up to under the bedsheets; indeed it was something she'd been resolute in *not* thinking about, but the steady flow of glamorous, sexy women in and out of his life had been pretty damning.

When had she gone from liking and hugely admiring

him but with an absolute determination to never get into bed with him, to marrying him overnight? She'd heard of whirlwind marriages before but from employee to wife in twenty-four hours? Her head hurt just trying to wrap itself around it.

Had Stefano looked at her with the same glimmer in his green eyes then as he was now? Had he pressed his lips to hers or had she been the one…?

'How will you help me remember us?' she asked in a whisper.

His thumb moved to caress her cheek and his voice dropped to a murmur. 'I will help you find again the pleasure you had in my bed. I will teach you to become a woman again.'

Mortification suffused her, every part of her anatomy turning red.

I will teach you to be a woman again?

His meaning was clear. He knew she was a virgin.

Anna's virginity was not something she'd ever discussed with anyone. Why would she? Twenty-three-year-old virgins were rarer than the lesser-spotted unicorn. For Stefano to know that…

Dear God, it was *true*.

All the denial she'd been storing up fell away.

She really had married him.

Don't miss
ONCE A MORETTI WIFE
By Michelle Smart

Available April 2017
www.millsandboon.co.uk

The perfect gift for Mother's Day...

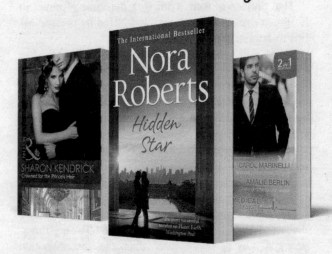

a Mills & Boon subscription

Call Customer Services on
0844 844 1358*

or visit
millsandboon.co.uk/subscriptions

MILLS & BOON®

Read on for an exclusive extract

How did she walk away? Lydia wondered.

How did she go over and kiss that sulky mouth and say goodbye when really she wanted to climb back into bed?

But rather than reveal her thoughts she flicked that internal default switch which had been permanently set to 'polite'.

'Thank you so much for last night.'

'I haven't finished being your tour guide yet.'

He stretched out his arm and held out his hand but Lydia didn't go over. She did not want to let in hope, so she just stood there as Raul spoke.

'It would be remiss of me to let you go home without seeing Venice as it should be seen.'

'Venice?'

'I'm heading there today. Why don't you come with me? Fly home tomorrow instead.'

There was another night between now and then, and Lydia knew that even while he offered her an extension he made it clear there was a cut-off.

Time added on for good behaviour.

And Raul's version of 'good behaviour' was that there would

be no tears or drama as she walked away. Lydia knew that. If she were to accept his offer then she had to remember that.

'I'd like that.' The calm of her voice belied the trembling she felt inside. 'It sounds wonderful.'

'Only if you're sure?' Raul added.

'Of course.'

But how could she be sure of anything now she had set foot in Raul's world?

He made her dizzy.

Disorientated.

Not just her head, but every cell in her body seemed to be spinning as he hauled himself from the bed and unlike Lydia, with her sheet-covered dash to the bathroom, his body was hers to view.

And that blasted default switch was stuck, because Lydia did the right thing and averted her eyes.

Yet he didn't walk past. Instead Raul walked right over to her and stood in front of her.

She could feel the heat—not just from his naked body but her own—and it felt as if her dress might disintegrate.

He put his fingers on her chin, tilted her head so that she met his eyes, and it killed that he did not kiss her, nor drag her back to his bed. Instead he checked again. 'Are you sure?'

'Of course,' Lydia said, and tried to make light of it. 'I never say no to a free trip.'

It was a joke but it put her in an unflattering light. She was about to correct herself, to say that it hadn't come out as she had meant, but then she saw his slight smile and it spelt approval.

A gold-digger he could handle, Lydia realised.

Her emerging feelings for him—perhaps not.

At every turn her world changed, and she fought for a semblance of control. Fought to convince not just Raul but herself that she could handle this.

Don't miss
THE INNOCENT'S SECRET BABY
by Carol Marinelli
OUT NOW

BUY YOUR COPY TODAY
www.millsandboon.co.uk

CB3